Henry's 7 Letters

Henry's 7 Letters

To PENNY & ERRIE
THANK YOU

M. P. Hanvey

Maurice P. Hanvey

Library of Congress Number: 2003099959
ISBN :   Hardcover   1-4134-4398-2
               Softcover   1-4134-4397-4

To order additional copies of this book, contact:
Xlibris Corporation
1-888-795-4274
www.Xlibris.com
Orders@Xlibris.com
19743

Contents

Chapter ONE

The Advert

"Ladies. Once a week you should spend some time in the arms of a man of your choice.

If you've lost yours, I can be available on specified days, for reasonably short periods of consolation. For further information, write:-

Adam;

P.O. Box 007 Gardiner WA. 98381

The above advert. appeared in the Olympic Pinnacle of 8/12/93 as a "For Sale" item in the 'Freebie' column for 'Under $50.00'.

Two weeks later, when the advertiser went to the Post Office in the rear corner of the Gardiner General Store, to see if there had been any response to the advert, he found a note in the box indicating that there was too much mail for the box and asking him to see the postmaster.

Fully expecting to be verbally chastised for misuse of the mails, he was somewhat taken aback when the postmaster, who knew him quite well, pushed three large boxes stuffed with letters across the counter to him with the jovial admonition.

"I hope you're going to reply to them all. Adam."

Mildly embarrassed, for as the postmaster well knew, his name was Robart, he was forced, by their size and weight, to carry the boxes out to his car, one at a time.

Each trip, he sought to avoid eye contact with the grinning faces of several older ladies, who had overheard the postmaster's remarks. The thought that some of them might even have responded to his advert and be, at that moment, discussing him amongst themselves, added further fuel for his burning cheeks.

As though in a dream, Robart Scanlon drove home. He unloaded the three heavy boxes and stacked them under the desk in the spare bedroom, which served as his 'Office', where he kept everything that didn't belong elsewhere. This done, he went straight to the refrigerator and mixed himself a strong Martini in a silver shaker. After taking a deep swig, he added three olives, fished from a tall jar with a distinct salt scum on it, topped up the glass and took his drink back into the 'office'.

He sat at the desk with his feet on the nearest box. Over the edge of the glass, he contemplated the amount of envelopes between his feet and sniffed the soothing aroma of the gin.

There was something deeply disturbing about the massive response his advert had elicited. Either there was a huge number of pranksters like himself or an incredibly large number of desperately lonely women. Somehow the idea of so many pranksters seemed implausible, and a gnawing uncertainty as to his right to meddle in the lives of so many unfortunate souls began to bother him.

The Martini ran out of sympathy, so he returned to the kitchen and poured himself another one.

When that was gone, he cleared a space on the desk with a sweep of his arm and began sorting the envelopes into piles according to the return addresses.

Every imaginable shape, color and size of envelope and stamp came out of the box. Robart had never dreamed there could be so many variations of stamp alone. Soon the desk was covered in loose piles, some of which were in danger of toppling over on top of smaller piles. Many were perfumed, and as the sorting continued, he began to imagine that they were all perfumed and all coming from a thousand sex starved women who would eventually descend on his house and tear him to pieces like little girls fighting over a straw doll.

He needed a third Martini. This time he didn't return to his office but stretched out in his tilt-back lounger and tried to shut the horror of the flood of letters out of his mind.

I first met Robart Scanlon when he was recovering from the loss of his wife, after thirty years of a happy though childless marriage. Three or four times a week, he and I played pool together at the local Navy club finding a common bond in our enjoyment of the game, our marital status and the fact we both worked for the same company. We became fast friends as the years passed, enjoying similar personal traits and interests. Since neither of us had any relatives or dependants, we went around together, like brothers and eventually retired within a year of each other.

After retiring, he became even more lonely and I would introduce Roba to lady friends of my own. By the way, he hated to be introduced as Robart, fearing they would question the spelling and he would be forced to confess his father had spelled it wrongly on his birth certificate.

I'm not ashamed to admit that these introductions often worked to my advantage, as few of these ladies ever measured up to the lovely wife I had also lost under tragic circumstances. However, I do not wish to infer that we passed our lady friends around. It was merely a matter of him being a few months younger, more 'dapper', and more attractive.

As time went by, the ladies usually failed to measure up to his lost love, and, since I refused to lower my standards, the supply simply ran out.

Painting, flying, writing and occasionally dancing, keep me from fretting over situations like this and as far as I knew, Roba's time was similarly satisfactorily occupied. But, even between the best of friends there are secrets.

When I dropped in on him that fateful evening after his overwhelming success with his advert, which he had never mentioned to me, I found him sprawled at his desk with several piles of letters towering like miniature paper skyscrapers around his head. My immediate fear was that he had suffered a stroke, until I saw the empty glass and sensed the alcoholic aroma surrounding him.

It was so uncharacteristic of him to succumb to drink to this degree that I wondered what had caused such heavy indulgence.

That was when I really took notice of the stacks of letters adding to the normal clutter. I concluded they must have some connection with his bout of drinking. However, it was obvious he was in no condition to explain, and as if to emphasize this, he belched loudly and began snoring. A small pool of drool or vomit began to form on the desk by his mouth and I picked up a small stack of letters which were in danger from this and went out to the kitchen for a cloth.

I set the letters aside while I filled and set the kettle on the stove to brew up some coffee for the two of us.

After cleaning up the mess on the desk, I returned to the kitchen, rinsed out the cloth and began reading the letters. I should say, envelopes, for there was no way I would invade my friend's privacy by opening any of them.

Even though I doubted that he would have missed any from the mass of correspondence on top of the desk and the obvious boxes full with more letters under his feet.

He was still unresponsive when I took the coffee to him so I returned it to the kitchen and began a careful scrutiny of my handful of envelopes. I counted seven, all from different places around the Olympic Peninsula.

Had he somehow become the target of some political or religious pressure?. Won the lottery?. Written something controversial to the papers and made himself a victim of poison pen activity?. He is prone to voicing strong opinions on such subjects as Abortion and Welfare for the Worthless, but it would not have been like him to write to the papers about it. Where had all this mail come from?. And, who was 'Adam'??

From the scented stationary, they were almost all from women.

Well, as I have mentioned, Robart has not been short of lady friends. Horrors! Surely to God they hadn't all decided to sue him.? Not all together at the same time? That would undoubtedly be enough to drive him to drink. I scanned quickly through the return addresses on the envelopes in my hand. Nobody I knew amongst them; and as already noted, I knew most of his Exes. I sighed with relief.

A loud snort and the sound of his chair moving panicked me. I didn't want him to think I'd been spying on him, so I quickly stuffed the letters inside my jacket and went to his room treading heavily and called out to him.

"Roba ! You want some coffee?"

He was swaying unsteadily beside his chair holding the back of it for support and looked at me blearily as I came through the door.

"'Lo Henry." He muttered as I handed him a cup of hot black coffee. He took it shakily and swigged it, almost scalding his throat.

"It's hot !" I warned him belatedly.

When his coughing subsided, I helped him out to the kitchen and we sat at the table while he slurred his way through the story of the stacks of letters.

Later that night when I got home and went to hang up my jacket I realized I still had the seven letters in the inside pocket. I put them, unopened, on the credenza in my bedroom intending next day to return them.

That was two years ago.

Why did the letters go missing for two years?

Because, early next morning, when Roba called me to say he was deadly sick, I dashed over to his house to help, completely forgetting about the bundle of letters on the credenza.

Of course, his sickness was no more than a hangover, deepened by remorse over the response to his advert.

Well, after dosing him with a glass of tomato juice, freely laced with Lea and Perrins and a stiff shot of Tabasco Sauce, I talked to him like a Dutch Uncle until he settled down and decided to go through the letters with my help.

He had begun sorting them the previous evening, putting them in piles according to the return addresses, before succumbing to the temptation to wash his conscience in alcohol; and for want of a better system we continued in this fashion. During the course of this therapy session, he explained why he had put out the advert in the first place.

"It was Free" He said rather lamely, in response to my question. "I wasn't looking for lonely hearts. I just thought there must be an awful lot of lonely old women out there who would like to have a little male company now and then. Or at least get a laugh out of the advert."

"Apparently you were right." I agreed sympathetically. The largest pile by far, contained those where the postmark or the return address was unreadable. These, we decided to open first and sort by contents.

Fully half of them were letters written by angry females, and a few males, who thought the advert, had been in poor taste. We put these aside for future action.

However, by lunch time, Roba, doubtless assisted by the hair of the dog that had bitten him the previous evening, was so incensed with the way his 'generous gesture' had been received, scooped the whole pile up, muttering something that sounded like, "Sanctimonious Bastards." and before I realized his intentions, dumped them into the fire.

"That'll teach 'em!" he added, heading out the room.

When I returned home that evening, I also, was fed up with the whole thing. I put all seven letters off the credenza into a folder, marked it "R's Folly" and stuck it in my filing cabinet at the back of the bottom drawer, behind "Old Tax Returns".

They'd probably still be there if Roba hadn't died.

It was almost exactly two years to the day of that deluge of fan mail that he died. I remember being struck by that fact later when I unearthed the folder of letters and compared the post marks with the date of his funeral.

You see, when he realized he was dying, he dictated a farewell letter which I was to send to a "Select Group" of the ladies he had been writing to, thanking them for their friendship over the years. As the executor of his will, I was to do this after he died. He didn't want to let them know he was terminally ill, fearing that some, if not all of them, would come to see him, and thus find out about each other.

"I'd rather die peacefully here," he said, "than have to witness forty-seven distraught women fighting over my carcass." I told him he was being a bit inconsiderate, as this would be a most fascinating spectacle for me to watch.

He gave a little smirk at my attempt at humor and reached for my hand, but his strength was fading rapidly and I could feel the weak tremors of his muscles as he tried to grip my fingers. His manner became serious.

"I want you to have my computer and the disks Hank." He pleaded. "You'll find everything's all set up with their names and addresses. Maybe my expression stopped him for a moment, as he smiled re-assuringly and then continued.

"Not to worry Me old dear, you'll find my manual, a blue, 3-Subject notebook, with everything you need to know about getting the computer to address the envelopes and match each one with the person you're writing to. On my desk. It's easy. The computer does it all. You only need to type out that letter I gave you, then select 'Merge' from the menu and press 'Enter'." The smile seemed frozen in place and his voice was barely a whisper. He heaved a deep sigh and breathed his last words. "Just make sure you have enough paper and envelopes in the printers and put the right letter in the right envelope."

It wasn't quite as easy as he had said of course. For one thing, I hardly knew how to operate a computer. As if that wasn't enough, there were several of his 'Harem' who had the same first names. there were four Janes, six Bettys, five Marys and eight, yes Eight Joans. Complex ? You bet it was. Especially as the Envelopes were ALL addressed in the form Mrs. J. Ettis, Mrs. B. Granslam, Mrs. M. Rissler, etc.

When he had dictated the letter, he had also instructed me to leave out the first name and type "My Dearest *.*" in its pla

"When you print it out, the computer will put the appropriate name in the letter and the appropriate address on the envelope." He had said. "Just follow the instructions in the notebook to the letter and everything will work perfectly."

Everything probably would have, except that, on my first try, there were only twenty four envelopes in the one printer. My mistake of course. He had told me to check.

People who write instruction books never write them for the truly ignorant. Although I know what to do now; if he had only included the remark." The first Letter and the first Envelope go together, and subsequent letters and envelopes likewise." It would have saved me from having to make two trips to the stationary store before I tumbled to such a simple solution. Maybe I tend to panic too easily when confronted with mysterious devices like computers.

I guess things really came unstuck when I realized that Whereas I assumed myself to be 'in the clear' after discovering only eight Joans, something was definitely amiss when there were twenty two envelopes addressed 'Mrs. J. Something or other'. Two Jennies, a Jacqueline, four Janes (I had forgotten) and several others beginning with 'J'. Julie, Judy, Jan, Janice, Jean, Jennifer and Jodie. Followed by a bunch of 'B's that weren't Betty either, which also appeared.

How he had selected that forty-seven out of over two hundred odd replies, I'll never know, because the day after our great 'Sort-out', I'd had to fly to England to settle my father's estate. When I returned, about a month later, Roba was off somewhere on a cruise ship with one of his ladies. Presumably she had offered to pay for him. Roba never said, and I wouldn't have dreamed of asking such a delicate question, knowing, as I did, that his pension could hardly be more than my own.

It took just a little more than a week to conquer his computer and fulfill his final request. All forty-seven letters, correctly aligned in the right envelopes and duly stamped, went into the post box in a neat stack. I put the flag up and went rather sadly back into his house to begin the miserable experience of disposing of my best friend's effects.

It was a typical wet cold Washington summer day, aptly matching my mood. Roba, neat and dapper though he may have been, was like myself, a pathological pack-rat. All the letters he had received in response to his original advert, were crammed into a cardboard box which he had undoubtedly salvaged from the Liquor store. I mean 'Crammed'. I could hardly lift it. I was in no mood to investigate it and at the same time it didn't seem right to possibly expose all those people to the chance embarrassment of their letters being found in the dumpster. I decided to burn them.

Roba's living room has a large fireplace and I balanced the box carefully across the grate before trying to set it on fire. I used up half a box of his best 'Diamonds' trying to light it. For your information, there are two hundred and fifty in a box.

Finally, I went down to his workshop and found his gasoline blowtorch. I set this in front of the box and literally incinerated the whole thing. As the flame ate its way like a cancer into the blackening mass, I followed his example and consoled myself in his recliner with the contents of his silver Martini shaker.

Disposing of one's best friend's effects is not the most enjoyable experiences in life. Yet, like any other aspect of living, it is up to the individual to make it what it is. At first, I was quite depressed. However, as the process evolved, I found myself getting more at ease and finally enjoying it.

Perhaps that sounds a bit callous until you realize that neither of us had any relatives to dump this burden on. No living parents, brethren, wives, or children, we were the ends of our genealogical lines.

"Los Ultimos", or "The Buffer Twins", as he jokingly referred to us, whenever the subject of children came up. Much as we made light of this, it was really a means of escaping the creepy sensation of finality, experienced when we discussed dying.

"All women, and some fortunate men, generate progeny to continue living through their 'genes' when their lifetime ends." He would say, giving a resigned shrug in closing. "In our cases, The Buck literally stops bucking, here".

Several months before his death, he and I had exchanged provisional powers of attorney and executorships. I can't blame it on him, for it was really my own idea. After finding out that I had to have my prostate removed, I realized that I had no one else in this world, other than him who I trusted to take good care of my affairs in the event of being incapacitated.

After putting it off for a while we signed the appropriate papers and had them legalized. It was all quite casual. I showed him the filing cabinet where my papers were and he showed me his.

My operation went off without a hitch; legally that is, as there was nothing for him to do beyond notifying the hospital of his power of attorney.

When my turn came to step into the legal shoes, events moved more swiftly than either of us had foreseen.

One night, he called 911 and was rushed to hospital in considerable pain. The Hospital called me next morning. When I reached the ward he had been operated on for Colonic Cancer. The doctors told me there was nothing they could do. The Cancer was so wide-spread in his system that they literally had to just sew him back up and administer pain killing drugs to ease his passing.

The martinis may have helped, I can't say, but I know I wept as I watched the surgical flame consuming the remains of what had perhaps been my friend's greatest achievement.

There's no need to bore you with the details of the disposal of his house, his stock market account and my trials and tribulations in complying with his will. I will note in passing, that a second mailing of forty-seven letters, each containing a personal cheque for one thousand, four hundred and forty-seven dollars and forty-seven cents, went out before I was released from my duties.

It's really strange how the spirits of the departed continue to exercise control over the living.

I was home in my little office, tidying up after my 'ordeal' when a tiny voice inside me, reminded me of the file marked "R's Folly."

I experienced a sensation as though the floor was dissolving into quicksand under my feet as I removed the file from the cabinet. For one moment I had a wild impulse to escape by flinging it into the fire along with the rest of his letters, but the ashes of that fire had long since been swept away and distributed evenly over the top of the compost pile in his garden.

Now, with the file open on my desk and the letters spread fanwise like a hand of cards, I wished I had been more thorough in the discharge of my duty.

It was almost as though I could hear him laughing at me, somewhere behind me, his high pitched giggle taunted me.

"Go on. Go on. Open them. They're yours, not mine any more. You chose to take them. Otherwise, they'd be ashes now. Go on. Chicken!. Open Them!" My spirit said. "Burn them." His said. "Open them Chicken!" and there was that giggle again, just as he used to laugh whenever he successfully snookered me behind the black ball.

I can only suppose a spirit, without a body to hamper it, must be much more powerful than one with a body, because I picked up my letter opener and did just as I was told.

Chapter TWO

The First Attempt

I have a habit of sniffing an envelope immediately after opening it. Smell is possibly the oldest of our senses and unless one has neglected it throughout life, it may be the most perceptive sense we possess.

Mrs. Mary Lykes, loved roses. Not the chemical concoctions that pass for that perfume, but real roses. All kinds of roses. She didn't smoke, but she had a wood stove in her house, which was not far from the beach. All this I sensed about her before I took the pale blue paper out of the envelope.

My Dear Adam,

I know that's not your real name but I'm quite sure it is a most appropriate pseudonym and I would dearly like to meet you. I have a nice little cottage, just across the bay from Gardiner at Beckett Point. My husband Walter, died several years ago, and, as you surmised, it would be nice to have a man to talk to once in a while.

Walter and I used to belong to a square dance group in Port Townsend but it was a long time ago and I don't dance now.

I have a beautiful garden which keeps me busy, but you can't hold much of a chat with flowers can you?

I shall look forward to hearing from you, either by mail or telephone.

Thank you for caring.

Sincerely,
Mary.

Obviously, it would be inappropriate of me to disclose her address or phone number so these details have been omitted.

I had a burning sensation between my shoulder blades as I read and re-read that letter. Mary Lykes came across as a very sweet personality and perhaps Robart was conveying his annoyance at having been deprived of the chance to meet her. I put the letter down and went into the kitchen for a re-fill of coffee, before tackling any more of the letters.

Somewhere along the way that morning, I caught myself asking Robart what to do. Speaking my questions aloud and then replying to them as though he and I were discussing the subject.

"Bullshit !" I told myself. "Get out of here and go for a ride in the fresh air. You're driving yourself batty."

One nice feature of the area where I live is the quiet, almost private, road system where I can ride my bicycle in relative safety.

I start out up the hills to the top and then free-wheel down to an empty cul-de-sac high above the cliffs where I stop and enjoy the wonderful vista across the water to the San Juan Islands. Away to my right, the morning sun was glittering on the collection of summer cottages that smother a sharp promontory jutting out from the opposite shoreline of Discovery Bay. Beckett Point.

'Which one of those cottages is Mary's ?' I wondered.

Although I had flown over Beckett Point many times, I had never been there, assuming it to be a collection of vacation shacks jammed shoulder to shoulder as often happens to the more desirable waterfront sites. I wished I had brought my binoculars with me. I never remember to take them when I set out for my cycle rides.

Back at home once more, I decided to just drive over to the east side of Discovery Bay and do a little exploring.

Nicely shaved and cleaned up, I put the letter in my pocket and set off in the car with the binoculars on the seat beside me. I had absolutely no idea what I would do, when or if I found her cottage but subconsciously I sensed a delicious feeling of suppressed excitement.

It took about an hour to arrive at the steep road down the cliff into Beckett Point and as I slowed around the first curve at the top of the road, I could look down on the whole long triangle of land that juts out into Discovery Bay. I stopped the car and studied the random collection of cabins masquerading as Vacation Villas, which sprawled all the way around the shoreline. Here and there a painted splash of color stood out incongruously bright against the general weathered cedar shake exteriors.

There was no sign of the vivid rose garden my senses and Mary's letter had led me to expect. The only place that had any sizeable garden was on the south leg of the promontory on the landward side of the road, and looked badly overgrown with brambles.

A rude blast of a motor horn shook me back to reality. I released the brakes and rolled slowly on down the hill signaling for Mr. Impatience to pass me. He turned out to be an auburn haired young lady in a fire engine red Ferrari who glared at me as she shot past, mouthing some witchlike imprecation in my direction.

At the bottom of the hill, where the road flattens out to the spit, barely six feet above sea level, I pulled over onto the shoulder just a few feet from the edge of the sea, to check the address on Mary's letterhead. Memory refreshed I moved ahead, slowly scrutinizing the mailboxes and house numbers.

Sure enough, it was the house with the overgrown front garden. And, as if confirmation was necessary, closer inspection revealed several rose bushes battling for survival amidst the blackberry vines. There also, in the narrow driveway, stood the red Ferrari.

The abandoned garden had already depressed my sense of anticipation to near zero and the prospect of being confronted with the hot-tempered young redhead pushed it well into minus territory. I carefully backed the Olds on to the shoulder and almost into the brambles in front of the house, switched off the motor and slid across the seat to the offside door to get out. The small voice inside me whispered.

"You've come this far, go in and find the rest of the story."

The front door knocker was a wrought iron heart pitted with ancient rust beneath its fresh black paint. It lifted easily and fell back with a resounding crash that echoed through the house. I didn't dare lift it a second time.

The years of rusting had left a dried bloodstain down the door that spoke of a long lost love. Or, I was beginning to wonder, a long trail of self pity. The door opening stopped my train of thought to reveal a stunningly beautiful transformation of the red-headed witch.

Perhaps my mouth fell open, or my eyes popped out, for the vision laughed and sang. "Yes ? Can I help you ?"

"Mary Lykes ?" I croaked. "Yes." The song continued. "Can I speak to her?" The frog asked. "You are." The princess replied.

"I was expecting someone older." My vocal chords responded at last.

"My Grandmother ?"

"I don't know." I replied hesitantly. "I've never met her. I came in response to her letter." Heaven knows why I said that. Probably Roba was still pushing.

"What letter?" The song had gone, replaced by a guarded prose. I fished it out of my inside pocket and handed it to her. She read it and then looked me over very thoroughly as if to see whether I was armed or dangerous in some other way.

"So. You're the mysterious Adam! Eh?" Her voice lowering menacingly. Then, as if to thwart any attempt at flight I might be about to make, the smile returned.

"Would you care to come in for a cup of tea ?"

"No. and. Yes." I said, feeling like the hypnotized fly invited in by the spider.

"I mean. No I am not Adam. and Yes I would like a cup of tea. Do I detect an English accent?" I added, hoping to regain any initiative I might once have had, but she merely motioned for me to enter and turned to walk down the passage towards the back of the house leaving me to close the door.

Her movements were so fluid, I seemed to be drawn along behind her like a piece of floating debris behind a boat. I half expected to see her grandmother bundled in an armchair somewhere, but the kitchen I entered was empty except for the two of us. She was drawing water for the tea when I asked.

"Is your Grandmother in? I was hoping."

"She's Dead!" She interrupted, with a sharpness that suggested she held me responsible. I was so taken by surprise, I could only stare at her until she turned to face me.

"I'm so Sorry." I said lamely. I had been looking forward very much, to meeting her." Perhaps I sounded as genuine as I felt, for her expression softened slightly.

"If you're not Adam, then who are you and what could you possibly want with my grandmother?. And, If you're not Adam what are you doing with a letter from Granny addressed to him? And why now? Granny's been dead nearly two years." She pondered a moment. Nineteen months anyway." I smiled and held my hands up in token surrender.

"Whoa!" I replied. "Too many questions all at once. Why don't you put those cups down. They look expensive. Your Granny's I presume. I'd hate to see them get broken." She did as bidden and turned to the stove to make the tea, leaving me to my mental arithmetic.

Her remark, besides confirming my growing suspicions, put Mary Lykes death at approximately three months after she had written the letter. Strange that in that short space of time, Adam had become a significantly prominent personality for her grandchild to know about him. Possibly the old girl had fantasized about him after writing, even up to the time of her death. That might well account for the enmity in the young girl's mind.

Mary, went through the tea ceremony and we sat opposite one another at her Granny's kitchen table, sipping politely while discussing our respective interests in the dead.

After white-washing Roba to the best of my ability in Mary's mind and confirming almost exactly everything I had suspected about the original Mary Lykes, our conversation drifted towards each other.

By evening, when I left, we both knew a great deal more and

had developed a much friendlier attitude. I knew, or thought I did, everything I now needed, to 'erase' the original Mary Lykes from my list of contacts, and my interest had definitely shifted to the delightfully present version.

Although I tried hard to tell myself to think of her more as a grand daughter I had been denied by a childless marriage, her image kept climbing up the genealogical tree. Or, as I lay awake in bed that night, was it I who was sliding 'down' it? Once I had accepted that it was most likely the latter, I went soundly asleep.

That night I dreamed in color. Roba and I were playing pool and he had me snookered and was fairly dancing with delight. Somehow he had contrived to turn Mary's head into a set of red balls that completely surrounded the cue ball. Whatever I tried would mean hitting her. In the end when I finally played my shot, all the balls turned back into Mary's lovely head and rolled about the floor while I tried desperately to retrieve them before they all disappeared down various holes in the floor which replaced the pool table pockets.

I woke feeling devastated, every movement seemed as though my soul had lost connection with my body. I plugged in the electric kettle for my coffee with no water in it. When I realized this, I filled it and plugged it back in without resetting it. Put the honey in my mug before the coffee and consequently plunged the sticky spoon into the instant coffee. After waiting long enough for the water to boil, I poured it into my mug before realizing it was still cold. In desperation, I put the mug full of cold mixture in the microwave oven, set it for two minutes and went to the toilet. I returned to find it boiling vigorously. I'd set the darned thing for twenty minutes; it was too hot to touch. Time for a cold shower.

After fighting my way through the initial shock, my soul began condensing back into my body. A brisk rub down, the wet towel wrapped around my waist, I padded back to the kitchen and began the task of cleaning up the mess in the micro.

From this inauspicious beginning, the day blossomed into a more normal routine as I entered the details of yesterday's encounter into the computer under a 'newfile' entitled; "Monday's woman." I stapled Mary Lykes's letter and its envelope together, printed the computer filename on the back of both and filed them once and for all in "R's Folly".

Blindly, I extracted a second letter before putting the file back, returned to the computer and opened another file which I entitled;

"Tuesday's Woman."

You see, with little knowledge of computer work to begin with, I simply adopted Roba's system of record keeping. After all, he had managed to organize and keep separate, the records of his correspondence with forty-seven different women in this manner. It should work for me. How little I knew. I hadn't even heard about such devices as 'passwords'.

Tuesday's Woman came from a place called Joyce, so I'll refer to her as Mrs. Joyce Reynolds. That's not her real name of course, but that's just between you and me. Joyce is a real place, like Martha, or Elmira, or almost any other little western town that has a sawmill or a grain elevator with some lady's name painted on the roof or the side to identify it from the air.

Joyce Reynolds letter read as follows:

Dear Adam,

What kind of dope are you smoking? Do you realize there must be a few thousand lonely women in the distribution system of this little paper? Suppose only one in ten of us replies to your note. What d'you think you can do about making good on your offer?

Why'd you put it in the 'For Sale under $50' ?? Or did you?

Sometimes the paper makes mistakes I'll grant you. You planning to charge for this? If so, how much?

On the other hand, I've been in this god-forsaken hole for the last forty years and I'm ready to take whatever chance there is of finding some sort of sympathetic relationship with any man that'll have me. There are plenty of loutish specimens around here that I wouldn't allow nearer than ten feet. Their stench alone would probably kill me.

I'll be honest with you. I'm not pretty.

My husband and I came out here from Seattle in our teens and homesteaded this place. We had two lovely daughters but after they grew up, Charlie began messing around with them, and some of the other women around here. I sent the girls to my mother in Seattle and I think they're both married and gone off somewhere with their husbands. I hope so anyway.

After they left, Charlie started getting drunk and violent, which is why I say I'm not pretty. Anyway, I ran him out of the house on the point of the kitchen cleaver and he hasn't been back in twenty years. I suspect he's drunk himself to death by now.

I taught school here in the house for several years, to keep food on the table, until the State forced me to close my class down because I had no degree.

I get a minimum welfare now and eat mostly from my own garden and the barnyard.

Well there you are, Adam, or whatever your name is, you know my life history. Now, I'd like to hear from you.

My house is a little over half a mile South of Joyce. It stands alone on the west side of the only road that runs South, out of Joyce. If you're ever in this area, drop in for some fresh eggs or a glass of milk.

Don't worry; with all the letters you'll probably get, I won't hold my breath.

Sincerely,
Joyce Reynolds.

P.S Anyone in town will direct you, but don't be surprised if they think you're crazy too.

I'd given her letter my usual sniff test without much success except to detect a certain earthy flavor consistent with her farmyard remark. Some scents have shorter duration of potency than others. I couldn't detect any trace of Tobacco, which pleased me. It's strange how both Roba and I feel the same way about women who smoke. Perhaps I should have said 'felt', but it was still too soon after his death, and my sense of loss was still with me. Perhaps I should have said 'is'. Either way, any indication that a woman smokes is a distinct turn-off and I'd bet my shirt, none of the forty-seven indulged.

Roba, bless him, was one who always had to be up with the latest in gadgets. Browsing through his disks one day, I discovered the copies of his ladies' letters were always in their handwriting instead of typed. After a careful search through the gadgets I'd put away, I found the hand-held scanner he'd used and with the aid of his blue-book and the manuals, I managed to hook it up and, after a few sour attempts, to make decent copies of Mary's and Joyce's letters. If nothing more came out of this experience, I was at least learning how to use a computer.

From its discombobulated beginning, the day had prospered into a sunny, interesting morning. I hadn't been to Joyce since my last fishing trip with Roba at Seiku, some ten years ago. Even then, I'm not sure whether we stopped in Joyce for breakfast or not. I vaguely recall, an isolated gas station cum general store/ cafe establishment, at an intersection on the highway some ten or twenty miles west of Port Angeles.

After breakfast, I combed my hair, put on a clean shirt and set forth with the map and binoculars. This time I also remembered to take my camera. I was beginning to get into the spirit of these new adventures.

Any lack of beauty Joyce may have felt about herself, she had compensated for in the exterior of her house, which sat back from the road, barely visible behind a screen of neatly trimmed trees and rhododendron bushes.

I parked in the clearing off the road and walked past the garage along a curved pathway through the trees which ended suddenly at a garden gate from where I got my first full view of the house and its attendant outbuildings.

I lingered there awhile to admire the neat rows of herbs and vegetables interspersed with clumps of vivid flowers, which surrounded a wire enclosure containing a flock of chickens. Beyond this, a strip of lawn separated the house from the farm. On the other side of the gate, a paved pathway surrounded the whole ensemble.

The two-story house was almost completely shrouded in creepers and vines, all carefully trimmed around windows and doorways, accenting their white frames in sharp contrast to the greenery. I found it startlingly reminiscent of fairy tale cottage pictures I've seen in magazines. I closed the gate behind me and chose the southern route where the gravel pathway ended in a sun drenched brick terrace with a wrought iron table and chairs that might well have come from a Mediterranean villa. After a momentary pause to absorb my surroundings, I stepped up onto the brick looking around for signs of life. Seeing no doorbells, I was about to tap on the glass door when a husky voice behind me asked.

"What can I do for you Mister?" The derogatory emphasis on the 'Mister' warned me to turn around slowly and I found myself facing a tall rangy woman in a long dress and apron, holding an ancient single barreled shotgun.

"Joyce Reynolds?" I asked, as calmly as my startled nerves would allow.

"Who wants to know?" She countered suspiciously. I gave my name which meant nothing to her, so I opened my jacket carefully, took the letter out of the inside pocket, and held it out for her to take.

"Please don't point that thing at me," I pleaded. I only came here to bring you this letter." She motioned with the gun, for me to set the letter on the table and to sit on one of the wrought iron rocking chairs. Then she took the letter to the other side of the table and sat down to read it with the gun leaning against her leg. I tried to relax back in the chair, hoping the damned gun wouldn't fall, as it would probably go off and blow my feet off if it did.

My legs began twitching in readiness to jump clear if it started to slip. Women with guns make me extremely nervous.

"So you're Adam." She said, looking me over contemptuously. "What took you so bloody long?" she added, picking up the shotgun and, much to my relief, un-cocking it.

We spent the next ten minutes in a question and answer session, while I carefully explained the situation to her. Naturally, I omitted my own responsibility for the delay, just as I had done in talking to Mary Lykes. A tactic I intended to follow religiously henceforth. I was beginning to understand why Roba had eventually restricted his involvement pretty much to Pen-Pal-man-ship. (If there is such a word.)

Hoping to turn the conversation in my favor, I smilingly asked,

"Would your offer of fresh eggs and milk extend to a stranger like myself?" and was rewarded with the first smile since our meeting.

Striking while the iron showed some signs of warming. I pointed to the letter on the table and added

"You were wrong you know. In your letter. You have a really beautiful smile. It lights up your whole face." My sincerity must have shown in my voice, for I declare the tanned weathered face actually blushed and her eyes misted slightly as she stared at me in silence, allowing the broken nose, split lips and missing teeth to reassemble themselves before speaking

"Flattery. Mister, will get your ass shot off." she growled and stood up clutching the shotgun. Then the smile came back like the Sun from behind a cloud. "How'd you like your eggs Henry? Over easy, poached or boiled?"

Late that afternoon, with barely an hour to go before dark, I watched Joyce's tall silhouette waving from the roadside outside her house, in my rear view mirror.

"You'll come back now," she had said, with a distinctly pleading tone of voice as she leaned through the door window to kiss my cheek.

"I promise." I'd replied, knowing I would and wondering about my sanity in the same breath.

Hell. I was supposed to be winding up the tail end of Roba's shenanigans, not embarking on a series of my own.

Chapter THREE

Wednesday's Woman

Wednesday dawned to a typical September morn with a low fog obscuring the normal view from my bedroom window. My sleep had been deep and restful and I peeled out of bed wide awake and ready to confront the day.

At the computer, I recorded the details of Tuesday's adventure, noting that Joyce's letter had been returned to her, at her request. No cross referencing necessary. Finished. Or was it?

I had deliberately left out most of what transpired after my meal of poached eggs on thick farm toast with fresh butter and a glass of milk to wash it all down.

Nothing to file away, I reached into 'R's Folly' and extracted the next letter, as though playing a crazy game of chance.

Wednesday's Woman came from Brinnon, some fifty miles away down the Hood Canal in the opposite direction to Joyce. The thought crossed my mind that there was small chance of any of them meeting each other.

Barbara Barranquillas. Fortunately, she had a printed return address, for her writing was almost illegible. I tend to rely on my sniff test before anything else and it told me that either she or someone very close to her was a fisherman. I spent best part of an hour deciphering her letter.

Dear Mr. ADAM.

You must be very kind person to sell you so cheap. Is you broke or defect some other way.? (except her question marks were at each end of the sentence.) My Enrique leaved me ten year. never come back. He take all the money I only got house. Can not afford big price for one time at a time too often. wish much to bargain with you. Have regular job in cannary. could pay in cans of salmon. ?You like shrimp? Enrique break heart. no can love no more but like Hugga Hugga.

At work and friends call me Bee-Bee. Like Tuna? You like Bee Bee?? I like Tuna? we do deelie.

come quik
BB

Wow! I thought, this'll really be a challenge to close up the loop.

If it had not been for the rather ornate return address label, I might never have found the place. It lay a mile or so south of Brinnon itself, on the canal side of Highway 101 down a steep driveway angled in such a way as to require entry by crossing the road at an oblique angle, on a curve against the oncoming traffic. If I had been asked to give it a name I would have called it "Suicide Court". After waiting for a break in the traffic, I squeaked through between a Semi and a Motorhome, traveling at fifty plus, leaving a group of angry drivers who had stacked up behind me, to start up the hill from a standing start. I settled my nerves by turning around in the narrow driveway.

Even with its small turning radius, the Olds needed about four zigs and three zags to accomplish this. The hubbub on the road and in the drive had alerted the inmates of the house to my arrival and I was met in the small entry courtyard by the lady of the house, a charming grey haired creature with a cultured Bostonian accent. After apologizing profusely for the harassment caused to me by the difficult entrance, she paused for me to state my business. By this time, I had convinced myself, Bee-Bee would turn out to be one of her Mexican servants, and I felt a little diffident at asking this 'Duchess' for her.

"My name is Henry Erickson." I began, extending my hand, "I was hoping to meet a Mrs. Barbara Barranquillas." I closed with my best Spanish accent.

"Oh how wonderful!" She fairly exploded with delight. "Please do come on in." Nonplussed, I allowed her to lead me into the elegant living room where she motioned for me to sit and asked, "Well, now you've found her, what can I do for you?"

"You're Barbara Barranquillas!?"

"Certainly. Have been, for almost all my life. Were you expecting someone else? Someone different perhaps?" She had read my face perfectly. And, from the delightedly mirthful expression on hers, I had a sinking feeling that I had been caught in some trap intended for Adam. My brain staggered under the deluge of probables on top of possibles for I couldn't believe she was aware of my reason for coming. It had been two years since she must have pulled this trick on Adam.

I smiled conspiratorially at her. There could be only one explanation; Barbara B. was a pseudonym she used when playing her trick. Anyone turning up asking for that name would have to be Adam. Very clever. No wonder she'd been so delighted to see me. She'd even had some labels made up for the trick. I felt genuinely sorry I would have to disappoint her.

"I'm sorry." I said gently. "I'm Not Adam."

Pure puzzlement muted her smile and slowly faded as my words sank in. Then the genteel smile returned.

"Well, I'm not Eve. So that makes us even." The smile became a throaty laugh at the impromptu pun, and I responded.

"I thought, you thought, I was 'Adam', when I asked for Barbara Barranquillas." I said, as the laughter slipped into guarded suspicion. She was either an accomplished actress, as I suspected, or completely baffled by my statement.

"Adam? I don't know anyone called Adam." She was very

positive about that. I produced the letter and she examined the envelope with care, before extracting the letter.

It also became visibly evident that although she recognized the return label and the letterhead as genuine, she could no more read it than I could. The envelope was readable because the writer had printed the address and when she reviewed it she noticed the date on the postmark. She showed it to me.

"This letter was posted over two years ago." She said, accusingly. "where has it been all this long?"

"In 'Adam's' filing cabinet." I lied glibly. She looked me over very carefully as I continued. "I only came to return it to you."

One more question and answer session. I was getting quite adept at it by now. Each one different, but each one ending up with a new acquaintance developing. Sitting with her in the gazebo overlooking the water, we discussed all possibilities regarding the authorship of the letter. Later we discussed Adam, her life, my life and various other topics, until the sunlight faded from the far shore and the evenings coolness drove us indoors.

The only person who had ever called her 'Bee-Bee', she said, had been her husband. However, we agreed the prankster could not have been him, because he had been drowned at sea in a storm, three years before the letter was written. While fishing in Alaskan waters, she told me sadly, his trawler had reportedly caught fire, capsized and sank with all hands.

The insurance had paid her a hundred and fifty thousand dollars, which, she declared, despite the fact the boat was already paid for, in no way compensated her for his loss.

I drove home that night with my mind in another world. Two letters actually delivered and I hoped, closed cases. Barbara had asked if I minded her keeping the letter in case she could ever find the 'Prankster' and confront them. Joyce had wanted hers back now that Adam was dead. Uneasily, in her case, I suspected I might have been designated as a substitute, but I hadn't given either of them my address and my phone is unlisted.

My 'Olds' was originally white but oil and road dust have sufficiently covered both number plates as to make them unreadable. I expect someday, the State Patrol will pull me over and tell me to get them cleaned. Meanwhile, short of one of them actually following me home, I didn't know how anyone of the seven, even supposing they wanted to, would ever find me.

It's amazing how a determined woman can out-sleuth the most elusive prey when they make up their minds. I'd delivered three letters out of the seven letters and had just finished off the details of Bee-Bee's file next morning, when I heard a car with a throaty exhaust pull up. A door slammed and light footsteps pattered along my deck, ending in a cheerful rat-a-ti-tat on the door. I hastily closed down the computer and shut the filing cabined before answering the door.

The low early morning sun, streaming directly along the deck lit up every strand of gold in her hair and my heart simply stopped.

When it started again, it must have shown for she chortled, "Surprise! Surprise!. Glad to see me Eh?. I Love your deck!. It's Such a Glorious Morning, I thought you'd like to take me flying". A verbal battering ram. I was down, and out for the count.

"Come in." I gagged, trying to shoo the wolf into the closet. "You caught me by surprise."

"'t wasn't difficult. You said you'd seen the Point from the other side of the bay. You kept your airplane in a hangar just outside your place. Two and Two. I just cruised around until I spotted your car. And here I are." She was right of course. All I needed was a good reason to go flying and here it was. I excused myself to get fully clothed while she cruised around the rest of the house like a cat sussing-out new quarters, or perhaps, checking for the scent of other females.

We walked across the dew coated lawn to the hangars and she helped me push open the heavy doors, exposing my pride and joy to the full warmth of the sun. I introduced Mary to Moonbaby, a name a distant relative had given my ancient Luscombe.

After I'd run my usual routine checks, we pushed her out onto the taxiway, and Mary helped to close the hangar.

Assisting Mary into the airplane and properly secured in the right seat was a heady experience requiring rigid, I mean strict, self control. As I've mentioned, I'm sensitive to scents and whatever she was wearing that morning should have been labeled "Instant Surrender" or such. Macho Me, I gave her the full cockpit drill before swinging the propeller.

Just before switching on and giving Moonbaby the final swing which I knew, would start the engine, I took her hand and showed her, like a child, how the four position switch operated.

"If the airplane starts to move before I can get back in, just reach across and switch her off, like this." I said, taking her hand off the switch. It was my standard patter for first time passengers. It gets them involved and feeling that I'm taking special care with them. They're looking for thrills and there's no better way of getting them than anticipating danger, real or imagined, and being involved. From her expression, I knew I had her full attention.

I skipped most of the explanations from there on because of the high noise level and also because I wanted to get airborne before the impending fog rolled in and made taking off, illegal. We lifted off to the west as the first tendrils of sea fog were reaching over the cliff to envelop the airfield, and turned out over what she had expected to be the sea. Continuing the climbing turn, she was just in time to pick out her cabin, before Beckett Point totally disappeared. There's probably no greater thrill than being lost over an overcast so I decided to give my little thrill-seeker a full treatment and headed west along the edge of the Olympic Mountains.

I was wearing earphones, she had on ear defenders. I could listen to the radio traffic and tell which airfields were open and which by default, were not. She could not. It was a skill I had developed flying back and forth across the Cascades in years gone by. Since I mostly flew alone, why go to the expense of installing an interphone system. I could yell in their ear if I needed to. This put me one notch above my hapless passenger, who, even if they had any piloting ability, had no stick or rudder pedals. I had removed these to make room for cargo I wanted to carry, such as a lawn mower or an eighty pound anchor I once took to the San Juan Islands.

She was worried, I'd made sure of that by pointing out that the airfield we had just left, had already disappeared. She wanted thrills and I wanted to provide as many as decently possible in the time allowed. Another thrill I had learned, is what I call 'The Drop-off Effect'.

Several mountains have steep sides, and if you fly straight and level close across the top of the mountain, when you shoot out over the edge of the precipice, your passenger will frantically grab something for support. Sometimes, if the winds are favorable, the updraft increases this effect. Although the wind was calm, Mary thoroughly enjoyed a couple of those thrills before I turned North across the Straits of Juan Da Fuca, hidden below the overcast, and requested a precautionary landing due to weather at Pat Bay on Vancouver Island. Wasn't she surprised to find herself in Canada!?. Customs and Immigration were sympathetic to our 'Plight' and gave us entry for the day, so we took the bus to down-town Victoria and had a late breakfast at the Empress.

Victoria habitually has great weather while Washington cringes under a cold blanket of fog, so the day passed all too quickly for both of us. It was Mary's first visit and she was enthralled. Since she hadn't brought her purse, it wore a little off my credit card, but just to be in company with this glorious creature in such a setting for those few hours was well worth it.

By mid day the fog had dispersed into small clouds and we left Victoria soon after for the bus ride to Pat Bay and a fair flight across the Straits to Port Angeles to clear American Customs. I deviated from the straight and narrow for my own interest in making an Ariel Survey of Joyce and points south and was surprised to observe an obvious grass runway that ran East-West through the forest, ending almost at the edge of Joyce Reynolds' property. I thought it strange she hadn't mentioned it in the course of our conversations. Perhaps her mind had been too occupied with other things. Ho Hum. But definitely interesting and accordingly filed away in some dark corner of my skull.

"Old friend's place." I shouted, in response to Mary's expression of curiosity as to why we were circling around some spot in what must have seemed to her a dense forest. We cleared Customs as planned and flew back away from the setting Sun for a smooth touch-down straight into the sunset.

"Perfect ending to a perfect day." Mary said, as she left. I could think of a better ending but I held my peace.

Chapter FOUR

Friday's Woman

Today is Friday. Somehow I have to keep things in order and since I dillied and dallied all day Thursday with Mary, The next name I drew from the file should have been Thursday's but wasn't, if you understand my reasoning. If you do, you are ahead of me. The computer welcomed me to Friday, so she became, Friday's Woman. Get it?

Alice Chalmers, (Somehow I connected the name with Diesel engines, possibly from the smell of the envelope.), had a return address on San Juan Island. 'C/o M.V Goliath, Poste Restante, Roche Harbor WA. 98049'

By air, in my trusty Luscombe, that's only twenty five minutes from take off to landing. And, what better excuse to go flying than to head out for one of my favorite haunts on such a lovely day. Less than an hour later, I was talking to the postmistress in the little Post Office under the veranda of the historic old Hotel de Haro at Roche Harbor.

"You've just missed her." The jovial rosy cheeked lady behind the counter responded to my query. "If you'd like to leave that letter for her, I'll see that she gets it."

"Well, that's very nice of you, but there's a lot of explaining to do so I'd like to deliver it personally. Any idea where she might be now.?" I asked.

"She just picked up her cheque this morning. She's probably

on her way to Friday Harbor by now to do her grocery shopping."
She replied thoughtfully. "Alice lives on her boat you know." I'd
pretty well guessed that much but it was nice to have it confirmed.
I asked if she'd gone by bus, thinking she'd probably docked in
the local marina.

"Oh No!" She laughed. "Alice couldn't afford to keep that boat
here. Heavens! It's fifty foot long!. That's why she calls it 'Goliath.'"

"Fifty foot!? I echoed in surprise.

"Yes." She nodded emphatically. "It's one of those old fashioned,
long, thin, swanky motor cruisers. How she handles it all by herself,
is a complete mystery to me." She concluded respectfully.

"Where'd the boat be while she's shopping then?" I asked, trying
to imagine the lady docking, single handed, in a busy Marina like
Friday Harbor.

"Oh, I expect she drops anchor out in Browns Bay and rows
ashore in her dinghy. There'd be no room on the visitor's dock. Not
this time of the season."

"How long is it since she left ?" I asked, mentally computing
the time required for her to travel, versus my time to fly there.

"I'd say about an hour. If you've a fast boat you might catch up
with her." I thanked the postmistress profusely and walked rapidly
back to the Moonbaby.

One quick circle over Roche Harbor gave me a chance to
confirm there was no boat matching the postmistress's description,
in or around the area, so I followed the coastline towards Friday
Harbor, scanning every vessel on the water. I spotted the Goliath
just before she anchored in Browns Bay.

Fifteen minutes later, I was leaning on the roadside rail
overlooking the harbor, near the top of the gangway that leads up
from the dinghy dock. I was watching a slim older lady tying up
her dinghy at the landing float. Alice was a picture right out of a
two tone magazine. From the felt brimmed hat with its bunch of
imitation grapes, to the ruffled blouse almost hidden beneath the
heavy overcoat, to the cream colored stockings, she was pure
nineteen thirty's. Her only concession to modernity and a sea
lifestyle, was a pair of pale blue yachting shoes that looked brand

new. She carried a ten gallon canvas shopping bag with a leather reinforced bottom in her right hand and a brown purse hung over her left shoulder. She moved easily up the steep gangway with only an occasional tug with her free hand on the handrail. Remarkably agile for a woman her age, I thought, as I stationed myself at the curbside diagonally across the sidewalk from the gangway exit where she'd have to pass me.

"Good Morning Alice." I called cheerfully as she paused for a breather. "Nice to see you looking so well." I added smiling broadly. She took a pace towards me and for a moment I expected her to clout me with the shopping bag, but she was only instinctively clearing the gangway and getting a closer look at my face.

"Do I Know you from somewhere?" She asked cautiously, and before I could reply, "Who are you?"

"I'm Adam's messenger." The words just came out, and I was as surprised as she was, until she smiled.

"Thank God for that! I thought you were Jehovah's Witness." She chuckled at her own wit and began walking past me. As I fell into step beside her, she smirked.

"What're you selling today, sonny? Apples?"

"No Dearie, I've brought you back a letter you wrote to my friend, ADAM." I hadn't timed my remark carefully enough for she stopped. Right in the middle of the crosswalk and some eager beaver in an open sports car almost ran us down. He began shouting obscenities at us, so I walked over to his door and made as if to slosh him. As he ducked, I whipped the keys out of the ignition and tossed them over the rail.

"Say that again, and I'll pack your ass straight into Jail." I snarled. "We've a Law in this State about stopping for pedestrians in crosswalks."

I suppose it was the collar and tie, and the navy blue suit that did it, for the kid jumped out of the car and ran to the rail looking for his keys.

"Quite a performance." Alice commented as I re-joined her. "You a policeman by any chance?"

"No Ma'am, Just a rather startled Senior Citizen, like yourself."

She looked at me as if to challenge my right to include her. "Well. You're the one who startled me." She accused me. "Not that young man. Who's this ADAM? you keep talking about."

"You don't remember writing to him?"

"No."

I began to think it would be better if I dropped the whole issue right there. Roba hadn't been involved. She had apparently forgotten her side, so why shouldn't I forget it? We walked on up the hill in silence while I debated this in my mind and were about to enter the supermarket, when she stopped, right in the doorway, and turned to face me. "Tell me about it." She snapped impatiently, as though aware of my indecision. "You got me intrigued."

'Damn you Roba.' I thought. 'I wish you'd stop messing with people's minds. I almost got away with this one.' For some reason, in my eagerness to go flying perhaps, I hadn't opened her letter. Now, I handed it to her, intact.

Shoppers going in and out of the door were jostling past us so I took her hand and led her aside, still staring at the envelope as in a trance.

"Where'd you get this?" She asked quietly, but we were in no place to discuss it, so I led her across the road to 'The Wounded Pig' and offered to buy her lunch.

"I'd forgotten about this." She admitted at the table. "I often wondered why I never heard back from my letter. Maybe you should explain." She faced me accusingly, and, so help me, I confessed.

I regretted the indiscretion immediately. As long as the victim thought the blame rested on some unreachable soul, the resulting question and answer session had been relatively unemotional. The Inquisition that Alice embarked on was pure Catholicism at its most intense. I almost had to take the blame for Roba's advert as well as his death.

To make it more difficult for me to gauge my answers to her accusations, I had no idea of the content of her letter. The interrogation lasted almost an hour and a half, and as if to exact immediate punishment; every time the waiter came over and asked about the meal, she ordered another delicacy. She had an enormous capacity for such a slim woman and the bill for what I had anticipated would be a light lunch, almost stripped my wallet. Finally she was either satisfied with my answers or too full to eat another bite.

"I've got to do my shopping now." She said, leaning back in her seat and patting her middle. "I only shop once a month. so there's a big load to haul and I'd appreciate having a big strong man to help me." She actually smiled at me as if to confirm that this small penance would satisfy her for the great loss my intervention in Roba's and her relationship had caused. I had no escape. By now, I was almost convinced Roba's ghost was at the table with us, giggling his little high-pitched laugh and probably popping over to call the waiter each time her plate had got about half empty.

"I always shop on a Friday." Alice remarked, as we loaded her shopping cart. "The fruit and vegetables are freshest on Fridays. To entice the tourists and the yachties." She explained. I wondered if she was making a bumper shopping spree this time since she had access to some help in carrying it, but she packed it all skillfully into the canvas bag and marched out of the store with it, before I could get around to offering. When I did, I wished I hadn't. I was glad when she directed me to;

"Set it down there, in the bows, and sit yourself back there." she commanded, pointing to the back seat and deftly untying the mooring line before settling herself in the middle of the dinghy. "Keep your knees down so they clear the oars." She added, pushing the heavily loaded boat away from the dock.

Resigned to dealing with whatever fate, or Roba, had in mind for me, I stretched my long legs, on either side of hers and tucked my feet under her seat. She grinned mischievously as we moved away.

"Don't look so worried. I'll bring you back." Then, as if to undermine any over-confidence, added, "When I'm finished with you."

I was down below decks, putting away the last of her tinned groceries, as she had instructed. Alice had disappeared somewhere on deck, when I heard the engine growl and then settle to a steady chug chug-chug. Surprised, I made my way up and out of the cabin to the after deck and looked out as the stern swung around to display Friday Harbor marina sliding out of sight behind Browns Island. We were moving out into the channel between San Juan and Shaw Islands. I realized then with a mixture of chagrin and amusement, that I'd been shanghaied. Other than some concern about how I'd manage to get back to Friday Harbor airfield, I was mostly amused at the notion of this crazy old dame kidnapping me in such a blatant manner.

When I found my way to the wheelhouse, there she was, perched up on a high stool, steering the boat with one bare foot on the wheel and the other tapping out the rhythm of some tune she was softly whistling.

I had to laugh. Her long grey hair, which had been hidden under her hat, now hung down her back. secured by a vivid red bandana. The ruffled blouse had been replaced with a worn denim jacket whose sleeves had been cut to elbow length and the wrinkled hose had gone, revealing the sinewy tanned legs protruding from knee length cut off Levis. The only thing missing was a motorcycle. She turned as I opened the wheelhouse door and positively beamed at me.

"Got everything stowed away ?" she asked, as though nothing had happened.

"Aye Aye Cap'n." I answered, entering into the mood of the moment. "Whose Galleon are we going to plunder today ?"

"Och Aye Me Hearty." She laughed. "Welcome aboard. We've a rendezvous with a flotilla of Canadian Pirates in Reid Harbor this evening. Sort of an annual reunion. I needed an escort, so

I've Deputized you for the job." She concluded with another wide grin. When I protested at the prospect of having to remain overnight, she brushed my arguments aside.

"You told me you had no commitments. No time schedules. Retired. How can it hurt you to spend a night here in the Islands." I shrugged helplessly. "I'll make it worth your while." She added, with a coy smile that left little doubt as to what she had in mind for payment. Maybe my expression betrayed me for she laughed merrily, leaning back relaxed in her high chair, looking so much younger, the prospect seemed far less daunting than if she'd said the same thing a couple of hours earlier.

Goliath cruised easily through the sunlit water for the next two hours while we chatted. Alice steered nonchalantly between the islands without reference to any maps, clear proof of her intimacy with the area, and we entered Reid Harbor about four pm. and dropped anchor, a little way outside the State Park. All the Park buoys were occupied, as she had predicted, mostly by Canadian power boats, and a party was getting under way on a small group rafted up together. As sunset approached, the tantalizing aroma of barbeques wafted in our direction.

"Let's go get invited." She said as she swung the dinghy out of its cradle on top of the aft cabin and lowered it neatly into the water.

She had replaced her denim tunic with a simple white blouse for the occasion and as we were going ashore to collect wood, she wore her deck shoes. The red bandanna, supplemented with a big matching bow, now gathered her hair into a pony tail. The overall effect reduced her apparent age by another ten years.

My jacket, shirt and tie had been confiscated and replaced with a clean white polo neck sweater, giving me a more raffish appearance. It fitted well and I didn't question its source. With the canvas bag stuffed under the forward seat, she rowed between the moored boats heading for the Park Dock. Ostensibly, we were collecting firewood, in reality, as she put it, "trolling for invitations".

Goliath, being a well kept vintage boat, is an object of

veneration to many yachtsmen and Alice had already flaunted her among the moored boats as we searched for an empty mooring before anchoring. Now, as she had anticipated, compliments and invitations came from several of the boats as we passed. Alice charmingly acknowledged the compliments and reluctantly declined the invitations, on the pretext we were bound for the State Park dock to replenish our supply of firewood.

While we were stacking the wood in the dinghy, she confided we would be going aboard the 'Chrysalis' on the way back.

"They've got the best Barbeque." She explained. I thought it was the obvious wealthy-ness. Just as she had planned, we were invited aboard. and an obliging crew man secured the dinghy as we climbed up the boarding ladder.

Chrysalis, was a floating Gin Palace with all the trimmings, and we were soon swept up in the on-board party atmosphere. I was introduced to and promptly forgot, the owner, a rather portly, balding individual in his mid fifties who, I thought, had already consumed far too much of the rum punch from a large bowl on the main cabin table. He, likewise, promptly forgot my existence and swayed off aft with his arm around Alice, eulogizing about the well preserved condition of Goliath. I was left to entertain or be entertained, by Sylvia, his wife, some twenty years younger than him. Certainly she was visually attractive, but her range of conversation was somewhat limited and I must not have hidden my boredom sufficiently, for she soon wandered off in the middle of some description of the Chrysalis, to talk to one of the younger male guests. I re-filled my glass and drifted off to explore for myself.

Forward, down a flight of steps were some six cabins, three on each side, and at the far end of the passage, an open door led into the crew's quarters, where, off to one side, four men were playing cards. Seeing me in the passageway, one of the men got up and came out to ask if there was anything I needed. From his dark skin and accent, I presumed him to be of Mexican origin.

"No gracias," I replied with a big smile, my half empty glass held chest high. "Solo mirando." I added by way of explanation.

He displayed a set of dazzling white teeth as he grinned and spread his hands in a generous acceptance, rattling something off in Spanish which I didn't understand.

I presumed it meant something like "Help Yourself." so I thanked him again and turned away with a cheery "Hasta Lluego." As I left, I heard the door close behind me.

On each side of the stair way, a sliding door marked 'Engine Room' attracted my eye. I love engine rooms in boats. Probably my Dad had carried me into every ship's Engine Room as an infant traveling between England and India, so I was happy when the door slid silently aside admitting me to Chrysalis's throbbing heart. At that moment the throbbing was a dreamy, distant sound of a small generator, the only power plant operating to supply lighting and galley power. The two main diesels were shining and polished with the same meticulous care that Alice apparently lavished on her little Gardner Four. The absence of the characteristic Diesel odor was mute confirmation of this care.

I went around the galleries between these big engines and peeped into all the cupboards noting the neatness of everything. A locker at the extreme aft of the room, held a huge supply of Mobil oil in quart cans. Enough I imagined, to meet the ship's requirements for the next two years. I was just closing this locker when I was seized by the arms from both sides by two men whose presence I was not aware of until then. One was the young man I had spoken to in the hallway. Their expressions as they led me out of the Engine room were anything but friendly. Like a prisoner between two silent cops, I was marched upstairs to the main cabin and out onto the deck, where, for a few moments, I was afraid they were going to throw me overboard. I'd been too surprised to resist, and I supposed that in much the same way I might have felt about someone interfering with Moonbaby, they resented my intrusion. However, it's difficult to apologize to someone when your arms are pinned behind you and no one has accused you of anything.

How the word had spread, I have no idea, but moments later

I was confronted by the Owner and another of the card players. Alice was hurrying some paces behind them.

"What were you doing in the engine room?" He asked quite civilly and soberly, indicating to my captors to release me.

"Nothing." I replied lamely. Realizing that this wasn't enough, I added. "I just love Engine Rooms. Yours is so beautifully neat and clean. I'm sorry if I intruded. I had no intention of offending anyone. I was just wandering around, looking at the ship." My answer seemed to satisfy him, for he dismissed his crewmen and after admonishing me not to forget that strangers alone in the engine room of a ship gives due cause for concern these days, invited me to come in and have another drink, mine having been taken away.

Rowing back to Goliath between the stars and the still black water, later in the night, after demolishing a delicious barbecued steak and two more glasses of punch, I was surprised when Alice quietly asked what it was, I had been looking for in the engine room.

The steak and the rum had undoubtedly blunted my wits, but I was sure she asked this because she hadn't believed my answer to old Baldy Whatsisname. And, for the life of me I couldn't think why. For once in my life I'd actually been speaking the truth. I repeated my earlier statement but she only responded with a sniff, which, in the darkness, I took to indicate she was still dissatisfied with my answer.

"What did you think I was doing down there."

"A guy doesn't just wander into an engine room and start looking into lockers and such unless he's looking for something". She hissed. "I'm surprised they dropped their interest in you so easily. It's not natural." She spoke in such a low voice as if afraid our voices might carry back to the Chrysalis.

"Maybe the truth triumphed for once." I replied, in my normal tone. Something about her secretiveness had penetrated my fuzzy thinking I suppose. If they had anything to hide, and drug smuggling jumped into place as first candidate, someone might be monitoring our conversation with a listening device. What had triggered her suspicions? I wondered, and was about to ask, when the thought of being overheard by some hyperbolic listening device stifled my speech. I'd wait until we were safely below decks. As though to confirm my wisdom, Goliath's ghostly white shape loomed protectively over us and I was relieved to climb up the ladder and act the part of some romantic gallant, helping his lady aboard. We lifted the dinghy with the hoist and swung it into its cradle with the firewood still in place and headed for the wheelhouse. After a last look around the darkened harbor with its shadowy flotilla of yachts, she put her arm around my waist and in an unduly loud voice, remarked,

"Time for bed my love," and opened the door. I didn't think it had been said for my benefit, since our sleeping arrangement had been settled earlier, so I presumed it was for the benefit of anyone she thought might be listening. However, I felt too sleepy to bother pursuing the matter. I said goodnight, I think, and went straight to my assigned bunk, stripped and climbed in. She could deal with her suspicions, as she pleased.

Rum has that effect on me, I barely touched the pillow before I was fast asleep. So deeply asleep, that I had no recollection in the morning, of what might have happened before I woke up to find the light of the early sun illuminating the naked breast beside the one I'd been sleeping on.

Fortunately, there was enough rum left in both of us to enable us to re-enact anything we might have missed.

All suspicious thoughts, and, or actions, had been satisfactorily accounted for by the time Goliath nosed up to the dock at Friday Harbor late on Sunday afternoon for me to disembark. As soon as my feet were firmly planted on the floating pontoon, Goliath backed away, leaving me to watch, with just a faint tinge of regret as she turned slowly and headed out into the channel once more. A vague movement behind the cabin curtains, was all that suggested Alice might be waving goodbye.

As far as I knew, she hadn't even opened the letter. It was back in her hands and my obligation to Roba was completed.

As I flew home, I spotted Goliath, heading North up 'Upright

Passage'. I resisted the temptation to make one low pass overhead as a farewell gesture. If we were ever to meet again, I felt sure Roba would arrange it.

Moonbaby purred steadily across the sunset, smooth as an armchair sliding across a polished floor. The sea moved under the wing like glittering glass. I felt suspended in space while the world passed me by, savoring the unreality of reality until Protection Island appearing below me, broke the spell and I had to take my part in the glide down to a landing.

I collected Friday's and Saturday's mail from the box and made my standard re-entry to normality, with a cup of coffee. Stretched out in my recliner, I scanned the mail, tossing most of it into the box beside the wood stove, unopened. The rest, I took to my office and set in the 'Inbox'.

My computer was still flying through the stars of the screen saver. I swore at my carelessness, touched the mouse, and, thank the stars, the unsaved file on Alice re-appeared. I hadn't lost it. One hiccup in the power during my absence and it would all have vanished. God's truth, I felt as if Roba was mad at me for taking my time disposing of the seven letters. Perhaps he was having to wait around till I finished. Assuming it took one day for each delivery, the job should have been completed today, the seventh day. If only I'd kept on schedule instead of fooling around with each new contact, he'd be free to leave. I imagined him holding me by the scruff of my neck and pressing my nose once more to the grindstone. Reluctantly, I plonked myself in the chair and began entering an account of what I've just told you.

There being neither letter nor envelope to file in 'R's Folly, I printed the computer cross reference on a file card and dropped it in.

I was about to extract the next random selection when I realized It was Sunday. Not Thursday, nor Saturday, and to select another, 'out of sequence' letter was simply inviting more trouble. I told Roba to go screw himself.

I'm not really superstitious, but I shut down the computer to further defy him, and the phone rang.

Hesitantly, I picked it up and was astonished to hear Mary's voice launching into a rather plaintive enquiry as to where I'd been for the last three days. Suddenly, I wondered how she knew my phone number, and realized she must have picked it off one of my phones while I was getting ready, the morning we went flying. What other information had she gleaned in that short time? Not that I had anything to hide, but the seeds of self protection, where these women were concerned, were beginning to sprout. My mind returned to what she was saying.

"I even ran over there this afternoon, when your answering machine didn't come on, in case you were sick. You weren't in and the airplane was gone too."

"I was visiting some old friends in the San Juan Islands." I lied defensively, as I recoiled from the implications of her words.

Warning bells, klaxons, flashing lights, and sirens, can fail to penetrate the screen of infatuation, or love, once a male is stricken with it. The human female is instinctively a predatory creature, and since education lies in the hands of women during the earliest and most formative period of life, men are indoctrinated to accept this as natural. It takes years of sometimes bitter experience before the fallacy of this early teaching comes to light.

However, the realization of all this seldom helps him, when it conflicts with the creative emotions. Had I been a much younger man I might have been overwhelmed by Mary's display of interest, and rushed to fling myself into her tender trap, come what may.

My, momentary pause before replying, must have alerted her, for she immediately changed her tone, asserting how glad she was to know I was safely home again.

"When am I going to see you again? She asked, in a tone that sent a tingle through my bones.

"You tell me." I replied recklessly. She was for coming over to see me right away, but the warning bells were clanging and I gently steered her away from that course, pleading fatigue, and the lateness of the hour. After all the 'flying' I had been doing in the Islands, I needed a good nights rest.

Chapter FIVE

The second Week

Monday dawned clear and crisp. I ate an early breakfast, and was in the hangar working on the airplane. The doors were wide open to allow the morning sun to warm and illuminate, while I'd unwired the drain plug to change the oil. It's a messy job, because the moment the plug is out, the oil runs onto the lower lip of the cowling before falling into the drain pan.

I also had to remove the oil screen between the engine and the pressure indicator tube to check for any metal flakes that might indicate the beginnings of serious internal wear. Knowing from long experience how much my life depends on that ancient engine, I make myself do this every twenty-five hours of flying time.

So. I'm wedged inside the cowling with both hands busy, trying to cut the lock-wire off the screen fitting, when I hear Mary's Ferrari stopping outside on the tarmac.

It should be a federal offense to bother a mechanic in the process of his work. The excruciating contortions necessary for getting at the job is more than enough irritation, and the possibility of making a mistake is enormously increased if one's mind is exposed to additional distraction, such as female chatter and the sight of shapely legs in the sunlight. Ask Mary if you don't believe me.

September is often a month of cool clear nights followed by

sunny days and morning fogs along the coast, as we had already found out. Consequently, we planned to take off early and go west along the coast before turning south to go to a fly-in at Ocean Shores. Port Angeles airfield was still fogged in as we passed and I flew along, following the edge of the ground fog, at an altitude that allowed us to look for a way to fly across the Olympic mountains. The first fresh snow of the year and the morning sunlight, etched their peaks in vivid contrast with the blue sky, and Mary, much to my delight, was entranced.

We had been airborne about twenty minutes when I first sensed the smell of hot oil. There's no oil quantity gauge on the Moonbaby but a glance at the oil temperature was sufficient to tell me we must be losing oil. How badly, I could only guess, as the temperature was rising rapidly. Instinctively I throttled back, hoping to prevent an engine seizure, while we still had some oil pressure left, and began looking for a place to land.

We were over relatively unfamiliar territory. Rugged mountains on my left, and the shore, where there might be a place to land, covered with fog. A perfect recipe for disaster.

Mary, bless her, remained calm as the engine noise disappeared and the nose dropped into the inevitable gliding attitude. Her innocent faith in me, helped me to restrain my own rising panic.

"We're going to have to find a place to land." I said, as calmly as I could. She smiled as though I was joking until I pointed to the instruments and showed her the oil temperature needle in the red range. Her smile vanished and to keep her from losing control, I told her to look down below and tell me if she saw any flat area on her side where we might land safely. At least, with the engine idling, it was nice not to have to shout at each other.

Ahead of us, the land seemed to be entirely covered in forest. No place to land, so I turned back to the east. Comparing the Altimeter and the Rate of Climb indicator, (Now showing the rate of descent), I calculated we had about four minutes of flying left, before we hit the trees. Time was being used up at a tremendous pace by my kaleidoscopic thoughts as I searched frantically for a place to land.

Suddenly, Mary grabbed my arm excitedly, pointing out of the her window.

"There!" She yelled. "Isn't that the place you were looking at the other day?!"

Sure enough, there was a slot in the trees where the road ran and at right angles to it, another gap which I had taken to be a grass strip airfield.

I judged we were too low to risk making a pattern so I made a diving turn towards the nearest end.

"Brace against the panel !!" I yelled, indicating where to put her hands, as I lined up with the strip. The ground was clear of obstructions, but we were too high and I had to make a steep right hand side-slip to get rid of our excess height. Sliding sideways, we cleared the tops of the trees by a foot or two and began the wildest fish-tailing I'd ever done in my life, to dump the extra speed I'd gained in the steep side-slip.

Once down inside the long box of tall trees that lined the clearing, there was no wind and all I had to do was get rid of the speed and stop in the available length.

I can hardly blame Mary for screaming, as Moonbaby sped sideways over the grass with her tail swishing from left to right, before settling down.

I was pretty excited myself. It's over fifty years since Flight Lieutenant Elgy taught me how to slow down by fishtailing a Tiger Moth. He'd have been proud of his pupil. In all my flying, I'd never had such desperate need of that piece of training.

I'd turned off the ignition and fuel in the last moments of the approach for fear of fire and there was nothing more to do except help Mary to get her feet off the instrument panel and climb out of the airplane.

We stood, holding tightly to each other beside the airplane, silent in the sunlight and I realized my legs were trembling as much as hers.

"Don't let go yet." I whispered into the golden curls against my chest. "Or I'll fall down."

"Me too." She lifted her head and smiled. "If we weren't wearing long pants, my knees would be clattering against yours like a set of castanet's."

Being down on the ground in one piece was all well and good, but there was still plenty to think about.

Before I opened the cowling, I knew we had lost all, or almost all of our oil, for the lower fuselage, from the firewall aft, was smothered in it.

Inside the cowling it was even worse. Engine oil was still dripping out from under the nut which secures the tube from the pressure gauge to the oil screen.

Like a condemning finger, the un-secured lock-wire pointed straight at me. I broke into a cold sweat. The evidence of my own negligence would have been impossible to deny if the landing had been somewhere else and the airplane had been damaged. Other possibilities flooded into my mind. One or both of us could have been killed or maimed. I must have put my hands over my face to ward off the visions accompanying the thoughts, for I was suddenly aware that Mary was holding my wrists and pulling my hands down.

"Are you hurt?" She asked anxiously. I shook my head and pointed to the piece of lock-wire sticking out of the nut. She didn't understand.

"Did you get oil in your eye ?"

"No. See the oil dripping out from under that nut?" She peered inside to get a better view.

"Is that where it was leaking from?" she asked with such innocence as to imply there was nothing to fixing such a small problem. "Can't you just tighten it so we can get out of here."

"We could both have been killed." I said as though it should have been obvious to her.

"Well we weren't. Though I did have my doubts." She replied with a smile.

"The resilience of youth." I said shaking my head.

It took the next ten minutes for me to explain how I had omitted to properly tighten and lock-wire that gland nut because my attention had been diverted by her. I couldn't blame it directly on Mary, but I felt justified in showing her and explaining how easily a tiny slip-up like not securing that nut had almost cost us our lives. She was tearfully contrite and vowed she would never, ever, interrupt an aircraft mechanic at work again.

She had wanted so much to help me, and partly to get her out of my way, I had given her the job of taking everything out of the baggage compartment and brushing the dirt out before putting things back. It had kept her busy, but not from talking.

Both our clothes had become soiled with oil when getting out of the airplane after the landing, so to help me unwind, I suggested we wipe the engine and fuselage down with pieces of rag soaked in gasoline. For some inexplicable reason, the rags I kept in the baggage compartment were missing, along with the small tools I always carry wrapped up in them. The cold sweat broke out again, and before long I was covered in oil and sweat, and Mary was beginning to pick up on my irritation. I took off my shirt, tore it up and used it in place of the missing rags but I could do nothing about the missing tools. I got the nut tightened up hand tight and the area cleaned up enough to work in. Mary and I pushed the Moonbaby, tail first, into the long grass and bushes at the side of the runway where she would be clear of any planes that might land, though there appeared to be none based on the strip. We couldn't tie her down because the goat-tethers I always carried for ground anchors and the tie-down ropes weren't there either. Somehow I had managed to forget to put all these vital items back.

"We make a fine team, don't we ?" Mary said very quietly, as we discovered each of these omissions.

"Let's not worry about it any more." I said, locking the airplane. "She'll be OK here. Nobody seems to be using the strip."

We walked in silence towards the road end of the runway. I noticed no ruts or tracks, other than Moonbaby's, and from the look of the grass, it had not been mowed for about a month. Definitely not a busy airport, and Moonbaby was almost invisible.

As I had thought, on the day Mary and I first saw this airfield, the only access to the field was via a track about a hundred yards long from the east end of the runway to the road. It was apparently used occasionally by a car or pick-up as the wheel tracks were almost totally bare of short grass and small seedlings, and there were traces of black engine oil on the longer grasses between the wheel ruts. At the road, the track was closed by a steel gate with a rusted sign on it reading, 'U.S.Govt. Keep out'.

The sign had a couple of bullet holes in it, but the gate was secured with a rusty chain and an equally rusty padlock. The gate was about a hundred and fifty yards further down the road than Joyce's driveway, and as we passed, Mary suggested going in to see if we could get help. I didn't want to do this for obvious reasons and dissuaded her by pointing out the absence of any cars in or around the driveway.

"We might as well walk. The highway's only quarter to half a mile up ahead from what I saw the other day." I replied without breaking step.

"Where does your friend live?" Mary suddenly asked, after we had gone past.

"I'm not really sure." I replied, "It's somewhere around here. I've only ever seen the place in the dark." I lied as the memory of Joyce's silhouette, waving from the driveway we had just passed, flashed across my mind. "I think we might be able to catch a bus up on the highway."

Mary said nothing and we walked on in silence.

One can travel, East and West across the north of the Olympic Peninsula from Port Townsend to the Pacific coast by the county bus system. It is inexpensive and reasonably well coordinated from county to county, and like most rural bus systems you can catch the bus wherever you find it.

We were lucky, an east-bound bus picked us up after less than half an hour's walking along the highway, and we completed the return to my house a little under six hours from departure.

Mary took a lot of fatherly comforting, to absolve herself from her growing feeling of responsibility for our predicament. She desperately wanted to make amends by taking me back to the airplane with whatever I needed to get it flying again. I had to repeat, over and over, that this was my problem, not hers, and in any case it was too late to drive back. I had a friend who would fly me back there tomorrow and more-over, I would rather have him accompany me, as he was a qualified Aircraft Inspector who would make a few checks to be sure the engine was fit to fly. Finally after a lot of hugging and forgiving, she drove off and I went back into the house and called my friend.

Kamm gave me a little lecture on the advisability of having my work inspected, and next morning we flew to the unmarked airfield at Joyce, checked the engine, refilled the oil tank and ran the engine. By the sheerest dumb luck, I had caught the problem just in time and there had been no damage. This time, I let Kamm tighten and lock-wire the gland nut.

We were unable to find the airfield marked on either of our sectional charts or in Kamm's Washington Pilots Manual, so he recorded the co-ordinates of both ends of the runway using his GPS, and marked it on his sectional, for future reference. State Emergency Fields are often located in far out of the way places, but, as we checked, the sign on the gate said, 'U.S.Govt.'.

I had brought some thinners and rags so I could complete the clean-up before flying home, but Kamm had another appointment so he left and I went back to work on Moonbaby's good looks.

An hour or two of cleaning, waxing and polishing was exactly what Moonbaby needed and it always gives me time to think about things other than what I'm doing. Some people knit or sew or wash cars or some other routine activity to get relaxed. Polishing airplanes relaxes me. Working the rags round and round, I began to see a pattern developing in my self appointed task of delivering letters.

Monday was the day I'd met Mary, and I had spent the following Monday with her. Today was Tuesday, a week from the day I'd met Joyce, and here I was, whiling my time away, with Joyce virtually next door. What could be more natural than to walk over to her house about lunch time and see if she was around. Perhaps she could also tell me something about the history of the airfield so close to her home. According to her, she'd lived there a long time.

Skimming over my recollections of my first meeting with Joyce, I experienced a growing sense of anticipation which kept colliding with other considerations. Again, it was as if Roba was reminding me that tomorrow was Wednesday, as if I didn't know. Also, if I stayed too long, I might not be able to take off in the dark since Moonbaby had no lights. Not that I would have tried, but, if I didn't show up at home Kamm might begin some kind of enquiry. He might even report me missing. The runway was plenty long enough. He'd had no problem getting off in his Mooney, but the Luscombe might find the long grass a detriment to picking up enough speed to get off and climb over the tall trees at the far end of the runway.

To check the engine and make a track in the grass, I taxied Moonbaby up and down the length of the runway a couple of times to roll the grass down. The ground itself, was exceptionally smooth, as though the runway had been laid with turf instead of just allowing the native grass to re-seed the ground once the tree stumps had been removed. Using the taxpayer's money I supposed. Obviously, whoever used the runway nowadays, seldom parked their planes here because the clearing on each side was never mowed. From the size of the brush which had sprung up almost shoulder high, between the runway and the trees, I deduced that some kind of brush cutter probably came and cleared this area about once every two years. It was about due for another haircut.

All this activity of mine saved me the need to go see if Joyce was home, for when I parked Moonbaby in the area I'd stamped down at the road end of the runway, I was surprised to find her leaning on the gate watching me. Apparently she hadn't recognized me until I was a few feet away. "Henry." she exclaimed, her face lighting up with pleasure. "Didn't know you were still in the Service." Then, to my surprise, she slipped the padlock off its chain and opened the gate.

I smiled even more broadly, recalling how Mary and I had climbed over it yesterday without even thinking of investigating that possibility.

Isn't it strange how we jump to conclusions.?

You've probably jumped to a few of your own by now, about Joyce and myself, so I won't bore you with details of how we spent the afternoon. I will say however, I learned a lot about the history of that little airfield from a delightfully congenial informant.

Pleading the absolute necessity of getting back to base before dark, I took off and flew home, landing just before lighting up time.

Wednesday dawned dull and overcast. Washington's weather pattern varies with the rapidity of a woman's moods. English weather is more predictable. Maybe the reason the English are regarded as 'Stodgy'. In the years before I came to the U.S.A. I had noticed how Monday dawns bright, and the week stays like that until Friday afternoon when the weather changes to the weekend's rain. That was why I left.

All night I had been thinking about that airfield and the stories Joyce had told me about it. It had been cleared in the summer before war broke out in Europe, by the company that owned the timber rights. A team of Forestry workers had leveled and planted the whole clearing with grass. Each week, some soldiers came and tended the grass. Before American involvement in the war, there bad been a lot of activity with airplanes landing and taking off. I deduced from her comments that it was used for some kind of short field training. By the time the big airfield at Quillaute was finished, the activity diminished and then only an occasional airplane landed. For many years, the airfield was virtually abandoned, except for an occasional crew that came and mowed the middle of the strip. Sometimes, usually in the middle of the night, an airplane would land, an army truck would meet it and then it would fly away and the truck would leave.

"Charlie and the girls used to have fun spying on them from the shelter of the forest." Joyce commented, a sad wistful mist clouding her eyes at the memories of a happiness lost. I held her close, bringing her back to the present. "Who looks after the place these days ?" I asked.

"I don't know. A truck used to come, now and then with one of those tractor mower gadgets, and just mow the middle of it." She drifted into her reminiscing again, while I caressed the back of her neck.

"We used to run a few cows there, for a while. Charlie did something to the padlock so I could just give it a bit of a jerk to open it. We never left them there overnight of course. Not while the airplanes were using the field anyway."

"Doesn't anyone use the field nowadays?" I asked, wondering if it might be possible to buy, rent or lease it. "I don't think so. I haven't seen anyone using the field except the man who mows it. Like I said. Not by day, or I'd hear them like I heard you. Sometimes in the middle of the night I wake up, thinking I heard an airplane. Maybe I did, maybe I didn't. Who knows, there's always airplanes flying around these days. I'm not getting out of bed to go look now, am I?"

"You don't run any cows there now, do you?"

"Not since Gertrude died."

"Gertrude ?"

"Yeah, Gertrude was the last cow I kept over there.

She must have eaten something. Something the mower man left I think, because she died only a few days after he'd mowed."

"What did the Vet think she died of ?" I asked.

"VET !? Joyce gave a harsh laugh. "What d'you think I did?. Carried her to the vet on my bicycle?

"When did this happen?" I asked.

"About three years ago. I don't take Florence over there. That's why the grass is so long now. Serves the bastards right."

I didn't fully believe her, as I'd noted a few of Florence's calling cards. Old ones I agree, but this year's for sure. The picture emerging from my conversation with Joyce, was of an old military airfield, abandoned, but possibly still on the government's books. Unless. Unless some other organization was maintaining it. The story of Gertrude's misfortune, didn't make sense. Why would a government employee want to poison a cow that was virtually working for him ?

While Joyce rambled on with her story, my mind was on making a visit to the County Assessor to find out who was paying the taxes on this airfield. I've always dreamed of owning one of my own.

The County Treasurer's office in Port Angeles, had no record of a tax parcel matching my description of the airfield, so I went to the Assessor's office trying to get a description. They had nothing on the books and the map of the area only showed the Reynolds's homestead. There was no boundary around anything where I estimated the airfield to be, but I splurged four dollars on a copy anyway.

Ariel photographs showed several small areas of cut forest nearby, but none I could define to my satisfaction. The entire area was still under the jurisdiction of the State Department of Lands and this particular section was mostly school dedicated land. The young lady clerk was as helpful as she could be, but quite convinced I had the wrong area. "There is no airfield in that area." She maintained, and suggested I go to Olympia and get a copy of the latest 'Satellite Photo' If I wanted to continue with my search.

I went, I saw, I found it, to paraphrase Caesar, and on my way back from Olympia, I stopped in for a cup of tea with Barbara Barranquillas. Why not? It was Wednesday, I was thirsty, and anyway, that's the day I'd met Barbara. I could almost feel the glow of Roba's approval.

She told me she'd spent quite some time trying to sleuth out the originator of the letter I had returned to her, without success. However, she made me very welcome and served an excellent gourmet meal which we ate together out in the gazebo overlooking the Hood Canal.

Thursday morning I aroused early and by breakfast time, I had entered all the current events in my computer, and with eyes averted, plucked the next letter out of the file marked 'R's Folly'.

Once again I had a desire to burn the whole wretched thing

but couldn't. It was as though Roba was there in my office accusing me of treachery if I didn't finish my part of the bargain I'd made when he asked me to take care of his affairs. 'I'd extracted those letters and I should fulfill my responsibility to him and the ladies who had responded to his advert.' It seemed suddenly so cold in the office, I turned on my electric heater under the desk and slit the damned letter open.

It contained a three by five file card, with a newspaper clipping of Roba's advert stapled to the back. As I glanced at the card, the fuse in the electric heater popped and I shivered with almost feverish chill as I reached down to re-set it before giving the card my full attention. The few lines typed on the card read:-

Dear Adam,

If I ever needed anyone, I need you now. My husband of the last fifty years, passed away eighteen months ago and I have been 'out of my mind' with grief ever since. The children write and tell me I should find someone if only to talk to, but the thought terrifies me. I'm sure this is what you put the advert in the paper for. Please help me.

Evelyn.

I was appalled. Here was the very thing Roba had in his mind when he sent in the advert. How many others he had received and acted on ceased to matter. By my act, I had deprived Evelyn of this chance to find her way out of her misery. How many similar chances had come along in the three and a quarter years that had elapsed? To say the least, Roba's gallant offer had been unusual. The response had proven that in our age group there's an enormous number of desperately lonely women.

In my fit of temper, I hadn't looked at the return address when I'd slashed the envelope open. Her letter had moved less than six feet, from where she'd posted it, to Adam's mailbox. They probably even knew each other, at least by sight.

No wonder my office had suddenly grown cold. I visualized Roba extracting all the loose energy out of the air in my office to fuel his rage when he saw the letter. I imagined him looking over my shoulder, and held the envelope up so he'd get a better look at the postmark.

"Look.!" I shouted at him. "If some dork in the Post Office had put this straight into your box instead of sending it to Tacoma for stamping, it'd have been somewhere else in the pile instead of in the stack I took." I turned accusingly towards him.

"In fact, if you'd faced up to the consequences instead of getting drunk, I wouldn't even have been involved!!" "Wow." I gasped, wiping the sweat off my forehead, as I realized I'd actually been shouting aloud. I reached under the desk and switched off the heater, tossed the letter on the desk and went into the bathroom. This whole thing was getting out of control, I needed to shock my system back to reality. A cold shower did the trick nicely and while toweling I decided to take the letter and return it with a full explanation. Evelyn could think whatever she liked. Sympathetic as I feel towards anyone who has lost their lifelong companion, I also admire those who can surmount their agony and go forward with their lives. I'm sure Roba's intention, with his crazy advert, had been to help such people, not become their nursemaid. I'd help Evelyn if necessary, but she and Roba, weren't going to send me on any guilt trips. I'd take all the cold showers necessary to see to that.

Evelyn Clearwater, according to the envelope, lived on in the same house she and her late husband had owned for the past twenty years. It sat on a knoll beside a small lagoon at the foot of the cliffs in Gardiner on the west side of Discovery Bay. When I drove down the lane that led to her house, she was out in her garden orchard, picking the last of the years apples. I had seen her somewhere before but couldn't place it right away. She was a robust, nicely shaped woman with a round florid face topped with a crown of pure white curls. As she came over to meet me, smiling brightly and then I remembered having danced with her on a few occasions when I had first started going to the Thursday dances at the V.F.W. She always sat in the same clique, with a tall angular gent who I'd assumed was her husband, though they didn't often dance together. I remembered also, how lightly she moved for a woman her size and I had wondered why they hadn't been there for a long time. Now I knew. The knoll lay directly across the Bay from Beckett Point, where the late Mary Lykes had lived. And, as Evelyn later mentioned, Mary had been a member of the same dancing group although I couldn't remember her from Evelyn's description.

When I told her about Roba's death, she already knew of it from the local obituary. When I returned the letter and explained my connection with Roba's estate, her only surprise was that he had never replied to her card. She seemed so casual about this, I felt safe to deny my complicity in that event and she took my standard explanation without question. We'd been sitting in the living room, looking out across the water, and from my chair I could see Beckett Point in the afternoon sunshine. Evelyn had gone out to the kitchen to brew up a fresh pot of tea. I was thinking about Mary Lykes, the living version of course, when a hissing that I'd only been vaguely aware of until then, suddenly stopped and a voice on a radio chilled my skin.

"Clearwater. Clearwater. This is Goliath. Do you read?" Evelyn was still out of the room, and I looked around for the radio with a momentary hope of silencing it somehow before she came back. Too late. She was returning with the tray when the radio repeated the call. She regarded me, smiling strangely.

"Startled you Eh?"

"Yes." I nodded, trying to appear nonchalant though my heart was thumping and I felt like fish caught in a net. My mind was racing. Three of the letters were from women who knew each other. I'd just lied to Evelyn whereas I'd told Alice the truth and suddenly they were talking to each other on the radio. Evelyn went over to the radio, picked up the microphone and answered.

"Goliath. This is Clearwater. What's on your mind Alice?" After a short pause, the radio replied, "Oh. Nothing. Just calling to see if you were on the air. Goliath out."

"Clearwater clear." Evelyn replied and hung up the mic. "Friend of yours ?" I asked, feeling as dumb as I sounded. Evelyn gave a funny little twisted smile. "There's a few of us old fisher-widows round here who keep in touch. It's nice to know someone out there checks up now and then. Same if you get a bit down, there's always someone to talk to. Doesn't cost anything either, not like the phone." "That's kind a nice." I said. "You always use the same channel I suppose." "Thirty nine." She replied.

Why I thought of the movie Thirty Nine Steps, I don't know, but I decided to take one step more, dig out my old forty channel C.B and hook it up, as soon as I got home.

Thursday evening, after I got home from Evelyn's, a mere five minute drive from my house, I went straight to my shed and unearthed the C.B., dusted it off and spent the next two hours hooking it up in my already over-crowded little office. Only after sitting for an hour listening to the fuzzy background hiss that came from channel 39, did I remember why I hadn't hooked it up long ago. First of all I had to find space for my spare car battery under the desk, and secondly, for it to be any use, I had to be there when somebody made a call. I switched it off in disgust and went to bed, frustrated.

During the night Roba paid me a visit. He sat himself on the little clock radio and kept switching the red clock numerals off and on until I woke up. At first, I didn't see him and thought the power had gone off for a few minutes. All the digital clocks in the house do that if the power fails. I reached over to reset the blooming thing and he had to jump out of the way. When he did, the numerals were back steady and I noted the time was exactly 12:00 midnight. Somehow, I wasn't surprised to see him reduced to the size of an elf about eight inches tall. He sat on top of the clock and dangled his legs in front of it swinging his feet. I had to ask him to stop swinging them because it made the numbers flicker and woke me up. Obligingly, he curled them up and squatted on the top with his arms wrapped around his knees.

He reminded me of Mr. Elfinstone, the little cement garden Leprechaun that sits on my rockery and keeps watch while I'm away from home.

"What d'ya make of that radio call yesterday Hank ?" He

asked, like he was enjoying my concern about getting caught in a lie.

"I suppose you set them up to do that." I replied indignantly.

"Not on your life. How you handle your affairs is your business not mine. They've been doing that for years."

"How do you know that?. You've only been." I was going to say "Dead" but stopped myself just in time. "I mean. It's only a couple of months."

"Hank." He said earnestly. "There ain't no such thing as 'Time' where I am. You know that. It's all. NOW !. No Past, Present or Future. It's just a matter of choice." I was amazed. This is something we'd often talked about when he was alive, and I wanted him to give me some first hand info. about it from his present standpoint. But despite my pleading, he wouldn't. He did want to tell me something though, if I'd just shut up and listen.

"You've got to keep an eye on those women Hank. Didn't you get the message yesterday?"

"What message?"

"Evelyn was telling Alice to 'Shut up'"

"Why ?"

"Because YOU were there." Suddenly, I understood why Evelyn had called Alice, 'Alice' instead of 'Goliath'. Code talk for: "Keep your transmissions on a personal level."

I'd heard it, without hearing it. However, that wasn't all Roba wanted to tell me.

"Look in the bag of my things, under your bench. There's a gidget in there you can hook between the radio and the tape recorder to record anything that comes on the radio."

He didn't even say 'goodbye'. He was just, gone, leaving me wide awake. I mean so wide awake, I got up and went out to the shed, right then and there, in the buff, and found it. Never tell me the dead don't talk to the living.

Friday morning early, I went into town, to Radio Shack, and bought myself another portable tape recorder, like the one I use to record my phone calls, some connectors and a twelve volt power supply, to replace the battery, and spent the remainder of the morning, hooking everything up. I tried different channels but reception seemed poor on almost all of them. (Another reason I'd given up on using it in the house.) When I had tried it out, some years back in my truck, reception had been far better. There was something wrong with the antenna and grounding system where I had mounted it in the office. The antenna had been mounted on the flange of the truck's roof where the six by four feet metal made a fine ground plane. Where I'd mounted it, on the window frame, just couldn't compete. I ended up screwing a three-foot by five-foot aluminum sheet to the roof of the house, grounded with a number ten gauge copper wire running down the side of the house and clamped securely to the grounding rod itself.

With the antenna mounted in the middle of this sheet and the co-axial cable spliced to some T.V. co-ax, and led in through a new hole in the wall, the rig worked like a charm, bringing in stations from as far away as Vancouver B.C. I finally felt confident that anything Goliath and Clearwater had to say to each other would be received clearly.

By the time I'd satisfied myself the lash-up would work, and recorded a couple of truckers somewhere on highway 101 talking on channel sixteen, I was dog tired and hungry. I erased the tape and re-set it to monitor channel Thirty nine. It was dark, by the time I'd tidied up and made something to eat. I watched a documentary on channel nine and fell asleep in the middle of it. Somewhere around midnight, I woke up and made my way stiffly to bed.

Saturday morning was another clear calm autumn morning with no sign of fog and I was tempted to give Mary a call. But, by the time I'd had my morning coffee, shaved and showered, I'd remembered it was Saturday and I was supposed to pick the next letter and deliver it. I went into my office, took the sixth letter out of "R's Folly" and opened it. I entered the usual copy of letter and envelope into the computer and sat down in the kitchen with a cup of coffee and Monica Carmichael's letter.

Monica had written the usual plea for masculine company

common to divorcees. However, she'd also enclosed a color portrait photograph of a strikingly attractive woman. She must have felt desperate I thought. A woman of that beauty should have no shortage of male suitors. Her return address, only given on the letter itself, was a post box on another San Juan Island. Lopez Island. Again, the envelope had a Tacoma Postmark. The address on the envelope was too smudged to read, but it was different.

I thought back to that distant evening in Roba's house when I'd found him in a drunken stupor, in the midst of his fan mail. I'd taken those letters from a single pile. Later when we went to work on the letters we had continued stacking them by return address on the envelope or by the postmark. I could understand letters from the Olympic Peninsula being franked in a central collection place like Tacoma, but letters from the San Juan Islands? They'd funnel through Anacortes, or perhaps Mount Vernon.

I pulled up the computer's copy of all the letters I'd already delivered. All had the Tacoma franking mark. So also did Sunday's letter, still in the file. Unable to think of a logical explanation, I put it down to 'Roba's Binge.'

In those days, I kept an old VW Square-back in a parking area alongside the airfield on Lopez Island. It had been there from the time I moved Miss Nomer, my houseboat, into the boatyard at Fisherman Bay for overhaul. I took the letter, and by one-thirty that afternoon, I was in the sunshine on Lopez Island, driving towards Lopez Village.

Of all the major Islands, Lopez is my favorite. At the peak of the summer season, it gets a little crowded with campers and cyclists, but there are few hotels or motels, so it escapes the saturation that Orcas and San Juan suffer.

Off season, it's a serene rural haven where everyone seems to know everyone else, and passing motorists wave to each other. I took about an hour to find someone who knew Monica and directed me to her house.

Monica's residence is one of those dream homes one imagines

for a retirement getaway. Dug back into the hillside, a little way back from the top of the cliffs overlooking a sheltered bay on the south shore of Lopez, it commands a superb view of the bay and a small island about a quarter of a mile out into the Straits of Juan Da Fuca. On each side of the island, the view encompasses the water stretching to the Washington coast with the Olympic Mountains on the horizon.

From the road, the house is almost invisible, as the roof is at eye level and completely covered with grass and vegetation. Its stone walls blend into the hillside and one would never know a house was there, except for the short drive and the parking space, where the grass is mowed. There was no car in the parking space, so I walked around to the seaward side, where the entry door and all the windows, faced the sea. Its stone wall about three feet high was surmounted, from end to end, by a gallery of small pane windows stretching to the top of the wall under the roof overhang. From that side it looked like the enchanted cottage from a fairytale book.

The Dutch style door, the lower half of which, was crowned with a wooden plaque on which the name "CLIFNEST" had been carved and painted in white, was not locked. Except for opening it and calling out to see if anyone was home, I didn't like to intrude.

The lady at the supermarket in Lopez Village had also mentioned that Monica sometimes worked part time at a farm where she made and sold Sheep Cheese, and other times during the summer season, she worked at the little general store at Richardson, where the main North South road ends. I went back to the car and drove the short distance to the store.

Richardson is another picturesque spot. The little general store, across the road from the Mobil tank, sells just about anything, and if they haven't got it, they'll direct you to where it is sold on the Island. Across the road, incongruously small below the huge storage tank, a solitary gasoline pump provides motorists with self service. After filling up, you go back to the store and find the store keeper, if you want to pay for what you've taken.

Between the store and the tank, the road runs directly onto the dock, where a shed houses a small ship chandlery and a fueling station for the fishing fleet and the occasional cruising yachtsmen.

Saturday turned out to be Monica's day at the farm. The storekeeper gave me directions, and when I arrived, she and two younger ladies were in the final stages of cleaning up for the day, so I bought some of the cheese and wandered around the little farm yard for half an hour, waiting for her to finish.

The photograph she had sent with her letter, although it must have been a few years old, didn't do her justice as far as I'm concerned. She displayed more focused energy than both the younger women combined, and seemed to sparkle, where they merely exhibited the glow of youth. She was, I guessed, in her early fifties, yet it was to her I was immediately attracted. Her hazel eyes were alive with the joy of living and her smile seemed a permanent part of her face, like a welcome sign, even in repose. I had not wanted to present the letter in the presence of the younger ladies and when I mentioned the reason for my visit, in the parking area after work, she immediately invited me to return to her house.

The low sun in the west, slanted through the window panes producing a pattern of squared rainbows on the east wall which added to the fairytale aura surrounding us as we sat discussing the letter. It was a perfect setting for an impressionable old fogey like me to fall in love and I did. I could feel it happening, yet powerless to stop myself. The witch of the west, wicked or otherwise, was winding me up in her web whether she realized it or not. Never has fish or fly been so eager to become entangled.

For her part, Monica seemed more saddened by Roba's death than disappointed that I was not Adam, and, unlike Joyce and Alice, was in no way inclined to make me a substitute. Although we talked until well after dark, she showed no inclination to have me stay the night or even come back for another visit.

I drove back to the airport and took off almost directly into the rising moon and flew through the stars, all the way back home, as if in a dream. I knew where to find her, but had no way to reach her, except by letter, or another visit, and what excuse could I drum up for that.?

Roba, it seemed to me, was exacting a rather stiff penalty for my having interfered in his affairs.

Chapter SIX

The Seventh Letter

As you might imagine, Sunday morning found me as discombobulated as if I was recovering from a massive hangover. The fact is, I'd gone almost straight to bed after getting back from Lopez. But unlike most nights, when I fall asleep as soon as I hit the pillow, I couldn't go to sleep at all. I didn't want to do anything; not, that is, enough to make me get up, so my mind wandered off into its random access mode, flitting from one theme to another, in connection with the letters.

Roba was apparently otherwise occupied for he didn't show up to add his two penny worth. I suppose he was regaling his ethereal buddies with tales of my predicament, punctuated by his high pitched giggle. They might even be making bets on how many of the seven I'd ultimately get involved with. Four out of seven so far, depending on your interpretation of 'involved'. One, if you think the way I do. Ethereals, having no physically generated emotions to contend with, are so much freer to play with ideas than mortals. They can influence the tides of human affairs more than most of us realize. To make an idea into a physical thought which can eventually flourish into a new creation requires a mind to plant it in. And, who knows how many Ethereals each one of us has hovering over us, with a packet of idea seeds in one hand and a trowel in the other.?

I could almost feel the root of an idea trying to wriggle its way into my grey matter, when the sound of a voice jerked me out of its reach, (which is another way of saying I promptly forgot it), and I heard the name "Goliath" coming faintly from the direction of my office. In an instant, I was out of bed and half way down the passage when I heard it again.

"Clifnest calling Goliath. Come in please."

Just that little extra emphasis on the word 'Goliath' had been all it had needed for the word to penetrate my consciousness.

Goliath must have been asleep, for after a couple more calls, Clifnest signed off.

By then, my heart was racing. Just the sound of Monica's soft southern drawl coming out of the speaker right there in my office, stimulated a series of ideas as though the mysterious Ethereal Gardner had dumped half a packet of seeds into my mind.

As I mentioned earlier, Roba always had to have the 'latest' in gidgets, and this one which interfaced between the CB radio and the tape recorder was no exception. You may have noticed whenever anyone uses a hand held microphone, they 'key' it about a second before speaking. That pause gives the gidget time to get the tape moving before the sound of the voice comes on. This gidget, also has the ability to turn the recorder off, if it senses no signal for the next five seconds. These two features make it possible to record several whole transmissions without using more tape than necessary. A 90 minute cassette, can monitor several hours of radio conversations, especially on channels like 39, which is often silent for long periods.

I spent the next hour playing back all the voice traffic on channel 39 since 11:45 am. on Saturday morning and sifting out those that concerned names like Goliath, Clearwater, Clifnest, and a couple of others that so far I had no experience with. All were women's voices.

I could not shake off a spooky uneasiness that three of them, were women with whom I had recently become associated, through the letters.

It was well after 2:00am. when I sagged back into bed, thoroughly worn out mentally and spiritually. If Ethereals were really running this circus I had been shanghaied into, they could get on with it without me.

When the early morning sunlight, reflecting off the mirror at the foot of my bed woke me again, I felt as if I'd rolled the last four hours away inside a tumble dryer. It wasn't purely the effect of my thoughts tumbling inside my head, the bed smelled like a stale sauna and the sheet and pillow were still damp from my sweating. I was de-hydrated.

Later, I discovered I'd left the electric blanket on all night.

Later still, after three mugs of coffee and a soothing shower, I also discovered I'd left my 'surveillance' rig on, without putting in a new tape. The old one was still in the stereo where I'd been dubbing the extracts from it, to another tape.

This was, I realized, the second time, since I'd started returning the letters, I'd suffered such a disorder on waking after I'd met one of the women and formed a romantic attachment. First Mary, then Monica. In each case, the woman had no romantic interest in me.

Was I suffering from an inability to accept such rejections? If so, how should I handle the situation.? First time, I know, the attraction had been, and still was, purely animal lust. Mary was young enough to be my grand daughter. Her only interest in me was some sort of 'Father Figure', who she sensed, could be manipulated to provide thrills and entertainment at no cost. A sort of sexless Sugar Daddy.

With Monica however, my attraction to her, had little if anything to do with 'Lust'. Maybe she had sensed this and therefore felt no urge to respond to me. What a mess. Unless I showed her some sort of Male-Female inclination, (the more inclination the better) she'd regard me as an acquaintance or maybe at best, a friend, for ever. Whereas, any more inclination or display thereof, would undoubtedly drive Mary away in disgust.

"Women are Strange Cattle." Is how my father had expressed it. I thought I was beginning to understand him at last.

I poached a couple of eggs on toast for my Sunday breakfast, to boost my sagging morale, physical as well as mental and washed down a handful of the vitamins I hadn't been taking since my last visit to the doctor, with some more coffee. Nicely replete, I settled down at the computer to record all I could remember of Saturday's Woman, before extracting the Seventh letter from 'R's Folly'.

Nora Transome, lived in an apartment in Port Angeles, yet the envelope was 'franked' with a Tacoma postmark. Didn't any of these women ever post letters from home? She'd also included a photograph; a smiling dark eyed brunette, in the mid thirties, wearing a black and orange long skirted dress and shawl, standing proudly, with one foot raised on the doorstep of a small motorhome. A typical old style Bohemian Gipsy with a modern caravan. One almost suspected the rear bumper might wear a sticker. "Have Van will travel." The Kodak paper was dated 1989. Along with the usual demographics, she also mentioned working in the Federal Building and included two phone numbers, home and office, with an invitation to call either one, at any time.

My watch showed 12:40. Lunchtime. Maybe she'd be home from church. I might be two years and three months late, but I called the home number and she answered on the second ring. After her first surprise at my reason for calling, she asked if she could call me back. She was busy with guests and would like to have time to hear more of my story. I gave her my number.

She had a slight foreign accent I could not identify and there was a wary quality in the way she spoke. It would not have surprised me if I'd never heard from her again. I copied and filed the letter and the envelope into the "Sunday's Woman" file in the computer and the cross reference in 'R's Folly with a sense of satisfaction. The job was almost finished, though I hadn't yet made up my mind exactly how I'd dispose of any hard evidence. Every letter, except the deceased Mary Lykes's and Nora's had been returned. If I didn't hear from Mrs. N. Transome before the end of next week, I'd mail it back to her with a letter of explanation.

At precisely 5:45pm there was a loud knock on my front door. I'd been snoozing in my recliner, waiting to hear from Nora and woke with a start. I glanced at the clock before opening the door.

It was as if she'd stepped right out of that photograph onto my front porch deck. The identical black and flame skirt with matching blouse and shawl. The same tall haughty stance and the regal smile in those jet black eyes, though the hooked Romany nose seemed more prominent here at close range. Her raven black hair was pulled back and hidden under the shawl. She was either pure Romany Gipsy or an Indian woman. Mighty impressive and handsome in either case. I wondered how she'd found my address, since my number isn't listed. Then I remembered. She worked in the Federal Building. I suppose my lengthy silent scrutiny prompted her smile to broaden and she asked in the same strange accent. "Aren't you going to invite me in."

"Oh! Yes!. Please do!." I stammered, stumbling out of the way like some unfortunate lackey who'd failed to acknowledge the Queen. "I thought you were going to phone. I hadn't expected you to come all this way."

She came in, slipping off her shawl and handing it to me as though I was her servant. Nonplussed for a moment I turned with it in my hand before realizing there was no place in my pad to hang anything up, and did as I usually did, hung it over the back of a chair.

"It isn't so far." She said smiling at my discomfiture, "Besides, I wanted to meet you in person." She seemed to swirl herself into my swivel chair as she spoke, and swung it round to face me, and somehow this action eased the stiffness in me and I managed a hearty chuckle.

"So here you are. What do you think of me and my pad."

"It's very nice. Very homey. I feel comfortable here, with you."

"Can I offer you a drink?" I asked, wondering if I was breaking some Federal law, by offering an Indian, alcohol. She nodded slowly as though not too sure of my motives.

"A small one please. Have you any liqueur?"

"Drambuie? Benedictine? Crème de Menthe? Scherezade?."

I rattled them off with a confidence I didn't feel, hoping I'd be able to find the one she chose, with some still left in the bottle.

"Scherezade? I've never heard of that drink. Is it nice?".

"Very nice." I assured her, marveling at the way women always seem to chose that one. "Just a moment," I added getting down on my knees to rummage under the kitchen sink amongst the Clorox, Lysol, and other Cleanser bottles. I was part way lying down, reaching to the farthest back corner of the cabinet when I realized she was standing over me watching my antics in amused amazement.

"I hope you don't keep all your liqueurs down there." "Sure do." I replied laughing at her expression of horror. "Nobody goes snooping around for liquor under here." I said, proudly emerging with the bottle in hand. The label on the bottle said "Cream of Kentucky" and it took a while to convince her I was not trying to poison her. Apparently it's not a well known brand of bourbon on the Olympic Peninsula and I flatly refused to divulge what I had done to convert it into a delectable Liqueur. I poured two small glasses and invited her to chose. I took the other and offered a toast.

"To Adam" I said raising my glass. "Don't take too big a sip. Hold your breath, and let it dissolve in your mouth." I added, taking a goodly sip and enjoying the sweet breath of heaven diffusing into my brain.

She went back to her chair and followed suit and I watched the colors changing on her face as its magic invaded her. We spent the rest of the evening and well into the night, discussing Adam, and Roba's well meant efforts to ease the lot of the lonely senior ladies.

Two refills each, of Scherezade's potent magic, soothed away any lingering discontent over the lost letter, lost time, and any other losses the world had incurred in the interim. Needless to add, it was too late for her to drive home so we curled up together like innocent babes in the wood, under my smelly blankets and slept like a pair of angels. In the early morning when I felt her wake up, I pretended to be fast asleep, allowing her to get up, dress and leave with dignity.

Although we'd done no more than sleep the night away,

cuddled together in the same bed, I felt she'd be too proud to ever want to see me again.

Once you retire, unless you start some new routine that is keyed to the days of the week, it doesn't take long before they cease to matter. Except for such inconveniences as weekend traffic, store and office closings, all days eventually become the same. Mondays, through Fridays, when the Nora's of the world must rise early to go to work, the retirees, as I was doing, can lounge in bed.

As soon as this thought crossed my mind, I felt thirsty and got up to make my daily coffee and toilet routine. Old ingrained habits, it seems, merely change their shape. I set my coffee mug on the tile I keep for it, beside the computer keyboard, and switched on.

I use "Direct Access", a nice little Menu program that welcomes me with the date and time, and an alphabetical menu of programs to chose from. I toggled down through the Main and Sub menus to 'Roba's Folly' and 'entered', "Sunday's Woman". The last entry, which I'd made after phoning Nora Transome read:- Letter returned.

However, I'd left out the date which would have completed the whole story, and enabled me to close forever, I hoped, the files on 'R's Folly'.

I had given Nora her letter back sometime during our discussion last evening, and I remembered her putting it on the coffee table beside her chair. Had she taken it with her?

I'd already typed in the date, when that damned little voice prompted me to get up and go look, before I 'saved the working copy'.

I must have stood for a full minute, looking at the blasted letter, while my mind went through the full gamut of reactions from rage at Roba for failing to remind her to take it, to relief at still having a reason to contact her again. The memory of her warm body against mine finally triumphed and I went back into my office and deleted the last entry.

I had hardly closed the file when the phone rang. I knew,

even before I picked it up, who it was, as surely as though there was a special ring to it and my spirit resigned itself to the inevitable. Monday had barely wiped the sleepy seeds from its eyes and here was Mary's cheery little voice, asking if we could go flying again on such a lovely morning. "SHIT !" I almost uttered the word aloud, I was so stressed. Mary's wheedling voice became a twanging pair of chords stretched from inside my ears, right down to my gonads, like the reins of a horse, while its rider jumped it over a hurdle. Mary, it seemed, was not going to take "No." for an answer. "Haven't I scared you enough with my flying.?" I asked, hoping to dilute her bubbling enthusiasm a little.

"I wasn't scared." She replied almost indignantly.

"O.K. Then why were your knees rattling? You said they were. Remember? not me." I reminded her.

"That was just the Adrenalin Rush after the excitement."

"Well I was scared, and I'm still scared. Something like that makes a man loose faith in his own ability, or competence as a pilot. It isn't something to take lightly you know." I laid it on rather thick, I admit, but she wasn't to be put off.

"Well it didn't stop you going flying on Saturday. Did it.?" She flung the last two words at me like a challenge and the alarm bells went off just as they used to whenever my Mother caught me out in a lie. How the heck did she know? She'd been checking up on me again. I could feel the hackles rising and spoke before I could stop myself.

"Been Spying again Huh?"

"Spying!?. Is that what you call my being concerned about my friend.?" I could hear the tear ducts beginning to fill up

"Honey." I gently protested, realizing that the vinegar wasn't working, "You shouldn't be concerning yourself about me. I'm a big boy. I can take care of myself." I have to confess, I'm no match for a determined woman, and as hard as I tried not to, I ended up telling her to

"Come on over Honey, I'll get the Moonbaby out and ready to go by the time you get here. Bye"

"Wimp.!" I said, as soon as the phone was down, but as I

looked at myself in the shaving mirror, I realized, I should have said.

"Wolf".

Everything would have gone just as I planned it, if I'd not decided to create another exciting experience for Mary.

Low Flying.

Except for a few obvious caveats, low flying over water, isn't any more dangerous than high flying and a whole lot more interesting as well as exciting. We were skimming along over the water between Orcas and Decatur Islands at fifty feet and a hundred and six mph., when she took hold of my arm and asked if we could go back around on the other side of the little island we'd just passed. She'd seen a boat there she wanted to have another look at.

Always eager to please, I banked round to the right and lined up for a low pass between Orcas and Williams island, (The little one she'd indicated).

Williams pass, isn't much more than a hundred yards wide between the shore of Orcas and the steep rock face of Williams Island, and Goliath was hugging the deep water close to the rock face as she steamed steadily westward. It was obvious from Mary's frantic waving as we passed, that she recognized the boat and probably the woman on board as well.

"Friend of yours?" I asked casually, once we had resumed our course.

"She's really a friend of my grandmother's, but I recognized her boat." The rest of Mary's remarks were lost in the engine noise and my own turbulent thoughts. I was trying hard to accept, or even rationalize, the idea that so many of the ladies whose letters I had picked up at random could be connected together. Allowing the mind to wander while flying is dangerous at any time. To do so at such low altitude is suicidal, and if it hadn't been for the sudden clutching of Mary's hand on my arm we might well have rammed the ferry pulling out of Shaw Island.

As it was, we cleared the mast by inches as I pulled up over it, and almost hit the water coming back down. I glanced at Mary whose face was white with shock and my grin must have scared the life out of her because my own heart was putting out almost as much horsepower as the engine.

As gently as my pounding heart would allow, I eased back on the stick and gradually climbed about fifteen hundred feet to allow both of us to regain some measure of composure. My mind was busy sorting out the possibilities of the ferry crew reporting the incident. Hopefully it had happened so suddenly that nobody had a chance to read the numbers on the side of the fuselage, and if anyone reported it, they'd probably call the airplane a Cessna anyway. Instead of landing at Roche Harbor as I'd originally planned, I made a wide circle overhead to allow Mary to see the place and then diverted towards Stuart Island and landed there.

Being a Monday, all the week-end visitors had already left. There were no boats in the State Park moorage, and apart from a wisp of smoke coming from the chimney of Littlwolf's cabin, no other signs of life on the island.

Stuart Island is almost the last island in the American San Juans, and in much darker times after my wife died, I haunted it like a lost soul. There are only a few cabins on the Island and I knew my way into all of them. In those dark days, I'd found where each of the cabin owners stashed their cabin keys. Some were up. Usually on a nail in the back of some crevice or cranny, while others were down. Usually under things, some obvious, others a little more subtly hidden. One guy kept his, wrapped in an old plastic bag and then made sure it wouldn't blow away by putting a brick on it. I often thought he must have brought the brick from home for that purpose as it was probably the only brick on the island.

I used all the cabins at least once, always leaving them in the same neat clean condition in which I found them. I never stole more than a cup of coffee and a few of their family secrets. I still have all the secrets because I never betrayed them, and as I was always alone, I had no concern about an accomplice ever doing so either.

There are two sheltered harbors on Stuart Island. Reid, where the State Park dock is, and Prevost, which has a less protected anchorage but a little bay with a moss covered bank and a fine gravel beach. By some quirk of the currents, the water is always calmer and warmer there, than anywhere else in the area, which is why I'd led Mary to this place after a long and strenuous walk.

We sat together at the top of the soft moss covered bank and luxuriated in the sunshine and the seductive fragrance of the pine trees, enraptured with the natural beauty around us. I had immediately shed my warm flying jacket on arrival, and after five minutes adoration of nature, decided it was now or never. I stripped off the rest of my clothes and stepped into the water. I took a couple of paces in to be sure it was as advertised and finding it so, plunged in and swam out into the deeper water.

We'd had a long warm summer, and the thermo cline, the demarcation area between the warm and cold waters, was about five feet down. One could dive down through it into the cold water and come up into the warm, giving yourself the illusion it was even warmer than it really was. Mary is no 'Piker' and it took no more than a few words of encouragement for her to take the plunge as well.

We frolicked in the sea for about ten minutes before the real cold began to make itself apparent. I prolonged the playfulness for as long as I could before we both stepped ashore onto the moss. Had it been the full heat of the summer sun I'd have laid down on the moss and let nature take its course. But the Autumnal sun doesn't have the stuff such dreams are carved from, so I gathered up our clothes, slipped on my shoes and led Mary to the cabin sitting back from the beach, under the trees.

The key was under the brick in its plastic bag and in less than a minute we were inside, the fire was alight, and we were crouched over it in our birthday suits soaking up the warmth as it blazed into life.

I'll not bore nor titillate you with the details of the rest of that day. But Mary has often suggested another visit. However, I don't have to go to such heroics nowadays. Confucius, he say. "Old

Age and Treachery, often triumph over youth and strength." Mary wanted to stretch her day at the Island with me, but I finally had to put my foot down and tell her we were trespassing in these peoples cabin. While she was still in shock, I got moving on the restoration of everything we had disturbed in the course of our fun and games. I set her to work, cleaning out the grate and re-laying the fire, though I had to help her a little as she hadn't registered exactly how things had been before we came in.

I suppose it's her sheltered up-bringing that made her feel guilty about what we had done and I was banking on her anxiety to get out of the cabin to extract the maximum effort from her. I wanted to get out of there for a better reason. Deer on the runway.

Stuart Island has a fairly short runway. As evening closes in, the deer move out of the trees into such open spaces, it's only prudent to roll up and down the length of it at least once to 'shoo' them off. Even if I'd been alone, I wouldn't risk taking off after the light faded too badly to see them. We got everything cleaned and restored to the AFC (As Found Condition) and made our way, via the short cut, to the airplane in time to get out before it was too late.

Mary was entranced with the beauty of flying across the water at night, and even though Moonbaby has no landing lights, she showed no nervousness during the landing. By the time we'd closed the hangar, her 'High' was so restored, she took off in the Ferrari as though it was an airplane.

I recorded the bare details of our trip in the computer file. Any subtle nuances, related to those events, that might later rise up to smite me, remain in the read only memories of my own head. With the file saved and closed, I luxuriated in a warm shower and slipped into bed, to sleep like the 'Just' are supposed to.

Tuesday morning, like Monday, dawned bright and calm. I turned on the answering machine and turned off the ringer on the phone in my office. Monday's mail which I had collected after Mary's departure was still lying on my desk, and I didn't want to be interrupted by any wheedling voices trying to seduce me into another 'Stuart Island Odyssey'.

Another feature of Roba's tape recorder gidget I forgot to mention, is a little red light that stays on if any calls were recorded. I hadn't noticed it last night, so I assumed some traffic had been recorded during the night. The sleep of the Just is not easily disturbed.

There was quite a bit of traffic but it was faint and hard to read as the squelch kept breaking in on the transmission as though it was far away. I could make out that the callers were women from the pitch of the voices, and someone calling herself "Risstaker", or something like that, was calling 'Goliath', I was unable to read the messages clearly because of the static, but what mostly impressed me was that the transmissions began at 21.00 hrs (9:00pm.) while I'd been in the shower last night, and lasted only three minutes. Was Mary 'Risstaker'? Or "Risk taker"? And was she calling 'Goliath' from a CB in her car on her way home.? Just to say she'd seen the 'Goliath' from the air?

She'd certainly been through a few 'Risky', or perhaps 'Risqué' episodes in my company. Also, the way she drove that Ferrari could definitely be described as, 'risky'.

I transferred the tape to my storage tape, rewound the cassette and re-set the system, before turning to the mail. A large envelope with an Olympia postmark drew first attention and contained the six by ten enlargement I'd ordered of the area around the 'non existent' airfield at Joyce, taken from the satellite photo. I put on my Jewelers bonnet with its high magnification lenses and studied the area of interest. Sure enough, the outline of the clearing and the lighter line of the runway was perfectly discernable. Joyce's house and farm were also quite distinct, and if the print was rotated so that the shadows were away from you, indicating the sun was behind you, even the buildings and individual trees could be picked out. I hovered mentally, over her place, for a solid five minutes, scrutinizing the entire layout until I felt so familiar with it, I could have found my way anywhere in the whole farm. 'So much for an individual's privacy,' I thought, suddenly realizing it was Tuesday again, and once more I was concentrated over Joyce's place. Time for another visit? If so, I'd better get going before Little Miss Muffet decided to make another check on the hangar.

I think I must have been developing some kind of a complex about collusion between all these unrelated ladies I'd come to know through those seven letters, for I decided not to announce my arrival at the little airfield. By arriving high, making a wide gliding approach, and slipping in over the treetops as silently as a Luscombe can, with its 85 hp motor at idle, I cut the switches as soon as it was safe and rolled to the far end of the runway. Unless Joyce was outdoors, listening carefully for an airplane, I doubted whether she would or could have heard my arrival.

With Moonbaby tucked back into the brush at the far end of the runway, it was unlikely anyone would be aware of her presence and I decided to do a little reconnoitering around the area before visiting with Joyce. One aspect that had intrigued me was her veiled suggestion that night landings might still be taking place. If so, how did the pilot 'find' the airfield in the midst of this forest? If the planes had landing lights on them, she'd surely have been aware of it because her bedroom had wide windows, without curtains, on three sides. Any airplane landing with lights would be visible in at least two of those windows. Probably the field itself had its own lights, dormant, until someone or something, on the ground, activated them. Some private airstrips have lighting that can be activated by a pilot keying his microphone a set number of times on a certain frequency. Such a set-up would require electrical power and a sensor of some kind. I hadn't seen anything like that. Yet.

As soon as Moonbaby was safely tucked away I began my search. Not too sure of what I was searching for. if this had been a Government operation, and Joyce had indicated it was, there should be plenty of hardware visible, but I walked the entire length of both sides of the runway without seeing any traces of runway lights. Doubtless in the forties, when the place had been cut out of the forest, the little mushroom lights you can buy today, from the Wag-Aero catalog, were not in existence. I next began a similar walk around the outer perimeter of the clearing itself. I hadn't gone more than a hundred yards from where the Moonbaby was concealed, when I saw what appeared to be a mound of wood debris about fifty feet out into the forest. It looked 'unnaturally natural', if you know what I mean, and a fairly distinct path through the undercover of the forest led almost directly to it from where I was standing. It turned out to be a small shed buried in forest debris with a door, covered in tree bark on the side facing away from the airfield. The door had a rusty padlock, similar to the one on the gate of the clearing, except that the hasp was already broken in half and turned easily to one side allowing the lock to be removed.

Inside, close to the door on a low platform, a small Honda Generator stood with two flexible wire leads running from its output receptacles. One ran out and under the wall of the shed, the other went to a light bulb under the roof. Eventually I found the wire outside, running up the trunk of a tree and about ten to twelve feet up it could be seen spanning the gap from tree to tree in the direction of the airfield. I followed the wire to a tree on the edge of the clearing where it went into some kind of a junction box about the same distance up from the ground, and split into two strands, each running in opposite directions from tree to tree along the side of the clearing. This wire was a brown twisted flex that had a standard brown or black light-bulb receptacle attached about every thirty feet or so, fixed to the trunk of each tree, facing the runway, and artistically covered with pieces of bark to resemble broken branches or bird's nests. I certainly hadn't spotted them as I walked the perimeter, and presumed that when switched on, the effect would have been to create a pool of light in the clearing, only visible from above. I had noticed a dead limb hanging down from the junction box, and when I pulled on it I could feel the click as it turned some kind of switch. I presumed this would allow for the indicator lights at the ends of the runway to be changed to indicate the direction for landing. In the daylight there was no way to determine how this would appear to an approaching pilot. Perhaps the switch reversed the colors of the end lights. I'd have to come back some night to find out.

Inside the shed, there were several five-gallon cans, full of gasoline. Many more, I thought, than would be required for the generator. Perhaps this spot was a refueling station for aircraft. In the subdued light of the forest, and devoid of any windows the only light inside, came from the door itself. But after my eyes adjusted, I could make out what appeared to be a single bunk, and a stack of bedding wrapped up in a sheet of black plastic. There were also five pairs of rubber boots lined up like soldiers under the bunk. I couldn't resist examining the boots and found to my surprise they were all different sizes of the same make and style. A real family gathering and only one bed!

I needed some time, and a little more historical information, to sort out in my mind, the significance of everything I had discovered.

It was noon, and having skipped breakfast to avoid being trapped by Mary, I was beginning to feel hungry. Poached brown eggs, fresh milk and pancakes were calling from just across the airfield. I restored everything including the switch to the AFC and headed out to Joyce's house for brunch.

As I had observed from the aerial photograph, there was a well-worn trail from the back of her barn, to the corner of the clearing. Although the continuation of this trail through the trees was not visible on the photograph, I found it without difficulty, and arrived on the brick patio un-observed.

In the South-East corner between the kitchen extension and the sliding glass patio door. Joyce was stretched out in the Sun on a chaise lounge, wearing nothing but a pair of panties. Patch, her ten year old border collie sleeping in the shade beneath the cot, opened one eye as my shadow fell on the ground beside her. Immediately her tail began to wag and Joyce started up, reaching reflexively for the shotgun lying on the bricks on the far side of the chaise.

"Gee whiz you're jumpy.!" I exclaimed. "Patch didn't even bat an eyelid when she saw me." I added, by way of justification.

"Mister. You'd better come-a-whistling, any time you choose to come in through the back yard in future." Joyce snapped in a tone as flat as the expression on her face. "Sorry. I came from the airstrip. I didn't think you'd mind."

"I don't. At least where you're concerned. I don't welcome strangers in this attire. Not as a rule." She said, a slow smile softening the hard lines of her face.

"Can't see why not. It's much more inviting than your 'Mother Hubbard' and that old hat. You've got a real nice body. And when you dress it up in a smile, you're damn near irresistible." I said, crouching beside her and giving Patch a gentle caress.

"You've as much Blarney as an Irish Tinker." Joyce responded with a merry laugh. "What's on your mind?. Food I've no doubt."

"Well it was. But some female around here is filling the breeze with Pheromones that make me think of less fattening diets."

"Must be Patch." she said, getting up and striding with a provocative wiggle towards the sliding glass door, with me in pursuit. She set the gun in it's rack and turned, giving me a look of pure devilment.

"What'll it be?" She said, holding me off at arm's length. "Food or Femme?"

"Both." I laughed, chasing after her as she eluded me and fled up the stairs. I caught her as she tried to shut the bedroom door and we tumbled onto the bed. I hadn't realized how strong she was until she rolled me on my back and ended up astride me. Pinning my shoulders to the bed and gleefully grinding her pelvic region against my middle, she proceeded to undress me, while I lay back enjoying the novel experience of caressing the tantalizing nipples she dangled before my face.

"You want food?. You better work for it." She whispered, shifting her lips from mine to my ear. We both worked for it, ending up in a gasping, sweating, heap on the floor. Never in my life have I experienced a woman having such a fantastic orgasm. She heaved and writhed, up, down, and sideways like a serpent, howling and groaning loud enough to alert the neighbors half a mile away. I literally had to grab leather to stay in the saddle, with the result that I'm still uncertain who won and, in the end, I was too exhausted to care.

In the tranquil aftermath of a good meal on top of our satisfied egos, we sprawled together on her over-stuffed couch and talked the afternoon away. I steered the conversation in the direction of the property boundaries she owned as well as more detailed memories of the airfield activity over the years.

She didn't properly know where the boundaries were, but as far as the airfield was concerned she was pretty certain it bordered their southern property line. They had homesteaded a quarter section which had its eastern edge along half a mile of the road. After Charlie left, she had never bothered to check the markers, and in fact, from what she told me, I was of the opinion she had no real idea where any of her boundaries, other than the road, lay.

From my observations of the plats and topographical records, I was beginning to think the airfield itself lay completely on her property. I had counted the paces as Mary and I walked from her driveway to the highway and it had been less than six hundred and fifty. If the highway itself was one of the other boundaries, the airfield must lie entirely on her property, which would account for the county records not showing it as a separate taxable parcel. In fact the clerk had denied its existence entirely. This highway is part of a military road system which was in existence before they bought the property, so if their northern border was on the other side of the road, there would probably have been some correspondence related to that issue, over the last forty years. Joyce had no recollection of any such.

Perhaps, I thought, I could superimpose a tracing of the map over the satellite photograph and find out exactly where the boundaries lay.

At that moment, it seemed inappropriate to say anything like that to her, but the idea intrigued, even excited me, and the thought of another trip to Olympia, reminded me that tomorrow was Wednesday and I should perhaps look in on Bee-Bee en route.

A pattern was beginning to develop, wherein each of the seven ladies was becoming associated with the particular day of the week on which I'd met her. I could imagine myself having to learn a new table for the days of the week.

Monday is Mary's day.	(that rhymed, somewhat)
Tuesday is Joyce's day.	(Rejoice)
Wednesday is Bee-Bee's day.	(Relax)
Thursday is Evelyn's day.	(Not far to go.)
Friday is Alice's day.	(Yo!Ho!Ho!)
Saturday is Monica's day.	(No. No. No.)
Sunday is Nora's day.	(Whoa! Whoa! Whoa!)

All of which served to alert me to break myself away from here and get airborne before it once more became too dark to risk a take-off.

Chapter SEVEN

The First Repercussion

I left early on Wednesday morning to get to Port Angeles by nine when the offices opened and went to the assessors office for the latest copy of the photo map covering the area of Joyce's homestead. These photos are taken at regular intervals by the Coast and Geodetic Survey Department, from airplanes flying at a set altitude, so the photo scale is approximately one quarter mile to the inch. Super-imposed on similar scale copy of the platted, area one can develop a fairly accurate co-relation between the two. It may not be quite perfect, but the error is probably less than plus or minus a hundred feet.

From what I found, the airfield was probably built on the North side, instead of the South side of her Southern property line.

I bought copies of both, and headed for Olympia, where I discussed these findings with the officials of the C&GS Dept. in Olympia, and their conclusion was much the same as mine. Namely, that some army surveyor, back before the war, made a simple error and effectively condemned or just, 'took by default', a chunk of the Reynolds's homestead for what had later become an abandoned training airfield.

They gave me some forms and Department of State numbers so we could fill in and submit a claim, to have the area restored to its taxpaying owner. This was all well and good, If Joyce wanted to do anything about it. She was still, after forty-five years, paying taxes on that property, and should have a good case for claiming it back, and possibly getting a sizeable refund. So, who was maintaining an operation there now?

I mulled over these questions as I drove back from Olympia and almost overshot the entrance to Bee-Bee's house.

Barbara was just as agreeable, in her aristocratic manner, as the first time I'd called in to deliver the letter, and promptly set about providing a cup of tea and some biscuits. She also had some interesting news for me, regarding its author.

We were again sitting in the gazebo overlooking the Hood Canal when she showed me a copy of the weekly Peninsula paper in which she'd placed an advert in the "Freebies" Section.

Bee-Bee where are you.?
Please call!. ADAM.
Phone xxx-xxx-xxxx.

The 'x's are mine of course, since I cannot divulge names addresses or phone numbers.

I looked up from the paper she handed me, wondering to myself what had prompted her to do this. She must have seen the question in my face for she said.

"I was getting nowhere asking subtle questions around here so I decided on using the direct approach."

"But its over two years since Adam put his Ad. in the paper." I protested. "Is it likely they'd remember doing it even if they see your Ad?. Whose number is this anyway?"

"It's an answering service in Sequim." She replied, giving me a smug little smile. "Adam's address was Gardiner, but there's no service there. The nearest one's in Sequim and they're the only ones with a Caller Identifying Capability." Her smile broadened proudly as she spoke.

"Don't you think that was clever of me?"

"Very. Have you had any responses yet?" She shook her head.

"It only came out in today's paper. I'll call them later in the week if they don't call me."

"Well I wish you luck." I said, though my tone must have inferred little hope. "Will you call me if you get any replies.?" She thought it over for a few moments and replied.

"Would you like to come with me if I turn up an address that seems worth investigating?"

"If you'd like me to."

"I would. I know you're not Adam, but you are the only one who knew him, so I'd appreciate your company."

"I'd be happy to." I was about to add 'Anytime' when I remembered. "I'm really only free on Wednesdays." I added hastily.

"I'd noticed." She remarked, as though there was more that she could say but chose not to. Then she smiled broadly.

"I don't know your phone number. It's not in the book." She concluded, eyebrows raised, waiting for my response. I didn't think she'd abuse the privilege so I told her the number and she wrote it on the table-cloth.

We spent another hour or more, talking in the gazebo until the evening sun began to recede from the shoreline on the other side of the Canal. Then I took my leave of her and continued homeward, sifting in my mind, some of the details she had spoken of, concerning her life with Enrique. They had met in Mexico, some twenty five years ago, when she and her first husband were on holiday in Acapulco. Enrique, a wealthy and attractive Mexican, had openly pursued her and paid her many compliments. They had a small intrigue together which apparently left Enrique with a deep desire for her, and after her husband, William Reynolds, died, Enrique had come up to visit her and she had gone back to Acapulco with him and re-married.

For a couple of years she had been in Seventh Heaven with him there. The house in Brinnon was virtually deserted, but Enrique had insisted she keep it as a summer retreat. During one of the political disturbances in Mexico, Enrique had suddenly found it necessary to flee the country and they had escaped to the States and settled in Brinnon.

The money Enrique had in Mexico was confiscated and the small amount they had escaped with, went in the purchase of his fishing boat and the Alaskan license. Although she had spent a couple of summers with him fishing, she had not liked the life in Alaska, and for some years before his accident, she had remained in Brinnon while he fished the Alaskan Salmon. He had been a successful fisherman and the boat was paid off before his accident, so she had been well taken care of by the insurance.

I had listened intently to her story and particularly when she mentioned her original husband's name. In the course of a few judicious questions, I came up with the realization that Barbara Barranquillas was, in effect Joyce Reynolds's Ex-Sister-in-law.

"When and where will this intriguing series of alliances between all these women cease?" I silently asked myself.

To cap it all off, I had become aware of an occasional hissing noise in the background while we talked, and as we were saying goodbye in the driveway, I distinctly heard it again followed by the sound of a voice.

"What's that noise I keep hearing?" I asked innocently,

"What noise?"

"It sounds like someone dipping a fish in a fry-pan for a second or so. Then it's gone.". Barbara looked puzzled.

"I don't hear anything." She said, and almost immediately, the hissing repeated.

"There it is again!" I exclaimed, and a smile broke across her face.

"That's the Sea Bee."

"The What!?" I said, trying to look mystified.

"The Citizens Band Radio. Almost all the wives of the fishermen have them in their homes. We talk to each other while the men are away, and to the men on the boats when they get back near home."

"I thought the fishing fleet has to use the Marine band, like the airplanes use the aircraft band." I said as though her information surprised me.

"They do, but we'd have to buy licenses for a set at home if we used that band, and there's nothing to say the ships can't use the Citizens Band, or walkie-talkies for that matter."

"Where is it ?" I asked, looking baffled, as though I hadn't understood her.

"Come." She said, taking my hand and leading me back into the house, and into her den, or perhaps I should have said her husband's den, for it still bore the character of a male's occupancy. The C.B. radio was neatly mounted above his roll top desk, within easy reach and as if to demonstrate its effectiveness it rasped into life as we looked at it, breaking squelch as though to rid itself of some undesired wind.

"I must have set the squelch too low." Barbara said, reaching up and giving the knob a delicate adjustment.

"Quite a gadget." I remarked, noting the channel selector was showing '39' in the window.

"Why's it set on channel Thirty nine ?" I asked. Barbara gave a wistful smile.

"I've never changed it. I've never turned it off either. I guess it's like a window of hope you never close." Perhaps I squeezed her hand a little more than usual as we left the den and again as I got into the car, for she gave me a peck on the cheek and said gently, "See you next Wednesday.? Unless I hear something interesting before.then." I thought I detected an inflection of hope in her voice.

As noted, I had plenty to mull over on the rest of the journey home.

It was a little after seven that evening when I got home and collected the mail. Amongst the usual assortment of bills, exhortations to take out a new credit card, and advertising circulars, was a note with no stamp on it, which had obviously been hand delivered.

At first I assumed it came from Mary Lykes, since I hadn't made any attempt to contact her, following our trespassing experience on Stuart Island. However, it was from Evelyn Clearwater. Just a card with the usual flower and robin design in color, tentatively inviting me to see her at the Thursday dance at the V.F.W. in Sequim.

As I hadn't given her my phone number or address, during our meeting last Thursday, I wondered how the note had been delivered. I decided the invitation to dance, would be accepted, but I would tread very lightly.

I went to bed early. In consequence I woke up around four in the morning and instead of getting up, I lay in bed, wide awake, looking at the ceiling. It's a condition conducive to clear thinking and I suddenly hit on the idea to install a C.B. in the Moonbaby, and immediately switched to visualizing the complete installation in my mind.

With that, I'd be able to hear, and if necessary, reply to any of the transmissions from any of the ladies on channel thirty nine, something I could hardly expect from the house installation. Of course, I realized, I'd have to give myself a different 'handle' for each one. But, from anywhere in the air, above a thousand feet or so, I'd probably be able to reach any one of the ground stations, whereas some of them, like Bee-Bee for instance, wouldn't be able to hear the replies from the more distant ground stations, because of the mountains between them and her.

The more I thought about the relative locations, the clearer the pattern developed in my mind. Ground stations Clearwater, Lykes or Risktaker, and Cliff-Nest, could probably reach each other at any time. And, Goliath too if she was in an area which was not screened behind some high ground. On the other hand, anyone in the area of Port Angeles or Joyce, would probably not reach Clearwater, Lykes, or Bee-Bee, and vice versa. Although they might reach Cliff-Nest and on occasions, Goliath.

The more I thought about the amazing co-incidence linking so many of the people I'd come to meet through Roba's letters, the more intrigued I became with the idea of equipping Moonbaby with a C.B. radio. In consequence, I made another trip to Radio-Shack, and spent all Thursday installing the equipment.

The V.F.W. dance begins at seven thirty pm. and ends at eleven on Thursdays. Habitually I dance three times a week, for exercise, and arrive at the hall about an hour and a half after the music starts, and stay to the end, for two reasons. Firstly, I avoid the period when the floor is most crowded. I prefer roaming the floor with a partner, instead of the stationary wiggle and semaphore style which a crowded floor tends to enforce. Also, later in the evening, the air conditioning, is better able to cope more effectively with the smoke from the smaller clientele.

When I entered that evening, Evelyn was sitting with her old friends, in the same area they always occupy. I made no show of having seen her, got my glass of draft beer, nodded to a few of my acquaintances and parked in a vacant seat. When the music started again, she came over to my table and we danced. She was still as light on her feet as I'd remembered although she'd put on a little weight, but we danced well together. She wanted me to join her table but I objected to the number of smokers there so she came and sat with me.

I find it difficult to converse in areas of high noise level, specially when I'm dancing. In consequence, I sing if I know the words. If I know my partner well enough I sometimes paraphrase the lyrics and create a little humor in the process. However I didn't feel I knew her well enough to give full rein to that talent, though she did get a laugh out my version of Blue Bayou. At the next interval, I asked her how she had found my mailbox and she told me she knew the Mail carrier and had asked her to drop it in there for her.

Strange, isn't it? how easily one is deluded into a sense of privacy where little exists. As we continue to populate the earth, Privacy will become an even scarcer commodity.

Not that I felt any particular lack of it, except where the developing relations with these seven women were concerned. One wonders, in the historical sense, how Henry the Eighth managed to juggle his six wives, until it becomes apparent that they were all in their separate time zones and he could arrange to kill off with impunity, any that wouldn't co-operate.

The seven ladies I'd acquired, while not exactly categorized as wives, were all semi disposed in that direction apparently and Evelyn's behavior could hardly be described as 'Indifference'. All that is, except Monica who I desired, with an almost adolescent infatuation, despite her obvious lack of interest. My preoccupation with these thoughts, prompted Evelyn to bring me back to earth by asking if I was feeling alright.

"Right as rain." I said, grabbing her hand and heading for the dance floor as the Midnight Blues struck up with their rendition of my favorite dancing tune 'Rock and Roll Angel'. When the dance ended we dropped back on our seats breathing hard from the exertion. I was sweating so badly I excused myself and went to the men's room to cool my face and wipe off the sweat. Otherwise, I felt exhilarated and really beginning to enjoy the dancing. When I returned to my seat, Evelyn was not there so I sat down, supposing she likewise, had gone to the rest room.

I sat out the next number, not one of my favorites, and waited for her to return. When the number ended and she hadn't returned I began to wonder if she was alright, perhaps the dance had been too vigorous for her and she was still resting. When she hadn't returned by the start of the next number I asked the waitress to look in and see if she was alright. In a little while the waitress came back to say she wasn't in either of the ladies rooms. Thanking her, I went out to the car park, in case she was resting in her car. She'd told me earlier that she'd driven herself to the dance, and although I had no idea what kind of a car she was driving, I looked in the half dozen cars still in the parking lot but she was not in any of them. It was ten thirty by my watch, I could only presume she'd gone off home. Something I'd said or done perhaps had upset her I supposed. I could think of nothing that should have offended her, yet it seemed somewhat rudely out of character for her to leave without saying she was going. The more I thought about it, the more bizarre it seemed. Eventually, I went out the front entrance and walked up and down the street looking in all the parked cars on the block. I then crossed the road and checked the few cars on the other side. Nothing. Zilch. At least she wasn't lying helpless somewhere around the V.F.W. The band was packing their instruments away when I went back inside. The tables were all cleared off, including my unfinished glass, but I was in no mood to complain about that since there had been nothing else of mine on the table, and I'd had enough anyway.

I only drink beer to lubricate the old carcass while I'm dancing, because Seven Up gives me a headache, and I can sweat away the little amount of alcohol consumed, just about as fast as I drink it.

Sober, somber, and a bit miffed with Evelyn, I drove home, figuring I'd done all I was supposed to do as far as Roba was concerned. And, if all the ladies wanted to be equally temperamental it was O.K. with me.

I had noticed, since Nora's departure early on Monday morning, that my awareness of Roba's influence on my affairs had diminished significantly. I no longer felt his presence or his influence in making decisions. It was as though he had been released from some sort of bondage with me after the last letter had been delivered. I hoped his spirit was now freed to do whatever the departed do in what we call The Afterlife. The seven letters which I had 'Purloined' were returned. In each case, Adam had been exonerated from any further liability. Whatever I chose to do about my relationship with any or all of them was my affair only.

As usual, after dancing, I stripped off my smoke contaminated clothing and showered before going to bed. I slept like a log, and woke next morning well rested but a little stiff in the mid section as occasionally happens after a particularly vigorous session. Tonight, if I decided to go dancing, I'd have to go to the Eagles in Port Angeles. As the Midnight Blues were playing at the V.F.W. Thursday and Saturday, and I wasn't sure who was playing in P.A. tonight, I'd leave the decision until this evening. Meanwhile I had the C.B. to test in flight, and today was Friday, Alice's day. Maybe I could go flying, and give her a call. I searched in my mind for a suitable call sign for myself. One that would be appropriate to use only when calling Alice, or Goliath.

'David'?. Maybe not, I was no stone thrower nor did I wish to imply any threat to Goliath, from above or below. 'Samson'? It also had a biblical tenor to it I didn't like. 'Oilcan'? For some reason the huge supply of Mobil oil cans, in the engine room of the Chrysalis still haunted me, as well as the unanswered question of what Alice thought I'd been looking for.

Should I have been looking for something? Drugs? Smuggling is always something one might stumble across. Especially here in the Pacific Northwest. Maybe Mexicans. There had been some Mexican crew members on the Chrysalis. Or Asians. Vancouver has a growing population of Hong-Kong's escapees. Maybe someone was flying them into Joyce's airstrip at night from Canada. The ideas festered on in my mind until I decided to light the fire and brew up some coffee.

Friday morning dawned pink and pretty in the bedroom mirror. 'Red sky in the morning, Sailor's warning.' The old saying goes. I rolled out of bed and hurried through the fire lighting ritual while the kettle boiled for my morning mug of coffee. I had to make a trip to the woodshed and the light southerly wind rustling through the cedars confirmed my expectations for a change in the weather. The high pressure system which had held the fine weather in place for almost a week was breaking down. Today would probably be the last really good day for flying to the Islands for some time. High clouds moving up from the South would be here, hanging over the hilltops by nightfall.

I can't see the need for me to fly in bad weather, so, if I was going to make a radio check of the C.B. installation I'd better get it over with now. Even so, I still didn't manage to get airborne until nine fifteen and swung out over Discovery bay making a wide enough pattern to look down over the Clearwater residence and confirm there was a large black car parked in the driveway. Wherever she'd been last night, it appeared she'd made it home. Cross off item one on my agenda.

Widening my departure pattern slightly, I could see Mary's red Ferrari in her driveway. Two located. I completed the sweeping left turn to 330 degrees and headed directly for Lopez Island airport.

Half way between Protection Island and Lopez, at three thousand feet, I triggered the microphone on the, C.B. holding the mike a little way from my face to allow it to pick up the engine noise, and speaking in as squeaky a pitch as I could manage, called out.

"Cliffnest, this is Risktaker calling Clearwater. Goliath come in please." and unkeyed the microphone. I waited fifteen seconds and repeated the squeaky call again "Cliffwater, this is Clearnest calling Goliath. Risktaker come in please." I only wish I could have recorded the ensuing confusion. All four were trying to speak at once and the squealing and whistling on channel 39 as one transmission overlapped another lasted almost two minutes before they sorted out who was trying to call who. Bingo! All four of them were at home. All four had been listening out, and only three could hear one another. Goliath was the one who, probably tucked in somewhere snugly sheltering from the Southwest wind, could only hear my transmission and thus in trying to get through, occasionally drowned out one of the other transmissions.

The hubbub apparently woke up several other 'Fisher wives' who joined in, wanting to know what the uproar was all about.

Smugly satisfied I'd confirmed my thesis, I flew on to Eastsound and landed. I walked into town and had a late breakfast in the Italian restaurant there before setting out to see if I could locate Goliath.

Obviously if Alice couldn't hear the other three distinctly, it was because she was in some spot where the high land between Goliath and the Discovery Bay stations intervened. If she'd been close to the south shoreline of Lopez, she'd have picked up Cliffnest. That left only one or two anchorages where a seasoned 'Island Hopper' like her would have gone for shelter from the impending Southwesterly. North. Possibly Stuart Island, Waldron, or Sucia.

Although Sucia has good anchorage, its shoreline is low lying and not much impediment to radio transmissions. Waldron is much the same so I opted for Stuart. If she wasn't there I'd go visit my old Indian friend, Little-wolf who I hadn't seen for many months. I picked up a six pack before returning to the airplane as a peace offering, for him.

As it happened, Goliath was there moored to the buoy closest to the State Park dock. I walked out to the end of the dock with my six pack and hailed her a couple of times, until Alice appeared. Once decided she knew me, she came and rowed me out to the Goliath, where we spent best part of the afternoon chatting and sipping Little-wolf's beer.

Again, she surprised me by asking if I'd found out anything specially interesting about the Chrysalis. I asked her directly what she had expected me to find, and again she surprised me by virtually accusing me of being some kind of under-cover cop. I spent several minutes, repeating most of what I had already told her of my life history, but I don't think it fully registered. In the end, I asked her if perchance, she had something shady in her past that she was afraid I might be looking for. At which point she laughed. "Nothing the statute of limitations hasn't run out on."

"The only thing I saw that seemed incongruous, on that ship," I said, was the number cans of lubricating oil they had, stored in the aft locker of the engine room." Alice almost sprang out of her chair exclaiming. "Ah Hah!" So you were snooping around. How much oil do you think was there?"

"God knows." I said, surprised again at her reaction and recalling that I'd estimated about four to five hundred, cans from the size of the locker. "Maybe four to five hundred quarts."

"In cans?. That much !?"

"I'd say so. Unless the locker has a false bottom." I added, watching her closely. "It's about three by five, and about three feet deep. And it was full." She was silent and I added. "I'd have thought the top layer would have been more than enough for a whole summer's cruising. Unless they change oil about every ten hours running time. Maybe they got it on special from Al's Auto."

"Did you see what kind they were,"

"Mobil I think. I didn't get a good look because the two crewmen grabbed me before I could pick one up to see. Not that I was going to." I added hastily. but there was a sort of blueness that made me think they were Mobil oil cans."

"You mean you don't know for sure they were even cans of oil." she said incredulously, and I had to think before replying.

"I suppose you're right." I admitted ruefully. "I couldn't swear to it 'On Oath' like. I just assumed they were Mobil oilcans as that was probably the most logical thing you'd expect to find in cans in an engine room. Isn't it?"

"You'd make a fine defense witness for the prosecution." She laughed. "A positively uncertain circumstantial eye-witness. Perry Mason would love you."

"Well, is it against the law, to overstock your ship with engine oil.?"

"Not if it is engine oil." Alice replied. "But suppose some, if not all of those cans, were full of Dope." I gave this some thought before replying, trying to imagine a customs inspector asking old baldy to open each of those cans to prove they all contained oil. He hadn't seemed too concerned when they told him I'd been looking in that particular locker when they apprehended me. But then again, come to think of it, he hadn't seemed as drunk as he'd been when I first came on board. Maybe the drunkenness was a sham. Perhaps the over-reaction of the crew, had been more genuine than his lack of concern.

"Do you know where the Chrysalis is now, or where it was going.?" I asked. Alice shook her head.

"I think they'd just arrived in U.S. waters. Those Barbeque parties, are a means of announcing their arrival, you know." I didn't, so I kept quiet.

"By the time they've settled down, they're usually just like the average vacationing yachtsmen. Busy exploring the port cities and buying what they can at better prices than back home. They're more interested in Smuggling purchases back into Canada, than smuggling dope into the States."

"You think the Chrysalis may be smuggling dope in cans of Mobil oil they picked up in the states?" I asked when she stopped talking. She looked quizzically at me for a moment and then laughed.

"I really started you thinking. Didn't I?"

"Well. You do seem to be very well informed about things the average housewife wouldn't bother her head over." I replied.

"I'm not your average American housewife. Am I?"

I had to agree. Her lonely lifestyle would never suit the average woman. I was on the point of asking her if she was connected, in some under cover way, with the Customs and Excise Office, when she stole my thunder by asking if it had been my airplane that buzzed her boat last Monday. My face made an answer unnecessary and she immediately asked who the young lady waving through the window had been. By then, the immediate shock had passed and I was able to reply evenly.

"So you did see us. Mary wasn't sure if you had. We were out joy-riding around when she spotted the Goliath and asked me to make another pass so she could wave to you."

Alice made no reply so I resumed my story. "She sometimes calls and asks me to take her flying if the weather's nice. I guess she gets a thrill out of flying. She's a proper little thrill seeker." I added lamely.

"Mary who?"

"Mary Lykes." I saw a momentary flicker of surprise in Alice's eyes and added. "I hadn't realized you two knew each other. She merely said she recognized the boat."

Alice accepted my explanation without comment watching me closely. then said softly.

"The Mary Lykes I knew, died some years ago."

"Mary is your friend's grand daughter then. Lives in the old house on Beckett Point." I tried to sound factual and somewhat indifferent, hoping to leave any revelations to Alice, as much as possible.

"I haven't seen her since she went away to college, I'm surprised she'd even remember the boat."

"How'd you meet in the first place.?" I asked.

"I used to tie up occasionally at a private pier across the bay from Beckett Point." Clarence Clearwater and my husband Graham, used to run a small purse-seiner together out of Tacoma in the fifties. Evelyn Clearwater and I worked part time together in the cannery there. We made good money and the Clearwaters bought the property across from Beckett Point and built a dock and a house together there. Later on, we moved the boat to Clarence's dock and fished the Straits and the Hood Canal, until Graham's accident. During the season, to save money traveling back and forth to our house at Dash Point, Graham and I moved Goliath up to Discovery bay and tied up at Clarence's pier, and lived aboard." As she was speaking, I suddenly remembered having seen those boats tied to that pier in the late sixties and early seventies when I had first started flying into the area. But I said nothing and she continued with her story.

"Clarence's wife Evelyn, and I used to be active in the Gardiner community association, while the men fished. All of us liked to go square dancing in Port Townsend, which is where we met up with Walter and Mary Lykes, and sometimes on a summer evening, they brought little Mary over with them in their boat. Those were very good times for all of us." she ended her story with a wistful sigh.

"And now ?" I prompted, loath to let her get the questioners edge again.

"Now?" She stared off into space, roaming her memories while I waited. "Now, everything's changed. Mary stopped coming over after Walter died, though I think Little Mary, as we called her, came over once or twice before her Grand mother died."

"What happened to your husband." I asked, a little hesitantly as I felt fairly sure the answer would evoke further unhappy memories.

"Graham and Clarence went down with the 'Allyn'." She said, as if it was an everyday occurrence and I got a measure of the woman's toughness in her acceptance of the inevitable.

"Do you ever see your friend now?" I continued the attack.

"Not since her dock collapsed. There's no place to tie up there anymore. I sometimes talk to her on the C.B. though. Fact I thought I heard her call this morning but the channel was full of static and chatter. I don't get good reception in here." she said, waving her arm around to indicate the harbor. "D'you have C.B. in your airplane?"

Her directness almost caught me by surprise but I answered without flinching.

"Sure do. I keep it on channel nine in case of emergency."

"You can give me a call on Channel 39 next time." She said, though I'm sure she didn't mean any reference to the morning exchange by her choice of wording. But, I can never tell with women, what they mean.

The wind was beginning to pick up a little and I began making a move to leave, though she insisted it would be safer for me to stay the night there than fly off in this weather.

"This is only a small front going through. You'll be safer here than flying into the wind all the way home. Besides you've been drinking. You can leave early tomorrow. Front will have gone through by then." She said conclusively.

We finished off the rest of Littlewolf's beer and spent the night, snuggled up in the forward bunk, rocking gently and listening to the soothing rhythm of the wavelets breaking against the bow, and chuckling their way aft along the waterline planking, just inches away from our heads.

In the morning, the soft rustle of rain on the deck above woke me. Alice was sleeping peacefully and I raised up gently and peered out of the porthole at the grey drizzle outside, that had flattened the sea into a motionless glassy black linoleum with a bottle bottom pattern of interlocking circles, where each drop formed a little peak at the center.

My movement disturbed her and she rolled over facing me, without opening her eyes. It was the first time I'd had the chance to see her face so completely in repose, and she seemed much younger than the Alice she presented to the everyday world. I studied the strong jaw line and the firm feminine lips that heralded her determination, and above these, the delicate nostrils and the slight upward tilt to the tip of her nose. The even tranquil symmetry of her brow line and the deep forehead, behind which lay the wisdom and strength of her personality, discretely screened by the waves of soft grey hair. An old, wise, courageous creature from another world.

Her eyes flickered open and for a second she seemed surprised to see me looking at her, then she knew where she was and smiled.

"Lie down honey, you're not going anywhere in this muck." She ordered gently, and I did as bid.

"Sleep O.K.?" she asked.

"Like a top." I replied, and wondered at the stupidity of the expression. All the tops I'd ever seen not spinning, rolled around at the slightest movement of whatever they were lying on. Alice's eyes continued to look at me as if she were thinking the same silent thoughts about me. Suddenly she smiled and slithered out of the top of the triangular bunk, slipping into her flannel nightdress as if to recover her modesty.

"Stay put lover." she said, as she drifted aft to the galley. "I'll have the coffee brewed in a couple of seconds. Might as well stay warm while you can."

I lay back looking at the deck planking above me and let my thoughts drift. How had I come to be here in this idyllic situation.? How had Alice come to be here. In both our cases, the spark that had initiated it came from the actions of others. In my case, Roba's idiotic, quixotic if you like, attempt to better the lives of others. In Alice's case, the careful teaching of her husband, Graham, who she had obviously adored, and which had prepared her for this unusual lifestyle. I pondered the relationship between the living and the dead and how the essential core of spirituality in each of us, influences and is influenced by the spirits of both.

There is no way I can dismiss the continuance of Roba's influence on me, even after his death, and I was beginning to sense the influence Graham might still be exercising to soften the life of his loved one. Even after his death.

When, where, and how, had the seeds of this moment been sewn? And, why? Karma? The influence of each moment on the following one, deals only with the 'How' of life's patterns. Time, and Space, the 'When' and 'Where' of physical existence, are only the result of the accident of creation.

The failure of the 'Creator' to know beforehand, the

consequences of the desire to 'Be'. To 'Exist'. Some flaw, in the 'Spiritual Personality' of the 'Creator'. A 'Lack of Willingness to Comply' that caused the 'Spiritual Energy', not to compress into an infinitesimal spot, but to miss doing so, by a minute fraction, and thus be drawn back into this orbital condition of 'Matter' by the intangible force of the Creator's desire to exist. Thereby, giving rise to Time, and Space, and How. Leaving the 'Creator's' 'Desire to Exist' as the one constant. An intangible force that holds the Universe in existence.

And what of the other components of the 'Creator's' spiritual personality? Were these perhaps, the foundation for each of the Elements from which the Physical Matter of the Universe is composed.?

Fortunately, Alice appeared out of the shadows of the galley with two mugs of steaming coffee and I was once more drawn back into the realm of reality.

Chapter EIGHT

Souls and Searchings

As she had predicted, the rain cleared away, the Sun shone and I was able to depart by about nine in the morning. Alice said she intended to remain in Stuart Island for the rest of the week if I cared to come back. She also suggested I call her on channel 39 any time and arrange a suitable meeting place, and we agreed on a 'Handle'. "Moonbaby".

The sense of freedom one finds in taking off from some place in your own airplane is incredible. No form 700 to sign, no set course to a defined destination or other set of orders, just the morning sun shining on the clouds. Billowy unsubstantial mountains with feathery canyons to explore, and rounded shoulders to slide over.

I blew the dampness off the runway and lifted away over the water between Stuart and John's Islands in a graceful climbing turn. Crossed the tip of Spieden Island and soared over the channel between there and San Juan Island.

Alice had been right. Rested and refreshed, I felt on top of the world. I was the GOD that had CREATED EVERYTHING WITHIN MY SPHERE OF AWARENESS. If I closed my eyes it would all disappear, and though I lacked the skill to close down each of my other senses in turn, I knew it could be done, and if done, nothing would exist for me. Yet, deep inside, I knew I could not create within my physical self, the desire 'Not To Exist'.

I and everything else, was one infinite experience, and I was here, now, to 'Enjoy' that experience for everyone and everything. And I did.

Below me, Roche Harbor displayed a few hardy boaters who chose to extend their cruising beyond the official boating season, though most of the slips were empty and only 'Corporate greed' prevented people like Alice from being able to find temporary shelter there. Slightly soured, I turned East towards Lopez Island. Fisherman Bay was similarly empty, though the storage yard was almost full.

I continued South across Lopez Sound to Mackay Harbor and Richardson, circling to see if Monica's car was parked beside the house. It was not. I surveyed the area around the store at Richardson without spotting her yellow Subaru station wagon and then followed the road to the sheep farm without seeing any sign of it. Five more minutes, flying over Lopez Village and the ferry terminal and I'd convinced myself she was not on the Island.

Disgruntled, I turned South again and commenced the long steady climb half way across the Straits of Juan-Da-Fuca, towards Discovery Bay. Twelve minutes later, I reached the end of my descent from mid channel, set up my pattern for landing and touched down on the end of the runway at home.

My sense of disappointment at not being able to spend Saturday pursuing my fantasies with Monica, dissipated after checking my answering machine and finding a message from Nora. She was intending to go to the Eagles, this evening, and hoped I might feel like meeting her there. The time of the message was two minutes after ten this morning, according to the machine. Only eighteen minutes before I'd arrived home.

I was on the point of calling back immediately to say I'd be there, but decided there was no need to. If that was her plan, I was free to do whatever I pleased until evening, but something indefinable niggled me about her call.

Today was Saturday, her day was Sunday. Was that it? Why this should bother me I could not imagine, and the problem wasn't resolved until I decided to run the tape on the C.B. system.

I had to sit through about twenty minutes of hissings, cracklings, and heterodyne whistles, to catch the few transmissions that did come through clearly, until my own transmission of yesterday morning suddenly boomed, clear as a bell despite the background noise of the engine. It was clearly an engine noise, and I'd certainly have to mute it somehow, unless I wanted to give myself away each time I made a transmission. Most of the call-signs, I didn't recognize but towards the last, there was a faint, but clear call, from 'Poopdeck' to 'Goliath' which absolutely galvanized me.

"Goliath please repeat. Did you say 'Premoth' is running short of lubricant?"

Goliath's short response was no more than a sizzling noise but apparently Poopdeck heard her for she replied. "thank you. Poopdeck out."

I hastily noted the counter reading for future reference and when the tape ended with no further transmissions, I stopped it and ran it back to see if I could piece together what had been said before that call.

With the volume turned up high I could make out enough of the one-sided exchange to conclude that Goliath had called Poopdeck first and reported receiving a message that Premoth, was out of oil.

Coming so closely after my visit with Alice I could only assume Poopdeck had something to do with the Customs or Narcotics Agencies and the report referred to had been my own. Was that the reason Nora had set up this evening's meeting?. Was Nora 'Poopdeck'?. She had told me she worked at Customs in the Federal Building in Port Angeles. 'Premoth' could easily be a code for 'Chrysalis'. Had the earlier transmission I'd been unable to make out concerned my visit to Goliath?. Why hadn't I heard it on the flight home?. I cursed Monica for not being home, and then, more soberly, my own infatuated anticipation of seeing her, which led to my euphoric take off from Stuart. In my excited mental state, I'd forgotten to switch on the C.B. If I hadn't missed that one vital act, I'd have heard both sides of the conversation.

Or, as I reasoned later, more likely, Alice's precautionary call to Moonbaby. It was a mixed blessing alright, but henceforth, switching on the C.B., had to be part of my cockpit drill.

The more I thought about the strange coincidences and connections between this group of women, the more I suspected that Roba's and my own spiritual forces had combined either to punish me for daring to steal any of his mail despite the the mitigating circumstances. Or, to create a set of connections only my intervention could modify. More likely the latter.

Neither Roba nor myself have adhered to the concepts espoused by the major religions in regard to defining a Deity. Nor on the other hand do, or did, either of us dispute the existence of an 'Overall Deity'. We both, in our separate ways, concluded that All of Existence is the physical manifestation of the One God, of which we are all a separate part. Each one of anything has a unique quality of being unique. A thousand coke bottles may all seem to be the same, but each one is unique. Unique means, there is only one of anything. And, though hundreds of them may have been formed with identical form, at the same exact moment, none of them exist in the place of another. Because of that feature, every particle of the universe is unique. There is only one of it. And, each particle is responsible for itself, for all time, whether they are manifest as a material form or an energy, or spiritual, form. Nor do we think this is a new concept, for it has been evidenced in prior civilizations and in the lives of isolated human beings since the beginning of human existence.

I do not mention this to suggest you change your concept of the Deity. Each one of us is responsible totally for what is in our minds because we were all born with the ability to think for ourselves, and in time we all reach our own conclusion. And, as the concept that you are 'GOD' carries with it a realization of the enormous responsibility this entails, I can sympathize with anyone who would rather shed this onto someone else's shoulders.

I mention it, only to provide a background to the many references to Roba's complicity in these events. Sometimes I sense him as leading me gently around some of the pitfalls I, a human in a body, have difficulty perceiving. At other times, he takes my hand and twists my arm up behind my back to propel me into those travails I'd rather skirt around.

I believe those seven letters were placed in the positions I found them, by Roba in his drunken state, being guided, or manipulated, by his spiritual guidance system or systems. With of course, the complicity of my own. All for a purpose, as yet undisclosed.

I had sensed Roba's satisfaction at the delivery of all seven letters and understood his lack of concern as to how deep I might be digging myself into a hole with seven angry women standing around ready to bury me when I'd dug it deep enough.

Both Roba and I have had our education at the hands of women. and we both find it (Found it) difficult to understand why, once they've lured you into their beds, or crept into yours, you suddenly belong to them. The usual expression is, "How can you do such a thing after I've given myself to you?" If they don't do it, I find myself smacking myself on the side of my head, trying to understand their concept of 'Giving'. Who gave what to who? or whom.?

Irregardless, (I love that word) and this is one oxymoron where it fits, I cleaned myself up after my dinner and dressed in neat clean clothes, set out with a light heart knowing I was heading right into the tender trap.

According to the impromptu schedule that had grown up around the letters, Nora was Sunday's woman. This was still Saturday and I arrived at the dance about five minutes before the band's nine o'clock break.

Everyone was, or seemed to be, on the floor dancing which gave me time to pick up my glass of Miller's Draft at the bar, and wander around looking for an empty table before the dance ended.

I saw Nora whirling around with some guy about a foot taller than me and reckoned my chances for the night's frivolity might be a little slim. However, my spirits revived when they separated at the edge of the floor and he went off to his own group. I still had three hours before Sunday anyhow.

Nora returned to her table across the dance floor from where I was seated. She was with another couple and an older man. Not the moment to announce my presence. I entered into conversation with the lady sitting beside me at the table, but it was difficult to concentrate on what she was saying while trying to watch what was going on over the other side. A few minutes before the band returned to the stand, a younger man came over and spoke to Nora, and she and her partner got up from the table and went towards the exit. I got up and made my way across the dance floor diagonally towards the rest room so I could see what transpired. Nora and the two men were talking to two more men in the lobby and I sidled across to the bar where I could watch, and ordered another beer. After some discussion, all three of the men left, and Nora came back into the hall. Beer in hand, I angled across the hall through the tables, and managed to intercept her at the edge of the dance floor. It took a moment before her expression of concentration changed to a smile of welcome, and she grasped my hand. "Been here long?" she asked.

"Long enough to get a beer." I replied noncommittally. I felt fairly sure she hadn't seen me enter, and allowed her to lead me across the floor to her table where she introduced me as an old friend to her two companions. After we'd cross examined the fact that I lived on the other side of Sequim, at least thirty miles from P.A. in the country and didn't know any of the friends they had there, the music started again, and thankfully, I asked Nora to dance.

"Your friends seem very protective of you." I remarked after we had settled into a steady rhythm. Her eyebrows went up in surprise and she studied my eyes carefully so I went on, "They have some proprietary rights in you.?". I thought I saw a momentary flicker of something in her eye as I said this and wondered if perhaps the man had more than a friendly interest in my dancing companion. Perhaps the wife had more than a casual interest too, as she had seemed happier about our 'Old acquaintanceship' than he had.

"You're very perceptive." Nora replied, smiling.

"Did you come to the dance with them?" I asked, mentally assessing my chances of starting Sunday with her. She nodded and my hopes sank.

For the rest of the evening I felt like some laboratory animal as they dissected my history. However, I had one ally in my effort to retain the contact I'd re-established with Nora and I wasn't giving up easily. I had one dance with the wife, while he danced with Nora and to my surprise, she suggested I ask Nora if she'd like to have breakfast. I had the impression she was desperately eager to drive any kind of a wedge she could between her husband and Nora, so I said I'd be delighted to do so. The dance was due to end at Midnight, so during the next dance, I asked Nora if I could have the last dance with her. Reluctantly, I thought, she said it was already taken, so I asked her if she'd like to have breakfast with me at Denny's after the dance. It was as if I'd offered a hamburger to a starving orphan, and she launched into an explanation of how they were insistent on taking her home. "I could meet you there." She suggested and I could see the pleading in her eyes as she spoke.

"I'll wait. All night if necessary." I said reassuringly, as the dance ended and we walked to our seats. Just to twist the guy's tail a little, I offered to drive Nora home. Gracefully, I accepted their announcement that they were going to do this, and, to relieve the ensuing tension, I said "Goodnight", and asked another woman, who was sitting rather disconsolately alone, if she'd dance. I understood why she was alone, as soon as we began dancing, for I almost had to hold her up throughout the dance. Unchivalrously, when the music ended, I led her back to her seat and took my leave of her rather hastily.

My coffee was almost cold when Nora joined me in Denny's. Almost at once, I sensed she was nervous about meeting me and I was not surprised when she asked if I'd mind driving back to her place so she could park her car there. I'm not in the habit of eating after dancing, so the suggestion was welcome and I followed her back to her apartment. At her request, I parked across the street in a different apartment block.

She has a little apartment in town, just the standard, sterile, one bedroom, $400.00 Dollars a month type, but she had decorated with bright fabrics covering most of the walls and installed harmonious lighting which gave the living and bedroom areas a snug, warmly intimate, appeal. Nora showed me proudly around and I spent enough time admiring her handiwork, to give myself the opportunity of discovering whether she had a C.B. installed anywhere. There was no sign of one anywhere. So much for the theory that she was 'Poopdeck'. I felt more relaxed. However, this was not the case with her, and I sensed she was still anxious about having me there. After she went to the bedroom, 'to change into something more relaxing' I was astonished, not to say dismayed, when she re-appeared wearing a one piece jump suit. I'd been expecting something like chiffon, at that time of night.

"I've a great thirst for some 'Scherezade'. Is there any left?" She said, coming close to me in that provocative manner a woman uses to virtually seduce a man into complying with her wishes. After the initial surprise, I realized she wanted to be invited to go to my place, since Denny's doesn't serve it. Anything to relax her. Even a thirty mile drive.

My house was cold, and we were both very tired. One large shot of Scherezade was all we needed to snuggle into a nice warm bed. When the daylight woke me, I found myself curled up around the back of a soft warm body with my face almost buried in a mass of raven black hair. My mouth felt as if Cox's army had marched through it in their sweaty feet, and I was in desperate need of coffee. Reluctantly, I slithered out of the bed and staggered out into the cold kitchen. While the kettle boiled, I stuffed some wood and paper into the Earth stove and lit it. In the bathroom, I was busy brushing my tainted teeth when Nora, looking like a Greek statue, came in and proceeded to use the stool. I glanced across at her delightfully naked form and she smiled sweetly, as though this was the most natural thing in the world for two relative strangers to be doing. Strangely enough, I felt exactly the same.

"Would you bring my bag.?" She said, as I rinsed my mouth. I found the soft bag where she'd left it, beside the bed under her Jump Suit. I put the suit to one side, she hadn't asked for that, and hefted the bag, surprised at it's weight. It was open and I looked in. There was a plastic Ziploc bag with a bunch of 'female accessories' on top of a folded uniform, but the weight came from an automatic and a Walkie-Talkie, lying side by side in the bottom. I put everything as I'd found it and taking only the plastic bag, returned to the bathroom, just as she flushed the toilet.

"Coffee will be ready in a moment." I said, placing the bag on the counter beside the basin, and giving her an admiring smile. She looked me over from top to toe and apparently liked what she saw.

"Cream And Sugar!" I said, as though describing what I saw, rather than asking a question, and left her to finish her toiletries. I carried both mugs of coffee back to the bedroom, piled the pillows against the headboard, and sat back against them and waited until she was likewise adjusted, before handing her coffee to her.

For a while we sipped in silence, enjoying the sunlight which streams into my bedroom.

"Why do you come here armed?" I asked quietly. "Are you afraid I would hurt you?"

"I wondered if you'd looked in the bag when you brought only the toiletries. Were you afraid I would threaten you with it. Silly. Didn't you see my uniform?. I told you I worked for the Customs." She said, reaching across and taking hold of my hand.

"I wanted to spend today with you. All day, and tonight too if you'd let me. I can go to work tomorrow on the early bus. You don't have to drive me home." There was something in the way she said this that made me think she had wanted to use me to get away from the couple she'd been with last evening at the dance. I wanted to ask her, but instead, I decided to let her tell me in her own time.

She was a very attractive lady and despite her proud bearing and demeanor, a very disturbed one at the same time. This was

the second time we'd spent the night in bed together and done
nothing more than sleep. Perhaps a full day and a night together,
would produce some more significant results. After all, this was
Sunday, and she was Sunday's woman. I pulled her towards me
and put my arm around her shoulders. Without any resistance
she snuggled in beside me and we moved into the harmonious
rituals of courtship.

It was mid day when we woke up and began taking stock of
our surroundings. Like two children we showered and dressed
together, breakfasted, and walked out in the sunshine. The
autumn air was cool and I'd dressed her in my padded jacket
and knitted cap so we could walk on the beach. The sea was as
calm as I'd hoped, inducing a sense of ease and tranquility in
both of us and we sat on a driftwood log in the sun and talked the
afternoon away. She unburdened her soul and I let her pour it
out with as little interruption as possible.

While she was talking, I remembered the Sony cassette
recorder I had in my Pea Jacket pocket. I'd taken it with me on
my last trip to the beach to record the sounds of the surf and the
sea birds. On the pretext of taking a pee, I went behind some
brush at the base of the cliff, rewound it and left it switched on
inside my pocket, to record the details for adding to my computer
records.

Born in the town of Hoquiam in Washington, she'd gone to
college in Spokane, married just after graduation, to another
student who had graduated in Forestry and found a job in
Raymond at the lumber mill. They'd lived there for eighteen years
until the children had left school and her husband had deserted
her and gone to live in Oregon with the other woman. She had
returned to her parents home, with her two daughters, to look
after her ailing father after her mother died. When he died, she
sold the house and moved to Port Angeles, where she had
managed to get a job in the Customs and work her way up to a
position as an inspector at the Port of Entry.

The constant study this required, had left little time for her
two daughters, who had left the nest and gone off to get into

trouble on their own. Roger, the husband of Alicia, in the triangle last evening, was her supervisor's Boss and also her lover. Alicia, who had become her close friend since her arrival in Port Angeles, knew nothing of all this. (I didn't see any point in disillusioning her.) Roger of course, felt that despite his love for her, he could not bear to hurt Alicia, who had no other means of support etc. etc. I, on the other hand, must understand that she truly loved Roger, and wouldn't do anything to hurt him. (In case she lost her job.?) I kept my arm around her, sympathetically encouraging her to 'let it all out.' Which she did, as indiscriminately as though she had been talking to her bedroom mirror. With a little subtlety, I introduced the subject of her armory and the radio in her bag and learned that her handle was 'Sternwheeler', not 'Poopdeck', that was Roger's wife, Alicia. Their house was high on a hillside above Port Angeles, overlooking the Straits. (Hence their reception would be able to cover a very wide area.) The C.B. organization I'd stumbled across, was titled the 'Thirtyniners', and everyone in it, had answered Roba's advert, because Roger had thought it might have been a coded message from a drug smuggling organization seeking contacts. I Ooh'ed and Ah'ed at each revelation to keep the flow going as much as possible without mentioning my 'handle', feeling a secret satisfaction that I hadn't installed the C.B. in the house before her first visit.

Surprising as these revelations were, what really amazed me, was the number of them that had fallen into my hands with the random selection I had picked up. The only one who was not part of this organization at some time or other, was Joyce, and she was related to Barbara. If the group had been an illegal organization, instead of an unpaid branch of the local Customs department, I'd have been in a fantastic position to 'Unmask' it, but the other way around was some what of an anticlimax. The only people who'd be interested, would be the smugglers themselves. And Roba. I know he'd have peed his pants with laughter if he'd known about this.

The first thing I did when we returned from the beach to the house, was to slip into my office, drop the tape from the Sony into the box of used tapes and disable the C.B. while Nora was in the toilet. I couldn't hide it, but I could set it up to a different channel in case she wandered in there and began looking around. I left it off and selected to channel 16, in case it got turned on.

That evening, we dined on my left over stew and finished off the last of the Scherezade before going to bed early. After all, she had to get up early to catch the bus. I didn't see myself obligated to taking her to work, and she ran less chance of being seen with me if she took the bus. I was relieved that she was relieved that I saw the wisdom in this.

By seven thirty, on Monday morning, Nora had gone. I had made no arrangement to renew our trysting, and lay back in my lounger, with my coffee, catching up on the 8am. news. Monday was Mary's day, but I had no intention of initiating the process myself. Old bodies aren't what they used to be, and my 'old grey mare' needed a rest, and Mary wasn't restful. Apart from that, it was raining, and I've no intention of going flying in the rain. There'd been no telephone calls from anyone and I was beginning to think I should best keep it that way.

Certainly, I'd dropped in on an established network of C.B. enthusiasts dedicated somehow to helping the authorities in their spare time but I had no intention of getting involved myself. That is, no more than I already was. Then I remembered, I'd switched off the recording set-up, and with no further thought to my resolution, I got up and went and switched it back on. Having compromised myself once more, I took yesterday's Sony tape and played it back on my stereo. Apart from a few passages where the sound was fuzzy from the movement of my jacket, almost everything of any significance was clearly audible.

I dubbed it onto a second cassette and put it away in the safe under my desk. Perhaps it was Roba or one of his agents that prompted me to do this, for I'm sure I would never have thought of doing so on my own. On the other hand, possibly there had been something about Nora which triggered my actions. Something which I can only describe as a sort of religious zeal about her work as a Customs Inspector. Had I been passing through customs myself, the awareness of it, might have steered me to another booth. If one were available.

Physically, she's an impressive and attractive woman, with a strong personality. Emotionally, she's a basket case, and I was thankful for the hiatus in our relationship which Roger could, in the foreseeable future, provide.

I began the task of entering up the record of yesterday's events in the computer and had just completed and saved it when I heard the sound of Mary's Ferrari pulling into my driveway. I never would have imagined I'd feel dismayed to see her but the sensation aroused, was similar to the rising panic a swimmer might experience if caught in a tide rip.

There's no back door to my house. Both entrances face onto the main deck, and the patter of Mary's footsteps told me there was no escape. I began a wild imaginary flight through the bathroom window and down the cliff face, for I could somehow not envision the idea of cowering under a bed or in the toilet until the tigress went away. Take it from me, Mary is a tigress, and I was sure she smelled my presence inside the house. I was just glad she could not have seen Nora departing. I'd seen her onto the bus myself.

Mary, I'd discovered, works late on Sunday, doing the accounting and store checking for the Safeway supermarkets in Port Townsend, Sequim, Port Angeles and Forks. Doubtless this is why she drives her Ferrari so fast, and probably knows all the State patrolmen on a first name basis, though I have no confirmation of this supposition as yet. Given the relative age difference between us, what she sees or saw in me is hard to imagine except my availability and the airplane. Obviously it was not the airplane right now and my weakened condition was as yet unknown to her.

I put on my brightest smile and welcomed her with open arms. "It seems like a century since I last saw you." She said plaintively, looking up from my shoulder where she'd buried her head. "What do you do? cut the telephone off.?"

"Oh lord!" I exclaimed, suddenly remembering I'd forgotten to reset the answering machine. "I was downloading some data the other day and I have to disable the answering machine so that it can't interrupt the transmission coming in. I forgot to reset it." Mary brightened, "What sort of data."

"Just a stock program database update" "You dabble in the market too?"

"Dabble is the right word. I've got to augment my pension somehow."

For the next half hour we sat in my office while I showed her how to analyze a stock.

"You shouldn't let yourself get so up-tight about it." she said suddenly and began rubbing the back of my neck.

"I'm not up-tight." I protested, in-effectively, for trying to dissuade Mary is like telling the Tide to back-up. I hardly had time to shut down the computer before I was prostrate on the living room floor with her astride my back rubbing me all over with Sesame oil.

I have to confess, it was good therapy, something I'd never given enough credence to in my life before. Massage was always some kind of treatment for athletes who had over-strained, as far as I'm concerned. But by the time she had reached my feet, I'd drifted right out of this world and came back, about two hours later, to the delicious smell of something cooking.

"C'monGramps." A soft voice in my ear commanded. "Wrap yourself up and let's eat."

She'd draped my bath robe over my nakedness, so I wrapped up as she'd ordered and sat down to a wonderful Spanish omelet and toast.

"Do you always go to sleep during a massage?" She asked.

"Couldn't say. I've never had one before."

"Hardly ever.?"

"No. Never."

"You don't know what you're missing."

"I do now. Thanks to you. You should be a Masseuse."

"I am. I qualified in Spokane during the College breaks."

Remembering our day at Stuart Island, I reached across the table and squeezed her hand.

"Your going to make someone a wonderful wife."

"Yes." She replied and the look in her eyes left little doubt about who might be the lucky man. With the weather the way it was, and the delicacy of the preamble, we went a long way down the road to her objective that day, despite my stuffy reservations as to the appropriateness of it all. When she left in the evening, I fell into an exhausted sleep without any reservations left.

That is until Roba put in another appearance. At first, it was only the ebony statue of the coconut cutter, which Mary had taken from the credenza and placed on my bedside table to 'watch over me' in her absence, that I saw. Why she had done this, I could not imagine. She'd told me she was going away to college in Spokane on previous occasions and It hadn't apparently registered with me that I wouldn't be seeing her for the next three months, until the statue spoke. "You need your heads tested."

"Huh?!!"

"You're supposed to think with the big one." The little shiny black face began, grinning at me in a way Roba often used when criticizing some particular miss-stroke of my pool cue. "You should be ashamed of yourself imagining you can kidnap that delectable lass. You ass." He sometimes lapsed real poetic. I watched in stupefied fascination as the head continued to swell like a balloon being inflated, until it became Roba's, full sized head, perched on top of that eight inch slender black body and began shaking from side to side in gentle admonition, like a parent chiding a small thoughtless child for some unkind action. I fully expected to see it fall over. When it failed to do so, I accused him of being a bit light headed in some of his own activities where women were concerned.

"At least I had enough sense to remain un-involved with children."

"Mary's over twenty one." I retorted defensively.

"So are you. A long way. You're old enough to be her grandfather. You'd damn well better be prepared to face that reality some day."

"Meanwhile." I replied getting up on my elbow and looking

him squarely in the eye. "I'm doing what she wants. And not by mail." I added unkindly, pursing my lips and blowing, to see if the balloon would carry the body of the statue over backwards and tip him off his high horse.

Instead, he simply shriveled up and disappeared, leaving me horrified; wide awake, foolishly blowing on an ebony statue. I lay back, feeling ashamed of myself for abusing our friendship.

Mary had left early, intending to drive to Spokane that evening to resume her studies at the University, and frankly I had felt relieved to know she would not be likely to come around for the next week or two to cause any further criticism from him. Eventually I must have dropped back to sleep again after my brush with Roba, for the sun reflecting in the mirror, woke me around seven on Tuesday morning.

Tuesday had somehow become Joyce's day, as though I'd re-written the days of the week to match my new lifestyle. Irrationally, I wanted to blame Roba for my predicament. However, any time I let my thoughts wander in that direction, he seemed to be up there, giggling as if he'd left my cue ball surrounded by all the colors, with all nine reds at the other end of the table.

Shaking off this distracting imagery, I settled down at the computer to enter Monday's events into the computer log as delicately as possible in case anyone should ever access them via the telephone connection or in some other way. Big Brother doesn't need to know. With that thought in mind, I decided to trans-scribe each file to a separate disk, labeled Monday thru Sunday and protected against access by a hidden file requiring a password before the disc could be read. The password of course would be the name of the lady of the day. Then I erased all the files from the hard drive. You and I know this, but only I know where those discs are.

Later, armed with the paperwork I'd collected relative to the airfield located on Joyce's property, I headed out by car for another visit, determined if possible to convince her to sell the airfield piece to me. I stopped at the surveyors office in Port Angeles on the way, to discuss the question of surveying the property and writing up a description. As a result, it was One thirty before I pulled into Joyce's driveway.

Once again, after the first guarded encounter, she seemed pleased to see me and I'd been careful not to eat before leaving so I was able to genuinely enjoy her cooking, which also pleased her. When both of us were fully pleased with the day, I felt it was time to introduce the subject of my researches. When I mentioned the possibility of a tax refund, her eyes lit up and the drift towards confirming my research with a survey also surmounted its cost barrier after I'd agreed to pay for this if she'd sell the piece to me.

I think the idea of having me as a next door neighbor appealed to her quite strongly and I eventually persuaded her to come with me and locate the corner stakes of her property if we could.

We walked the length of the road up to the highway before we discovered a survey marker we could read and I noted the numbers down for the surveyors information. They'd told me roughly where to find it and how far from there, the homestead corner should be, so we set about measuring the quarter mile with the hundred foot tape I had brought.

There were thirteen chalk marks on the road before we began a really intensive search for a corner marker, twenty feet from the last mark. Eventually we stomped enough of the undergrowth down until we found the small cairn of stones, almost buried by the humus they had accumulated since they had been set there, some forty five years ago.

Although Joyce could not remember putting it there, we also found a rusty piece of Iron pipe in the middle of them. Patch, her old faithful collie, who had accompanied us throughout the search was as excited as she was, and marked the spot appropriately. Hand in hand, like two happy children, we walked back to her house. Even at a rough estimate, the airfield definitely had to be on her property. Just pacing it off from the corner marker, put the house in the middle of the quarter section. It was dark by the time we had finished measuring and Joyce asked me to stay for supper and beyond. I didn't object for several reasons, all valid.

In the wee small hours of the morning, Joyce woke me to say she had heard an airplane, which she thought, had landed on the strip. I was out of bed like a shot and into my clothes ready to investigate and we were whispering as though whoever was out there might hear us.

Beyond the window was a faint glow from the lighting on the runway which I had seen on my last visit and I could barely detect the faintest murmur of the generator in that hidden shack.

Joyce insisted on coming with me though I tried to dissuade her. It would be better if she remained here on watch, I argued to no avail. We did however agree on leaving Patch behind and tied up so she wouldn't break out.

In almost total darkness I let her lead me through the yard to the path she used when 'taking the cow to the meadow' as she described it.

We reached the edge of the trees just in time to witness a biplane at the far end of the runway, start up its engines and take off without lights into the darkness. As it broke above the trees, I gasped in amazement as I recognized the momentary silhouette of a De-Havilland D.H.84 against the lights on the trees, before it disappeared into the dark sky. Nor could there be any mistaking the subdued purring of its two Gipsy Major engines. A few moments later, the runway lights went out and the faint sound of the generator ceased.

"Come." I whispered in Joyce's ear. "Lets get to the road and see if we can see the car before he takes off." Joyce set off and I followed as best I could, holding her clothing, for we had agreed not to use any lights. It had been easy on the way out because of the runway lights but it took a little longer going back. We scurried across the barnyard and down the path past the garage to the road just as the car passed us. Obligingly the driver turned his lights on in time for me to see the rear number plate and read the letters 'AGE 794' as he headed in the direction of the highway.

"So much for that." Joyce said as we stood in the road watching the tail lights turn right at the highway. "We still don't know who they are or what they're doing."

"At least we know it wasn't a government vehicle." I said. and asked her if she'd been able to read the number plate as it passed. "It went too fast for me." She admitted, so I kept quiet and merely told her it had the wrong format to have been a military car.

"Should we tell the police?"

"Tell the Police ! What for? It isn't a crime to land an airplane and then take off again even if you don't put your Navigation lights on.That's an FAA matter."

"Well, they're trespassing on my airfield aren't they?"

"You've let them do so for forty five years. How're you going to justify stopping them now?" I laughed, surprised at her sudden display of assurance that this airfield was hers, and she should be controlling what happened here. I took her hand and began moving towards the house.

"Let's go back to bed. They've gone, they didn't do you any damage or injury. We know nothing about them or why they landed here. Let's take it real easy and just set up some kind of watch on the field and see if we can find out who, and what, and why, and all the rest of the unknowns, before we make any noises." I urged her along with me and we went back to bed and I cuddled her up close while we talked. "For all we know, this might be some kind of CIA activity and those guys act outside the law anyhow. If it is, we might find ourselves in 'protective custody' or some other nasty situation depending how secret they want to keep it." Joyce said nothing but I felt the tension building in her as the idea of falling into ungovernable hands, affected her. Seeking to dispel this, I continued in a lighter vein. "On the other hand, they might be doing something totally illegal like smuggling drugs, in which case we might find ourselves wearing concrete bathing costumes at the bottom of the Straits."

I rambled, on suggesting other potentially unpleasant results of too precipitate action. I wanted to discourage her from getting the authorities involved. If, as it looked, this operation had been in progress for such a long time, I had a lot I wanted to find out before calling the cavalry in, to trample everything, including us, into the mud. Gradually, she relaxed and began snoring gently, and I realized I was talking to myself.

When the dawn lit the windows, I awoke with Joyce's head still on my shoulder. She slept peacefully, occasionally giving vent to a soft popping sound whenever her lips fell apart as she exhaled and I watched her face, musing at the ease I felt within me. I gently stroked her eyebrows and cheeks until her eyelids flickered open and she smiled her lob sided welcome at seeing me there.

"Did I dream that someone came to the field last night and we went out to spy on them.?" She asked.

"No. That all happened. Someone landed and took off in a De-Havilland D.H.84. Then someone else turned off the runway lighting and left in a white car with a Washington license plate."

Joyce made no comment but looked at me for a long time as if uncertain whether I was kidding her or not. As she had mentioned in her letter to Adam, the damage her husband Charlie had inflicted on her face, had not improved the regularity of features normally associated with a pretty face; but in some mysterious way, it had enhanced the qualities of strength and resolution. The face I saw portrayed sincerity and compassion. I found myself moving my fingers delicately tracing the lines of eyebrow and the various creases in a gentle caressing motion as though in some way to erase the pain that once was had been there. She lay motionless, watching my eyes. Her pupils wide open, revealing the depth of her contentment.

Undoubtedly we could have lain there all day but I was anxious to continue with my researches into the legality of her possession of the airfield.

"Coffee ?" I asked, fully intending to get up and make it myself, but she sat up and pushed me down, as if to insist I stayed in bed while she fetched some. However this was my chance to escape and I dressed and followed her down to the kitchen before the coffee was ready. She registered a slight disappointment but said nothing, and after coffee and some toast and poached egg for breakfast, we walked out to the airfield and began an inspection in depth similar to the one I had conducted after Kamm left. She was astonished at the discovery of the camouflaged shed and its contents and we examined the airfield lighting system in greater detail. While she watched in some wonderment, I traced the wiring to a point where I thought I could hook in a connection to whatever we used as a monitoring device. My thought was to set up a hidden video camcorder which would come on as soon as anyone started up the generator and actuated the switch to the runway lights.

I made some notes of distances for wiring, and other items I would need, on the back of an old supermarket receipt I found in my wallet, marveling at how well I was prepared for every eventuality. At least I didn't have to write it on some part of my anatomy.

On the pretext of gathering all the equipment needed, I bade Joyce a tender farewell and set off on a shopping expedition. Port Angeles had only one outfit in the security business and they were only interested in selling their particular system. However, I learned there was a supply house in Shelton, where I could probably buy the sort of equipment I had in mind.

I stopped in at home to check the mail and spent an hour sketching out my scheme for placement of the cameras and the wire routing. From this, I derived the length of wiring I'd need, about four hundred feet, somewhat more then I'd originally thought. Better buy a whole spool.

At a rough estimate, the runway lighting itself consumed about five hundred of the five hundred and fifty watts available from the generator, leaving me only fifty to do what I wanted. After that, the four hundred feet of wire I needed to reach the cameras would use up another five or ten more, just from its own resistance. I needed at least four relays to physically actuate the cameras so it became obvious I'd have to provide my own power source locally.

I drew up two schemes. One using two twelve-volt car batteries, located near the cameras. And a second using a power line from Joyce's house.

At Mason Security Systems in Shelton, I discussed the pros and cons of each system with their engineer and finally decided on the one using power directly from the house. The small relays would work on 110 volt and were less expensive than six or twelve volt equivalents so I bought the necessary relays and rented a camera. I also bought a neat little dual deck VCR they had there, made by an outfit in Phoenix, called Go-Video. This unit, will accept the 8mm. camera cassette and a standard VCR cassette and transfer the pictures directly from one to the other. Ever since I've owned one of those little 8mm. camcorders, I've wished for such a machine and now I had one. On my return, as I approached Brinnon, I suddenly realized it was Wednesday, Barbara's day on my revised calendar. The roadway was clear so I made the suicidal turn into her driveway without incident. Once more she expressed delight at my arrival and made tea for me out in the gazebo. We had been sitting together only a few minutes before I sensed she was suppressing her excitement at something she wanted to share with me.

"Any news?" I asked innocently.

"I think I've made contact with Adam." She blurted out excitedly, pulling a letter out of her pocket.

> Dearest Bee Bee,
>   You can never know how long I have waited for your call.
>
> Adam.

Short and sweet. The letter had been typed so whoever wrote it didn't want to chance writing it by hand. And, there was no return address. Presumably, the joker wanted to keep the initiative.

"Have you got the envelope?" She handed it to me and once again, the postmark was Tacoma. However, the stamp was one of those new fangled self sticking labels they put on at the post office.

"Ah!" I exclaimed this letter was posted from the post office in Tacoma." Barbara looked at me as if I were a small child. "What I mean is it was physically taken into that office for posting, whoever posted it didn't post it in Sequim for instance."

"Do you think it was the same person as wrote the original letter to Adam?" She said dubiously.

"Hard to say." I muttered. "Is this the only reply you've had?" She nodded her head. "So far. It came this morning." She said sadly. "I think it's someone who knows me."

"Who?"

"My husband." She replied almost inaudibly."

"Your Husband!?. I thought you told me he died years ago."

"He did. At least it was officially stated that he died. Some wreckage and the bodies of two of his crew members were recovered."

"Do you think he may still be alive?" I asked, watching her intently. She shrugged her shoulders slightly and softly replied.

"I've never really believed him dead. We were so close. I'm sure I'd have known long before they told me he had been lost."

"What did the insurance people say? They paid you a pretty large compensation didn't they?"

"A hundred and fifty thousand. But that was only for the boat and I had to get a lawyer to force that out of them after a year." I didn't want to suggest that the likelihood of him still being alive after the investigations the insurance people would have conducted before paying out such a sum was extremely slight. But you never know. Stranger things have happened and I admired her tenacious belief he would someday come back. She seemed so radiant with excitement one minute and despairingly sad the next.

"You think both these letters were written by him?" The radiance began returning even as she shyly nodded her head.

"Why."

"He was the only one who ever called me 'Bee Bee'."

"None of your friends.?"

"Everyone calls me Barbara."

"Some of your friends must have heard him calling you Bee

Bee though." She nodded again and the radiance dimmed. What was I doing I thought, destroying the straws she clung to so systematically. But, it seemed, I couldn't help it. My logic told me that she must face facts. After almost six years, he just wasn't coming back. Why live in this fantasy world, waiting forever. I began to hate myself for ever bringing her letter to her.

"Surely Bee Bee isn't the only clue you have to base your hopes on is it?" I was becoming desperately anxious to help her back to reality but she smiled and shook her head again. "No it isn't." She got up and went into the house leaving me to my thoughts. In a few minutes she returned and dropped the original letter on the table in front of me.

She had penciled a circle around the words 'Bee Bee' and 'Hugga-Hugga'.

"What's this?"

"Hugga-Hugga" is what Enrique called Making Love." I sat and stared at her. My God I thought, what tiny fragments of hope some people live on. I couldn't bring myself to disillusion her. My silence must have disturbed her for she picked up the letter and read it aloud.

"None of our friends knew we called it that." So what if he is still alive, how come the son-of-a-bitch hasn't contacted you before this in a more normal way like a simple postcard, or just come home some night after dark and knocked on the door. My thoughts raced on over all kinds of unsavory possibilities, none of which I cared to share with her.

"What's next ?" I asked gently, as I wondered how to extricate myself decently from this crazy situation.

"I think I'll just wait until the next move."

"You can't do that." I protested quietly. He's left the ball in your court."

"What can I do? There's no return address."

"Another advert?"

"Saying what?"

"Depends on what you want. After six years. How's about? 'All is forgiven Adam, come on Home.' Or something like that.?

Always supposing you want him home. If not, why waste anything on continuing the game?"

"I like that" She said brightly, "I really do want him home." It was said with such simplicity it almost brought tears to my eyes.

"Keep me posted." I said, hastily getting up from the table and forgot to thank her for the tea. "I have to be getting along now. Give me a call if there's anything I can do to help." I ended lamely, hating myself for being a false friend. She'd just have to find her own way out of the mess I'd so innocently got her into.

The rest of the way home I ranted and raved at Roba for involving me in this fiasco. Finally I told him to find the S.O.B. and lead him home to her or get one of his heavenly pals to do it, but DO IT!!! Maybe that's not the approved way to pray but in my mood it was all I could manage. It's funny how one can drive a known road without ever seeing a single tree, light, or crossing; but after I closed the door of the house I came to, wondering how I'd got there. I unloaded my purchases into my work shed and went back into the office and began a more detailed plan of the surveillance installation I intended to make at Joyce's place.

With the cameras in hand, I made rough drawings of the extra parts I had to make, for coupling the solenoids to the camera controls and the switching requirements to make them operate in the correct sequence. Since both camcorders would focus automatically and adjust to the lighting themselves these parts could be simple levers and push rods to take the place of my fingers.

By the time I'd finished, it was time for bed. I'm not sure whether it was all the ruckus I'd stirred up on my drive home from Brinnon but Roba and a couple of his pals came and gave me a rough time during the night. Apparently they felt I should be paying more attention to each of my ladies, instead of trying to weasel my way out of my indebtedness to them.

Exactly what my indebtedness was, or how it arose or could be evaluated wasn't clear. In consequence, I slept extremely badly and woke with a raging headache, to find the heavens weeping profusely.

Thursday! Evelyn's day? My foot.! This was Aspirin's day. I took two with my morning coffee. Whatever Roba and his pals thought about it, I was not about to call that supercilious character today. If she wanted to contact me with an appropriate explanation for her sudden disappearance last Thursday, all well and good but she'd have to make the first move.

I dressed in this frame of mind and after a bowl of Oatmeal, went out to the shed to cut and glue together, the detail parts I had drawn up last evening.

I fitted them to the acrylic case I'd made for each camera and ran a trial with the power connected. It all worked as planned and as the aspirin diffused the headache, my spirits rose from the ashes of the night.

From some slabs of pine bark salvaged from splitting logs, I fashioned a couple of boxes to house and conceal the cameras high in the trees, where they would overlook the runway and the parking area. I loaded the finished products into the trunk of my car with the wiring and all the tools I might need, plus my new dual deck VCR, and set off for Joyce's in the early afternoon.

The guy in Mason's, had tried to convince me to use motion sensors to trigger my cameras but though this would have been easier to do, I rejected the idea because animals moving in the zone of the sensors, might trigger them and waste our time. However he did save me a roll of wire by pointing out that I could tap into the runway lights much nearer to the cameras than the place I had planned. Not only did I save the cost of the wire but it saved me having to hide about 400 feet of wire which the suspects might discover and thus be alerted to the surveillance. Joyce was not at home when I arrived but Patch apparently accepted my presence and I was able to get the wire from the house to the parking area of the airfield strung into place before she came cycling back from her shopping expedition. She was a little surprised to find me there but showed only her pleasure in doing so. Together, we installed the first camera about ten feet up on the trunk of a tall fir tree and disguised the bump with a collection of twigs and forest debris. It looked like a large bird nest at the base of a limb, and I felt satisfied it would adequately cover arrivals and departures at the parking area, without being detected.

By the time we had finished and connected it to the runway lighting, it was too dark to install the other camera. We gave up for the night, went into the house for a light evening meal, played Gin-Rummy for a while and went to bed. The night passed comfortably without disturbance of any kind. After breakfast, we moved my car into the parking zone to test the operation of the camera. I hooked three 100 foot extension cables together, to bring power from the house to the camera and plugged in a wire connected to the joint where I had wired the camera to the runway lights. Immediately all the lights came on and we walked around by the car to get pictures of how well the camera was covering the area. I left Joyce sitting on the front of my car to identify the end of our program and disconnected the power.

With little difficulty, I collected the cassette without disturbing the camera. I'd inserted a brand new tape and one glance at it, showed me the camera had been triggered. Excitedly, we tied the ladder to the car roof, collected the power cables, removed all traces of our activity and hurried back to the house.

Since Joyce has no TV, I'd brought my portable and we played the tape through my latest toy, the Go Video dual deck. When the picture came on, I was dismayed at how dark it appeared. The car was barely visible but looked further away than I had expected, indicating a need to change the position of the camera to get an adequate shot of the area.

"It's too dark to get a look at the number plate." Joyce commented, staring at the screen in disgust. I was about to agree, when the car jumped forward about a yard and the picture became bright and clear with the number plate easily readable.

"That's better." Joyce exclaimed happily. and read off the number "DGV 693. Oh! There I am. See. I'm on TV.!" She squealed with delight, but I was too preoccupied with trying to understand the sudden change in the picture, to fully appreciate her enjoyment.

My first thought was some kind of obstruction had moved

away from the lens. But that wouldn't account for the car jumping like it had. I stared at the screen watching us walking around the car. Occasionally, one or the other would move out of the picture and then come back but it seemed we were able to cover most of the parking area with the camera situated and aligned where it was. When the picture went off I decided to rewind and re-run the first part. Exactly the same thing happened again. I rewound and re-ran it a second time. This time I tried to enhance the picture with the brilliance control. What I saw made the hair stand on my neck. It was not my car. I said nothing to Joyce for she apparently had not noticed the difference in the cars.

"I'm going to run it again, so I can time the dark part." I said, taking my watch off to get a better look at the sweep of the second hand. I wanted to know exactly how long the runway lights had been on last night, especially since we hadn't heard anything. I timed it three times getting one minute and twenty five seconds within a couple of seconds each time. Joyce said nothing until the end of the third run when she asked me what I was up to.

"This camera was on for one minute and twenty five seconds sometime during last night." I announced to her surprise. "I wonder why.".

"How do you know?" She demanded suspiciously. "Watch the cars. They change. The first one isn't my car. It's about a yard or more further back than mine and it has round headlights while mine has square ones." I started the tape again and pointed out the changes as she watched, open mouthed in amazement.

"It can only mean one thing. While we were either playing cards or asleep, someone, probably the guy we saw leaving on Tuesday night, came and turned the lights on for a minute and a half and then turned them off."

"Why'd he want to do that?"

"Who knows. Maybe he saw us and wanted to know if it was the light that alerted us or the noise."

"It's always the noise. I've heard it many times but never noticed the lights until last time."

"Last night?"

"Not a sound." She shook her head emphatically. "If I'm awake, I sometimes hear them land. Usually I only hear the airplane taking off. It makes a lot more noise then." "Maybe someone landed and the airplane's still there." I said, a small germ of excitement beginning to arise in my gut as I remembered she hadn't heard me land and the airplane had been there all night. She hadn't heard anything until I'd started rolling the grass next day for my take off.

"Let's go look." I said, trying to suppress my excitement.

Chapter NINE

More Repercussions

The DH-84 had been pushed back, tail first, into the long grass at the far end of the airfield on the left side of the runway. From where we stood at the gate, she was almost invisible in her brown and green camouflage colors. We walked up to meet her and Joyce stood looking on in awe while I walked all around testing the fabric of the wings and fuselage with the care and reverence one should feel for the priceless antique she was. Her legs in their sleek streamlined pantaloons looked as new as the day she had rolled out of the factory at Hatfield. Her fabric as taut as the newborn skin she had worn on the day of delivery. I literally drooled at the thought that she was waiting for me to fly her away. The door was not locked. I entered and climbed up to the sloping floor to the controls where, to my amazement, the keys were dangling from the master switch.

"Take Me, I'm Yours." I heard her saying. At least that's what I'll tell the Judge, if I'm ever caught, my fevered brain decided as I slipped them into my pocket.

"Want to go for a ride?" I said jiggling the keys in front of Joyce's face. She took a step back as if I'd struck at her with them.

"You can't do that!" She gasped. "It's not yours." "'It is now." I replied jiggling the keys again.

"You don't know how to fly one of those. Do you?"

"Sure do. I've got umpty-ump hours in these. Used to fly them during the war."

"Oh My God! You're serious aren't you.! Where to?" She asked, squeezing her knees together as if to stop herself urinating and smiling excitedly at the same time.

"Where to?. I thought it would be fun to take it and hide it in my hangar. Nobody 'd know where it was if we took it there and landed just before dark."

"We'd go to Jail."

"Why?. This is your airfield. Someone parked it here without your permission and all you did was ask me to impound it until the owner showed up and gave an account of his actions. At which time, you might or might not, return it to him depending on whether he's willing to pay you for the use of your airfield. All perfectly legal I assure you."

Joyce looked torn between the rights and wrongs but the more I thought about it, the better it sounded.

"Hell they've been sneaking in and out of here for years without your consent and at last you've caught them. I'll vouch for that."

My mind was freewheeling in overdrive and I could see a vast interesting scenario developing, as long as she didn't have time to develop cold feet.

"What if they're crooks." She asked.

"Even better. They haven't got a leg to stand on."

"But. Crooks don't play by the rules."

"O.K. Then why should we?"

"Oh My God!".

Time for action before she weakens.

"Can you drive a car?"

"Yes."

"Then you can drive my car to my house with all the evidence of our activity, including the tapes. While I fly this baby out of here."

"But."

"No Buts. Do you know what this baby's worth?"

Joyce merely shook her head, but I could see the clouds of indecision gathering behind her eyes.

"I'd say a million, maybe two, in the right hands. There probably are less than a dozen of these in existence today and most of those will be in museums." Joyce's eyes widened in wonder.

"Is that the same one that flew away the other night?" "I'd stake my life on it." I replied, nodding affirmatively. Joyce still appeared doubtful and anxious to keep the brakes on my impetuous desires.

"If it's that rare and valuable." She said dubiously, "How do you think you'd be able to sell it?. Or even fly it around yourself?" She added, raising one hell of a good point I thought, as I tried to imagine the uproar this bird would cause if Kamm ever set eyes on it. Nothing I said to justify our actions would keep him quiet.

"Well. If we just leave it here, they'll just fly it away again and we'll have no choice in the matter." I countered. "If I hide it in my hangar we'll have a pretty good trump card to negotiate with."

"On the contrary Henry, We'll have defeated our own objectives and alerted the 'Enemy' (She added the quotes manually) to the fact that someone is on to them. They'll come straight to my house looking for whoever took that airplane."

I hated to listen but I knew she was right. I tried to argue that this might be the only chance we'd ever get to lay hands on the airplane. Again she pointed out that if they felt so secure in leaving the airplane with the keys in it, we could assume they'd done this before and would probably do it again.

"If they were the least bit suspicious someone else might even see the airplane, they'd have taken the keys for sure."

I should have known when I was licked but I kept arguing the case for stealing it now until she raised her hands and silenced me with.

"Henry! It's my airfield!." I stared at her open mouthed, feeling like a schoolboy confronted by a determined teacher.

"You're wasting time." she said, grinning her twisted smile.

"Lock the airplane and take the keys to the workshop behind the gas station in Joyce. They've a machine there to cut keys. Hurry! We don't know when they'll be back."

I was fairly sure they wouldn't fly this rare an airplane in daylight but again, she was right. Who knows when they might return.

I spent twenty anxious minutes, getting there and back, with a new set of keys. Joyce assured me nobody had even passed by the airfield, so we checked out the new keys and put the originals back in the airplane, leaving it exactly as we had found it.

I regretted not having been more careful walking around the airplane, but any trampled grass would probably not be noticed if the pilot and his airport manager came back after dark. However, since we could not guarantee this we took extra care moving the ladder and keeping in the cover of the trees while I set up and camouflaged the second camera. Both cameras were set to record date and time in operation, and would both begin recording simultaneously.

It was almost dark by the time I had also run a lead, from the joint between the second camera and the runway circuit, over to the house so that a night-light in the bedroom, would alert us if the runway lights were turned on. Whereas the cameras would shut off as soon as the runway lights went off, this bulb would remain on, triggered by a different kind of relay which switched it to the house power until we manually reset it. That way we'd know the runway lights had been turned on, even if we weren't otherwise made aware of it.

Highly satisfied with our labors we congratulated each other over a bottle of wine which I'd thrown in the car with my tools. Between this and my expectation the airplane would be flown out after dark, Joyce had little difficulty persuading me to stay the night.

Around three am. the light woke us and we heard the sound of the take-off. Less than a minute later, the faint light in the trees went out and we could just discern the sound of a car starting up and driving away. I would have dressed there and then to retrieve the tapes from the cameras, but Joyce had other plans.

Saturday morning, we woke late after the night's disturbances. After coffee and toast, we took the ladder to the two cameras, and retrieved the cassettes. I replaced each with a blank tape, reset the cameras, and re-adjusted the camouflage, leaving no trace of our activity.

The picture covering the runway, was somewhat darker than I had anticipated, but the video clearly showed the DH-84 taking off to the west as we had witnessed. The footage stopped less than a minute after the plane disappeared. The other tape showed nothing but the car parked in the driveway with the number plate hidden in the long grass, though I was pretty sure it was the same car I had seen passing on the road. We had learned little or nothing more than our ears and eyes had already told us. I regretted not taking the advice of the engineer at Mason Securities, to install the driveway camera controlled by a motion sensor. Joyce was as disappointed as myself and perhaps some of the aura of superiority she bestowed on me was tarnished. However, The wiring was in place and I could easily adapt it to give us a better picture of the total activity for the next encounter. Consequently, I spent most of that day rigging up the revised surveillance system, triggered by a security light I bought that afternoon, from the electrical store in Port Angeles. Joyce helped enthusiastically in each phase of the installation including the trip into P.A., and expanded it into a shopping expedition, since she so rarely had the chance to go there except by bus.

As luck would have it, we bumped into Nora, Sunday's Woman, accompanied by her two friends from the Eagles Dance Hall, in the supermarket.

Being the common denominator in this complex equation, left me no option but to introduce them to each other. I've never seen a cockfight, but I'm told the handlers of the birds introduce them to each other in order to stimulate the enmity for a fight to the death. However that hadn't been my intent so I swiftly steered Joyce out of the store, on the pretext that we were running short of daylight. I told her a few little white ones as I drove back to her place, hoping to defuse her interest in Nora's existence. I felt very thankful Nora's triangle was all present and intact, as it enabled me to shift myself out of the Star role in the show. Still, I'd seen the sparklers and had no intention of waiting around for the rest of the fireworks.

As soon as the installation was completed, I told Joyce I'd be back to see what fish we had trapped, if any, by next Tuesday and fled.

Saturday evening was getting ready for one of those perfectly still autumnal sunsets which call me to get up in my little ultra light amphibian and just cruise across the tranquil waters of Sequim or Discovery bays. This little single seat amphibian, is known as an XTC. (Extacy) a most appropriate name. It was designed by a company in Jenks Oklahoma and I bought it fully assembled from the gentleman who built it from one of their kits. It has a 25 HP motor, driving a three bladed pusher type propeller through a two-to-one belt drive, which gives it a cruising speed of 55MPH.

Normally, she's tucked away in the back of my hangar with the wings off, because I'm too lazy to push it out of the way each time I want to take the Moonbaby out. However this Saturday evening, as I rolled her out and bolted the wings on, I had visions of flying over to Lopez Island and showing it, and myself, off to Monica, in the hope of stimulating some sort of interest in me. Old men are just as crazy as adolescents when they become bitten by the love bug. This condition can be exacerbated in the extreme by A Full Moon.

I was blissfully ignorant of the imminence of this dangerous coalition, as I took off directly into the last blaze of the sunset and retracted the gears before setting course for Lopez.

Twenty six miles of open sea whose water temperature is around 45 degrees Fahrenheit lay between me and Lopez Island. It never occurred to me that I was insane. I was just going to put on a little local air show for Monica, and, if she saw me and waved, I'd land at the airport and drive out to her house and talk with her. Fifteen minutes later, I was half way across at a height of sixteen hundred feet when I became aware of the Moon rising like a huge orange lantern above the Cascade Mountains away to my right.

What more could a lovesick swain wish for. I put the nose down and headed for the exact point of land where her house would be. There was still too much daylight to see if there was a light in her window, but at my top speed of 65 MPH. and losing height at 100 feet per minute, I visualized myself flashing across her rooftop. A steep pull-up to the left and swoop around to whiz across her lawn along the cliff edge. 'Cliff nest'. That ought to wake up the little chickadee inside.

It certainly did, and as I turned for a repeat diving pass from her left, I saw her come out and stand with her hand above her eyes as I came diving down. I waved; she waved, and immediately dashed back into the house. As I pulled round for my next pass, I began slowing down so she could get a better look. (In case she'd dashed in to get a camera rather than call the police or take a pot off the stove.) I passed, a foot above the cliff top again, coming to her, out of the sunset's afterglow at a stately 35MPH. She was waving her arms vigorously as I approached and I was about to yell out her name when I realized she wasn't alone. A tall man, with his arm around her waist was standing beside her and waving just as happily except his right arm was around her waist and her left was around his.

That took the wind out of my sails alright, and strangely enough, it seemed to take the breath out of the 'Ecstacy' as well, for she refused to gain altitude as readily as before and I turned disconsolately out to sea and set course through that perfect Moonlit night sky, for home.

Habitually I climb across these cold waters to the midway point and only descend when I'm sure of my intended landfall. 'Extacy' seemed to have lost her enthusiasm for the night's flight and after we reached one thousand feet of altitude she refused to climb any higher even at full power. in fact I had to maintain full power, just to remain at that altitude. Despite the fact that as the flight continued, the rev-counter showed we were still at max revs, I couldn't maintain height. Something more than emotions was amiss. I was ten miles from home and losing height at a steady fifty feet per minute. At 55mph., I'd be in the sea in about nine minutes, at least a mile from home with no hope of climbing high enough to land on the airfield. For the first six of those minutes, I thought I might just make the airfield on Protection Island, a hundred and fifty feet above sea level. But, as the altimeter needle passed that point, while I still had time to turn away from the island's steep, dark, cliff face, I elected to go around the northeast side and land in Discovery bay. At any other time, a moonlight landing on the placid dark waters of Discovery bay, might have seemed a romantic, charming, even exciting experience; but tonight, the romance had just shut itself out of my life and all I felt as I gracefully touched down on the water at about thirty five miles an hour, was foolish.

During those sobering minutes when my safety hung in the balance, I had gradually deduced what was wrong with my little sea bird. The propeller was not putting out all the power being put out by the engine. It is driven by a set of three flexible belts. The belts were slipping. Most probably brought on by the frequent power changes I'd been making in my crazy air-show. They were old belts and, as I later remembered, the tension adjustment was at it's maximum. Months ago, I had bought three brand new belts, which were still hanging on a nail in the wall of the hangar.

However, it ain't hard to be humble when you realize you're sitting in a little flimsy amphibian on the dark cold hungry water as a direct result of your own carelessness. At least, the engine was still running, and despite the weak link to the propeller, the XTC was steadily motoring across the water towards the forbiddingly dark, but Oh! So welcome cliffs ahead.

There's a road which runs down through a ravine to a boat ramp. It starts about a hundred yards from my house. and I planned to taxi across the bay to this ramp, beach the XTC there and walk home. I won't belabor you with the trials and tribulations of beaching the little airplane. The tide was in, and though I got soaked up to my waist, the exertions required to pull the little machine up the ramp and out of harm's reach, kept me from thinking about it. Having no ropes to tie her with, I blocked all three wheels with big stones and set off squishing my way home up the steep road through the dark tree lined ravine.

I walked as quickly as I could to keep warm, but the road is very steep and I was soon totally out of breath. I stopped to get my breath back and realized that the clear sky was bringing the air temperature down severely. I could feel the cold night air flowing down the road, and knew I'd not be surprised to see frost in the morning.

Between the breeze and my soaked clothing I was losing heat faster than my exertions could replace it and I desperately needed to pee. I could not afford to stop and rest so I began walking backwards up the road, just to ease the cramping in my legs and keep moving in the right direction.

The final humiliation came when I could no longer contain myself and literally peed my pants. Strangely enough, the relaxing warmth seemed to revive my legs and feet and I was able to turn around and continue up the hill to my house.

I marched straight into the bath, stripped and ran the hot shower as I did so. I set my wallet and credit cards on the counter top to dry, and sat on the pile of soaked clothes in the bath absorbing the heat until the full warmth returned to my body.

About an hour later, warmly dressed in my sweat suit and a heavy jacket, I returned to the boat ramp in my pick up with ropes and planks and tools, to retrieve the XTC. By this time the moon was directly overhead and it was as bright as day. So bright in fact that I could see to remove the wing attach bolts without the need for a flashlight. The pick-up was backed down the ramp and the front wheel of the XTC was already on the tail gate when another pick-up with a boat in tow, came down the road. With the willing help of the two young fishermen who could not launch their boat until I was out of the way, we lifted the XTC into the truck and set each wing on top of the stub wing leaning against the twin tail fins and securely lashed in place against the cab. Fortune had finally relented and smiled on me. I reciprocated in helping them launch their boat and watched them head out for a night's fishing.

In their excitement at this unusual airplane, its peculiar shape and predicament, we had neglected to exchange names and addresses. They were from somewhere locally but not members of the homeowner's association and really not authorized to be using the boat ramp, but I was grateful for their help. With no other thought than perhaps being able to buy them a drink some time, I made a note of the license number of their pick-up in the sketch pad I keep in the truck, and set off, driving very slowly up the rough road to the top.

Un-loading, alone outside the hangar was an even more strenuous job than the loading had been with two helpers. Each wing weighs about fifty pounds, is cumbersome to handle and fragile in the extreme. I did a lot of huffing and puffing and had worked up a pretty good sweat by the time I had both of them out of their cradles in the truck and safely stored in the hangar. The main hull rolled easily down the two planks on its wheels and was tucked away inside the hangar in a tenth of the time.

Undoubtedly, some will wonder why I put myself through this labor when I could have parked the laden truck in my driveway and had some assistance from my friends next day.

Pride. I couldn't face their unspoken derision at my utter stupidity. As dear old Dad remarked on more than one occasion.

"Pride and Vanity, are the hardest of taskmasters." I guess I'm a slow learner. Not until I drove the truck back to the house, did I realize how late it was and how dog tired I was. As I crawled into bed at almost three in the morning I could only think of one redeeming factor. I had been thoroughly cured of my infatuation for Monica.

Sunday morning's frost had long since dried up before I woke. Probably, I'd have missed the whole day if Sunday's woman hadn't interrupted my sleep with a mug full of steaming coffee. Perhaps my total lack of enthusiasm for another encounter with a fickle female of the species registered in my insipid response to Nora's cheerful greeting.

"Hang one on last night?"

I made some noncommittal grunt in reply, deeming it

inappropriate to open a discussion of the night's miserable experience with the raven perched on the bed beside me. She reached out and began a muscular massage of the back of my neck. I was too lethargic to protest and gradually it began feeling better. When I tried to reach the coffee she'd placed on the nightstand beside me, my muscles, collectively, went on strike.

As the CEO of my corp. I must have made some suitable comment on this union action, for she immediately joined the strikers and ceased her ministrations. She hopped off the bed as though I'd struck her and watched as I struggled to turn over and retrieve my arm, which had almost made it to the coffee. Her expression slowly shifted from contempt to concern.

"You're Hurt.!?"

Statement or question? I didn't care, but my facial muscles who were not on strike must have supplied the answer for she slid an arm under my shoulder, lifted and rolled me over onto my back. As the pain subsided and my breath returned, I tried a smile of thanks and with my hands under the backs of my thighs I helped the tummy muscles pull my knees up to relieve the pain in my back. Nora, folded the other pillow and slid it in under my legs. At last, I was able to relax and consider trying to move to a more suitable configuration for drinking coffee.

"Over exerted myself last night." I offered, with a weak smile.

"You should have come to the dance, I'd not have been so hard on you. Anyone I know?" she added under suggestively raised eyebrows.

"You haven't met her." I joshed. "She weighs about three hundred pounds and she fell in the sea at the bottom of the road. I had to carry her up the hill."

"What did you do with her?" Nora asked, looking around. "I saw Your wet clothes in the bath."

"I left her in the hangar."

Nora sat down again on the bed and pressed me to tell her all about it. I left out the reason for my foolish behavior and substituted the superb flying conditions as the total explanation. Nora is never satisfied with the superficial.

Since she'd seen the pile of clothes, I presumed she'd also seen the contents of my pockets drying on the counter top. It wouldn't have required too much imagination on her part, to realize I had been in pretty deep.

"What time was that?" She asked, in response to my story of the fishermen helping.

"Bout midnight." I estimated, from the time I hit the sack about three hours later.

"Who goes fishing at that time?" I could see her Customs Officer mind working, and shrugged it off.

"They do I suppose. Anyway I was damned glad they did or I doubt if I could have managed without them. It was hard enough getting the airplane out of the pick-up let alone into it, by myself."

She wanted more and more details and I began to regret telling her anything. After an interlude where she seemed to be thinking, she suddenly asked.

"Want some more coffee.?" I nodded and then asked her to get me some Motrin from the medicine cabinet. It seems to be the most effective of my drugs for this back condition I get after sudden or unduly prolonged exertion.

"I guess, if you want to ask the fishermen yourself, you can find the license number of their pick-up in the glove compartment of mine."

She brought the coffee, the Motrin and the sketchpad all together. I found the entry and she copied it down.

"Don't tell them you got it from me, I only took it because I thought I'd like to buy them a drink sometime for helping me." Somehow, the thought of 'betraying' my good Samaritans, bothered me, and it occurred to me that if she let me know who the owner was, I might be able to warn them. I asked her to let me know the name and address of the owner as soon as she could, explaining I was sure they were not from the development and we were trying to discourage the use of the boat ramp by outsiders.

"The homeowners association has a letter that's sent to the owners of vehicles using the boat ramp, explaining that they are trespassing. What good it does, we're not sure, but it's bound to discourage some and spread the word." Nora thought about this for a while and asked how we get the names of the people who are using the ramp.

"Same way I did. It's not very effective I know, but if the homeowners want to protect their privilege they've got to do something."

"Huh!" She replied, eloquently conveying her contempt. "If your letter noted that all unauthorized boaters using the ramp are automatically reported to the Coast Guard, it might have more impact."

"Great idea. I'll mention it at the next board meeting." Suddenly another idea struck me. "And by the way, while you're getting the address of these guys, you might as well get the address of another one I saw some time ago. A white car, Washington license number 975 NKB You've probably got much better connections with the State Patrol than I have for getting such info without a lot of unnecessary explanations."

"Were they fishing too? At midnight?"

"Who?"

"The ones in the white car."

"No. They were parked on the airfield with the lights off. I was walking back late one night from some friends at the other side of the field and saw the car. As I approached, the guy in it started up and drove away as if I'd startled him. So I memorized the number." Nora gave me a strange look as if to challenge my memory, but jotted the number down beside the other on her little notebook.

"Can I use your phone?"

"Sure. Use the one in my office. There's paper there to write on." There's also a tape recorder which will record your call and who you dialed, so feel free. But I didn't say that part aloud. When she came back after calling someone, she gave me a slip of paper with both names and addresses on it. I traded the empty coffee mug and she went to fill it. I slipped the note under the pillow.

I waited, hunched over my knees to relieve the ache in my

back and mid section until she brought the mug of coffee. and asked if she hadn't called her 'Lover-Boss', an epithet she obviously didn't appreciate, for the information.

"No." She seemed surprised "Why'd you ask?"

"Just thought you might have. Get a few brownie points so to speak." She wasn't amused. "Sorry. Just my sick sense of humor I suppose. And, I just thought it might not be a good idea to call him from here. No offense meant." I put the coffee on the nightstand and slid my leg off the bed preparatory to getting up. The pain elevated immediately as I tried to stand and I grabbed her arm for support.

"Help me to the toilet." I gasped.

Had any of the neighbors glanced through my living room window they'd have seen a strange procession with me naked and her holding as we passed. She left me to perform and only returned to help me back to bed. I took a couple more Motrin with the remainder of the coffee and settled on my side with my knees pulled up to my chest. Though I tried to participate in the conversation, I must have fallen asleep, for it was dark when I woke up again. The pain had gone, and so had Nora.

I made one more trip to the toilet and checked the front door as I passed. She'd locked it, bless her, so I got back to bed and slept until Monday morning.

When the first gleam of sunlight echoed off the mirror into my eyes, I thought of Mary's golden hair and remembered it was her day with a tinge of regret, muted with relief.

She'd be away in Spokane at College and today was mine alone. I got up, made myself the usual heart-starting cup of coffee and settled into my office to review my options.

The little red light on the CB. was blinking. I ran the tape and listened, with slight interest to the staccato chatty conversations between my various songbirds.

As I listened, I began hearing the different days of the week talking to each other. Monday and Tuesday were missing and accounted for. Wednesday was also silent, too far away. However, Thursday Friday and Saturday were on the air fairly regularly.

Most of the conversation dealt with how each one was and the weather, which was apparently changing for the worse. Friday was getting ready to head south for the winter. Saturday wanted to be sure Friday had enough fuel and oil for the trip. Sunday, I suddenly realized, had been sitting on the edge of my bed; probably, I suspected, listening, while I, doped to the gills, slept. The tape stopped. I ran it back and listened again, faintly more attentively as it seemed I had been missing something. Pow! All of a sudden it hit me. Monica, Saturday, ran the Mobil dock at Richardson. She was checking with Friday, Alice, about 'enough oil' and the tall gent she'd been holding so close to, on Saturday evening, was none other than 'Old Baldy Whatsisname' the skipper of The Chrysalis. I remembered the way the light from the window behind them, had reflected off his head as I flew past.

Then, the glimpse of the boat moored at the Mobil dock, which hadn't fully registered as I'd made my turn almost overhead, suddenly became significant.

Alice, in her persistent questioning that night aboard Goliath, hadn't been interested in what I'd seen, so much as what it might have meant to me. Baldy, suddenly very sober, had played the incident down. Alice had been with him all the time, silent, but had not been able to resist digging me about it later, when we were alone. I began to feel sure the whole thing smelled fishy. There were just too many co-incidences for it to be otherwise. It was about time I had another chat with Roba. What I needed to know, was what had motivated him to stack those seven letters in a pile just where I'd be likely to pick them up? I'm fairly sure he didn't know then, but maybe he does now. "Come in Roba."

You see, I just don't believe everything in this world happens by chance. Neither does Roba. We've hashed this subject over many times and we are both convinced there's a reason for everything that happens. Darwinists, (Roba's title for those who blindly follow the Darwinian theory) think otherwise. But, given the known facts, and the opportunity to think about it for oneself, everyone 'knows' instinctively that this is wrong. Nothing happens without thought. Every stage of evolution was initiated by a thought. Each one of us came into this world as a consequence of thoughts that went through the minds of our Daddies and Mummies.

We ourselves, built ourselves within our Mummies Tummies by following the trail of thoughts that were the laid out for us in the DNA manual. And we know we've done a good job when we wriggle out into the daylight.

That's why the Religionists, (another of Roba's epithets), have such a difficult job convincing us of their particular warped ideas.

A thought came into my head and was followed by a series of others, so that I moved out into the kitchen and put the kettle on for another mug of coffee. With this in hand, I stretched out in my recliner, with my feet extended to absorb the warmth of my wood stove and mulled over the jumble of thoughts which the C.B. conversations had stimulated.

Pretty soon, I saw Roba. He was squatting on top of the Earth Stove with his arms around his knees. For some time, I watched him, waiting for him to react to the hot surface but he read my thoughts and advised me there was a shortage of fire-wood. "Down there." He added, gesturing with a thumb.

He claimed we were cutting so many trees and turning them into plywood and particle-board, there wasn't enough left to fuel the furnace.

He said he was glad I'd called, so he could enjoy the heat for a change, and asked me if I could turn it up a little. I reached out with my foot and lifted the stove door handle so the door opened a crack. Immediately the fire surged into life and Roba shuffled his bottom and smiled contentedly. I also relaxed with the increased warmth on the soles of my feet.

"So you want to know why I piled those letters there for you to pick up.?"

I nodded.

"Hell. I don't know. The Devil made me do it I suppose." He could see I wasn't satisfied so he shrugged his shoulders and continued. "I think He and the Boss are having some kind of a dispute about the speed with which the next evolutionary change is coming about."

"So?". I couldn't think of anything more significant to say, if they wanted to argue, who am I to interrupt? Roba and I are fully aware of the next evolutionary development in the mill so to speak. We've been aware of it for a long time. "So?". I repeated.

"What's the problem?"

"It's technical."

"Technical!??"

"Si!." Roba sometimes slips back into his native tongue under stress. "El Diablo. Well he's a bit anxious to speed the process up because he's afraid that once the New Species takes over he'll have a surplus of candidates for his empire and this will make his fuel shortage even worse."

"That's pretty high level stuff for the likes of you and me to be involved in don't you think.?"

"For you maybe, but things are different for me. "Remember?""

"Sorry."

"Just don't open any of those cans of oil."

"What's in them?"

I didn't have time to finish the question, for there was a sudden pain in my foot and the fire alarm went off with a piercing whistle. Roba disappeared in a puff of smoke which I realized was coming from my sock. I hastily snatched it off and crushed it against the brick hearth. Fortunately, all my socks are one hundred percent cotton and my hot-foot was no more than that. However I managed to spill my coffee all over the carpet in my excitement.

"So the secret's in the oilcans." I muttered, mopping up the mess with my charred sock. What had those oilcans got to do with the next development of evolution?.

According to Roba, the next phase of the evolutionary development would be some inanimate organism which would be capable of living (inanimately of course) for several hundred, maybe thousands, of years.

Mankind, the spearhead of evolutionary development he maintained, had reached its ultimate usefulness as far as the Creator was concerned. It simply had too many weaknesses. The damned creature, managed, despite itself, to last for less than a hundred Sun-cycles, by which time all the experience it had gained was lost.

Progressively, over the centuries, it had managed to pass on proportionately less and less of what it had learned to its children. And periodically it would slip, En-Masse, into emotional overdrive and destroy most of its cultural and intellectual development.

Finally, having penetrated the barriers of its terrestrial restraints, it was now probing the rest of the universe, carrying with it, the viruses of its own making, to contaminate the remainder of creation. The next evolutionary development, would have none of these faults. It would last for thousands of years continuously refining its structures and talents. It would suffer no emotional disorders, primarily because it would not be required to reproduce sexually. It would retain all its experiential knowledge and thus be able to relay everything to the Creator.

Thereby, the original purpose of Creation would be achieved. Roba was certain that we as creations are in fact the material substance of the Creator and exist solely to experience the phenomenon of BEING.

We flip periodically between material and spiritual existence, evolving in both dimensions. We have been in existence as long as creation and in each stage of this process we have had, and still bear the full responsibility of being the creator of ourselves.

He has written all this, and much more, explaining the process of arriving at this conclusion. In consequence he had little patience with the missionaries that came around peddling their version from door to door and used to trade a copy of his version for theirs. He told me once that one of the more enchanting missionaries had come back alone one evening for a further infusion of his doctrine.

I miss that old fart. He had such a way of enjoying life. I bet he had the greatest difficulty containing himself while he watched my sock beginning to smolder and flew off into his current dimension giggling happily about his ability to still give me a hotfoot.

So what did he mean with all that guff about the devil?

Roba maintained that the transition from animate intelligence, to artificial intelligence would presage the next stage of evolution.

Had he been inferring that something to do with artificial intelligence must be connected with the cans of oil? Were they contaminated with some virus? Why had he warned me against opening them? Was the hotfoot a joke? Or possibly, a much more serious warning?

Chapter TEN

One False Step

When I tried to put a fresh sock on my foot, I realized the Hot-foot had been more severe then I first thought. After bathing it in ice water, I dried it and applied a coating of Betadine to the sole before pulling the sock on. It felt much better, even bearable to walk on. At least I would be able to drive since the Olds is an automatic.

Fully aware that it was not Tuesday, I told myself, as limped out to the car, that Joyce wouldn't raise any objections if I came a day early to see what might have happened at the airfield. I was right. My reception was almost overwhelming, yet I saw from the glow of happiness in her eyes that she was genuinely delighted to see me. After our first breathless embrace, she was fairly bubbling with eagerness to tell me our trap had been sprung on both Saturday and Sunday nights. Since she had no phone, she'd been unable to let me know and hadn't felt competent to get the cassettes out of the cameras and examine them herself. As we retrieved the cassettes from the cameras, I cautioned myself to remember to weigh in this anticipatory effect, when assessing why she'd seemed more than usually pleased to see me.

With suppressed excitement we watched as the pictures appeared on the TV screen. The parking lot camera came on as soon as the gate was opened, and I realized the hinges had made no sound. The car drove in and stopped. Three men got out and moved around silently. I could just distinguish the sound of the car doors closing and realized the camera mechanism was making enough noise inside it's enclosure, to depress the auto volume control to the point where the fainter distant sounds, which I had hoped to record, like conversations etc. were shut out.

The men walked past towards the airfield and even though the light was inadequate for a good picture, the impression I got was they were Orientals or Indians. After about four minutes of no activity on the screen, the camera shut down and then came on a second time as one man, presumably the driver, walked to the car, got in and backed the car out through the gate. Suddenly there was a momentary blaze of light and the camera shut off. Before I had time to understand what had happened, the camera came on again as the gate was being opened a second time. I realizes then that what we had seen was the compressed sequence of Saturday's activity and the beginning of Sunday's activity.

The blaze of light was probably due to the driver switching on his headlights before shutting the gate. The motion sensor I'd adapted from an area light control, had a light sensitive element which prevented it operating in daylight. Poor confused little cheap-y gadget couldn't tell the difference between day light and headlight.

This time, only the driver got out of the car and walked into the airfield. After another four minutes watching the inactivity, the camera shut off and then came back on as the original three men walked to the car and got back in. This time the driver didn't put his headlights on before shutting the gate and backing out of the picture. a few moments after the car went off the screen, its lights came on illuminating the area and faded away into the darkness once more.

In another three minutes the camera shut off again leaving a blank raster pattern until I stopped the recorder.

"What do you make of that.?" I asked.

"Very confusing." Joyce replied looking blankly at me as I explained the sequences and the reasons for the special effects.

The second cassette began its program with the airfield in darkness and a message saying there was insufficient light for what seemed like an eternity, until the lights of the field came on. This completely mystified me for the wiring had been simply connected in parallel with the light wiring.

The audio, which had been turned up on the previous cassette produced the sound of aero engines and the screen became clear and bright as the sound increased and the DH-84 swiped across the picture landing from the eastern end of the field with its landing lights on.

Since the telephoto zoom action is manually operated, the view of events at the far end of the field was too small to discern clearly but from the movement of the lights, the plane apparently turned around and put its lights off. These cassettes provide at least an hour's coverage and I was afraid it would run out before the plane took off but in fact it was only ten minutes later when the lights blazed up and came rushing back down the field as the plane took off.

The airfield lights went off and came on again, and the sequence repeated itself except for a much shorter interval between the landing and take off.

I had synchronized the time on both cameras within a second, so with the aid of my new Go-Video Dual Deck VCR, I was able to transform the fragmentary events recorded by the two 8mm camcorders into a complete time-edited sequence on a VHS cassette for playing on the TV.

I had fun employing some of the editorial capabilities like fade-ins and fade-outs to make a neat little episode showing the arrival of our mysterious Orientals and their take off and return.

"Big deal." Joyce commented contemptuously, after watching the whole procedure with well restrained patience.

"So a couple of 'Chinks' take a midnight flight to some secret rendezvous and come back in the early hours of the morning."

"Put like that, it don't sound much like a police matter. Do it?" I replied, wondering why it had taken them ten minutes to load two able bodied passengers. "I think I'll move the camera to the other end of the airfield where we can see what they do down there. Or maybe what happens at that woodshed of theirs."

Joyce came over and put her arms around me.

"I'd rather we put them up in the bedroom and made a porno movie of ourselves. I could watch it when you're away." Her remark took me completely by surprise, but there was no denying the sincerity of her desires. So I didn't. In consequence, it was mid-afternoon before I left her sleeping and went out to move the cameras to new positions, where they could monitor the activities at the other end of the field, and in the woodshed.

In order to expedite the changes, I took the camera monitoring the parking area down and connected the motion sensor directly to our warning light in the bedroom. I already had all I needed to know about the car and the parking area. My main concern was what happened in the woodshed.

The camera covering the runway, I simply cut its cable to the lighting system and transferred the whole rig to a tree overlooking the far end of the field. To save time since it was getting late, I simply pinched its leads around bared areas of the lighting wires without even bothering to insulate the joints. It was a temporary installation anyway, and the chances of anyone seeing it, I decided, were remote. The camera for the woodshed I installed at the top of a stack of bedding on a shelf at the far end and covered it with a folded pair of overalls so that only the lens was exposed, aimed to cover the inside activities, relying on its ability to auto-focus on its background or on objects closer in the line of sight. I connected its solenoid lead to the wire leading to the overhead light.

At least, I think I did, for the next thing I remembered was the strange sensation of being dragged along the ground by my feet which seemed to be tied together, and my bare back sliding on wet grass.

I must have yelled out or made some other sound for whoever was pulling me stopped and stood over me, shining a flashlight in my face.

"Still alive eh?" A foreign male voice remarked out of the darkness. "We'll soon take care of that." I was aware that my arms had somehow been dragged up above my head as if my jacket sleeves were tied together leaving my torso bare and presently the voice muttered "There." and I felt his hand on my chest, feeling the ribs.

As if in a dream he was suddenly illuminated and I saw with horror the terribly burned face and the teeth bared in a sort of surprised grin as he held a long knife against my chest and was feeling for the appropriate point of entry to kill me.

A dismembered voice I knew I'd heard somewhere, barked "Hold it Mister!!."

Distracted for a moment, he drew back the knife preparatory to the plunge, and I remember wondering what it would feel like, but there was a tremendous explosion and he was blown backwards off me and seemed to sail away into the darkness. The knife flew out of his hand and spun twinkling into the night that had descended on every side.

For a while I lay petrified on the cold grass unable to move either hands or feet and a terrible pain spread from my head, down my neck and arms into my hands.

In the background I heard a strange keening noise and feared he was coming back to find me and finish me off. I could see stars above me but they were steady and I realized I was looking up at the sky. A shadow came across the stars and someone stumbled and fell almost on top of me. The strange groaning and wailing was coming from this person and moments later I felt hands groping and someone trying to lift me up.

Still fearing it was this same murderous gargoyle, I decided to play dead, and went as limp as I could under the painful circumstances.

Eventually I realized this person was trying to free my arms from the clothing that imprisoned me and pick me up, and appeared to be terribly distressed over the inability to do so. It gradually penetrated my mind that it was Joyce who was holding me.

"Joyce.?" I asked, hopefully.

I barely remember how we got from there to the bedroom but somehow she'd freed my arms and legs and assisted me home.

She washed the back of my head where a huge knot had appeared causing the pain and dosed me with Asprin before she tied some kind of an ice pack to my head. As things began to come back to normal, I asked her what had happened to the guy who'd been going to skewer me with the knife.

"Oh, I shot him." She said, in such a matter of fact tone that I thought she was joking, and that I'd somehow banged my head on something and had been dreaming the whole episode. But the vision of his disfigured face would not go away.

"You shot him!? What with!?"

"The shot-gun of course. Silly. Lie back down and don't excite yourself."

"Excite myself !?" I shrieked. "Where is he now?" I was coming back to reality and the vision of a bullet riddled corpse lying out on the airfield when the plane came back, convinced me that our troubles were just beginning, instead of ending as she seemed to think. Worse yet; if she'd had birdshot in that gun, as I'd imagined, he was probably still alive and maybe even capable of coming after us again. Right now in fact, if he'd seen her take me away.

"Where he should be!. In Hell I expect." She looked at me as If I'd lost my mind. "How would I know? I hit him because I saw him fall. But the shock of the gun made me drop my flashlight and it went out. I couldn't find it and I was trying to find you. I didn't care where he went." The picture was coming clearer in my mind as she spoke.

"He was about to kill you with a dagger." She was getting close to tears remembering her terror.

"Did you find the flashlight?"

"No. I stumbled over you."

"So it's still out there.?"

"And the shotgun." She admitted ruefully.

That abashed announcement stopped my questions, and I wrestled with the possibilities.

No weapon. No flashlight. One very dangerous, make that murderous, wounded man out there looking for revenge. He'd had a flashlight, I remembered seeing it. Very bright. Blinding in fact. By now he might even have two flashlights. And a shotgun. Make that an empty shotgun. Please.

Add to that, the probability he'd been there to welcome his buddies. I had to assume he'd been alone, or there'd have been no need to drag me around with him. My head ached even more from the effort of trying to concentrate.

Would the pilot of the DH-84 dare to land if the runway lights weren't on? There seemed no end to the questions.

"Do you have another flashlight?. In the house?"

Joyce nodded her head. My terse questions seemed to convince her that danger might still be somewhere out there.

"Better get it. And the box of shotgun shells. Bring them all here and turn out all the lights." Without lights, if he was looking for us, he'd almost have to use the flashlight and that would warn us. "Be quick."

When Joyce left, I began to realize that despite the throbbing pain in my head, I could still function and perhaps the effort of thinking about our predicament was helping to clear my mind.

The two minutes it took her to return with the flashlight and two boxes of shells seemed like an eternity. I hated being alone and the thought of her possibly being confronted by that murderous gargoyle, while I lay in bed, troubled me even more. Together we might have a chance. I reached out my hand for the boxes of shells and she gave them to me and switched out the light.

"Whoa!. Wait a minute." I suddenly realized that all this hysteria revolved around what kind of shells our assailant had been hit with. I once spent an hour picking Number six shot out of my padded hunting jacket when a friend fired at a duck, passing between us, across a small pond.

"Put the light back on."

"Oh My God!!" I was staring at a box of Double-Naught Buck shot. Hopefully, I suppose, I looked at the other box. For some reason, although I feared it, I wanted to believe he was still alive. Solid Slugs. There wasn't a chance. No wonder he'd sailed off me in that airy fashion.

Joyce had her hands over her mouth, looking wide eyed at me as though I was the Judge condemning her for a murder.

"Honey, it's almost certain you killed him."

"I Had To!! The Son-of a bitch was about to Kill You!!!" she flung her arms around me sobbing in my ear.

"I had to. I had to."

"I'm eternally grateful," I said gently into hers, "but there's a mess out there we'd better clean up, before anyone finds it."

For several minutes we sat there on the side of the bed holding each other and discussing what we should do next. It's fortunate that Joyce had no telephone, for in my weakened condition, I might not have been able to stop her phoning for the police.

"Honey, as far as the police are concerned, you should have called them instead of shooting him." The sheer idiocy of my remark stopped her protestations. Suddenly she smiled and asked casually,

"Aren't you glad I didn't?"

"So. Let's leave them out of it as long as we can. Eh?"

"I can dig a hole and bury him."

"Not anywhere around here. And! Don't forget! We'll have to get rid of his car too." I warned. "If his buddies come looking for him, and find it here and him missing, they'll probably come here first. We're the nearest other people. If they get suspicious, we could have even more trouble with them than with the police."

"You're certain they're crooks aren't you.!?

"Well you were pretty certain of that when you pulled the trigger. Weren't you ?" I felt a bit unkind saying this but she seemed to want to talk about it whereas I felt we could be running short of time in which to act.

"We'd better go and remove the body right away in case someone else comes to find our why the lights haven't come on."

"Is the airplane coming back again tonight?"

"I don't know. If not, why was he here.?."

"Wouldn't they talk to each other on the radio." She asked, surprising me. I hadn't seen any sign of one in the shack, so if they were in radio contact, it would have to be via his car.

"We'd better go look in his car. There's no radio in their shack."

By this time, I was up on my feet, still a little rocky, but my headache had diminished enough for me to contemplate serious action.

Joyce steadied me as we went downstairs, and I slipped a couple of the Solid Slugs into my pocket. Just in case.

"How'd you come to find me?" I asked, as we went outside. "It's so dark tonight."

"It wasn't so dark when I first went out. I woke up and the alarm light was on and you'd gone. I knew you'd gone out to do something to the cameras. and I wondered if you were out by the parking, so I went there first. When I saw his car there, I went back and got the shotgun and came looking for you. I was walking at the side of the runway when he came along dragging something towards me. I ducked down at the side in the long grass, and just after he passed me, I heard him mutter something. He stopped and put his light on and then I saw you. When he got that knife out and was going to stab you with it, I shot him."

She related her story in such a matter-of-fact tone, as if it were a normal occurrence, that I wondered at all the emotion she had displayed upstairs.

Since I felt somewhat dubious about my ability to carry the body any distance, even between us, we fetched a blue plastic tarpaulin from my car with the intention of rolling the corpse into it and dragging it in much the same way he'd dragged me around.

He was lying on his back almost in the middle of the runway, mute testimony to the force of the shotgun blast at such close range. His arms and legs were stretched out like a starfish and though I shone the light over him there was little signs of blood except for a trickle from the side of his mouth into his ear and beyond. With his eyes half closed, he was less hideous than the last time I'd seen him just before the shot. His pale features were scarred and distorted by what I took to be surgery, following a severe burn all over his face and it was difficult to determine whether the eyes were open or not.

I felt in his pants pockets for his wallet and the car keys, surprised that they still felt warm as it was getting quite cold in the night air. He had a heavy padded jacket on so I assumed the insulation had kept the body warm. I got Joyce to stand on the edge of the tarp while I dragged the body onto it and we rolled him up in it like a sausage.

We collected both the flashlights, his knife and the shotgun. Then, half carrying, half dragging, moved the heavy burden towards the gate. I opened the trunk of his car, but there was no room in it for him so we pulled and pushed, dragged and lifted him into the back seat and folded the ends of our blue 'sausage skin' over on top of its contents. It was a pretty untidy pile, but at least it bore no resemblance to a body.

Since we dared not leave the car with its macabre occupant where it was, in case other members of his fraternity should come looking for him, I deemed it better to take the risk of being stopped on the road and decided to drive it to my place where I could take my time disposing of the 'evidence'. Joyce declared she could drive my car and after shutting up the house and leaving it tidy with Patch on a long leash, we set out in convoy with me in the lead.

We kept strictly to the speed limits and though the drive took forty minutes, and our thoughts seemed loud enough inside our heads to alert every patrolman in the state, we made it without incident. Sometime after midnight, we had him and his car tucked safely into the corner of my hangar on the side opposite the amphibian's center section, and were back in Joyce's place.

The only evidence of our complicity in his disappearance was his wallet and car keys, which I felt confident would not be recognized even if his pals raided the house looking for him.

Tuesday morning, about four thirty A.M., I woke in a cold sweat remembering he had surprised me and knocked me unconscious inside the hut in the woods. Had he found the evidence of our surveillance.? I could not remember anything after connecting the camera wires to the light wiring.

Had I completed this before he hit me?

What sort of a mess had we left inside the shack which might alert anyone who came searching for him.? If they found the camera, it wouldn't take long to connect it to the other one, and then to the house next door. I sat bolt upright with fear, cursing my own carelessness.

"What's the matter ? Head bothering you?" Joyce asked solicitously, turning over.

"You could say that." I answered, getting out of bed. "I need to go check on the camera in the woodshed."

"At this time of night!?"

"We need to know whether he found it, before or after he laid me out. Or if he found it at all, for that matter. I just don't know. I can't remember whether I'd finished hooking it up or not."

"Quit worrying Pet, It doesn't matter. He can't tell anyone either. Besides, no one else has been here since we moved his car or the alarm light would have been on."

"All the more reason we'd better check now. Before anyone does come."

I was half dressed by this time, and Joyce must have realized the futility of trying to hold me back, for, without a word, she got up and dressed.

Nothing had been disturbed in the shed.

I must have finished the hook-up and been outside before he hit me. Probably he'd arrived and waited to see who was in there and waylaid me when I came out. I don't even remember getting hit. Thinking about it later, I realized the blow must have concussed me severely. Probably he thought he'd killed me. I shone my flashlight on the forest floor but there was no sign of a struggle near the entrance and only a slight indication of where he had dragged me out into the clearing. I scuffled my feet over that area to erase the tracks and meekly allowed Joyce to lead me back to bed.

By five A.M. I was wide awake again and decided to go back to my place to figure out how to dispose of the body. Joyce, more concerned about the possible after effects of the blow to my head did all she could to dissuade me, but finally compromised by insisting on accompanying me.

"You're not fit to be out alone."

"I made it all right last night."

"That was an emergency. This isn't." We argued all the way to my house. The disposal of the anonymous marauder's body taking top priority.

I felt fairly comfortable with the idea of disposing of the car by leaving it parked in some distant town, like Port Townsend, where, if anyone set up a police search, it would be found and possibly lead the searchers away from the airfield arena.

We'd not seen any signs that the people who were running their clandestine operation out of 'Joyce's' airfield, were even aware of our interest in them, much less having any interest in our existence. The unfortunate Mr. Who, hadn't had a chance to alert them before Joyce had filled his heart with buckshot.

"I think our best plan is to take the body from the hangar and put it in the deep freeze at my house until a suitable time to take it out into the bay and sink it. The local shrimp will dispose of it in a few days. If a fisherman ever pulls the remains up in a trawl net there'd be nothing to connect them with us."

"Well you can't leave him where he is". Joyce stated flatly, and I was intrigued to realize how easily he had become my responsibility now. I felt it fair to retaliate.

"I'd appreciate your help getting him out of the car into the pick up so I can move him without exposing the neighbors to the sight of me driving a strange car this morning."

"They'll see you driving the pick up. Won't they?"

"They see that every other day. Nobody will notice it."

We drove in silence while she thought about this. "What'll they think if they see me with you.?" I was about to say this too would go un-noticed, when I remembered I'd asked for her co-operation.

"They'll be jealous."

She relaxed and I went on. "Once he's nice and frozen. We can saw him up and sell the meat."

For some reason, the vision of the federal agent scoffing the steak in the movie 'Fried Green Tomatoes' popped into virtual reality on my windshield and I laughed. But Joyce had her hand over her mouth and for an uncomfortable moment, I thought she was going to throw up in my car.

"Henry! Sometimes you can be too gross for words!"

"Got a better idea.?" I asked cheerfully.

"Perhaps he's got a wife. Maybe someone is worried about his disappearance. Who is he anyway?" Her question jerked me back to reality and I remembered having taken his wallet and keys. We'd become so stressed out with our desire to get rid of his body, I'd not even looked at the wallet to see who he was. I slipped off the seatbelt to get the wallet out of my pants pocket, and handed it to Joyce.

"See what you can find from the driving lcense or credit cards."

His name was Henry Barkeel. He had four credit cards and a California handicapped drivers license showing an Address:— in Solana Beach, California.

"No Washington license?" I asked, figuring we could cross check against the registration in the car. or possibly an insurance policy card that should be in the glove box.

"Sounds like a Swanky address, wonder where it is." Joyce continued the search in silence, until she'd counted his money.

"There are sixteen $100 bills, four twenties and a folded cutting from a newspaper." She announced in some awe, ruffling the stack of greenbacks in her lap.

"Eight forty apiece. I'll split it with you." I said jokingly. However, it didn't seem to amuse her for she stared in apparent disgust at my assumption we would keep it.

"I shot him." She said indignantly.

"Ah. But the burial costs have yet to be paid." I countered, raising an equally indignant eyebrow.

Suddenly she smiled. "Listen to us. You'd think we were Bonnie and Clyde, out for a picnic, instead of two responsible citizens, discussing the funeral arrangements for some guy we'd just bumped off."

"You bumped off." I corrected, as I pulled into the left turn lane and stopped, long enough to let some early commuters headed for Sequim, to pass.

"I saved your life. You don't seem very grateful." I reached across the car and squeezed her hand.

"You were absolutely wonderful. I don't know any other woman who I could have been sure would have pulled the trigger like that. Never a moment's hesitation when the chips were down. I am most grateful to be here, now, with you, instead of in a box, at a funeral, even if you were attending. I mean that. Now I want to do everything I possibly can, to shield you from the after effects of your action."

I held her hand all the way to the house to confirm my statement.

The old Chevvy pickup sprang into life at the first turn of the key and we took advantage of the early hour to get to the hangar before the locals were up and about.

I parked with the tailgate down beside the joint between the two sliding doors and together we pushed the one door open, just far enough for us to carry our burden out and slide him into the box. We would then put the gate back up before anyone could see the contents of the box, shut the hangar doors, and drive him the long way round, back to the house. There, my plan was, to back down to the store room where the big chest type freezer was and together we could slip the whole bundle out of the truck and into the freezer with the minimum of effort.

The first thing I noticed was the awful stench that assailed our nostrils as we opened the car door. I had no idea a body could putrefy that fast at such low temperatures, and the thought of carrying it into my house horrified me. Certainly I couldn't leave it here either, since all the hangars are open to a common roof and the other tenant pilots, who would soon be coming to investigate. The next thing I noticed was that our wrapping had come undone somehow and his head was visible. I must have frozen in place for suddenly Joyce was looking over my shoulder at the body, with her hand over her mouth.

She turned to me, white as a sheet, with eyes that were several sizes too big for her face.

"My God!" she whispered hoarsely. "He's still alive."

I could not move. Mental and physical paralysis set in without invitation. What worse scenario could develop now?. When he had been faced with the fact that I was still alive he'd set about putting that straight without hesitation, but had killing me been his original intention?

Or had an attempt to merely neutralize whatever threat I represented to his operation, been all he'd wanted, and the blow he struck had been too hard? Killing him, certainly hadn't been my intention, and I doubted if it had really been Joyce's either. True, she'd been faced with what appeared to her as the immediate necessity to use whatever power she held in the shotgun, to remove the threat from me. but that's not quite the same as an intent to kill.

All the way here we'd been psyching ourselves up to dispose of a dead body which apparently wasn't quite dead. I suppose a similar train of thought was plowing its way through Joyce's head, for she hadn't moved either. We looked at each other, each expecting some miraculous decision from the other.

Joyce shook her head as if to refute the thought that might be in my head, to finish him off.

"We'll have to get him to a hospital." We said in unison.

"The nearest one is in Port Angeles. That's thirty miles away!" I said, suddenly realizing I was no longer holding my breath. "And," I added cautiously, "We'll be in a hell of a mess whether we get him there dead, or alive."

"We can't just kill him!. Can we?" Joyce responded in a hushed whisper. There was just enough pause between the 'him' and the 'Can' to make me wonder if she could. I knew I couldn't. I shook my head, and the die was cast.

"Help me lift him out of the car into the pickup as gently as possible. We'll move him to the house and see what we can do for him there, before rushing into something we'd rather avoid." I said as calmly as I could.

I won't risk nauseating you with the details of our struggle to lift him and the pool of excrement in which he was lying, out of the back seat of a two door car and carry the whole mess, carefully contained in the tarpaulin, and get it up into the pick-up. But we did it without spilling much on the hangar floor. I shut the door hoping the stench would dissipate fairly quickly, before my friends accused me of indecent behavior in my hangar. Given time, I could slip back with a bucket of Clorox and a swab the area, later.

I backed the pickup into the garage where we peeled his clothes off and washed him with warm water before sliding his now naked body onto a blanket and carrying him into the house where, after removing the shower doors, we laid him in the bath in a few inches of well warmed and disinfected water.

His whole chest was black and blue, he was unconscious, and his breathing was very shallow but there were no puncture marks I could find. Later, we discovered several of the buckshot had fallen out of his clothing in the pickup. Apparently the shirt he was wearing was made from extremely tough fiber for there were no holes in it at all. I reasoned that the padding in his coat had cushioned each pellet and spread the load enough to prevent penetration.

In combination, they had acted like a bullet proof vest. Doubtless if Joyce had loaded the gun with a single solid slug the outcome would have been different. He should be grateful for small mercies.

I conjectured that his lungs and possibly his heart, had been severely bruised and perhaps there were some broken ribs which had caused the blood that had run out from his mouth. I figured the best place to keep him for a while would be the bath as we could maintain adequate warmth and the water would support his injuries better than a bed. My bed.

I somehow felt a deep aversion to letting him lie in it.

Although I felt sure there was little chance he would become violent, I decided to bind his lower legs together, using a large towel wrapped around them and secured with a belt.

Joyce was a little caustic at first until I explained it was as much for his protection as anyone else's.

"He shouldn't be encouraged to get up just yet." I said, leaving her to watch over him from the vantage point of the toilet seat, while I went to tidy up the pickup and the garage.

Closing up the car, I noticed his wallet and the money lying on the seat and picked them up. The folded piece of newsprint fell on the floor and idly, I opened it up to see what it was he was carrying around.

What at first glance seemed to be a single piece, turned out to be several pieces joined together with mystic tape. I spread the strip out and read it in amazement.

"How's he doing?" I asked, poking my head around the bathroom door.

"Seems to be breathing a little easier." Joyce replied, "Need any help."

"No thanks. I'm going to make a couple of phone calls. Holler if you need anything."

I left her and called Barbara Barranquillas. When she came on the line I asked her if she'd heard anything more from her adverts.

"As a matter of fact Henry, I have. I was going to ask you tomorrow if you'd come with me to Forks as it seems that's where these strange letters have been coming from.

I've an address there but I'm afraid to go there on my own. Would you mind.?"

"Not in the least, I'll be glad to Barbara. Does the name Henry Barkeel mean anything to you?."

I distinctly heard her sharp intake of breath but she didn't answer right away.

"You still there ?". Still no reply.

"Barbara?." There was a squeaky sound from the phone and I imagined my 'Duchess' desperately trying to re-compose herself for she eventually answered in a husky voice.

"Yes. It does. It's a direct translation of. of Enrique Barranquillas."

"Have you located him !?" I asked, my voice rising in the vague hope that there were perhaps two of them.

"Not yet. But that's why I was hoping you'd come with me."

"To Forks?"

"Yes."

"How'd you find him?"

"I asked a friend in the state department of licensing to try and find out if they had anyone by that name on file."

"And ?."

"There's a temporary license, issued to a disabled person from California with that name. Living in Forks.

"You think he might be your husband?"

"I'm almost certain it is. I remembered years ago how he translated his name into English. Barra, is a ridge or a bar, and Quillas, is like breastbone, or the keel of a ship. So Barranquillas, translates almost directly into 'bar-keel' . . . How did you find out?" It was now my turn to be silent, thinking about the battered, black and blue breastbone I'd just been looking at. Was there a chance it could be the same one she yearned to cling to?. What chance did he have of recovering?. They say a woman's love is the greatest healing power on earth.

"Henry?"

"Henry.!?"

"Sorry. I was just thinking."

"Well. Tell me!. How did you find out.?"

I just couldn't bring myself to tell her the awful truth. That we might actually have her husband, who she had adored, and so desperately wanted back from the dead, lying almost dead. Here. In the bath.

"Henry!!".

"Barbara. How badly do you want to see him.?"

There came that silence again. The awesome tortured silence wherein a bereavement is accepted or a lost hope acknowledged. Then the brave strained words seeking the painful reality.

"Henry. You're my friend. Tell me what it is you're not telling me."

"Barbara. I don't want to raise your hopes, but we have a Henry Barkeel here at my house who just might be the one you're looking for. But. He was a burn victim at one time and he's not very well at the moment."

"A burn victim?. They said there'd been a fire. I'll come right over."

It was hopeless trying to dissuade her, so, I gave her directions as to how to find my place, and went back to the bathroom.

Henry Barkeel was still far away in La-la-Land. Joyce, bless her practical heart, had solved the problem of supporting his head, which had been prone to loll to one side, thus putting its unconscious owner, in danger of drowning, by creating a makeshift life preserver out of some plastic sacks. I knelt beside her and put my head on her knees, studying the floating face in the bath, while she ran her fingers soothingly through my hair.

"We can't leave him here." She said as though reading my thoughts. "Haven't you got a folding canvass cot or something like that we can put him on?"

"There's a chaise lounge somewhere out in the garden. I'll go get it." Why hadn't I thought of that? Too busy preparing my thoughts to meet the prospect of dealing with Barbara's arrival and it's possibilities, I suppose.

After dusting off the spider webs etc from the plastic webbing, I brought the collapsible chaise into the back bedroom and set it up.

Then, I applied myself to making a couple of bridge type supports from some two by fours, to stand on each end of the bath so I could lay a fifty nine inch length across them, above the centerline of the bath inside the sixty inches the walls allowed. My Idea was to make a pole to which we could attach Henry, with towels and similar strap supports and carry him, like the natives of Africa are always shown carrying the game animals they've killed. I had a little difficulty convincing Joyce that it was in his interests to do this, as her idea, lifting his sodden carcass out of the bath by the arms and legs had been messy and stressful enough getting him into the bath in the first place. In view of his enhanced status as a potentially valuable 'prize' for a faithful wife, I felt it imperative to minimize the risk of doing any further damage as much as possible henceforth.

To get him lifted as close as possible to his 'Watusi-Shoulder-Pole', (Joyce's name for the fifty-nine incher, after looking at my sketch of the rig), I taped over the overflow hole in the bath and we literally floated him up to the rim before strapping his lower legs to the pole. His knees hung over a piece of 'one and a half inch black plastic drainpipe' resting across the two-by and a similar piece across his insteps, under the two-by. All light-weight equipment, but I didn't want his feet to flip up as soon as we lifted.

Similarly, we laid an eighteen inch piece of one by six across the pole and strapped his forearms to this, so he was virtually embracing the two-by. Joyce wrapped a wet towel around the pole and his head, which kept the center of his attention up against the underside of the two-by, and we let the water out. By sliding the 'pole along the two end bridles we moved him to the edge of the bath and as soon as the water was gone, we were able to step into the bath and lift him up and over onto the bathroom floor. The moment his bare wet back touched the cold tiles of the floor he began to revive making small twitching movements of the feet and hands and a soft gurgling sound as though trying to clear his throat.

We dried him, and wrapped him in the remaining dry towels before setting him on the chaise with as many blankets and quilts as I have extra, folded double and piled on top. As a reward for all this labor, he opened his eyes and began moving them around as if to establish his surroundings, though from where I stood, it seemed as if they moved independently, like a chameleon's. I tried to smile reassuringly, but his facial muscles didn't or perhaps couldn't function though he switched his attention to Joyce and followed her every move. Anyway, he didn't seem to want to move from where he was, and the sound of a car stopping hastily in my driveway, alerted me to Barbara's arrival.

With a whispered, "Keep an eye on him." to Joyce, I left and went out to intercept the Rushing Duchess Express.

We met on the corner where the path from my garage emerges through the trellis arbor to the main deck, bumper to bumper.

"Where is he ?!"

"Whoah !" I gasped, wrapping both arms around her as I pushed against the surprisingly powerful momentum her body possessed.

"Barbara. Wait!. There are things I have to show you and tell you before you dash in there and create chaos. He's in intensive care. Any shock such as seeing you might kill him." I laid it on thick and heavy, as the situation seemed to dictate, almost ending up under the 'Cow-Catcher' before I brought her to a halt.

"Where is he?" She kept repeating, as I forcibly steered her to the patio table and sat her down in the nearest chair. No mean feat, considering our relative size and my weakened condition.

"He's going to be O.K." I said breathlessly. "My Nurse is with him and he has just 'Come-to.'. I don't think he knows quite where he is yet and it's important not to subject him to any sudden shock. Such as seeing you. Not just yet."

She began to relax under the pressure of my hands and seemed to understand what I was driving at, for she set her purse on the table and made no more effort to get back up on her feet. I stroked her head for a while, telling her to relax and listen to what I had to tell her about him, before she jumped to her own conclusions.

"Sit here a minute while I get you a cup of tea."

She nodded and began reassembling the 'Duchess' from the ruins.

"I'll be right back." I said from the doorway and closed it behind me, colliding with Joyce who had pumped herself up the haughty level of a 'Baroness' and demanded, in a stage whisper, "Who is that woman?!".

I guess I'll never learn, so I replied,

"Never mind. You're supposed to be looking after our victim," and pushed past her heading for the kitchen. Somehow, Joyce seemed to float about three inches taller and remained in front of me, demanding in a savage whisper.

"Who is she?!. And what's she doing here.?!"

I reached around her and began filling the kettle, pressing my body against hers until she was almost sitting in the sink.

"Her name is Barbara Barranquillas. She thinks our friend Henry, is her husband. And she doesn't mean fiddly squat to me." With my grip on the faucet I was able to exert considerable leverage against her so that our faces were almost touching and with her arms above mine, she had no purchase on anything to resist, so I kissed her and said.

"Honey. Go on back and see to it our friend doesn't do himself any damage trying to get out of bed. There's a dear. I'm going to make a cup of tea for our visitor and get her calmed down so she doesn't become hysterical on us." Her eyes were wide and dilated, so I knew I had her attention for the moment and continued. "I think she's convinced herself that Henry Barkeel is her husband who disappeared about six years ago in a fishing boat accident."

"Barbara Barranquillas?. That name is strangely familiar." Her eyes became unfocussed and far away. "Where have I heard that name?"

"I don't know honey. Please go back and look after our patient, while I get things out here under control." I had to release her to plug the kettle in and she pushed away from the sink, demanding,

"How did she know he was here?"

"I told her."

"You Told her!!?. When?"

"About two hours ago. On the phone."

"So That's who you were talking to. You knew all along who he was."

"No. I had no idea who he was until I read that newspaper cutting you found in his wallet." her hand went to her mouth and she exclaimed through her fingers.

"I left all that money on the seat of the car!" Then, with the ease of a woman, she accused me.

"Why didn't you tell me?" I shrugged helplessly.

"Too much to explain right then. Remember?. We were busy trying to figure out how to get him out of the bath." Abruptly, she strode to the window and peered out at the forlorn woman sitting nervously at the patio table.

"I know that woman from somewhere." she declared, and

with her mind preoccupied with this problem, went back to the shambles in the bedroom, while I brewed some tea for the Duchess. I waited until Barbara set the cup down before giving it to her with both barrels.

"Henry Barkeel is a cold blooded murderer." I said slowly and distinctly, watching Barbara's eyes widen in horror and indignation. I held up my hand to stop the impulse she had to denounce my remark and went on. "Last night he bludgeoned me from behind." I bent my head forward so she could see the damage for herself. "And then, when he discovered I wasn't dead, he was on the point of plunging a dagger into my heart, when Joyce shot him." I pulled up my shirt and showed her the scar where the point of his knife had actually pierced the skin. "I was that close to being dead now, if it hadn't been for Joyce." Barbara's face was a pallid white mask of horror, and the hands clasped across her mouth trembled visibly. I felt sorry and a little ashamed of myself for being so brutally direct. But desperate situations require desperate measures as Henry himself must have been painfully aware of, by now. Barbara's role as the Duchess, was crumbling rapidly to a frightened mouse, so I felt it was time for the 'good' news. "Fortunately for him, he must have been wearing a bullet proof vest of some sort. The shotgun blast never penetrated his body, though his chest was massively bruised, and for a long time, Joyce and I thought he was dead. As soon as we realized he was alive we rushed him here and brought him back to consciousness a little while ago. In fact he opened his eyes just a few moments before you arrived." The frightened mouse was beginning to emerge so I brought out his wallet and passed it to her.

"Here's his wallet." I opened it for her and took out the driving license. She had to see the burned face sometime and this would break the shock a little. Perhaps. She studied it for a while and silently put it down. I handed her the money. "Sixteen hundred dollars. All in hundreds." She put them down beside the license, uncounted. "This is the newspaper cutting I mentioned." I said, passing it to her. I watched the gradual disintegration of her self control as she read the copies of the adverts he had taped together in sequence displaying Adam's original advert, a miniature copy of the letter he had sent Adam on her behalf and the remaining sequence of exchanges he and she had inserted in the paper as they sought to re-establish contact with each other. Finally she put her face in her hands and broke down in tears.

I left her to cry it out and brewed up a fresh pot of tea. Joyce had the situation in the back bedroom tidied up, with the two room doors and the shower doors, stacked neatly against one wall and the lumber and wet towels all dumped in the bath. She had Henry's head lifted up on some extra pillows and he had a less pallid appearance, which, I hoped, indicated a return of normal blood flow to his face. He opened his eyes when I spoke to Joyce but didn't seem to understand when I told him there was someone to see him. I didn't pursue the topic.

Barbara was busy rebuilding the Duchess when I returned with the tea and a handful of paper towels, which she accepted gratefully.

"What are you going to do with him now? She asked hesitantly, doubtless thinking we were intending to turn him over to the police.

"Hard to say." I replied. "He's quite a liability to us at the moment, in case his 'friends' come looking for him." I emphasized the quotations around 'friends' manually.

"What Friends? she asked.

"We don't know exactly. We've had them under observation for a while. In fact it was yesterday evening while I was changing the observation cameras that he caught me and whacked me over the head. I. We, think they're up to some kind of smuggling deal. Maybe drugs or such. Henry appears to be the ground base man for a dope or drug operation involving secret midnight flights into and out of the airfield next to Joyce's house. It's been going on for a long time. We were trying to get some proof of our suspicions before going to the police."

"You feel you're in danger from his. Associates.?

"Hell Barbara. He was going to commit cold blooded murder

to keep me quiet. What do you think his pals would do if they found him with us?"

"Is the airfield you're talking about, an old army airfield near Joyce?" Barbara asked, suddenly coming alive with curiosity. "And. Is Joyce's name. Reynolds?"

"Yes. And. Yes."

"She's my sister in law."

Somehow, I wasn't surprised. I could just imagine Roba rolling around on a cloud somewhere, simply pissing himself with laughter.

I got up from the table and went inside. Joyce was still nursing her invalid so I sent her outside to talk to Barbara. "See if you can persuade her to take Henry away. And keep him away." I said as she left. A few minutes later, I got up from his bedside and went to the window. The two women had their arms around each other and both appeared to be bawling down each other's neck. I'll never understand women.

I have never thought of myself as a nurse, or a social worker, but as the afternoon wore on I found myself becoming steadily more eager for Henry to recover and somehow heal the rift he had created between himself and Barbara. When he began struggling to wriggle out of the bonds we had around his arms and chest I was desperate to calm him and held his hand saying things like

"Take it easy Pal. You're safe here. We've wrapped you up so you don't hurt yourself." and patting his hand like a old friend, despite the fact the bastard had almost murdered me less than twelve hours ago.

Somehow I managed to get through to him and he relaxed again, to the extent I thought it might be an appropriate time to introduce Barbara into his area of consciousness. That is, if he was conscious, for he hadn't so far uttered a word. His eyes were following me, so I said.

"Henry. Your wife, Barbara, is here. Would you like to see her?" For a moment I thought he had not heard or understood what I had said, but suddenly he became quite agitated and his facial muscles began to quiver as if he was trying to say something but couldn't.

"Take it easy." I said, gently stroking the back of his hand. "She is outside. She wants to see you." His eyes suddenly watered and I hastily added. "She knows you have been burned. She still wants to see you. Personally, I thinks she still loves you." I didn't add that I couldn't understand why. That was for them to work out. I left him there, feeling reluctant to have to wipe his eyes for him, and went out to fetch Barbara and Joyce who had by now separated and were busy talking.

"I believe he may be up to seeing you now." I said, taking Barbara firmly by the shoulders and speaking slowly.

"Don't expect too much. He's a very sick man." I then stepped aside and motioned for her and Joyce to go inside.

I had no desire to witness what might happen in there so I busied myself in the kitchen making a mug of coffee which I took outside and sipped while the three of them decided the fate of all of us.

I drove, while Barbara sat with Henry, still in his cot, under the canopy in the back of her pick-up, and Joyce brought up the rear with my car. We negotiated the 'suicide entrance' without mishap and loaded Henry and his cot, into the house, where the three of us shifted him from the cot to a bed. Despite all the care we exercised, he groaned frequently with the pain caused by the movement, and I wondered silently how much damage Joyce and I might have inflicted, on top of his 'shotgun injuries' by all the heaving and dragging we had subjected him to. Hopefully if he had any broken ribs, we hadn't ruptured his lungs. After Barbara decided she wanted to take him home, I had cautioned her severely about the necessity of keeping his presence there a secret and explained that if she didn't, and he or his pals came after us, we'd prosecute him for attempted murder and trespassing. I made her promise to call me each day with a status report on his progress. She fully understood also, the consequences of anyone finding out about him being at her place, and what would happen if the insurance people ever got wind of the changed situation. From a beloved asset, he had suddenly become a beloved liability. But as I've said repeatedly, "I'll never understand women."

While we were packing the cot and all the wet and dry towels we had bound him with, into the car, the clock struck midnight. I turned to Barbara and said,

"It's Wednesday." She looked at me in surprise for some time then started laughing.

"So it is." She said. "I hope it won't be our last."

"Call me every day." I replied, getting into the car.

"Leave a message if I'm not home. Don't forget!"

"I won't. And. Thanks again Henry."

As I started the engine, Joyce asked,

"What was all that about.?"

"Much ado about nothing basically. I've asked her to report on Henry's condition every day so I, We, can know how much threat to our safety exists."

"I don't think Mr. Barkeel is going to be much of a threat to anyone for some time." Joyce replied contemptuously.

"Maybe not directly, but if he tries to contact his 'friends' we may have more trouble than we've already got." Joyce, deep in thought, said nothing for a couple of miles then asked.

"Where are we going?"

"Back to my place."

She lapsed back into another couple of miles of silence before announcing her recommendation that we go directly to her place.

"Nobody," she declared, would be looking for us at my place, whereas if anyone was searching for Henry Barkeel, they would be more than likely to scout out her place before anywhere else. We should therefore go directly there and be ready to defend ourselves against their invasion. Besides there could possibly be more information on the video cameras, and Patch had been locked in the house all day. Tired as I was I couldn't fault her reasoning.

Just before we turned into her road, she suggested I turn out the headlights and coast down the road scouting out the area before driving up. Probably, if I had not been so tired, I would have remembered how difficult it is to steer a car with power steering with the motor shut off. We were doing about twenty five when I turned the corner and with only the parking lights to guide me, slipped out of drive into neutral and switched off the engine.

Fortunately, the road is dead straight from the corner to her place, for I could not possibly have steered it round even the slightest bend, and lest I tried to, Joyce rasped,

"Turn the lights off."

Zombie-like, I complied and we swished along in the dark, unaware of our speed or direction and only the lighter sky above us between the tall tree tops, showed we were still going straight. By then I realized belatedly, that power brakes don't function with power off.

"Use the handbrake!" She commanded, in the same rasping whisper, doubtless realizing that I was losing it rapidly.

"Gently!" We stopped about fifty feet short of the entrance to her house.

The fresh night air brought back some of my reasoning capability. Enough that is, to caution both of us to get out without slamming the doors, even though the courtesy lights did their best to betray our presence in the neighborhood.

With Herculean strength and willpower, mostly hers, we pushed the car the last few yards and turned it into the driveway, parked it in park, and locked the doors as quietly as we could, even though the windows were not rolled fully up.

Patch welcomed us into the dark house with a soft whimper in response to Joyce's hiss to silence her enthusiasm. Her presence there assured Joyce that there had been no 'investigators' prowling around the house since we had left. It felt like a bit of a let-down after all our elaborate caution, but I was extremely relieved to get inside and lock up for the night, which we did without turning on a single light.

I developed a great admiration for the care and wisdom of my companion that night, as she shepherded me gently up to bed.

In the early hours of the morning, Joyce woke me, asking for the car keys. Numbly I found them for her and she went and retrieved all the towels and ran them through her washing machine. Only the fold up cot remained in the trunk as tangible evidence of our ambulance activity, and as Joyce remarked,

"Why should anyone connect that with Henry's disappearance?" I rolled over and went back to sleep.

Wednesday, which after all had become Barbara's day in my new calendar, had begun with the midnight chiming of her clock, and had lasted about five minutes of shared time before Joyce and I hit the road. I felt no guilt at short changing Barbara in favor of spending the rest of her day with Joyce. Hadn't we done her a tremendous service returning her lost husband to her?. It was something she had wished for and we'd granted the wish. I woke feeling like the 'Genie' who granted the lamp rubber a perfect back-hander for his last wish. Possibly Joyce felt likewise for she hadn't returned after taking the car keys. I fumbled for my watch and was surprised to find it was almost nine o'clock. Since there are no curtains in Joyce's bedroom I felt it should be much lighter. I looked out the window at a pea-soup fog pressed up against the outside of the glass so densely I could not see the trees that surround the house, nor the ground on which it stood. It was as if the fog had erased the rest of the world.

I slipped into my robe and went downstairs to find Joyce and promote a cup of coffee. There was no sign of either Joyce or Patch in the house, which had an aura of emptiness that began to un-nerve me. I hastily put the kettle on, for companionship. While It heated, I opened the sliding glass door a little way to scan the patio and see if there was any sign of Joyce or the dog to be seen or heard. Visibility was down to about six feet and the dense moisture seemed to drown my voice as I called her name, for there was no echo or response of any kind. I could feel my insides tensing as my imagination flitted from one ominous scenario to another. Leaving the kettle to gather steam I raced back up to the bedroom and dressed. I carried my shoes back downstairs with me and put them on as the kettle burst into its shrill warning. I leapt to its side and silenced it.

Making the coffee seemed to calm me and I carried the mug to the window and stared into the grey-ness willing her to appear but my power to do so failed miserably and the creepy scenarios crept back across the grey movie-screen of the fog. I knew she had returned from the car, because I had heard the washing machine running and later the steady monotonous beat of the drier. I'd just assumed she was still inside the house and could think of no good reason for her to leave in this dense damp fog.

I hoped she hadn't gone out to check the airfield and the woodland bivouac of our mysterious fliers. I had little doubt she could find her way there and back blindfold but if there was anyone lurking around she could have run into the same trouble I landed in. Since the shotgun was also gone, this seemed like a fair possibility. I shuddered at the realization of my own inability to go to her assistance. If it were needed that is, for I'd learned a great respect for her ability to cope with nature in the raw. As a youngster, I worshiped 'Deer-foot the Indian', who could run like a deer and move through the forest like a shadow. But as I matured, I found my own ability along those lines to be more like Hugo the Hippo. If I blundered out there now I might end up being 'shot-at' from both sides. I took my steaming coffee out on the patio, ostensibly to listen for any sound that might indicate what was going on. In reality to escape the eerie emptiness of the house. I sipped my warm comforter, listening to the sibilant hissing of the millions of distant crickets that have lived in my ears for several years now and whose song never varies. Day or night it's there, inaudible, except when I try to listen for something else. I had to do something. The cold had drained all the comfort from the empty mug in my hands and there was still no sign of Joyce or the dog. I set the mug on the wrought iron table and set off in the direction of the car. So far so good, I found it cold and damp and locked. Big help. Out to the road, turn right and follow the edge until it turns into 'the parking' as Joyce calls the un-mowed entry to the airfield. Look up occasionally to see if anything else is there except the road. Follow the wheel track. Whoa! A red something gleams ahead. It's a car's back bumper. Others are here. Stop. My own breath adds to the fog. I stand still, trying to direct it into my shirt front in case anyone else sees the movement of it. Also, it warms me.

Unlike Henry's white Chevvy, this is a sleek dark up-to-date Japanese model. A rental car, from the Budget sticker in a corner of the back window. I have an immediate urge to disable it in case Joyce is a captive of whoever brought the car here. But I'm loath to touch it in case it has a warning beeper on board. Footsteps swishing through the wet grass and subdued voices. I step quickly into the brush beside the track and crouch down in the wet grasses. Four men. No sign of Joyce or the dog. Relief or panic? Have they caught and killed her as they would have done with me? I'm desperate to thwart their getaway now. Tires. My hand falls on a dried twig on the ground. I snap it in pieces as the car doors slam. Crawling on my belly I'm beside the right back wheel the valve cap spins off easily and a piece of twig jammed into the end gives off a satisfactory hissing. Dare I chance the front wheel? I slither forward as the engine starts and the valve almost jumps into my hand. I jam the twig in as the wheel starts to turn, breaking the twig for me. Flat on the ground. The wheel rolls past my arm and tugs the flap of my jacket. The headlights come on, blindingly bright and the car slows. Head on the ground, I don't even breathe. The lights go off and the car keeps rolling. I hear the tires gritting as they turn on the hard surface of the road and the car moves slowly away up towards the highway. How far will it get before the tires deflate and they have to stop? I'm running along the wheel track past the gate and along the edge of the runway where Joyce found me I blunder left into the long grass and veer right back onto the shorter grass I have to keep to the edge or I'll get lost. My breath is cold and hard to draw. I slow down involuntarily. God! I'm out of shape. Barely able to stagger above a walking pace I reach the end of the runway and follow the path out through the trees. Somehow the trees seem to keep the fog up off the ground and I can see the shack. Inside there's no light and I call loudly,

"Joyce!"

No sound. I feel my way to the generator and pull the starting chord. The light fills the room. There's no sign of her or the dog. I shut off the generator and close the door behind me. Nothing had been disturbed and I grimaced at the thought of seeing my panic stricken self on the video sometime.

Nothing for it, but to head back to the house. I won't bore you further with the description of my meanderings through the forest, but I got back to the house somehow.

Patch, bless her, accepted me with her usual welcoming lick, but Joyce looked at me as if I was a ghost.

"What the hell happened to you this time?!" I was so overwhelmed with her greeting I just put my arms around her and buried my face in her neck. Unkindly, she tried to push me away, but I held on grimly, letting myself flood with relief.

"I was looking for you." I said softly. "Where did you go?"

"Patch and I took a walk to the gas station for some milk."

"You get milk at the gas station?!"

"Out here, you get everything at the gas station. You'll just have to get used to it honey." At least she'd stopped struggling to get away from me.

"You'd better get out of those wet clothes and take a bath. Did you fall in a cow pie? You smell pretty ripe." I let go of her then and asked if it was normal of her to go out in such a fog?

"That's something else you get used to out here at this time of the year. I always take Patch though. She never gets lost. Or falls into cow pies." She added pointedly.

Standing under the soothing warmth of the shower, I felt extremely foolish, and even more reluctant to tell her any more details of my little adventure or its possible ramifications. I just hoped the men in the rental car got a long way away before the tires went flat.

Chapter ELEVEN

The Third Repercussion

I might have stayed in the warmth of the shower all day if the tantalizing aroma of bacon and eggs hadn't lured me away. In a matter of moments, I was dried, powdered, dressed in fresh clothes and salivating at the door of the kitchen.

"I thought it might have the desired effect." Joyce laughed as I appeared and gave her a big hug. "Feeling better?"

"Much better. Thanks to you."

"What'd I do now.?"

"Nothing. You don't have to do anything. I just like finding you here." She turned and gave me a funny look.

"Like I've said before, flattery'll get you a second helping." She smiled at the variation in her usual retort, which prompted me to ask why she'd taken the shotgun with her on the trip to the gas station. My question stumped her for a moment until she realized I really had been out, looking for her.

"Sorry. I should have told you. I'm keeping it in the broom closet now." She came up to me and squeezed my hand.

"Ever since the scare we had the other night, I decided to keep it hidden rather than standing by the fire-place, where any Tom, Dick, or Henry could find it."

"Good thinking Kiddo. Glad to know that. I was worried when it was gone, and you and the dog too."

After the meal I broke it gently to her, I'd better get going back to my place and clean up the residue of our little escapade before the smell in the hangar aroused too much interest.

"Drive carefully in this fog." She said, after I'd persuaded her it was best I go alone. "It's not so bad on the highway. Traffic was moving pretty steadily up there."

Just about a mile from the junction with highway 101, I spotted the dark blue Toyota Corrola with a severe list to starboard, at the side of the road. I slowed enough to get the number and scribbled it on the ferry schedule as soon as I was safely past.

Maybe Nora could usefully check on who was renting this vehicle today, I thought as the buildings of the city of Port Angeles began displacing the trees along the highway.

I parked at the Federal building and went to her office. She seemed mildly embarrassed by my presence, so I asked her quietly to;

"Check on this number for me please. More midnight trespassers. I explained. "Perhaps you'd be kind enough to leave the particulars on my message machine.?. Thanks." And I was on my way with a casual farewell, for the benefit of any interested observers.

When I opened my hangar door, the smell was almost overpowering. I went to work with a bottle of Clorox and a stiff broom on the hangar floor and as soon as the contaminated area was fizzing nicely I backed Henry's car out and drove it to the back lawn of my house, downwind of the house and the neighbor's and parked it with all the doors open. For starters, I hosed it out thoroughly and left it to mellow a bit, before attempting to scrub the back seat and carpet where most of the contamination had congealed. Alternating between these two strategies, I had the job done in an hour and left it in the sun to dry out.

I had no idea how 'hot' the car might be by this time and hesitated to go ahead with my plan to ditch it at Port Townsend. Suppose there was Heroin, or some other illegal substance aboard and I got stopped by the State Patrol.?. Nasty thought.!. I hadn't even looked in the trunk since determining there was insufficient room in it for 'Henry'. In addition to the spare tire, the trunk contained five cardboard boxes, labeled 'Mobil Oil, One dozen cans'.

All except the middle box were unopened, but this one had been opened and closed again by overlapping the flaps. It popped open easily and I was surprised to see it was full of rectangular packets wrapped in brown paper. Definitely not Oil cans.

I spent a few minutes checking the packets which were all sealed with paper tape, sniffing them cautiously in case I snorted a blast of 'Snow' or some equally noxious substance but could detect nothing. Not that I'd have known what 'Snow' smelled like anyway. The packets felt firm not like a powder so I decided to carefully open one to see what was in it.

Money!. In $100 bills. About $10,000 in each package. At a rough guess, $480,000 in all. I was about to open one of the other boxes which by its feel and weight, contained cans of oil, when I recalled Roba's warning. I won't swear to it, but maybe my feet felt just a little sweaty. Anyway, I decided to heed his warning and left all four of them unopened. I carried the other to the house.

I was still no nearer to the solving the mystery of the oil cans, but close to half a million, in $100 bills, was pretty conclusive evidence that something underhanded was going on. Both by sea and by air, and, probably each was related to the other.

Once you make up your mind that the other guy is a crook, It's only a small step to making up your mind to out-crook him. $480,000 is a sizeable prod in the right/wrong direction, especially when it's already in your hand in $100 bills.

I make no excuses for my decision. The box went swiftly into the trunk of my car instead of his, and the remaining boxes 'closed ranks' easily.

From there the money went into a couple of black plastic trash bags which I buried in a large bag of peat-moss in my garden shed. The Mobil box went up in smoke from the incinerator.

Joyce, I decided, wasn't in any way to be involved in this little bit of larceny on my part. Barbara wasn't even aware of the existence of his car. Unless. Unless he had become more communicative. I thought it might be about time to check with her on that score.

The 'dear sweet man' was still sleeping, but more peacefully since she had been able to slip some chicken soup down his badly bruised esophagus.

"No he hasn't spoken yet but I think he knows he's with me and seems more relaxed." I thanked her and encouraged her again to be extremely careful when he returns to health.

"His recent activities may cast some shadow of doubt on his sanity you know."

I then called Nora. She, bless her dedicated heart, had done more than just check on the renter. She had also run a 'make' on him and found that he and his companions were. "Chemical engineers employed by a Californian company engaged on, "Research into Artificial Intelligence."

"Chemical engineers?! In an Electronics company? Working on the digestive system of the Artificial Intellect no doubt.? "Nora would doubtless not understand my humor, so I asked if she thought Mobil might be supplying cans of oil used for cooking baked beans for the nourishment of 'Arty'?" Naturally she didn't get that either and I ended up explaining to her that from my observations of the Canadian yachting fraternity, someone was shipping large quantities of Mobil oil in cans between here and Canada.

I made no mention of the cans in the car but the germ of an idea was sprouting, as to where to park it. I could almost hear the questions fizzing between her ears but I hastened to close the discussion and leave her with something in the way of a 'mole-hill' to work on.

Back to Henry's car. This time with gloves on and a spray-can of WD-40. I wiped the whole car from end to end and anywhere either Joyce or I might have touched it. Carpets, seats, headliner, even the boxes in the trunk, in case I'd touched them in the re-shuffle. I had a pretty fair recollection of where I'd handled that area so I left areas I knew my prints could not be.

I 'Windex-d' the inside of all windows, the mirrors and all the outside glass before giving the car a thorough wash down. I vacuumed the rugs and pedals again, and after checking the bus schedules, slipped some plastic bags over my shoes before driving it to Port Angeles.

In the visitor-parking area, behind the Federal building, I stuffed the bags into my pocket, put the keys in the ignition, locked up and strolled nonchalantly in through the back door. I rode the elevator to the top floor and used the Men's room. I took the same elevator back down and left via the front entrance. I strolled up the road to the bus stop, sat and waited for a ride to Sequim, and was back at Diamond Point by five fifteen in the evening.

"Where have you been, I've been calling for the last hour." Nora sounded quite upset.

I'd hardly got inside when the phone rang, so, instinctively, I lied.

"Sorry, I was in the hangar. Guess I forgot to set the machine. What's on your mind?" All spoken very casually while I filled the kettle and plugged it in. Do something routine while you talk. It's a trick I learned from dealing with jealous lady friends.

"What do you know about Mobil Oil that you aren't telling me.?" She continued, her curiosity well aroused. "Nothing. It's a good oil. Beyond that, I was hoping you might have some idea why the Canadian yacht Chrysalis goes around in these waters with a few hundred or so cans of that brand stored in the locker of her engine room?"

"How do you know that.?"

"I was on board and saw them. The crew was a bit upset when they found me in there."

I ended up having to tell her the story of my kidnapping by Alice, and after a few references to her, and to the Goliath, had passed, Nora slipped up. In one chance remark, she disclosed that she already knew all about the Goliath, and the oil and, some of the other events particularly those pertaining to channel 39. I was suddenly very relieved I had never mentioned Joyce's airfield, the car, the Mobil cans in the car, much less the money.

Even if she suspected I had stumbled onto some connection, between Oil and Artificial Intelligence, there was nothing to connect me with the car that had been left, virtually in her back yard, so to speak.

Feminine intuition would undoubtedly lead her there, but I was forewarned. I would innocently allow her to tell me all about it when they found it. I had plenty of experience at 'being innocent' I remember one schoolmaster telling me I looked like a sick sheep when I professed innocence. From then on, I practiced a wolf-like countenance.

Oh how the trials of infants prepare them for the real world.

It was still early evening though the sun had set and I had a sense of reluctance to head back to Joyce's. After all it was still Barbara's day and in her hands lay much of the future safety for all of us. Sometime, possibly already, Henry would be returning to full functioning. Always supposing his brain had not been significantly damaged by the coma he had been in for the last forty-eight hours. It was time to renew contact with Barbara and find out.

I called. It seemed like the phone rang a long time before she answered. I asked after Henry's health and waited for her to provide whatever she felt like in the way of information about Henry's condition. I wanted to seem concerned from the standpoint of his and her well-being, rather than how these aspects affected my interests. I expressed pleasure when she told me he had regained consciousness, recognized her and wished to restore their lost relationship.

"He's an extremely lucky man to have a wife like you. There are few women I've known who would have remained so steadfast in their belief that he was still alive and would come back to them."

"I always 'knew' he would come back."

"That's wonderful and I'm so happy for you. My only regret is that we had to be so violently involved."

"Joyce told me all about it." She said thoughtfully. "I'm glad it happened the way it did instead of the other way round."

"How's he doing now.?"

"I'd just finished feeding him when you called. He may have gone back to sleep. I left him lying down."

"I shouldn't keep you talking then. You should try to keep him awake for a while, talking to you if possible. He was unconscious for a long time and a little mental stimulation is desirable before letting him go back to sleep. Go on back to him and give me a call in the morning whenever you can."

'Patience!' I kept telling myself despite my eagerness to know anything he might have said. I'd asked her to call but the more I thought about it the more I felt it would be better if I talked to him myself as soon as possible. I'd go and visit, first thing in the morning.

Joyce has no phone. This inability to reach her disturbed me. I wanted to be with her in case of any nocturnal disturbances, amongst other things. At the same time I had other things to consider and do rather than drive all the way to her place, just to keep her company for the night. Barbara knew nothing about Henry's car. I'd not mentioned it and doubted whether Joyce had either. If questioned later, I'd tell both of them that it had been left on the highway and someone, probably the police had removed it.

I suppose you could consider the federal parking lot as an extension of the highway system. I also imagined that, by now, confiscation, was a reasonable supposition. Furthermore, It would certainly discourage much discussion on the subject. Especially by Henry, who undoubtedly knew about the box-full of money, even if he 'forgot' to mention it. I'd also tell Barbara the police had been advised of the incident and the disappearance of the mysterious wounded marauder, in the night.

If she relayed this to Henry, it would further dampen his eagerness to go reporting the loss of his car. I desperately wanted to talk to Henry and see what all the activity at the airfield was about. Whatever his part in the game was, he obviously knew enough to decide to kill me on the spot when he discovered my intrusion. But, I'd have to exercise my patience, and wait. In the end, I set the answering machine and went back to Joyce's for the night. We were both happy I did.

October mornings come blearily into focus and the late night events were not conducive to early activity. I lay cuddled around Joyce for a long while before moving.

"What was that ?"

"What was what?" I hadn't moved or heard anything.

"I heard something moving. Outside."

"Probably a deer." I volunteered sleepily.

"Deer don't come in the yard. Patch sees to that"

As if to confirm this, Patch nosed the bedroom door open and came over to Joyce, who announced confidentially.

"We've definitely got visitors."

Her quiet statement brought me wide awake and I was out of bed almost a soon as she was.

Dressed and downstairs, I headed for the broom closet while she went into the kitchen and filled the kettle as if we were totally unaware of the presence of strangers.

I had just closed the breech of the shotgun on a 'solid-slug' in favor of 'buckshot', when the doorbell rang. I set the gun back and waited just outside the closet, as Joyce and Patch went to answer it.

The rising note of the kettle's whistle, jerked me to attention. Despite my desire to overhear the conversation at the entry door, I went quickly to the stove and shut it off. In support of our apparent unconcern, I forced myself to make the coffee, and had just finished stirring it when Joyce returned to the kitchen, grinning broadly "Jehovah's Witnesses." She laughed. "I told them we were Mormons."

"Have some coffee."

"Good job the smell of this hadn't reached the door before they left." she smirked, taking the mug. "Otherwise they might not have believed me, even if they really were Chinamen."

"Chinese!?"

"Orientals. American variety, they had no accents."

The warning bells were literally clanging in my ears.

Undoubtedly, these 'Missionaries, were the same bunch whose tires I had 'Spiked' yesterday morning and they were back looking for the spiker.

Thankfully Joyce and I had been too concerned with other things and I'd forgotten to mention anything about my conversation with Nora, or her expression might have betrayed us.

"Oriental Jehovah's Witnesses !?. How many?"

"Two." Joyce smiled at my concern. "What's so significant about that?. There are a lot of them around here these days."

"Orientals? or Jehovah's Witnesses?"

"Orientals. Ever since the Mill at 'Pee-Ay' changed hands." Her response disturbed me for some reason I could not clearly define. Nora's information had been intriguing enough, but somewhere, inside my subconscious, a demon was trying to tell me these Orientals were all the same.

Maybe a flashback recollection of a Tokyo subway platform crossed my mind and I couldn't differentiate one face in the crowd from another, especially as they were all dressed alike for the office.

"I'll bet these Jehovah's Witnesses are the same guys we saw on the video of the parking lot." I'd been on the point of saying they were the guys in the car I'd spiked, when I remembered I hadn't told her about Nora's phone call, or other items I'd decided not to mention. D'you ever get that sinking feeling when you find yourself traversing a 'bog' of your own creation? I did, until I rationalized,it was for her protection.

My conscience cleared like a burst of sunshine dispersing a morning fog, and she smiled as she remembered.

"I thought I had seen them somewhere before." she said slowly, her smile fading to concern as I announced.

"I think I'll go look-see if they've left yet." "No! That'll only make them more suspicious of us."

She was right of course but I was burning to know if it was the same car and the longer I delayed the more chance they'd have left and I wouldn't ever know for sure.

198 | Maurice P. Hanvey

"I'll be careful."

"Like last time." Joyce laughed scornfully. "We can see them from upstairs." she added, heading for the stairway with me in hot pursuit.

We bounded up the stairs like two squirrels in a treadmill. Instead of heading for the bedroom, Joyce opened a door I had never been through, into another small room, still furnished with the twin beds and residual trappings of teenage girls. I had scant time for a survey, for Joyce pulled the drapes from a window which I had not previously noticed, providing a view of her parking area where my car and a second white car behind it, were clearly visible through the treetops.

Our visitors had not left. The driver, was in the car, but the other was bending over, doing something to the back bumper of my car. For a moment I was afraid he might be putting sugar into the gas tank and a wave of anger flushed over me. I let out a word not often used in company and turned to rush out and accost the villain, but Joyce, anticipating my intent, grabbed my arm, spinning me around so that I fell on one of the beds with her on top of me.

"Whoa! there tiger! Where do you think you're going.?"

She said pinning my arms so I could not get up.

"He might be putting sugar in my gas tank." I gasped, but her grip slackened and she burst out laughing.

"Sure. I suppose they bought a pound of it at the gas station on their way here. I think he was checking the number on the car. If they're the ones you think they are, they probably want to know whose car it is." she concluded, getting up and returning to the window. "They're leaving thank goodness. Their car looks mighty familiar. I'd swear it was Henry's, except it looks much cleaner than his." I was beside her at the speed of light. It was Henry's car, and I broke into a cold sweat.

"You alright?. She asked You're white as a sheet. Where did you leave the car?" The decision to keep certain things to myself was about to swamp me and I forced myself to regain control.

"I left the car in the parking lot of the Federal Building in Port Angeles."

"Yea Gods! Why? I thought you wanted to keep the Police out of our affairs!?" Her tone was now one of hurt feelings as if I had betrayed her to the authorities.

"The trunk was full of Dope. Sealed up in Mobil Oil cans." I began to wish I'd leveled with her from the very beginning. But. Well too late now. I wondered which would be better, facing her with tales of the other six letters, or trying to wriggle out of my present predicament. The uproar about Barbara had been clear indication how thin the ice was where other females were concerned. Since she already knew about Nora I thought it fairly safe to admit I'd expected the Federales to glom on to the abandoned car and begin investigating. I certainly hadn't expected it to fall into the hands of the smugglers so quickly. Unless . . . unless this was some clandestine C.I.A. operation we had fallen into. That was a Hell-of-Thought! Maybe Henry was a C.I.A. agent!! Before she could stop me I sprinted for the door shouting over my shoulder.

"I'm going after them!. I want to see where they go."

She yelled something after me, but I was making too much clatter on the stairs to hear.

It had been raining and the road in front of Joyce's house was still wet from the overhanging trees. The highway was dry and the wet tire tracks told me which way they'd turned. West. At least they weren't high tailing it back to the Federal Building in P.A. I put my foot down and soon spotted their white Chevvy a long way ahead. I slacked off and kept that distance behind them all the way to where the road for Sappho joins highway 112 where I lost them. After shattering the speed limit for a couple of miles and failing to see them I decided they had turned off at the junction and I had to back track, cussing myself for being too cautious. When I reached the Highway 101 at Sappho, I opted to follow the road to Forks. Remember?. Barbara had invited me to go with her to a 'contact' at an address in Forks.

I had no idea where this address might be, except for the address Nora had given me, in exchange for the license number of Henry's car, and both of which were written on a slips of paper at home. Though I racked my brains trying to remember, I couldn't. I drove slowly around the town hoping to spot Henry's car parked in a driveway somewhere, feeling as though everyone in the town was eyeing me suspiciously. I'd taken a quick glance at my rear number-plate which had confirmed Joyce's suspicion. They'd been checking the number-plate sure enough. It had been wiped clean. Cruising this town like this was definitely not a good idea. I thought of returning to Joyce's but a more intriguing idea was festering in my head.

Although I'd scrubbed and polished Henry's car, my car hadn't had a wash since I bought it.

If Joyce hadn't remarked how clean Henry's car was, I might never have noticed it at all.

If I cleaned mine, it might, however, make it less conspicuous, to the opposition. Better yet, suppose I had it painted a different color!?

I drove back along the main Highway 101 to Sequim, intending to take advantage of the beautiful Fall sunshine.

I would spend five bucks on the car at a carwash, pick up half a dozen spray-cans of paint and exercise my artistic talents.

A roll of masking tape, some newspapers, a joyous afternoon on the lawn in the warm autumnal sun and I had become the proud owner of a beautiful new, Midnight-Blue, Brougham. All I needed now, was a secure place to hide a D-H 84.

I was dying to show my new treasure to Joyce and see her reaction to the transformation, but sometime ago I had fallen from grace, although she wasn't yet aware of this. Undoubtedly Roba was, or would be, as soon as his spirit re-entered the sphere of my activities. Not that I expected him to express too much disdain for my actions as he himself had never hesitated at 'taking down' a bad guy. However, now that all the letters had been delivered I suspected his sprite had departed in search of more interesting pursuits. I imagined him shrugging nonchalantly and saying,

"So you robbed the robbers. Why stop now ? Go for it! Do it big!"

"In for a penny, in for a pound," was one of his favorite expressions. I just 'knew' he would approve of my larcenous intentions where the DH-84 was concerned. However, my hangar was just too narrow to accept the 'Dragon's wingspan, and the only one I knew of locally, that was, was on a small private strip at the southern end of Lopez Island. I had landed there once, in the halcyon days of my early flying career in Washington. The gentleman who owned the strip, had initially been rather abrupt when I landed, but mellowed somewhat in his admiration for my ancient Luscombe and my 'British' accent. He had shown me around his facilities, which had impressed me with their size and emptiness, but despite my earnest appeal to be granted entry and exit authority to his airfield, had insisted that 'insurance considerations etc. etc.' prohibited his doing so.

We had parted amicably, but I had never been back. I wondered if he was still there, and might possibly be cajoled into housing a vintage Dehavilland Dominee or Dragon as it was sometimes called, in his empty hangar.

The straits of Juan Da Fuca was a sheet of glass in the sunset below me as I approached Lopez Island. I have a severe case of Flyer's Delight. Having flown in so much 'bad' weather, the prospect of pure silky smooth air and a moonlight night, are like an addiction and I had to fly my little amphibian, if only to try out the new drive belts. This time I was sure of the tightened drive belts and not bent on some idiotically romantic mission. I was going to see the 'owner' of a rather large hangar on a small private airstrip near the south coast of the island, which, purely by co-incidence, was near Monica's house.

I landed at the Lopez airport, started up my VW Square-back and drove to the South end of the road at Richardson. The road to my intended destination, turns East at that point, and passes directly in front of Monica's house. Acting on impulse, although it was not Saturday, her day, I parked beside her yellow station wagon, walked around to the seaward side and with some slight trepidation, knocked on the door.

As she recognized me, her face lit up with a stunning smile

and my heart skipped a beat when she invited me to come in. The rising euphoria immediately evaporated as I spotted old Baldy Whatsisname, comfortably ensconced with the inevitable glass of liquor, in the armchair by the fireplace. He rose from his hiding-place and extended a hand in greeting.

"How's our favorite stunt pilot?" he asked with a derogatory smirk which made me wonder if, somehow, he was already aware of my subsequent discomfiture.

"Fit as a fiddle." I replied, exerting sufficient pressure in my handshake to cause him a momentary wince. I declined his offer of a drink on the pretext of flying. Monica, to my surprise, virtually insisted I join them for their evening meal which was already prepared.

Baked Halibut and cottage fries were well on the way down, when Baldy asked me if I remembered the party aboard the Chrysalis, and reminded me of my entrapment in the engine room.

I apologized for the incident, re-iterating my fascination with ship's engine rooms. However, he persisted, much as Alice had done, in his attempts to find out if I had observed anything peculiar in my 'study'. I made him lead me to the subject of the aft locker's contents, and only then acknowledged that I had thought the ship's supply of lube oil was somewhat extravagant.

"Were they on 'Special' at Canadian Tire?" I asked innocently, "there did seem to be rather a lot of cans in that locker, now you mention it."

I wasn't sure he hadn't swallowed my story until he asked me how many cans were in the locker. I made quite a production of my attempt to guess, mumbling calculations with my eyes closed as if visualizing the scene in the engine room.

"Well of course it would depend on what was under the top layer, wouldn't it?. I'd guess if the locker was full of them it would hold about five or six hundred. That is a lot for two engines on a short trip between Vancouver and Stuart Island. By the way, did you know that Alice had kidnapped me on that trip?"

They obviously didn't, so I related that episode, limited of course to the events following my helping her with the shopping.

They thought it was quite funny, and I thought it was time to ask a few questions of my own.

"Well? How many were there? If it isn't a rude question, and how many have been used up, so far on this trip?. Not many I'd estimate, considering how nice and clean the engine room was, I can't imagine those engines burn much oil either and there wasn't even a smell of leakage. In fact I thought it was the cleanest engine room I'd ever been in. So. Why do you carry such a lot?. It's a fair question."

Baldy took a deliberate, but slightly longer slug of his brandy before replying and I sensed rather than saw a signal of some kind pass between him and Monica. The sort of question and answer signal when a secret is to remain a secret or to be shared.

"You're right." Baldy continued condescendingly. "It is a fair question, and," (a second opinion on the original question flashed and presumably got a confirmation) "though the number is immaterial, all of the cans of oil have gone."

A pause to allow me to register surprise, followed by further curiosity, before he continued. "Delivered. Safely to their destination."

I remained silent in case he had more secrets he wanted to share with me but my mind was working so fast on what he had given me, it was unable to snag any of the possible conclusions from the whirlpool. Extreme caution seemed to be indicated.

"What I don't know can't hurt me, so I won't ask." I said,

"But you did have your suspicions. Didn't you? He sounded disappointed.

"Not until now." I demurred, "Was there something to suspect about the number of cans?. Or. Maybe what was in them?. Instead of oil?"

He hesitated just long enough before replying, for me to hold my hand up to stop him. Perhaps the momentary flicker of anxiety on Monica's face prompted me to wonder if Baldy was one of those people who can appear sober when dead drunk. He had refilled his brandy twice since my arrival, and I didn't want him to say something I might have to react to.

"Hey. Listen. I really appreciate you taking me into your confidence like this, but if there's something I don't need to know, I'd rather you didn't tell me."

"Nonsense my dear fellow. Those cans are precisely what they appear to be. Mobil oil."

I stared at him unable to decide whether he was fooling, lying or too drunk to differentiate.

"Since when has an expensive yacht like the Chrysalis been employed as an oil tanker?" I asked, concealing my contempt with a broad smile. "Come off it. You know there must have been something special about them." I stretched my smile as wide as I dared. "And, you're just dying to tell me what it's all about. Aren't you?"

He gave a sickly smile and sort of fell towards me, pawing at the table to set his glass down, as Monica reached for it protectively. The booze had finally hit him and he toppled into my lap. I looked up at Monica's distressed expression and remarked,

"A little early in the evening for this. Isn't it?"

She made no comment and between us we hauled him back to the armchair and propped him up in the corner of it. With him comfortably out of the picture for the moment, I asked if there was anything more I could do, supposing she would guide him to bed after I left, but she asked me to watch him for a while so that she could go to the dock and summon a couple of his crew to come and collect him.

Apparently this was a fairly routine occurrence and she had simply been playing out the sequence until it reached its inevitable conclusion. In about five minutes, she returned with the two stalwarts who had arrested me in the ship. When they left with Baldy, I prepared to depart, but she again asked me to wait until she returned, saying she had some things to talk to me about. I went back into the house and spent the estimated available time looking around for anything that might indicate what had prompted their inquisition.

I drew a complete blank until I noticed some papers and

pamphlets from an organization calling itself, 'The Pacific Rim Independent Artificial Intelligence Forum'. I barely had time to jot down their address, and park myself in Baldy's armchair, before she returned, and launched right into another inquisition, asking me if I would kindly tell her what all the talk of 'oilcans' had been about. That floored me as I felt sure that she and he had definitely participated in some kind of charade for my benefit. However, she steadfastly maintained that she knew nothing about any 'six hundred cans of oil' in the Chrysalis, and simply wanted an explanation. Baldy, she insisted, had never previously mentioned them, or the incident in the ship, to her. I sat, for twenty minutes, carefully discussing selected details of my part of the story as if mesmerized by her big brown eyes. When I left, I felt sure she believed I had not originally suspected anything, and that I believed her sudden interest in me was genuine. She was wrong on both counts. Since neither of them had asked me where I was heading when I stopped in, I decided to play things extremely cautiously from this point on. Whatever was being transported in Mobil oilcans, by sea and/or by air, had to be a joint project. It would be simple for any such organization to find me through the car registrations; they'd had opportunity to learn both of these. I could not discount the VW square-back, because it's normally parked at the Lopez airport. Monica, Baldy, or either of his crewmembers could easily have jotted down its number this evening.

My once white whale, had definitely been scrutinized by the airborne sector. If both sectors cross checked with each other, my unannounced visit to Monica, might be viewed with grave suspicion. Ooh! Bad choice of words; Druggies or CIA-ies are notorious for taking a 'grave' approach to obstacles.

Also, if Lopez Island was a focal point of both organizations the large hangar I was thinking of renting for the nesting place of one DH-84, on which I had larcenous designs, might in fact, already be its nest.

I know there are no empty hangars big enough to house it at Lopez Airport, and everyone on the island would soon know of its existence there, if there had been. I shivered at the thought of how close I'd come to a potential disaster. It's one thing to filch half a million bucks in cash, but another to swipe a million dollar rare antique airplane, and then have the gall to try and hide it in the original owner's hangar. I needed to do some more thorough research. I was gradually developing two new sensations. One, of becoming a highly visible irritant to these people, whoever they were, and two, a deep desire to vanish; at my discretion, not theirs.

Mulling over these thoughts on the flight home across the Straits, I barely noticed the serenity and tranquility surrounding myself until Protection Island loomed under the canard and I set up for a landing. XTC has no lights. She was never intended for night flying. She has no radio either. But, she makes lots of high pitched noise with her high revving engine. There being no other traffic visible, I closed the throttle and made a long, gliding approach to a landing on the grass taxiway and rolled to the tarmac outside my hangar. Unless they were outside, I doubt if anyone would have observed my arrival.

For the first time since I'd begun the task of returning Roba's seven letters, I felt scared. I mean really scared. Evil forces seemed to be at work both outside me and, I realized, inside me too. We'd almost killed a man, almost been killed myself, a couple of times if you include the incident of my forced landing on Joyce's airfield, and I had severely compromised mine, and probably Joyce's, security by 'glomming on' to almost half a million dollars of someone else's cash.

On top of that' I'd become obsessed with the desire to hijack a million dollar antique airplane, with, as yet, no place to hide it.

"Where in Hell does one hide a thing like that?" I asked myself, standing by the stove waiting for the kettle to boil for my coffee after returning from Monica's 'spider's web'. To my astonishment, I heard Roba's voice say,

"In a museum."

I looked round to see where the voice had come from, expecting to see him somewhere, perhaps on top of the refrigerator, or possibly warming the seat of his pants on the kettle, but saw nothing.

The kettle boiled, and as I was pouring into my prepared mug of 'instant' and honey, the steam obscured my glasses as it sometimes does when the house is cold. I was about to remove the blinders, when I saw him, as if in virtual reality, sitting on a cloud, complete with feathered wings and a harp.

"Time for a chat." he said, plucking at a few strings, which I couldn't hear.

"I didn't know you could play a harp." I said, to cover my astonishment.

"I can't" he replied. (Which probably explained why I hadn't heard it.) "I was only issued the darned thing when you finally delivered the last letter."

"That was a long time ago." I protested.

"Time!" He said contemptuously. "How long do you think it takes to learn to flap these wings and play a harp at the same time?. Get some more steam on your glasses before this cloud dissipates."

I stuck my face back in the steam hastily. We had a lot I wanted to talk about.

"What did you mean about a Museum?"

"Perfect place to hide a vintage DH-84."

"Damn it! I want to fly it."

"Dangerous. People will see it. And talk about it. The previous owners might find out you've got it and come looking for it." He was right, as usual. However I sensed he was here to help me so I asked him for advice.

"If you had the proper paperwork showing your ownership, or could fake it up, enough to convince Henly Aerodrome you owned it legally, they'd store it in the Museum and let you fly it occasionally as the donor's privilege. Or. Depending on how much you want to fly the Damn thing, you might try applying to the present owners for a job as the pilot of it."

"Wait.!!" I yelled anxiously as his cloud started to disappear.

However, my glasses had warmed up to the extent the steam

would no longer condense on them, and I ended up shoving my nose right into the spout of the kettle in a desperate attempt to maintain his cloud.

I recoiled in pain and tears with my ears ringing to what might have been the pinging of a harp or a peal of high pitched laughter. But; he had given me an answer.

A handful of ice cubes alleviated my immediate concern and the coffee restored some of my equilibrium, but when I blew my nose I found the paper I'd jotted down the data on the Pacific Rim Artificial Intelligence Society, in my handkerchief. PRIAIF inc. and a phone number which I dialed right then. It had one of those 'Tin' voices which informed me that the next meeting of their society would be in June three years ago. I played back my tape recorder for confirmation and indeed it was as related.

The Artificiality of it amazed me. How could a current organization leave, a recorded message on their phone like that? Unless, maybe they were defunct, and the phone company hadn't cottoned on to this reality yet.

Being artificial of course, there would be no odor of decay to alert the living Eh?. I decided that all this was confusing enough for me to get into the 'Blue Bomber' and drive out to Joyce's place, to seek some creature comfort from the living.

Parked in her turnaround the car was almost invisible in the darkness.

I saw no particular need to apprise her of my trip to Lopez at that time of night. She had other interests, and, the new color scheme could better wait for daylight.

Once she was soundly back to sleep, I lay still, dreamily mulling over my thoughts until the airport warning light came on. She didn't wake as I slid out of bed and stood at the window watching the glow in the trees until the treetops lit up in the landing lights as the airplane of my dreams drifted down like a ghost out of the darkness.

So. Henry or no Henry, 'Operations' were still on for tonight. There was little doubt in my mind that the four boxes from the trunk of Henry's car would be on their way someplace, accompanied by the one or both of the 'Orientals' and a substitute driver would extinguish the lights and drive off, probably to Henry's place in Forks as soon as they'd left.

'No harm in checking.' I thought, dressing quietly, and slipped quietly out to the parking area to watch. Henry's empty car was there as if nothing had changed. I took up a station midway between the two driveways to watch, and waited. By cupping my hands around my ears, airplane engines idling at the far end of the runway could just be heard, and before long they came up to speed. There was a sudden glow in the trees from the landing lights, which went out just before the plane rushed into the darkness above me. A few moments later the airfield lights also went out.

It took the driver about five minutes to close up shop and find his way to the car, giving plenty of warning of his approach by liberal use of a flashlight, due doubtless, to his unfamiliarity with the place.

I hid behind my car until he drove away lest he decided to investigate. When his car reached the highway he turned west, headed like his predecessors, towards Forks. If he followed their route, I could go east to the highway and be waiting for him at the Sappho junction and follow him to his destination.

It was worth a try, and I'm happy to report that we met as planned and journeyed, loosely in tandem, almost to the house. In Forks, he turned off the main drag into a dead end street and pulled into the second driveway on the left just as I was passing the end of the road. A little way further down the main street, a 'U' turn and coast back with the lights off to see if he'd changed his mind, concluded my first successful 'Tail'. It's really amazing how much one learns from watching the boob tube.

Half an hour later Joyce was sleepily complaining again, about my feet being cold.

The Sun was well up when Joyce woke me with a cup of coffee. She sat on the side of the bed like a hospital visitor listening to the patient describing his operations. I described most of mine. (The paint was drying during the visit to Lopez, and who wants to listen to a description of paint drying ?).

She'd already seen the result of my artistry and seemed unimpressed. However she did congratulate me on my discovery of where the enemy base was in Forks.

"No wonder you're sleepy. You've been a busy boy." I sensed she was feeling a bit 'left out' so I brightened up the day with the promise of further secret discoveries from the camera in the hut. "That's one of the Jehovah's witnesses.!" She exclaimed as the camera focused on the face of the Oriental who had apparently just started the generator in the forest shed and was trying to get accustomed to the sudden brightness.

"I couldn't swear to it," I said, "but it could have been the driver of the car last night. I didn't want to get too close in case he recognized me or the car."

Except for a couple of interludes when an indistinct figure came into the shed and picked something up and then left, the picture remained a boringly steady view of the shed door. Eventually the same guy came in and did something out of sight and the screen went blank.

Joyce started clapping.

I was momentarily dismayed at her reaction until she smilingly asked if it had been worth getting my head bashed in just to make that 'Masterpiece'? I ruefully caressed the still sensitive bump and tended to agree with her.

"What do we do now Cowboy?" She said putting her arm around my sagging shoulder.

It seemed like a good time to broach the subject of Roba's suggestion and I replied.

"Well. If we can't beat them, we might as well join them. Isn't that what they say?"

Apart from a sudden tensing of her arm, Joyce made no comment regarding what she thought about my remark.

Chapter TWELVE

Four Loud Percussions

Over breakfast, we discussed various scenarios in which we had already participated in this clandestine operation, but my mind was busy sorting out future possibilities which would be better if they excluded her. This was not based on any deficiency in her but because it might, and probably would, expose her to dangers of various intensity.

The first priority seemed to be to establish whether the airfield was a 'U.S.Govt. Operation' or had it been abandoned by them or, if it was on her property what could we do about this. By our measurements it seemed the Government had inadvertently built the airfield on her property, since local authorities have no tax records of the field and flatly deny its existence.

The second avenue of approach seemed to be through the Artificial Intelligence community and the Oriental's Company. However that might take us to California whereas the number on Monica's paper was here in Seattle. Again really a one man operation, since she has no phone. Third, Roba's suggestion, to apply for a job as the pilot of the airplane which really appealed to me. Again, a one man op. The added advantage would be a penetration of their organization, with the glamorous lure of 'undercover espionage'.

This alternative seemed to offer easiest access; especially if we owned the airfield. I borrowed paper and pencil and began writing down the alternatives.

Objective :—(General)

1. To eliminate the continued use of the airfield for illegal/immoral purposes.
2. To restore use of the airfield for legitimate purposes.

   2a Get paid for its use.

3. To get hands on the DH-84 for flying.

   Objective :—(Personal)

   3a. To fly the DH-84 anyhow.
   b. To get O.K. from Joyce, to put a hangar on the field and keep my airplanes there.

Methods. :—1. Confront the present users.

   1a. Claim the airfield belongs to us. Demand to know what they're doing.
   1b. Threaten to call the authorities. Offer to come to an arrangement.

   2. Call the authorities anyway. (Narcotics?)

Joyce came to read the paper over my shoulder, and began laughing.

"That's interesting. Now I know what you're really after. and all along, I thought it was me you were interested in." It took a moment for her remark to sink in, but as soon as I caught the drift, I slipped my arm around her waist and grinned at her.

"I've already got you. This is a joint project. I've put down my personal reasons. What are yours?" Joyce became pensive for a while before announcing that she'd been quite content for these people to fly in and out at night so long as they hadn't bothered her, and it had only been since my arrival on the scene, that she'd become involved. Deeply, as I pointed out.

"Even if you wanted to build a hangar and keep your planes here it would be alright with me. And these jokers could continue with their games without disturbing us."

"Well they were the ones who became violent in the first instance." I reminded her. "We were only trying to find out what they were up to. Something we have every right to do." I could see she was about to protest so I added.

"Don't forget, you were the one who fired the first shot."

"That's not fair!." She exclaimed almost tearfully. "If I hadn't you'd be dead now."

"So?. As of this moment, who'd be involved with them?? Me?? I'd be out of the picture and you'd have it all to yourself." I know it was brutal logic but. It was logic. Life's like that, and I had to have her on my team. Sensing how appalled she was feeling at my stark analysis of the state of affairs, I pulled her down onto my lap and took her chin in my hand gently pulling her head down to kiss her.

"We're in this together sweetheart, thanks to that twitch of your finger. Don't ever think I'm not grateful, because I am. Very. But we have to go forward together, and decide what to do next."

She brightened up at this and I pressed on.

"What I'd like to do is to swipe their bloody airplane and fly off with it to some place where we could sell it for half of what it's worth and live in warmth and comfort for the rest of our lives."

"Got some place in mind?" She asked, and again I was surprised at the resilience of her spirit, for her demeanor had done a complete reversal.

"If we planned it carefully enough, we could load up the plane next time they leave it overnight, and, DV&WP, we could fly it our of here; hop across country all the way to Miami and then pop over to Grand Cayman and sell it there."

"You're Mad. Completely, utterly, and delightfully mad." She sighed, shaking her head sadly in my hand. But, I could see from the glint in her eyes that she wasn't completely sane either. And, she didn't yet know about the half million we'd be carrying in directly negotiable cargo.

To reassure Joyce I was not solely interested in her airfield, I led her upstairs to the bedroom and let nature take a hand in convincing her how deeply I felt for her, personally.

Later she went downstairs to clear the breakfast dishes while I leisurely showered and dressed. I'd just tied my shoes when there was a thumping sound, followed by frenzied barking from Patch, which was cut short as though she'd been suddenly muzzled in the middle of it.

Immediately after that, I heard Joyce scream and more thumps.

I raced down the stairs coming to an abrupt halt as I saw Patch, lying by the front door in a pool of blood and struggling feebly to get up. Then, I recognized, Henry, of all people, with his hands on Joyce's throat, bending her backwards over the kitchen table, his threatening voice demanding to know,

"What have you done with the money?".

Unsure of my physical ability to overpower him I ran, heading for the broom closet, shouting at him,

"Leave her alone! She hasn't got it.!"

He rose from the table whirling towards me and flung the butter dish at my head. It came apart in mid-air leaving me a choice of three missiles to dodge. Fortunately the hard parts missed, but the half pound block of soft butter hit me squarely in the face. I clawed at my eyes to clear them, stumbling towards the broom closet to get a more convincing argument than a handful of butter, and turned to face him clutching the slippery shotgun at waist level, like a lance. He had drawn his knife and was bringing his arm back as if to throw it at me. My thumb slipped as I tried to cock the hammer, and the gun tore itself out of my fingers as it recoiled with a tremendous roar and skidded across the floor into the corner.

Through one greasy eye, I saw the top of Henry's head exploding like a kicked watermelon while his almost headless body hurled the knife like nothing had happened. Fortunately, his aim was off and the knife thudded harmlessly into the wall above me. Spun by the force of the throw, his body seemed to envelope Joyce in its arms spewing blood all over her and she fainted.

If events hadn't moved so quickly, I might have had time to be appalled at what I had done, but I rushed to her rescue, and the three of us slithered into a tangled motionless heap, under the table.

When I recovered my senses, I could not determine whether Headless Henry, or Joyce was the source of the movement until I realized that Joyce was attempting to crawl over to Patch.

Patch and Henry were dead. He had slashed her head almost off and I remember sitting on the floor watching Joyce clinging to the body of her dog with the tears streaming down her face in rivulets, washing the blood of the killer off her cheeks.

"How appropriate" I thought, as she stood up with the broken dog held to her chest and stepped over me to Henry's body and kicked him violently in what was left of his face.

I will neither bore, nor nauseate you with all the messy details of the clean-up, but after both of us had partially recovered from the shock of realization, we went out into the yard and buried Patch. Then we dragged Henry's corpse out of the house and after removing the four boxes of Mobil oil, flung it into the trunk of his car. Finally, we showered together, removing our clothing like some macabre striptease act, slipping and sliding around the tub, frantically scrubbing ourselves, and each other, with every kind of soap, brush, and shampoo available.

Our sodden clothes, trampled heedlessly underfoot during this dance, were left to soak, while we, still wet and naked, tackled the mess in the kitchen, the living room, the passageways and the stairs.

Fortunately, Joyce had never been able to afford carpeting, and the varnished wood cleaned easily except for the crevices between floor-boards. These, she worked over with a toothbrush as though obsessed with the dread of one corpuscle of Henry's blood remaining in her house. His knife however, remained embedded in the wall, above the broom closet door, as if invisible to her.

One might very well wonder why we didn't immediately call the police. As I drove up to the Gas Station, on my way to call Barbara and find out why she hadn't kept that homicidal maniac under house arrest. The thought had entered my head and been immediately abandoned. Nobody would have believed our story. I wasn't yet ready to do so myself.

For openers, this was the second time we had shot him and there was no question he was finally dead. Premeditated Murder? No Question!

Secondly, we had completely obliterated the 'scene of the crime.' Even the shot gun had been scrubbed clean of all the mitigating evidence that might have supported a 'Plea' of "Accidental death."

Barbara didn't answer her phone. I had the eerie sensation of listening to it's ring, echoing in an empty house, and decided not to leave a message on the answering machine. We would just have to take Headless Henry home and hope she wouldn't call the cops.

"What will Barbara say now.?" Was all Joyce could say, staring at the body, crumpled up in the trunk of Henry's car. I made no comment, except to say.

"The car and the body are on their way back to her. She agreed to look after him and failed. She let us down. These disastrous consequences are her responsibility." I was determined to show Barbara that sentiment and murder don't mix. Joyce was still too numb from shock to protest. I felt no qualms about my own brutality. Henry had twice shown himself to be a cold blooded murderer, willing to extinguish my life as casually as if I'd been a salmon caught in his fish net.

Furthermore, his treatment of Joyce and Patch had angered me beyond compassion.

We drove, carefully observing the speed limits once more, in tandem. My blue beauty, with Joyce at the wheel and the four cases of oil in the trunk, following me, at the wheel of Henry's 'Hearse'.

Barbara was in the bath, looking very pale, when we arrived. In fact she'd been there quite a while, from the sickly odor which assailed us on entering; courtesy of Henry's keys.

She was naked, naturally, with her bloodstained clothes flung carelessly all over the floor. The tub was full to the overflow and the cold tap was still running. Both her wrists had been slashed and a kitchen knife was lying between her legs on the bottom of the tub.

Despite her severely bruised eye, Henry had apparently wanted to suggest it was a suicide, or perhaps he'd hoped the water would wash off his fingerprints.

I hated to see the water running to waste, so, although I was wearing gloves, I wrapped my handkerchief around the faucet handle and shut it off.

I searched the house, methodically leaving everything as we'd found it, until I located Barbara's collection of papers relating to 'Adam's letters', and her subsequent efforts to locate the author of 'her' original letter to Adam. She also had a telephone diary with references to my involvement, which I borrowed as well as her file of telephone bills. I saw no point in making any connection to myself readily available to subsequent sleuths. I had the cheerful notion to bring Henry's corpse and sit it on the toilet, watching over his lost love in the bath, as though it had been a suicide pact.

Joyce put her foot down hard on that idea, effectively squashing it. She pointed out that the physical condition of Henry's memory might throw some doubt on that conclusion.

Before leaving, I backed Henry's car into the garage and

shut the door, leaving the corpse in the trunk and the keys in the ignition.

We locked up carefully and departed, grateful they had a paved driveway which would bear no imprint of our passage.

At my house we burned all the incriminating evidence in my incinerator, along with the junk mail from the mailbox and the accumulated newspapers.

There not being enough food in the fridge for a decent meal, we drove on to Port Angeles and had dinner in the restaurant overlooking the harbor.

I felt the need to sit amongst sane people doing sane ordinary things, and a restaurant meal with wine in elegant surroundings, would be a relatively new experience for Joyce.

I hoped it would lift our spirits, which had become vindictively vicious towards Henry, and his gang, ever since she and I had buried Patch's body and pitched Henry's into the trunk of his car.

We walked on the pier after the meal enjoying the view across the placid water to the light-house on the end of the spit.

"It would be nice if every night could be as peaceful as this." Joyce said wistfully. "I wish my head and heart could be like the sea out there."

"They will be." I assured her, putting my arm around her, though I had no idea how I could make good on such a promise.

"I don't want to go home." Joyce whispered softly, as we reached the car. I could understand why.

"Will you come back to my place with me?" I asked gently.

"I would like to go somewhere that has no connection with all this hideousness that's happening to us. Somewhere where its warm and sunny and people are happy instead of killing one another for no reason. No reason at all. Poor little Patch, she was only trying to protect me." With that she broke into tears and I held her close to me while she sobbed it out.

'So much for the steak and the wine.' I thought to myself. They hadn't helped, what she needed, was time away from this area where she could heal herself.

After a while she settled down so I ushered her into the car and began driving. There was no point in going east so I didn't and shortly after we left P.A. she became agitated again and tearfully repeated her plea, not to return to her house. I stayed on the main highway instead, and we drove in silence past Crescent Lake and Forks, and onward towards Asylum.

The gas tank needed refilling and we literally coasted into the only gas station open in Hoquiam. I filled the tank and we continued Southward into the darkness. Shortly after leaving the gas station, Joyce fell asleep. I drove mechanically through the deserted night, across the Columbia at Astoria, and onward towards, 'Asylum'.

In Pacific City, I almost fell asleep myself, so I pulled into the Motel in town and woke the landlady. I booked us in as Mr. and Mrs. V. Gingham.

Don't ask me why, I don't know why. Probably I also wanted to separate myself from this present reality. I almost had to carry Joyce to the room and the landlady may have wondered about two exhausted travelers with no luggage at all. I noticed her watching us but I was past caring. Next morning, we had a late breakfast in a cute little cafe two doors down the road and set off in somewhat better spirits.

We had been on the road for little over a half hour, when the oil light came on and I pulled over to check. There wasn't a trace on the dipstick and we were miles from anywhere, on the coast, at the crest of a hill overlooking the sea. I had no oil, except the Mobil oil in the four cases I'd transferred from Henry's trunk to mine, in order to make room for Henry. I'd have to use a couple of them for sure. If they contained oil.

I had my doubts about opening them, but the cliffs were high and deserted. If they had dope in them, I could pitch them all over. No sense risking some alert Oregon Trooper asking why I was 'out of oil', with four cases of it, sitting in the trunk.

The cans were the old fashioned kind that needed a church-key to open them. Fortunately I had one and, bearing Roba's warning in mind I opened the first one carefully and tipped a little out. It was oil, engine variety, and I poured it in carefully through a cloth in a funnel. The second, third, and fourth cans were O.K. as well. I ran the engine, and rather than leave the empty cans in the trunk or at the roadside, I carried them to the sea wall and tossed them, one by one, far over onto the rocky shore. I was almost back to the car when there were four violent explosions, and a veritable cloud of seagulls erupted, squawking and screeching out of the cliff side.

We both ran to the wall and looked over but there was nothing to see, except some blue smoke and the whirling birds. I grabbed Joyce's hand and pulled her back to the car.

"We'd best get going before the Audubon Society connects us to the disturbance."

"What on earth caused that?" Joyce demanded, as if expecting me to know.

"Something must still have been left in those cans." I replied, still wondering what it could be and recalling Roba's warning once more. I just hoped there was nothing in the oil I'd poured into the engine, which might have the same inclination to explode.

Torn between a desire to 'get the heck out of there', before anyone came to investigate the explosions, and a nervous disinclination to have a repeat of the pyrotechnics right under the hood, I sat trying to make up my mind to start the motor, until Joyce asked me what was wrong.

By then I had rationalized that if it hadn't already exploded when I ran the engine to check the oil pressure, the explosions must have been caused by something that had stayed in the cans. The oil was only there to protect it against violent impacts or such. I licked my lips and nervously started the motor. By the time I'd driven a mile I was certain the oil was oil and whatever had exploded was what was being smuggled across the border in that fashion.

We discussed the situation guardedly, for I'd not told Joyce about many things and I couldn't remember exactly how much I had or hadn't told her. In the end I think she believed my explanation and was mildly concerned that we might be ferrying Nitro-glycerin across state boundaries.

She wanted to stop and put the cargo out beside the road but I couldn't see doing that since we were running through more populated areas, and someone else could get hurt, or worse, if they found our garbage.

"The sooner we get rid of it the better. That Horrible Man." She added, as if everything that happened, was his fault. I wasn't prepared right then, to discuss the finer points of responsibility with her, for we were entering California and I'd remembered Nora Transome's remarks about a certain Californian Research Company, which, by my reckoning, wasn't too much farther down the coast. I might just deliver the contraband myself.

At Eureka I decided to find us a Motel for the night. Although it was early afternoon and Joyce offered to take over, I pleaded tiredness from yesterday evening's marathon drive, and since we had no set destination, it made better sense to rest early. I could not tell Joyce my plan, largely because I didn't have one, but also because she knew nothing of my discussions with Nora about the identity of our mysterious visitors. Shame on me I should have mentioned it, but there always seemed to be more interesting events to concentrate on.

A good healthy belt of Sherry after our meal sent her off to sleep and she barely responded when I told her I was going out to make a few enquiries. She didn't even ask why.

Nora assumed I'd flown down to Eureka when I told her where I was and what I wanted to know. Fortunately she was still in her office when I called and had ready access to the name of the firm; Praif Inc., and a different telephone number. When she asked my intentions, I told her I'd decided to apply for a job. In the silence that followed, I added,

"Maybe I'll find out what's going on."

*　　*　　*

"Artificial Intelligence, is an oxymoron." The bespectacled, long grey haired youngster informed me from behind the desk. I could not see his face to decide whether he knew or cared if I knew or cared what an oxymoron was, but if I wanted the job, I'd best take his pontificating at its face value and not argue.

"Intelligence is a living thing. Always has been and always will be."

I nodded understandingly, despite a rising desire to reach over and tip his feet off the desktop to where I could look him in the face. But I wanted that job. So I didn't ask him if it also smelled bad after it died.

"Evolution has brought intelligence to its present stage of investigative development, in the human carrier.

Unfortunately, it can't progress beyond that stage without ridding itself of all the failings inherent in the human being." I shook my head sympathetically to show my acknowledgement of this piece of wisdom.

"The next stage of evolution will embed intelligence into an entity constructed from materials that will last several hundred, maybe thousands of years. It will not have to reproduce sexually thus ridding itself of the emotional aspects involved in that process."

I nodded or shook my head to signify my agreement with each of these announcements. As I said, I wanted that job. "Naturally, it will require the human species as its life support system in the same way we rely on cells and corpuscles for our life support system."

Ugly thought; but I kept my cool and said nothing to interrupt his monologue.

I was here to learn and I was damn well going to stay until I did. It was comforting to learn that the humans would still be around to enjoy the situation, probably the same kind of relief the corpuscles must have felt when told that the human being was to be evolved. But, he still hadn't told me what exploding oilcans had to do with it.

"Part of intelligence comes from feeling." I'd go along with that. "But computers can't feel." No questions there mate. "So our part, in this company, is to provide the nerves and sensory organs to enable the 'AI' to feel things and ultimately to provide it with qualitative analytical capability."

Hence the Biotech and Chemical engineers I supposed, nodding vigorously to keep the flow going.

"Here, in this facility, we are trying to make what might well be termed Artificial Nerves." I brightened up; maybe I'd get to see one of these miracles after all. My mind leaped ahead to artificial noses and tongues, but I kept mine still and listened intently.

From time to time, he would turn an ankle so that he could see me through the gap between his feet, and occasionally he stopped to read what I presumed was the resume' I'd typed on the computer and printer I'd rented from the local office supplies store in Eureka. Such Qualifications!. He was almost drooling at the prospect of hiring me. When he took his feet off the desk I held my breath and only released it under strict control when he said,

"Come! I'll show you around." I was in!.

Somehow I'd sensed there was a direct connection between these mysterious oilcans and the nervous systems of Artificial Intelligence experiments, and I was not as surprised as I might have otherwise been, when he proudly introduced the experimental nerve fiber.

It was a foot in diameter and made entirely from oilcans joined together, end to end, and wound like a three strand rope sixty or more feet long. It ran from one desk sized computer to another.

Remembering photos I'd seen of ENNIAC, 'Artif-Intel's prototype, despite all the advances in miniaturization, is destined to fill a football stadium, if this was one nerve. My curiosity got the better of me and I leaned closely enough to discern the remnants of Mobil labeling on the sides of the cans. A cluster of short plastic tubes linked the middle of each end of each can to its next in line, giving the flexibility needed to wind the strands together.

Apparently my interest pleased him for he launched into a treatise on the exchange of Potassium and Sodium 'Irons' in nerve fibers, during the passive transfer of nerve impulses along the motor nerves of the body. This process, he said, had to be reproduced in order to transmit sensory stimulus from one computer to the other.

Fortunately I didn't understand a word of it but the mention of Potassium and Sodium triggered a clue, as to what might be inside the cans.

'Gadgets' of one or the other of those metals, possibly both of them in an oil, specifically to exclude air and moisture. I shuddered, thinking of what had been happening inside those four cans while I was carrying them to the edge of the cliff top.

"Makes you nervous?" He asked, smiling for the first time since we'd met. I nodded. hoping he wouldn't ask me to explain why.

"What are you using as sleeves for the fibers?" I asked, "They look like oilcans."

"Precisely. This is only a prototype to prove the principles and later when we can import the raw materials here in bulk, we'll manufacture the 'Dend-Rights', 'Gangly-Irons' and 'New-Rones' right here."

"Getting them in such small lengths must be extremely expensive." I commented solicitously.

"Very." It was like pulling hen's teeth to get much out of him, but some quick mental arithmetic, dividing the estimated length by the height of a can, came up with about four hundred and eighty cans in the whole skein. I took a wild guess at about a thousand dollars a can!!

Wait a minute!! There were forty eight cans in Henry's trunk and four hundred and eighty thousand dollars in the fifth box.!? Ten thousand dollars a can ??!. Never!. But, it would sure make it worth smuggling six hundred cans at a time. No wonder old Baldy Watsisname could afford a yacht like the Chrysalis and get pie eyed every night.

Author's Note.:-

I've deliberately omitted the name of my prospective employer and given a minimal description of the gentleman who interviewed me. Partly because the most prominent part of him that I saw during the interview, was the soles of his shoes. (Size thirteen). And partly, because I don't want any repercussions after this story gets published, because someone thinks they know him.

I'm sure you realize the idea of 'Artificial Intelligence' taking over the prime spot on the food chain, is abhorrent to most people, and, as a result, their reaction to it's development is likely to become somewhat more 'personal' than even the most rabid environmentalist could imagine. Witness what happened to Henry.

My resume', hastily written on the computer the previous evening, had included my piloting experience, with heavy emphasis on my familiarity with the DH-84. I was particularly gratified when he began asking questions about that airplane. Hopefully, I gave him the impression; I could 'Fly it with my eyes shut.'

I suspect by the end of the interview, Mr. Bigshoes, as I'd nicknamed him, had determined my knowledge of anatomical and chemical biology was virtually non-existent, despite my skillful avoidance of specifics in answering many of his questions, and any real utilization they might expect from me, would be as a substitute pilot for their courier airplane.

Later that afternoon I was introduced to their 'Chief Pilot' a small, taciturn, wizened old man, Chip Mason, (The originality of some parents is Awesome) who took me in his Rolls Royce to the airport, barely a mile away, where to my intense delight, the Beautiful Lady was tucked safely away in a hangar. I tried not to drool but Chip sensed my delight at meeting her immediately and became quite expansive from then on.

Whereas I had assumed the DH-84 was on some kind of ferry service, originating from Joyce's airfield to some point on Vancouver Island or Lopez island, the truth seemed to be that it flew between her place and this area.

The cases of oil and the money we had found in Henry's car obviously had been destined for airlifting from Joyce to this hangar right here. Our little 'altercation' had interrupted the flow by making a landing impossible. Since, from Baldy 's stupefied remarks, the flow of 'oil', was southward from Canada to some destination in the Washington area maybe Seattle or some place on the Olympic peninsula.

If these two operations were really one, it was then shipped in smaller quantities, via Henry's operation in Forks, by air to this place. All very confusing.

I wondered what would happen if they ever learned that those cases were sitting in their car park right now. Had those 'Orientals' passed on my license plate number? Had Henry's resort to terminal violence been an aberration of his own? Or was it likely to be typical?

I could feel that old sensation returning. You know, the one that tightens your purse strings, when you are standing outside the Headmaster's study, prior to reporting to him for what inevitably became a dose of either four or six of the best, across the seat of the pants.

I forced the thoughts out of my mind. Primeval thoughts like those are too easily transmitted from mind to mind.

Chip finally rescued me, by suggesting I took him for a 'turn around the patch', in the DH-84.

Since at this point, I was not presumed to even know where Port Angeles was, I left most of the talking to Chip, hoping he might mention the route structure of this operation I'd joined. Eventually, it paid off.

The turn around the patch convinced me I'd lost none of my old familiarity with this airplane and apparently Chip approved, and told 'Bigshoes' I would do, immediately after we landed. They asked me to come back tomorrow and begin familiarization with their operation.

I could hardly wait to share this exciting news with Joyce. However when I got back to the motel and told her, she seemed distinctly uneasy about it and suggested we leave right away and return to her house, since, as she said,

"You don't know when to quit. Do you? Mister Gingham." I was dumbfounded, which gave her the opportunity to tear off a little more of my self esteem.

"As if we aren't in enough trouble already, here we are in California gallivanting around as Mr. and Mrs. Gingham with those phony identifications you made up on that computer. Driving around openly in Mr. Erickson's, car all painted blue; which the local police in Washington are trying to trace, in connection with a double murder he's wanted for." Still dumbfounded, I stared open mouthed at her until she snorted.

"Remember, It was you who pulled the trigger this time."

The unfairness of this stung me back to speech and I replied hotly.

"I didn't pull the trigger. My thumb slipped off the hammer of your ancient blunderbuss, as I was cocking the gun."

"Which you didn't know was loaded I suppose." She retorted angrily. "I know I hadn't loaded it since the first time, so you must have."

I was appalled at her accusations and gradually it was seeping into my mind that she had made definite statements about police activity instead of suppositions.

"What makes you think the Washington police are looking for anyone ?" I asked warily.

"It was on the T.V." She blurted out, bursting into tears. I was overwhelmed, instinctively reaching out to hold her, but she brushed me aside and I have never felt so lost in my life.

"I knew something like this would happen to us. That evil man. What are we going to do?" She poured out her distress in a torrent of angry questions, none of which I could even begin to answer. In the end she let me put my arms around her and I clung to her as much to quiet my own alarm as to soothe her anguish.

"Tell me what you saw on T.V." I said softly, several times before she settled down, wiping away her tears on my shirt.

"It was on the news."

"So? What did they say.?" I asked impatiently. She began talking, but she wasn't making coherent sense to me so I took the remote from her and began flipping through the channels for the next ten minutes, hoping to catch a repeat.

Suddenly she grabbed my arm, exclaiming,

"There!" and pointing at the screen.

It was a local station newscast. Apparently, a man had murdered his wife in some small rural community called Washington and then committed suicide in his garage.

Joyce, with her mind full of vivid memories of a similar scenario, must have convinced herself it related to our episode. It took a lot of effort, quieting her down, as I pointed out the differences.

However, it brought me to an awareness of my own potential predicament, much more forcibly than I had previously appreciated.

In the newscast, a reference to neighbors observing a blue car leaving the residence shortly before the bodies were discovered, had confirmed her fears the police would be looking for us.

I explained it would be best if we returned to her home and carried on as normal.

We could get another puppy. She'd be involved in its upbringing which should take her mind off the loss of Patch.

However, I didn't want to miss my chance of getting hold of the DH-84 by severing my new connections and returning with her right away.

'One step at a time'. Another of Roba's favorite comments. I reminded myself.

Much gentle caressing, mixed with plenty of rational explanations and generous applications of Harvey's Bristol Cream, soothed the turbulent soul and we went out into the late afternoon sun.

Joyce and Pooch took to each other like mother and daughter at the local pound and we snuck the two of them, somewhat theatrically back into the motel room under a coat.

Fortunately, Pooch took to Harvey's like a fish. She and Joyce were soon asleep in each other's arms, while I slipped out and made arrangements for the morrow.

Dawn was spraying the eastern skyline with a fringe of gold along the mountain-tops as we took off in the rented Cessna.

My two passengers were still comatosely wrapped in a motel blanket that had somehow followed us into the darkness. A little over two hours later we landed at Joyce's airfield. Soon after settling them there, I flew to my own base, to liberate a bundle of greenbacks from their burial place in the peat moss, and collect a few other essentials from the house. Fifteen minutes later, some of the locals may have wondered who was taking off, but, after all, a Cessna is a Cessna is a Cessna.

I had to make a pit and fuel stop at Hoquiam, but by noon, the wandering blanket was back on its bed and I was in Chip's office, freshly shaven and ready for work.

I had expected a mild reproof for turning up so late but nothing was said, nor was there any of the usual bureaucratic indoctrination of a new employee. Instead, Chip took me into what served as his office and began showing me, on the map, over the route of the flight I would be making. It was almost exactly the same as the flight I had just returned from, with some minor modifications, specifically to avoid entering the various FAA Control Zones.

The phone rang and he excused himself and left me to myself. Sensing this might be a test, I gave a cursory glance around the office and returned my attention to his maps, studying them in detail. It took a little effort of self control but I was not going to appear on some T.V. screen, as anything but a Pilot whose sole interest was in his job. Especially, I didn't want to make accidental Eye Contact with some unseen Oriental who might, just by chance, recognize me. Chip returned some fifteen tedious minutes later and asked me if I was ready.

I waved the piece of paper on which I'd noted the details of the various 'emergency' airfields along the route and a few 'safe altitudes' for crossing the mountains, and agreed.

"OK. See you back here tomorrow evening at eight." he said, dismissing me cheerfully. I walked out into the hangar and climbed aboard My Beauty, as I now thought of the DH-84, and inspected her thoroughly from rudder pedals to the rear cabin wall inside, before going over her from nose to tail, on the outside.

For the benefit of any observers, I was the quintessential conscientious pilot. Satisfied with my pre-flight inspection, I was free to return to the motel and break out the computer and printer. I needed a current Medical Certificate. Mine had been expired, almost ten years, and someday Chip might want to examine it more thoroughly than the flash glance he'd given it in my wallet. Such Faith in a fellow pilot, I almost felt bad deceiving him.

It took little more than a couple of hours to re-equip myself with a complete new identity and my originals went into a manila envelope which I mailed to myself for safe keeping at my Sequim P.O. Box. Later, it would be placed in my Bank Safety Deposit Box, if I ever had any free time.

I'd come a long way in computer duplicity under Roba's remote control. The remainder of the afternoon was spent writing a letter with many careful instructions for Joyce. I managed to catch the post office, in time to post it with top priority to be delivered directly to her house.

Next morning, I began laundering the first two thousand, from my 'ten pack' in a series of 'performances' at most of the big stores in Eureka, buying small purchases, under ten dollars, and apologizing to the cashiers for having to break into my 'Mad Money' for lack of sufficient small change.

In consequence, I spent time, sorting the pile of small greenbacks into something more manageable in my wallet, before depositing the residual stack of twenties into my 'portable bank account'.

I used the last hour before reporting to the hangar at the airfield, in writing a long overdue, love-letter to Joyce, just in case things didn't turn out quite as planned.

Chip was waiting when I arrived at 7.50 pm. and handed me the maps we had reviewed earlier.

"Let's go." He snapped, as if I had been late.

"Something wrong?" I snapped back. "You said eight."

"We've a problem at the other end." he replied sharply, as if this too was my fault. It might well have been, but he didn't know that and I rebuked him on principle.

"Hey don't get mad with me about it."

"Sorry. I'd been wanting to make it in good light. Couldn't get in touch, so we'll just have to try and get there on our own resources in the dark."

'Some hopes' I thought, remembering my own daylight landings there. Finding an unlighted hole in the forest at night!?. But I wasn't supposed to know that so I kept quiet with a mental reservation to wait till we got there, before refusing to land.

"You could have reached me at the motel office, they'd have given me a message." I said, to let him think I'd assumed his sour mood was from being unable to reach me in time for an earlier take-off.

He made no comment until we'd been airborne for several minutes, when he decided to unburden his soul.

"Nothing to do with you old chap. Fact is, the buggers who were supposed to meet us at the airfield haven't made contact and we've been unable to reach them.

"Perhaps there's been an accident. Have you called the police?"

Although we were wearing headsets and speaking over the plane's intercom, rather than facing each other, I plainly saw the tensing of his jaw muscles as I mentioned 'police'.

"Can't say." He replied after a few moments. Then he turned towards me and continued explaining that he himself hadn't made the enquiries, apparently this was 'Bigshoes' department. All he had to do was be sure the plane arrived at the pickup airfield on time and brought the cargo safely back to base. The pickup time had been scheduled before my arrival and only the last minute confirmation was adrift.

They were assuming the cargo would be there when we arrived. Somehow, I had my doubts. Henry had been driving his own car when he came to Joyce's and got himself killed. Had he simply taken over again from his substitutes? Was that why he was so incensed over the missing money? Even to the extent of killing.? Had he mentioned Joyce and my own involvement to them? Or anyone else.? I mulled these matters over in my head as we purred northward. Chip, in the driving seat, had also relapsed into silence.

The countryside below us had become a pool of darkness sprinkled here and there with small clusters of lights, which drifted slowly backwards under the wing. The moon had not yet risen but the stars were intensely bright and supplied all the light required to see the exterior of our graceful aircraft. Roba, bless his heart, had indeed given me the right lead once more and I reveled in the joy of flying her.

The desire of possession thus temporarily sated, I gave thought to this strange situation. To all outward appearances, this trip was perfectly legitimate (Bar my paperwork) so why had Henry flipped his wig? Had they been dealing in Drugs, I could have understood, but Oilcans loaded with Potassium and or Sodium.? Just didn't make sense. On the premise that our activity was legit, I asked Chip what our cargo was to be.

"Nitro-glycerin." He replied. "Handle it carefully and make soft landings." My mind flashed back to the way I had slung those boxes around from one trunk to another and I blessed the 'Saviors' who had allowed me to escape from the Federal parking lot in Port Angeles without detection. Perhaps I shuddered or gave some other outward sign of agitation, for he looked across at me and asked,

"Cold feet?"

"Na!. It's not the first time I've sat on top of twenty thousand pounds of high explosives."

"Think of it as just another mission. Only this time you'll be landing with it still on board." He added with a sly grin. I remembered the four 'Bangs' in Oregon, from what I'd assumed were empty cans, and suppressed another shiver.

As the flight progressed, the lights below us became less frequent and less brilliant, as the eastern silhouette of the Olympics lightened with the rising moon.

We had another hour to go so it would be high enough to pick out more detail of the terrain in the vicinity of Joyce and the pool of light in the dark forest should be fairly easy to find, easier perhaps than in daylight.

When we arrived, there was no pool of light, only the eerie green of the forest, glowing like a million spear-points in the moonlight.

Circling overhead I could discern the highway, and the junction of Joyce's road, but I was not supposed to know this area, so I said nothing and waited to see what Chip would do. Occasionally, Joyce's house was momentarily visible, but there were no lights on and I wondered if she'd got my letter yet. She had. Chip had finally turned the C.B.radio on and was about to make a call when the airfield lights came on. He replaced the microphone with a visible sigh of relief and we set up to make the landing.

"Where the *** hell are they?" Chip finally exploded. We had parked the DH-84 in its usual turnaround at the far end of the runway, where he had obviously expected to meet the ground operators, but the place was deserted. In the shack, the generator was running and the airfield lights like a string of 'fairy lights', hung on the trees giving a festive appearance to the clearing. There was no other sign of life even in the parking area.

"What do we do now?" I asked innocently. Joyce, bless her heart, if she had followed my letter to the letter, would be tucked in bed and probably trying hard to go back to sleep.

'If anyone comes to the house, stay in bed unless they try to break in. If they do, you have the shotgun, but for God's sake, turn the lights on before shooting.' Had been my last instruction before committing, in writing, to the fact that I loved her.

If Chip didn't know about the house so close by, I wasn't about to tell him. We could sleep in the airplane if necessary.

"Is there any other place they could be? It's pretty cold here. Maybe they've gone for a cup of coffee somewhere."

Chip stared at me as if I'd lost my mind, and shook his head. "Don't be absurd. They must have heard us circling and started up the generator. It's standard practice. We were only a few minutes ahead of our 'ETA'. They were here, they put the lights on and must have left right away for some reason.

"Probably forgot to bring the cargo and went back for it Eh?"

"They'd have left a note or one of them would have stayed to tell us."

"How many of them are there?"

"Two. There used to be one but he disappeared mysteriously and we sent two to replace him."

"Perhaps a 'Sasquatch' got them."

"Then drove off with them in their car I suppose. For Christ Sake!. This is serious!. We'd better get out of here while we can."

As if to emphasize his concern, the generator slowed down and stopped, leaving us standing in the dark forest. Lulled into false security by the airfield illuminations, neither of us had a flashlight. "Shit!"

"Is that a comment or a command?" I asked. "Where the blazes do these guys live?" I added before he could decide.

"Forks." the voice in the darkness answered angrily.

"Swearing isn't going to get us anywhere." I commented quietly.

"Forks. you idiot." He sounded exasperated. "It's about twenty miles west of here. (As if I didn't know)

"That's a long walk. Maybe we should just sleep in the plane until daylight. I don't fancy trying to take off from here in the dark." Chip made no comment, but I felt sure he had no intention of trying to do either alternative.

Dark as the forest had seemed when the lights went out, my eyes had adjusted sufficiently to discern lights and shadows cast by the pale moonlight filtering through a thin upper cloud layer. We made our way in relative silence back to the airplane and crawled back into the empty cargo area and lay down to try and sleep.

That same cloud layer, thankfully, prevented a really frosty night so the temperature, around forty degrees, was not unbearable despite our light clothing. However, Chip began shivering with the cold. I got up and went into the shack and pretended to discover the bed and blankets in there. Much to his relief, we stretched out on it, head to toe, fully dressed, like two sardines on a biscuit, and he was soon fast asleep.

I pushed aside a strong urge to slip out and exchange my present bedfellow for a more comfortable situation in the house, but decided to stay put, rather than risk exposing Joyce any more than necessary. She had performed her part well, but I had grave misgivings as to what had happened to put Henry's two Oriental replacements out of commission.

I thought I'd prod Chip, in the morning, to go in search of them rather than just return to base empty handed.

"Jesus its cold!" Chip was irritable as well as cold and not too receptive to the idea of a long walk. I had to play the 'Company Man' to the hilt, insisting that as long as he actually knew where their base was, Bigshoes would hardly expect less of us than to go and investigate.

All his leadership seemed to have evaporated after landing and I ended up wrapping him in one of the dark grey blankets with a wire belt, draping the loose end over his head and shoulders. To hold the blanket securely around the head, I stuck a second piece of the wire through the blanket under his chin drawing it closed. Similarly attired, we looked more like a couple of Monks or Mongolian peasants than American Pilots as we set out on the long walk. Our 'Habits' had the added advantage of limiting his field of vision, and by walking half a pace ahead of him, I prevented him from being able to see Joyce's house as we passed. At the cafe in Joyce, it was almost ten o'clock. Nobody seemed to want to notice our strange attire, but as soon as I produced a twenty, the atmosphere became quite relaxed. Hot coffee, bacon and eggs, worked wonders for both of us.

When we mentioned that we were headed for Forks, the man who apparently functioned as cook, waiter and probably owned the joint, informed us there would be a bus along in about fifteen minutes, which cheered Chip immensely. He had earlier rejected my suggestion of calling Bigshoes from the cafe, so I hadn't pressed the point, easing him back into the role of leader once more.

From the bus station at Forks, it was a five minute walk to the house where I'd seen the Oriental park Henry's car. Although a pick-up was parked in the drive, the window shades were all drawn and the house had a deserted appearance.

"Doesn't seem like anyone's home." I volunteered when there was no response to our hammering on the front door.

"You wouldn't have a key by any chance?"

Chip shook his head glumly and went ahead of me down the pathway between the houses to the back yard. The wicket gate opened easily and we went into a typical Northwest enclosed yard with a high laurel hedge all round. Very private. He banged on the back door with the same result as the front. I watched as he produced a large pocket knife and jiggled it into the space between the lock and the door jamb. The door Popped open, letting out the terrible stench of death. Chip got the full blast of it, and recoiled, dropping the knife. He slapped his hands over his mouth, staggered back from the door and leaned against the wall, heaving as though about to lose his breakfast.

Covering my nose and mouth with my handkerchief, I reached in around the door and released the lock before shutting it. I put my arm around Chip's shoulders and pulled him away from the wall, leading him out through the gate into the driveway and over to the vaguely familiar navy blue Chevvy 'step side'. I guided his rump onto the step and sat him there, looking as green as an unripe tomato and, despite the cold breeze, he was perspiring as if it was midsummer. I retrieved the two blankets we hadn't needed since breakfast, from the back bumper of the pickup where I'd parked them before our excursion to the back door, wrapped one around him and fanned him with the other. After a few minutes of this, he waved his hand at me to quit the fanning and gradually recovered his composure.

"There's something terribly wrong in there." he said, in a hoarse, hesitant undertone. "I don't think I could venture inside without a gas mask."

By the way he looked at me, I read the unspoken request for me to do this for him. Suddenly it all came together in my mind.

The pickup he was sitting on, was Barbara's. I remembered seeing the canopy hanging from the rafters of her garage when I parked Henry's hearse; doubtless why I hadn't recognized it immediately. Henry must have killed her, driven her vehicle to his house, and probably, from the smell of things, killed one or both of the Orientals. He had then retrieved his own car and driven to Joyce's place. From the cursory glimpse I'd given the kitchen when closing the door, there were no bodies lying there. I hesitated to imagine what might be the scene in one of the other rooms.

"Maybe we should call the cops?" I ventured. There had to be some point where his reluctance to involve the authorities ended. He looked up at me then and shook his head.

"NO." He said firmly, not yet."

Given the fact that he probably had no idea of the magnitude of the carnage he might be about to discover, I refrained from pushing the question. I shrugged my shoulders in a gesture of submissive disapproval and said nothing.

They say serial killers are usually caught because they develop a thing called a 'Modus Operandi'. Henry was no exception. The awful stench came directly from the bathroom. The bath contained two pajama clad oriental bodies floating like two bloated sardines in a can. The only difference between the modus operandi here and at Barbara's was that he had left the hot water running instead of the cold. The bodies were definitely overcooked. Both throats had been cut clear through the windpipes and only this and the fact they were wearing pajamas, had restrained them from bursting. With what remained of the deep breath I'd taken before entering, I shut off the water and fled, out of the house through the front door leaving it wide open behind me. I sat on the step of the pick up beside Chip waiting for my heart to slow down, and for the wind to cleanse me of the dreadful odor, which seemed to have invaded my whole being. After the desire to vomit subsided, I got up and walked into the street facing into where the wind was strongest.

Presently, Chip came out and joined me still wearing his blanket. He sounded stronger though he still looked drawn and pale.

"What did you find?" he asked.

"Two stiffs. In the bathroom." I answered, trying to sound as if this was an everyday occurrence. He looked at me quizzically as if to question my statement so I continued,

"Go look for yourself. The smell's not so bad now the doors are open. I think it's time we called the police."

"NOT YET!" He sounded almost panic stricken. I shrugged again.

"It's your decision. You're the Boss. I just don't want to be charged as an accessory after the fact."

I didn't want to press the issue for obvious reasons. But at the same time, I wanted to maintain his concept of me as a law-abiding citizen. He began walking towards the garden gate and I followed, advising him to soak his handkerchief and hold it over his nose to filter out the smell.

At the bathroom door he hesitated, and peeked in before closing it hurriedly. I saw his body heave again but he controlled it immediately and moved into the bedroom. The room was a shambles, as if Henry had searched it after killing the two occupants. Obviously he hadn't found what he was looking for there, (I suspected I knew why) and had done a similar, though less destructive, search of the living room.

Chip was also searching for something though he said nothing to that effect, moving around casually looking into drawers and cupboards. I quietly followed him around, keeping one hand in my pocket, the other holding the handkerchief over my nose.

After a while I decided to leave Chip to search for whatever he was looking for and went to the kitchen, found a dish towel and made a complete circuit of everything I had touched, wiping it thoroughly to remove any fingerprints.

This done I went out to see what I could do about getting into the Pick-up. The door was unlocked so I searched around for a key and finding none, sat wondering which wires to disconnect to hot wire it. Maybe Chip would know. I lolled back in the seat and must have fallen asleep for I woke up to find Roba sitting beside me. We chatted a while though I can't remember all we talked about but when we talked about my problem with the pickup, he asked me if I'd looked under the frame below the radiator.?

"Many people put a small magnetic box under there with a key in it, just for occasions like this."

I got out of the cab, felt under the frame where he had said to look, and there it was, with three keys inside. Two of the keys were Chevrolet car style, one square end for the ignition the other hexagonal end for the door, and the third, a small cabinet lock style which I assumed would probably fit the lock of the wooden toolbox that spanned the forward end of the pick-up's bed.

I closed the box, put it in my pocket and climbed back in to thank him but he had gone, so I just lay back and waited for Chip to come out of the house. I must have gone right back to sleep for the next thing I knew, Chip was shaking my shoulder.

"Come give me a hand with these boxes." He said eyeing me strangely. I went back into the house and saw three boxes of Mobil oil lying on the kitchen table.

I was about to ask where he'd found them, but he started handing them to me and piled all three on top of one another as if I was his slave. I just couldn't talk. It was all I could do to hold them and I staggered out to the garden and tottered to the pickup and dumped them on the step to get my breath back.

I'd heard the house door slam behind me but I was surprised when he immediately ordered me to put them in the cab. I turned to look at him and he snapped.

"Come on man, Get them inside. On the floor." I was speechless. Finding these boxes had transformed him from the debilitated old man into a vibrant commanding individual again. However I wasn't his slave so I opened the passenger door and held it for him to put the boxes in if he wanted to, and stood thus until he perceived the message.

He compromised by picking them up and handing them to me, one at a time, to put on the floor.

"Get in." He commanded, skipping around the back of the pick-up and into the driver's seat as though some magical power had restored his youth. Then to my further amazement, he produced a bunch of keys and searched for one that fitted the ignition and started the engine. Hanging from the key-ring was a silver owl. Barbara's keys.

"Where'd you find the keys?" I asked grinning at him.

"They were on the floor of the cab. I picked them up while you were fooling around in the house."

"Amazing." I gasped, still trying to maintain my smile. The crafty old bastard had appeared to be at death's door one moment and while I was occupied, had revived enough to check the cab, found the keys and then returned to his charade in time to await my return. It would be well to keep an eye on him henceforth, I decided. I had stacked the boxes, two below and one above, resting between my feet. As we drove away from that house of death, I looked down at them. All had been opened and re-closed by interleaving the four flaps. Just like the one that had been so delightfully different from the sealed cases in Henry's original shipment.

Maybe that's what had resuscitated Chip so dramatically.

It was just after One O'clock by the time we were back on the road with Chip driving. He looked a different man now, perky and smiling to himself from time to time, like the proverbial cat who'd just swallowed the canary.

"How long has your medical been expired?" He suddenly asked, breaking into my train of thought. I stared at him in astonishment, and my sick sheep expression was in place before I could summon the wolf. I tried recovering by opening out my wallet and handing it to him. He gave a short laugh as he looked at my New Medical certificate.

"It's very good." He said, handing it back. "Do it on a computer?". He asked with a grin.

I knew I'd been caught fair and square, so I nodded weakly.

"How'd you guess?"

"Never mind." He replied, and I wondered if he'd been making phone calls to California from the house while I was loafing outside. I should have been more careful.

"Going to Fire me?" I asked, trying to look dismayed. He pursed his lips as if contemplating, then shook his head.

"No. You're obviously a competent pilot. At least as far as the DH-84 is concerned. I can use you."

I wondered what he had in mind with 'I can'. Perhaps Bigshoes wasn't included in his plans, and I suspected he had plans, so I waited patiently and said nothing, hoping to appear ashamed of myself.

It was obvious to me that if these cases under my feet were what I thought they were, Chip possibly had other intentions than simply flying them straight back to Bigshoes. I waited. He apparently didn't know his way back to Joyce because he stayed on the highway instead of turning off at Sappho and seemed a little surprised when we began to drive along beside Lake Crescent. I said nothing and maintained my submissive demeanor. Presently he pulled off into the parking area of a roadside restaurant and stopped by the entrance.

"How about some lunch?" He asked cheerfully, getting out of the cab. "Lock your door." He added slamming his. Inside the restaurant, his mood of joviality extended to a ten-ounce top sirloin, while mine remained at hamburger level. We were the only customers and he chose to sit at a window table where he could see the parked pick-up. I was facing the opposite way.

Halfway through the meal, I saw a state patrol car pull into the parking lot and heard it pull up, apparently alongside the pickup. Chip's forkful stopped in mid air as he froze, watching the events outside. I turned around to see what had attracted such concentrated interest and saw one of the officers looking the pickup over with more than casual interest, before they both entered the restaurant.

"Your lunch is getting cold." I said quietly, as Chip, who had remained in his statuesque pose, appeared to be about to melt.

The officers were behind Chip and removed their hats as they entered. They greeted the owner and were settling down at a table on the other side of the room, when the one who had been studying the pickup turned and headed towards our table.

"You eat, I'll talk. I added quickly, as Chip put the fork into his mouth.

The patrolman smiled as our eyes met.

"Either of you gentlemen own the pickup outside?"

"I do." I replied cheerfully, smiling back at him.

"Ever think of selling it?" He asked.

I shook my head vigorously, adding pride of ownership to my smile.

"What year is it."

"Sixty two."

"It's in great shape."

"I guess I baby her quite a bit. She's only got seventy thousand miles on her.

"Well, if you ever want to sell it I'd be interested. Name's Brian Morris." he added extending his hand.

"Henry Barranquilla." I replied, half rising to shake hands. "Why don't you give me your address." I added, sitting back down. "Just in case I change my mind."

We exchanged a few more pleasantries, he gave me a card with a Shelton address, so I didn't volunteer any un-necessary information and he politely said goodbye and went back to his table.

Chip swallowed the mouthful he'd been chewing throughout the conversation, wiped his forehead with his paper napkin, and relaxed.

"My God you're a cool bastard." He hissed quietly. "Where'd you come up with a name like that?"

"It's on the registration slip." I replied in a soft undertone. "If they took the number, and check later, they shouldn't jump to any un-necessary conclusions."

By unspoken mutual consent, we wolfed the remainder of the meal and called for the cheque.

"You pay." I said, grinning at him. "I forgot to bring my wallet with me."

He looked at me quizzically for a moment, then it came to him and he smiled. He opened his wallet, thumbing through a wad of hundreds to find a twenty.

He took the single dollar out of the change, and put the coins on the table.

"Gimme that." I said, snatching it from him before he could put it away. I put it down on the table, and hustled him out of the restaurant.

"Christ!" I said in a savage undertone as the door closed behind us. "I put on a performance like that, and you want to give them something to gripe about after we leave. For the sake of a dollar!?. Get with it man! We're accessories after the fact. Fleeing the scene of a murder, and possibly driving a stolen car into the bargain."

We had driven in silence for several minutes after leaving the restaurant and were in the middle of Port Angeles. I was about to ask him where the hell he was going, when he pulled into the Safeway parking lot and headed for the liquor store. He came out with a bag-full of bottles.

I had deduced by now that he was under some considerable inner stress and his first act after settling the bag on the seat between us, was to open a bottle of bourbon and take a healthy swig. I needed no further confirmation, and reached across to remove the keys from the ignition.

"You drink. I'll drive."

We changed places and I asked him if he'd talked to Big-shoes yet. He shook his head.

"Give me the number, I'll call him and see what he wants us to do."

His manner darkened, and for a moment I thought he was going to hit me with the bottle but he only removed the cap and took another swig before closing it and turning slowly to face me. All semblance of his earlier jollity had gone and in a deadly serious tone he demanded.

"Listen Friend. How much is Big-shoes paying you.?"

"Twenty-five grand." I replied meekly, leaving him room to make a better offer. He'd already tipped his hand and I guessed he was about to cut me in on a deal. I waited as he took another swig from the bottle. The more swigs, the better the deal would probably be.

"D'you know what's in these boxes?" he asked, tapping his foot on them.

"Cans of oil. I guess."

"Wrong." He replied, tapping his foot on them again.

"There's about a million and a half in cold cash here and I'll split it with you if you'll help me 'Liberate' it."

I waited, open mouthed, in an expression I hoped would convey my surprise.

"Whaddya say?. I've got a plan all worked out. but I need someone to help me." He grinned at me as if he'd made me an offer I couldn't refuse. "Come on man I know you're on the run. False papers and all that shit. I checked on your car. Henry Erickson." He sounded very smugly pleased and though I felt some concern; from the current sequence of events, he probably hadn't mentioned any of his findings to Big-shoes. Not yet anyway.

"Let me think about it." I said, starting the engine.

"We can discuss it on the way back to the plane. I don't think the Safeway parking lot is the place for this kind of discussion."

He put the bottle between his knees and reached across, grabbing the wheel, twisting so his face was close to mine, and with his right hand, switched off and pulled the keys out of the ignition.

"This is the Perfect place for this discussion." He said emphatically, puffing alcohol fumes in my face. All these nice people around us will keep it on an even keel. I feel safer here. I know you're a crook. But, I've no way of knowing how far you might go for another million. Besides that, as I said earlier, I have a plan in place. You don't, which makes You, dangerous." He let go the wheel and sat up straight, watching me closely. We must have remained like that for two whole minutes before I let go the wheel and slid into the corner of the seat so I was facing him. My mind was real busy, and he waited patiently, confidently, and not the least bit like the drunk he had portrayed a few minutes earlier. Finally I let my self relax into a broad smile.

"O.K. What's the deal and what's the plan.? If I like both, I'm in.

"And if you don't.?"

"Cut the cards and start again. I'd like to see the money first. If you don't mind."

He put the bottle down by his foot and opened the flaps of the top box, taking out one of the bundles, which, from what I'd seen in his wallet, he had obviously opened earlier, and passed it to me to examine.

"Don't flash it around." He warned, indicating the other cars parked around us. "There's forty eight of those in each of the boxes. Ten grand in hundreds per packet"

"I thought you said half a million." The mathematician in me blurted out before I could stop it. He shrugged, his contempt for my exactitude written all over him.

"Just setting the record straight." I replied smiling, "There should be another four hundred and sixteen dollars and sixty six cents in each packet." No harm in having him think I could do that sort of calculation in my head.

"Maybe there is. I was talking in round numbers. You want to count them or are you in.?" He growled scornfully.

"What's in it for me?" I countered, figuring I could draw him out slowly without committing myself. Obviously there would be no written contract between us thieves later.

"One box is yours. the others are mine." Then, seeing I was about to make a counter claim, he continued. "My plan calls for us to separate and we'll each keep our share with us until we reach our destination."

"Which is?"

"Are you in? Or not?"

"I haven't heard the plan yet." I replied, figuring he was leaving things open to later negotiation, possibly at some destination where I might be at a serious disadvantage.

"We fly the Dominee to the Cayman Islands."

I'd expected something like that, so I just sat quietly expressionless and waited for him to make the next move. Obviously the DH-84 wasn't going to make a 3,000 mile flight in one hop so there were details of his 'Plan' still missing.

After a one minute silence, in reverence for his lost sanity, I uttered the word, "How?"

"You're going to have to trust me on this part." He said, "I've set up a series of landing places where the Dominee can refuel. One of us flies, the other drives and sets up the refueling program."

It was just about the sort of hare-brained scheme I myself might have planned, given my larcenous inclinations. In fact, as I suddenly recalled, it was almost what I'd proposed to Joyce. Was Roba in on this somewhere, I wondered.

"And. When and if we get there. Even Stevens." I said, without the interrogative inflection. He nodded.

"O.K. Then I'm in. We can get down to the fine details later. Right now, I'd feel much safer back at the airfield than driving around in what may be a stolen car."

He gave what I took to be a deep sigh of relief and handed me the keys, before taking another swig at the bottle.

"Try and be a bit more discrete with that bottle." I said, exerting my authority as an equal partner. "Someone just might report us drinking and driving. We might not be so lucky if the cops stop us after that."

He must have been working on his plan for a long time, for he'd written it down in two school notebooks. One page of the blue notebook was dedicated to each leg of his flight, with carefully drawn maps of the location of each of his five rendezvous points. Similarly, one page of the red notebook to each leg of the road journey. Careful details of where to get the necessary gasoline to refuel the plane was included in each case.

He produced the notebooks from his flight bag after we had loaded the boxes from the pickup to the DH-84. I just chanced to notice the flight bag also contained a small revolver. Whether he intended me to see it or not, I wasn't quite sure.

He had apparently calculated each day's journey, based on the road, for each page of the road version also included the name, location and phone number of what I presumed was the nearest motel. I wondered, who had been his original co-conspirator before

I so conveniently came along. On the principle of 'least said, soonest mended', I decided to let him tell me, at his own convenience, and why his plans had been changed to include me. It occurred to me that perhaps, his original associate might somehow have 'lost interest' and been abandoned as a result. On the other hand, since the first leg of his planned route began here and ended in California less than thirty miles from the home base, maybe Bigshoes himself was involved. That was about the only thing that made sense of his reluctance to call him after discovering the bodies. Despite Chip's claim to having checked my references, and, having found them false, deduced that I was a criminal on the run, and therefore potentially an accomplice, I sensed he'd been almost too anxious to get me to join him. Perhaps I was being set up as a patsy to take the rap for all these murders.

By the time we'd loaded the Dominee and the truck and gone over the maps, it was too late to consider starting out. The fuel for the airplane was stashed in ten five gallon Jerry-cans behind the shack. Probably the last act of the two dead Orientals.

After refueling, Chip had instructed me to stack them in the back of the pick-up, to be refilled at some convenient point along the way to the next rendezvous. We lit the tiny wood-stove in the shack and as twilight deepened, retired into the warmth for the night. I discovered there was a battery lamp in there which was connected to the twelve volt output of the generator and we arranged for Chip to sleep on the cot while I, the junior member, bunked down on some of the spare blankets, on the floor. By this time, he had consumed about four of the five fifths in the fifth of Bourbon, and went out like a light. Ten minutes later, I couldn't even wake him while taking the keys of the airplane out of his pants pocket.

Joyce was so relieved to see me, she threw her arms around me as though I'd just returned from the dead. Pugsley, as she'd named the puppy, joined in the excitement by trying to climb up my leg. After they both settled down, I filled her in on the details of the latest escapade and our plans for the next few days, before enlisting her help.

I'd borrowed Chip's revolver and when I showed it to her, she laughed and showed me a cake of soap which had been perforated with a series of holes.

"This morning, after you two Monks left, I got into the airplane with our keys and found that revolver. I knew it wasn't yours so I emptied all the shells, filled them with soap, and put everything back in the A.F.C."

I threw my arms around her and hugged her with delight. "Where'd you learn that trick."

"Charlie." She said, explaining that long ago, he'd liked to fire a service revolver and she'd helped him with the re-loading of the empty cases. In later years when he had become abusive and threatened her with it, she'd had the idea of replacing the cordite flakes with soap flakes, in case, during one of his drunken rages, he tried to carry out the threat.

Not having any flakes handy at the moment she'd used the cases like a cookie cutter on the bar of soap, before re-inserting the slugs.

"Did he ever try firing the soap laden cartridges?"

"I didn't keep him around long enough to find out. He always claimed he needed to carry it, in case he was ever attacked by a bear."

She gave a little giggle and continued. "I hope for his sake he never had to use it."

I wasn't too sure just how soap flakes would react to the firing of the percussion cap, but felt solid soap would be less likely to ignite as readily as flakes might.

"Perhaps the bubbles would scare the bears." I said, and she laughed.

By the time I had finished outlining my plan and explaining how she could assist me, she was as excited as Pugsley had been. I had to use every trick in the book to get her calmed down.

On my way back to the shack in the woods, I put the gun back in Chip's flight bag, hoping I'd never have to find out how soap acted as a propellant.

We woke as might be expected, hung over, cold, and unshaven in the dark shack and stumbled out into a foggy morning. Nobody in the cafe-cum-store at Joyce seemed to care and I ate a hearty breakfast while Chip drank all the coffee he could hold.

Before returning to the airfield, Chip also bought a roll of two inch masking tape. Back at the airplane he took the opened bundle of notes and divided it between us. Instructing me to use the notes to buy gas for the truck and fill the cans with 'regular'.

Then he taped the box shut and sealed them all with the tape. I was to drive the truck to the next waypoint and meet him there. He put the one opened box in the truck and the two unopened boxes in the plane. I retaliated by taking his bag of booze, taping it shut and parking it behind the seat in the truck. He then took the roll of tape and put it in the plane. It was all so dramatic, I didn't dare to laugh.

I had figured it correctly. The plane would be unable to take off until the fog lifted clear of the runway, about midday. The drive would take all day. I'd have to leave right away for us to meet at approximately the same time. He'd have no problem making a solo take-off, he'd done it many times. We shook hands and I drove away.

Joyce and Pugsley were waiting for me with a bag-full of groceries at the store and we set off together on our next big adventure. We hadn't gone far before it became evident that Pugsley was not going to settle down and we stopped and set her on the tool-box with a short leash, tied to the handle on top of one of the 'jerry-cans'. She struggled for a while to get comfortable and finally lay down with her nose against the back window of the cab.

The wind and vibration soon had her asleep and Joyce was at last able to relax.

"You're going to need some money." I said, passing her my wallet. "Take about eight or nine hundred in hundreds and another couple of hundred in twenties." Her eyes were wide with surprise at the bundle of hundreds Chip had passed over to me. He hadn't made any attempt to count them, merely dividing the bundle in half. Fifty of them together with the wad of twenties and a few fifties I'd collected in exchange for the two thousand I'd changed earlier, made the wallet unduly fat.

"I've never seen so much money in all my life." She said finally.

"Well don't flash it around, or someone may want to steal it, while others might ask awkward questions as to where you got it especially around Joyce."

She picked out a few and I made her fold each one separately into quarters and put them away in a fold of her purse. The twenties she stacked in the same purse unfolded.

"After you put the car in my driveway, take the boxes of Mobil oil out of the trunk and stow them under the saw in the workshop. You can't miss it. It's on top of a big white stand in the middle of the shop. There's a door on the back of the white stand, which just lifts up, so you can remove the sawdust, which falls inside. Stack the boxes inside the stand and cover them with the sawdust so they're hidden.

O.K.?" Joyce nodded her head and I carried on. "Catch the bus at the crossroads, just by the house, and go back to Port Angeles and buy yourself a ticket at a travel agent from P.A. to Garden City Kansas. Get a return ticket. Tell them you have to travel right away, first possible flight. Leave the return date open. If you have to explain the rush, tell them your mother has suddenly been taken critically ill and you want to go see her immediately. If there's any question about paying in cash say you haven't got a checking account and this is your life's savings or some-such."

"I'm not a very good liar." Joyce said reluctantly.

"I know dear." I replied sincerely. "That's another reason I like you so much. "But you're a wonderful actress. Don't give you're your address or mine, remember. I expect the Ticket will cost about four or five hundred dollars. at least." I added, seeing her surprise.

As the miles rolled by under the wheels, I schooled Joyce on more details of my plan. I had to liberate my car from the parking lot at PRAIF inc. and she would drive it back to my house. She was not to go near her house or the airfield, on the way there. Also, I needed her to pick up my mail at the P.O.Box, put the packet of my Ident. papers in the safety deposit box, for which I had to give her a note and the key and bring the keys and the rest of the mail to join me somewhere along the route.

Garden City was the nearest place of any size to our third destination and she was to book in at the motel nearest to the airport there. I'd find her there under our assumed name.

We cracked another hundred in Astoria filling the Jerry cans and the truck, and another in the little restaurant there by the bridge. She hadn't seen this part of the route on our first trip down and was very impressed with the beauty of the countryside.

It was almost quitting time at the 'factory' when I picked up my car without incident, the guard at the gate barely looked at my badge and I wasted no time in searching for Big-shoes or hanging around to talk with anyone. I didn't even ask for my paycheck, just joined the crowd and quit my job for what I hoped would be a more lucrative pastime.

I collected the rented computer, printer, and other gadgets, and locked them in the wooden toolbox in the back of the pickup, before checking out of the Motel.

The rental store was closed, so I put another hundred in an envelope with a note requesting extension of the rental for another month, and slid it under the door.

I kissed Joyce passionately in the parking lot and we parted on our respective missions. Pugsley made quite a fuss when she realized Joyce had gone, but I cuddled her on my lap as I drove and she soon went back to sleep. Joyce had made me promise to look after her when she realized we hadn't time to get the necessary immunization papers for her to travel by airline.

Chip raised quite a ruckus when we met at his private airport, but I told him it was a case of 'Love me, love my dog' and he threw his hands up and said.

"If it pukes in the airplane, you get to clean it up. It ain't traveling with me."

By that remark I gathered he was driving tomorrow.

After filling the airplane tanks and tying her down, we drove to the designated Motel. Chip, having retrieved the bag of bottles when we got back in the truck, had finished off the remains of his bottle of McNaughton's and was almost asleep by the time we reached the motel.

As I drifted towards sleep myself, I imagined Joyce still driving North across Oregon and prayed she would have enough sense to stop somewhere and take a motel for the night. Roba, put in an another appearance and talked about the developments that had taken place since his last visit. He seemed very pleased, that I had found a happy bond of companionship with Joyce, and, by taking his advice, I had been able to renew my acquaintance with an old friend.

However he did advise me not to get too attached to the DH-84.

"She's feeling her age." He said, cryptically. "Look to the ladies to outlast her."

I tried to 'pump' him for more explanation but he only inferred that Joyce knew how to swim. I couldn't quite grasp his meaning. In any case I woke feeling disturbed by his visit, to find Pugsley curled up in bed beside me.

The 'Airfields' Chip had established, were rudimentary twenty-foot wide grass strips, well off the beaten track of the automotive culture. Each had a metal gate with a sheet steel notice; "U.S. Government Property" welded to the middle rail.

It must have taken him months of preparation to have set them up approximately five hundred miles apart from the northern California seaboard, to southern Florida. He must also have had help, and although I'd made several references to this fact, he studiously avoided telling me anything about it.

In the end, I deduced that he and Henry must have been conspirators in this venture.

Henry's sudden disappearance must have upset Chip's plans, and the murder of the two replacements had probably been the last straw. Things had obviously got completely out of hand and Chip had decided it was time to cut his losses and run. Did he know about the other box of money? I didn't think so, but the more I thought about how fortuitous for him, my induction into the company had been, the more suspicious I became, that somewhere along the line, he intended to 'dump' me.

Such is the tenuous nature of the relationship between thieves, that I found myself beginning to hone my own larcenous instincts to a razor's edge.

There was also an incongruously parsimonious aspect to his character that surfaced again at the motel. He wanted to share a room to save money. I almost laughed in his face as I insisted he snored too loudly for mine and Pugsley's comfort, and in any case, the extra cost was coming out of my share. I however conceded to getting rooms with an adjoining door, so we could react more quickly in an emergency.

We each carried our boxes into our respective rooms rather than risk leaving them in the truck. Other than them, we had no luggage except our liquor and our flight bags. On the trip down, I had bought a bottle of Harvey's Bristol Cream Sherry. Actually I like it, but the main reason was that Pugsley liked it too. So much so, that I suspected we'd turned her into an alcoholic the first day we picked her up.

Sad, but it was much easier sneaking her into a motel asleep. The rented computer and accessories were packed into the fancy toolbox across the front of the pickup bed, which was locked, and both the keys were in my pocket. In addition, the Jerry cans made access to it almost impossible. I felt quite safe leaving it there. Even if Chip decided to break into it sometime when he was driving, I doubted if he would tamper with anything. My only concern was that he might have an accident. But, I had at least a month before the owner might get excited. Even then, by that time, one more looking for Mr. Gingham, wouldn't matter.

At six am. I got up and shaved. Chip was still snoring so I woke him and gave him one of my disposable razors to shave with. Meanwhile, I confiscated the remaining bottles, put them back behind the seat in the truck, and stacked the three boxes on the floor.

The motel didn't provide coffee, but a small cafe next door did, so I fetched him a couple of cups, and let Pugsley out to relieve herself. We ate a rather greasy breakfast there and throughout the meal, under cover of the loud music, I badgered Chip about his excessive drinking.

"Having a drunkard for a partner in this operation wasn't part of the deal." I snarled in my best Bogart whisper.

"We're a team. Until we split at the islands.

You're damn well not fit to fly today, and if you don't sober up and cool it with the drink, you won't be fit to drive either."

He started raising his voice in protest but I shut him up, hissing that I was taking charge of the operation until he sobered up.

"I'm flying the plane today! With All the boxes!.

If you expect to see any of them again, you'd better meet me there." He simmered down then but I caught the momentary flash of malevolence in his eye. 'Another Henry.' I thought, reaching across the table and clasping his right hand between both of mine.

"Listen Chum. We'll never make it by fighting." I said quietly smiling at him. "We need each other. I can't make it alone any more than you can. It's you and me, against the rest of the world. Remember?. There's no place for drinking or any other weakness until we've done it. I'm totally on your side; and I need you on mine." I ended, squeezing his hand warmly before releasing it.

I think this must have been a turning point for him. The sudden show of warmth on my part seemed to relax him and for a moment his eyes misted before he looked down at his plate and continued eating.

It was strange to find myself alone with Pugsley and the Dominee on a small private airstrip. Chip, more relaxed and cheerful than I'd ever seen him, had been gone almost an hour before the sun came out and warmed the ground mist off the runway. I'd left the bottles behind the seat as a measure of my 'trust' in him, feeling fairly sure he trusted me to be there when he arrived at 'point C'. Now it was my turn to search my own conscience.

The steam rising off the wings as I made my final preflight inspections was like my own desire to own this beauty, dissolving before the lure of wealth. Here it was, all mine including almost two million dollars in cash. But with no effective plan of my own, I had no chance of ever escaping with it alone.

I strapped Pugsley in the right seat and settled her down before starting the engines. During the run-up I had to reach over and pet her again but she soon relaxed and I just let her struggle during the take off until I could throttle back in the climb out. After cowering down, she gradually relaxed and sat up to survey her new surroundings. When I leveled off at my cruising altitude she seemed to be quite at ease.

I think it was during this flight that I realized how shallow my desire to steal this airplane had been. I enjoyed the beauty of the mountains below me, as I had done so often in the past when flying across the Cascades between Seattle and Colville in my Luscombe, and suddenly, I felt sated with it. This was, I decided, just another operation. I named it 'Operation Loot-Squared' since I was really stealing what had already been stolen, and my whole future depended on it's success. I arrived over Ely Nevada almost exactly three hours after take off. Chip's Landing as I decided to call these fields was six miles southeast of the little town. Like the others in the book it was about half a mile long, half a mile into the fields from the road, running parallel to the road and clearly identifiable from the air by the broad white line along each side. There were no other markers, wind socks on masts can be seen too easily from the roads. On arrival, one must look for natural indicators like waves in the grass, dust, or smoke to determine the direction for a landing, and be prepared to go around or buzz the strip if stray animals are in evidence. I gave the strip a thorough examination from low level before touching down. I taxied back to the downwind end, turned around, shut down the engines, got myself and Pugsley out and then tied the airplane down securely with the goat tethers. (Big cork-screws that needed a piece of steel pipe to turn them in the hard ground). It would have taken a full gale to pull her loose.

Where it had taken little less than four hours for the flight, it took Chip almost ten hours of hard driving to get there. He was tired and hungry but sober when he arrived and he could not have doubted the genuine pleasure I displayed when greeting him. We wasted little time unloading the boxes into the pickup and heading for town.

The next day, it was my turn to drive. The flight to rendezvous 'D', about fifteen miles south of Garden City in Kansas, was 540 miles. The distance by road, was 680 miles and we agreed it would be well after dark by the time I arrived, so Chip would use the crop dusters airport at Sublette and stay at the motel at the junction of highways 83 and 56. If I could make it there before midnight, I'd drive right through. If not, I'd find a motel somewhere along highway 50 for the night, and meet him at our rendezvous airfield by noon next day. I had to give him credit for the meticulous detail of his plan, it even included the phone number of the motel he'd be using. Naturally this arrangement suited my own plan to a tee, and I drove light-hearted, at the thought of meeting Joyce in Garden City.

I was, none the less, unprepared for the elegant curly haired beauty that greeted me at the door of room 124.

We swept into a crazy dance in the confined passage between the credenza and the beds, finally tumbling onto one of them in a passionate embrace. The alcoholic Pugsley who had been wrapped up in my jacket, came back to life, yipping excitedly and trying to lick Joyce's face in place of me.

I surrendered, and got up to close the door before the ruckus alerted the motel security. Joyce with Pugsley folded in her arms eventually managed to get up and I wrapped myself happily around the two of them.

Joyce had arrived early in the afternoon and after signing in at the motel, had gone on a spree in the town to a beauty parlor where she'd had the full treatment, including even her toenails, which, like her new fingernails, were a vivid rose color.

She'd bought a new dress in a bright black and orange design reminiscent of Aztec paintings, with a loose blouse and a full skirt.

Her toes peeped elegantly out from between the leather straps of her new sandals.

Back at the motel she'd carefully assembled all this below a pair of gold earrings that must easily have cost a hundred dollars, and just waited for this moment.

Pugsley and I were successfully swept off our feet.

We breakfasted gaily together in a small cafe on the road to Sublette and arrived at the airfield at eleven o'clock. The gate was open and we drove right up beside the Dominee. I had expected some reaction from Chip when he saw Joyce, but I was totally unprepared for what actually took place.

I have never in my life, seen two adults so suddenly and utterly smitten with one-another. Though Joyce immediately tried to hide it from me, I knew right there, that I'd lost her.

Numbly, I participated in the loading and refueling of the plane. I even joked about carrying Chip's share of the loot to make room for Joyce and Pugsley in the truck, and watched in dumb dismay, with the taste of her last kiss on my lips, as they drove away.

When they disappeared from sight, I closed the gate and walked on rubbery legs to the plane. My breakfast decided to leave me as well, and I clung weakly to the wing tip for support until my strength came back. I felt like I'd been shot in the stomach. Such is the power of our emotions. I sat in the pilot seat unable to take off. I think I laid my head on the controls and wallowed in self-pity until it all left me drained. Maybe I slept it off. Maybe Roba came and chided me for my weakness. Whatever. I found myself flying again at eleven thousand feet, over the sprawl of Oklahoma City, headed for destination 'E' of the plan. Presently I saw Texarkana below me and began the search, for Newelton on the Louisiana side, and Port Gibson on the Mississippi side, of that mighty river. I spent almost half an hour flying at under a thousand feet along the Louisiana side of the river between Newelton and Clayton as the sun went down, before I spotted the strip along the edge of a cane-field. The surrounding terrain looked pretty wet, but the strip was dry and I put the Dominee down in the gathering darkness at exactly five pm by my watch. Allowing for the time change, and the four hours it would have taken to fly the 540 miles, I must have taken off at one o'clock Kansas time. I judged it had taken me best part of two hours misery to come to my senses, and I still had no recollection of taking off.

Outside the airplane the mosquitoes were murderous. Inside, with every vent and window closed, I sprayed the 'Off' that Chip had thoughtfully left with me, on every part of me that wasn't covered and then covered myself with a blanket and tried to sleep on the sloping floor of the cabin. Between the whine of the insects and my fevered thoughts about what Chip and Joyce were probably doing; I could not decide which tormented me the most.

By morning, I could have decapitated Chip, Cut Joyce into ribbons and sprayed every living thing in Louisiana with concentrated DDT.

As the light of day returned, my bitterness seemed to have congealed inside my heart and I lay on my back on the hard sloping floor with my feet against the aft bulkhead thinking about the loss I had suffered. Chip had, without even trying, robbed me of my companion and my crazy dream of an exotic future with her and the money behind the bulkhead.

I sat up and unzipped the cover panel to have another indifferent look at what now seemed an empty, purposeless project. What could I do with my share? Or theirs for that matter?.

All I truly wanted had been stripped from me. The three boxes were securely stored there by the cargo tie downs, bungee cords with hooked ends, and two to each box. They weren't going anywhere.

Then something about the way they were tied down struck me like a blow in the stomach.

Chip, bless his sweet trusting heart, had secured the three boxes inside the baggage compartment with the bungee straps provided for that purpose. It should have taken only a few seconds to free any box, except for the fact that he had taped the bungee cords to the top of each box.

Any attempt to remove a box would tear the tape and reveal that the box had been tampered with. If either end of a cord was detached from its anchorage, the resulting tension on the other end, would likewise tear the tape. To ensure that I did not tamper with this set-up, he had also written his name across the tape where it crossed the cords. Even a slight distortion of the tape would thus be exposed. In addition, he had taken pliers and pinched the metal hooked ends shut.

I think it was this overt lack of trust that finally decided my course of action.

I puzzled over the problem for several minutes, visualizing what would happen to the tape if I tried to release the cords. Finally I hit on the solution. If the cord must remain in its stretched condition while I removed the hooked ends, all I need do would be to tie the bungee cord fast to both ends of a length of stiff material such as a piece of cane. There was no shortage of cane at hand.

In the lid of my briefcase, there are two partitions for holding manila files, or thin books. In the course of much traveling I have learned the need for a tool kit. In the early days, I carried the tools loose in the case.

Airport security persistently required me to 'open up' and show them what all this metal was.

Finally, I got smart and made a thin toolbox from a 'how to do it' book. I glued all the pages together and routed out the middle of this block with my router. This gave me a nice thin tool case with a place for each tool and a perfect X-Ray display of the contents without the need to open up and go through their routine search. If Chip had looked in the brief case, all he'd see would be a book in the file holder.

I bound the bungees tight to the canes with fishing line and straightened the hooks at each end with a small pliers.

Then, working both ends at the same time, I freed each bungee cord without disturbing the tape.

Two minutes with the box upside down on the cabin floor, my razor-knife opened up the bottom of the box. I replaced the blocks of money with a matrix of sugarcane and earth to approximate the weight and volume of the removed material and glued the bottom back as slick as originally, with superglue.

I set each box back in the rack with the bungee hooks closed as before, around the anchor rings, and carefully removed the braces. You could not tell it had ever been moved. The third box, the one we had already dipped into, I left untouched, figuring that if they needed money before ditching me, they'd take it from this box rather than open either of the others. And, there was still one more leg before showdown. Besides, this was supposed to be my box, so why rob myself?

Each bundle of ten thousand was individually wrapped in waxed paper and I packed them, in blocks of ten, inside one of the black plastic garbage bags I'd transferred earlier, from the truck toolbox to my briefcase. I then extracted the air from this bag by sucking it out, until it collapsed tightly around the stack. I twisted and tied the neck and placed this bundle inside a second bag and repeated the vacuum packing. After nightfall, I carried it to the corner of the cane field and, having no tools to dig with, buried it carefully, under a stack of old dried canes.

The second night was worse than the first.

I do not recall such mental torment since my wife Mary died. That agony had been spread over four long weeks of increasing hopelessness, watching the precious flame of her life, dwindling like an exhausted candle, until it finally flickered out, leaving me in empty darkness.

This severance, had happened in an instant.

It was as if a huge knife blade had fallen out of a clear blue sky, across my forehead, slicing down through eyes nose mouth chest belly knees and somehow missed my toes, leaving me standing like a sectioned anatomical dummy.

The cold wind entered all my open pipes as my soul slipped through the missing facade, and fell, face down in the Mississippi mud.

Soulless, my love for Joyce, which had grown steadily since our first encounter, turned in a few seconds, to a bitterness that poisoned every worthy aspect of my being.

Only my hearing survived, rendering me intensely aware of the infernal noise of all the insects in Louisiana clamoring to break through the taut fabric of the Dominee's fuselage, and consume what was left of me. I cowered under my blanket, firing occasional blasts of 'Off' at the imaginary invaders, until the can was exhausted and I fell asleep.

I was awakened by voices outside the plane.

The sky was overcast with a light drizzle falling. My watch said, nine thirty. Adjusting for the local time that was nearer eleven thirty. Chip, Joyce and Pugsley, looked fresh and full of life. Why not, they'd been sleeping in a nice clean bed in an air-conditioned room somewhere.

I stumbled out of the plane, looking like a hobo disturbed by the railway cops, bleary eyed, unshaven and dirty.

"What the hell took you so long?" I asked accusingly. Chip shrugged, not meeting my eyes, "It was a long drive." he replied non-committally, as Joyce moved between us and put her arms around me. "Was it that bad honey?" She asked, holding me tightly and kissing my forehead like a mother consoling an aggrieved child.

"This place isn't exactly the Ritz." I replied trying to respond with warmth I didn't feel. All through the lonely night, I had been schooling myself not to make a scene, and yet, when the time came, I felt awkward and clumsy.

"I'm hungry and filthy," I said by way of an excuse, "not to mention tired, and bitten to buggery by mosquitoes." I tried to smile, but it must have looked as phony as it felt. "I'd like to get the hell out of here as quickly as possible." I concluded with real sincerity. "This wasn't one of your better choices." I said, turning to Chip. "There's nothing but mud if you get off the runway and the motel is on the other side of the river."

"There's a boat across the road. Didn't you?.

Obviously not." He stopped, in mid sentence as I retorted

"There's a post. and a piece of rope. but no damned boat. I hope the next place is better organized."

From the corner of my eye I saw Pugsley trotting off towards pile of dried cane at the edge of the field and called to her to come back.

I looked back to Joyce, and with what I hoped was a smile said, "Perhaps you'd better grab her before she gets bitten by a snake or an alligator. Chip and I'd best be refueling and getting things ready for the next leg so we three can get on the road. I need a bath and a shave."

I knew instantly, by the sudden change in her face, that, as I'd suspected, I'd be making that trip in the truck alone.

"Pugsley! get back here!" I yelled as the pup started in the direction of the pile of dried canes. "Cum-ere!!. You call her." I pleaded with Joyce. "That ditch is full of snakes and alligators."

That got some action and Joyce started in the same direction calling and coaxing Pugsley while Chip and I set about refueling.

When the Jerry cans had all been emptied into the airplane tanks, Chip announced that this next leg would need more fuel because of adverse prevailing winds across the Gulf and he'd decided to carry four extra cans of fuel that could be pumped into the tanks in flight. That meant he needed Joyce to go with him since it couldn't be done by a solo pilot. I argued that I could just as well fly again with her but he pointed out my condition and my need of rest. It would be a long flight. He was familiar with the destination area, and would more able than I to find the rendezvous, etc. etc. I argued just enough to convince him I wanted to fly and keep Joyce with me but each of my suggestions got shot down and in the end, to the relief of them both, I surrendered.

We drove to the gas station, refilled the Jerry cans, and secured four of them to the backs of the two seats in the plane.

Before going to the baggage compartment to take out the middle box from the bungee cords, I made sure the arrangement of rubber pipes and squeeze bulbs was working O.K. and that Joyce knew how to transfer the fuel.

"What the hell's all this for!?" I exclaimed as though seeing his tape job for the first time, and turned to face the two of them with a look of disgust. "What did you think I was going to do? Take it out and play with it while waiting for you.?. You dull shit!"

I turned my back and ripped the bungees off the middle box and started for the door with it. "I've a Damn good mind to take it all with me just to make sure you turn up at the next rendezvous.!" I shouted from the doorway before carrying it to the truck.

Pugsley made her usual fuss as I set the box on the floor and I was just petting her when Chip started the engines. I saw Joyce getting back into her seat and realized he'd told her to secure the door, and would probably take off before I could carry out my threat.

I rushed from the passenger side round the front of the truck and jumped into the drivers seat and realized he'd also taken the keys with him knowing I'd try to drive the truck in front of the plane to prevent him taking off.

I jumped out of the truck and ran to get in front of the plane making frantic signals to show I needed the keys, but he just continued with his run-up. I raced round to Joyce's side making pleading gestures and miming myself trying to turn the keys and pointing at the truck. I saw her say something to him and he laughed and started the take off roll leaving me with every appearance of despair.

I sank down on my knees as she passed, clasping my hands in mimed prayer. It only resulted in a more distressed expression on her face as the plane gathered speed.

Halfway down the runway the graceful bird lifted off and climbed straight ahead to about three hundred feet and then banked into a shallow turn.

I had time to pick up Pugsley and climb up onto the hood where I stood holding her watching the plane circle the field and come in for a low approach over the runway.

I could see Joyce at the right aft window and as the plane passed over along the left side of the runway; she tossed something white out of the window. It fell streaming to the ground a few yards from us and I jumped down and told

Pugsley to fetch it. She came back to me triumphantly dragging Joyce's scarf with the keys tied to the other end.

Chip treated us to one more fly-by and a farewell wave from

Joyce, before he and the Dominee flew away out of our lives forever.

When, at the end of an hour they had not returned, I retrieved the hidden plastic bags and stowed their contents, evenly spread over the bottom of the tool box under the plastic, with the tools, fishing gear, my computer and other office equipment covering them completely.

Pugsley I think, sensed my state of desolation and tried to comfort me on the long drive to Florida, lying quietly beside me in the cab with her head in my lap. The skittish puppy we had bought at Eureka, to compensate Joyce for her loss, had suddenly grown up into a loving companion.

I knew in my heart, Chip had no intention of showing up at the next rendezvous. The extra fuel had not been special extra to account for adverse wind but to give them the extra range needed to reach the Caymans directly. However, I kept my side of that bargain, just in case, and we arrived at the 'Jump-off' airfield in good time for the planned rendezvous, for the final leg to the islands.

After ten days, moping, loafing and fishing in the Florida swamps around the rendezvous, I gave up hope.

I bought a camper-van in Fort Lauderdale, transferred our treasures to it and sold the truck to a Cuban in Miami. We drove our 'luxury home', back to the rendezvous airfield in the Everglades, and spent several extra days camped in that area just in case they came back. but as hope of this dissolved in the wet weather conditions, I decided that a boat would be a better vehicle and bought a thirty six foot motor sailer in Fort Lauderdale boatyard.

In a little publicized, ceremony we re-named her 'The Sugarcane'.

After surreptitiously moving most of the treasure aboard, hidden inside concrete casings, which we made, to augment the existing ballast, we secured the campervan into a long time storage facility. and Pugsley and I went on a two year long odyssey in a fruitless search for our lost love.

Somehow, it seemed that Roba never showed up again either, so I don't know if he was satisfied, or just disgusted.

Epilogue

Those ten days of idleness in the Florida Sunshine on the edge of the Everglades did much to mellow the hurting inside me at losing Joyce. I rationalized finally that it was my bruised pride that I was tormenting myself with, rather than any deep love I had lost. However, I really enjoyed her down to earth nature and the obvious pleasure she had shown in our intimate moments which I presumed were now being enjoyed by Chip. My anger diffused and was replaced by a growing sense of concern that she and Chip must have gone down at sea. I had not wanted such a disaster to enter her life as a result of my nefarious activities.

Unheralded as their flight to Grand Cayman had been, there would be no search called for. I was sure no Flight plan had been filed. I wanted to raise the alarm only for her sake. Chip deserved whatever fate had sent him. I finally decided there was no point now in possibly involving myself with the authorities over what would, in all probability, result in a fruitless endeavour and a whole lot of needless publicity.

If they hadn't crashed in the sea, I felt sure they certainly would have come looking for me as soon as they discovered what had happened to the cash.

I'd given them ten whole days after my arrival, added to the three days the road journey had taken. Plenty of time to get from Grand Cayman back to Florida, by almost any mode of transportation. They were not short of money. That I knew from the fact that at least three of the blocks of bills which should have been in the box which was supposed to have been my share, were gone.

I scanned the papers every day for any possible indications of a plane crash elsewhere along the overland section of their route without success. Much as I normally deplore the hysteria given by the media to plane accidents, in this case I felt frustrated by its absence.

After securing the money and the camper in a safe mini storage at Fort Lauderdale, Pugsley and I went on a two year jaunt in the motor-sailor I bought there. If anyone had ever asked either of us why we never rested long in any harbor, we'd both have admitted we were hoping to find Joyce. There was always that unspecified motivation for our journeying.

Even on sandbars and coral atolls which were barely awash, Pugsley had to jump over, swim ashore and make a complete circuit before returning to the boat. I didn't need to ask what she'd been looking for, or explain why I left these particular trips to her alone. I talked to her a great deal of the time and I swear she understood most of what I said.

In Puerto Rico, I bought and installed an Auto-Helm (Sailboat autopilot) and Pugsley even sat watches at night and would only awaken me if something extraordinary occurred.

We scoured the Caribbean, visiting every major and minor port on every island, starting with the Cayman Islands, without finding even a trace of either Chip or Joyce. When Pugsley came of age, I had to have her sterilized, not neutered. Consequently, she enjoyed enormous popularity among the ever present strays that seem to haunt every port and village we visited. At some ports, potential suitors even swam out after the boat as we motored out from the harbor, with her standing on the transom railing, howling farewell or encouragement to the swimmers and scolding me with her big mournful eyes, as I increased power, leaving them behind.

For a young lady she had a very complete education in canine infidelity and heartbreak, but throughout all this, she remained faithful to me and never had to be brought aboard by force.

The possibility of the authorities getting wind of my connection to Henry and his malevolence, had haunted me for a few days until I decided to buy the boat and lay a false trail for them by sending a Fax from my computer to Kamm. I told him I was leaving from New York to go to England to take care of family matters there and would get in touch later from there. I gave a fictitious New York address in case he ever got around to sending a reply, which I hadn't asked for. If he did, of course the connection would not have worked, and I presumed he would make no further attempts, attributing the problem to some stupidity of mine.

Despite our high profile and constant enquiries as to their whereabouts, and given the fact that I'd 'stolen' their share of the loot, if Chip or Joyce ever saw us, they failed to make contact.

Finally I was forced to accept the sad probability that they'd gone down somewhere at sea. Victims of some mystical Oceanic peril such as the infamous Bermuda Triangle perhaps.

As far as I could ascertain, they had never been heard of in the Caymans or anywhere else.

Each April, I sent a postal draft to prevent delinquent taxes from accumulating on Joyce's property, and also contacted the Electricity Utility and paid a year in advance.

I could tell you I felt impelled to do this, to assuage my sense of responsibility for getting her involved in my 'caper'. In truth, I was more concerned to avoid the authorities having a reason to investigate her absence. And then again, she might have survived, penniless, in the Caribbean (Roba had inferred she knew how to swim) and if that meant anything, she might eventually make her way back to her home only to find it had been sold by the County for back taxes. I did the same thing for my own electricity water and taxes and it seemed the most prudent thing to do to protect my interest in her airfield, under the circumstances.

Finally, convinced that neither she nor Chip were anywhere in this part of the globe, I decided to return to my old haunts in the Pacific Northwest.

Who knows what strange forces propel us to do the most irrational things ?

Every indication had lead me to conclude that Chip and Joyce must have been lost at sea. Otherwise, they'd have been searching for me and their money, even more assiduously perhaps, than I'd searched for them. They'd expect me to eventually show up in my old haunts sometime, and Chip at least would have laid a trap. He, I felt very sure, would not let me get away with the money he'd worked so long and so hard to purloin.

He'd been counting on making it to Grand Cayman and going to ground out there, into a secure and well funded retirement.

Meeting up with Joyce would have been the frosting on his cake. But when they got there they'd have realized that I had the cake. So, why did I decide to plant myself and the loot, right where they'd have the best chance of finding me? Was I simply torturing myself with the faint hope that Joyce was still alive? Still caring? I felt I could understand Barbara's mind a little better now. But look where it got her, with my assistance of course.

On the long journey, diagonally across America, taking in the sights I had neglected to see, like the Grand canyon and Yellowstone Park, I allowed my beard and hair to grow until I became a disreputable looking old man. My residual British accent, I masked, simply by mumbling.

Even Kamm failed to recognize me when I walked up to his hangar and asked if he could direct me to Henry Erickson's place.

Kamm is fond of dogs, and made an immediate fuss of Pugsley and I suddenly realized that she was part of my disguise. I'd always declared; "I'd never have a dog," citing the many reasons why not.

He followed us as Pugsley and I wandered off in the direction he had given, and as I surveyed the unkempt garden, he asked me where and how I had come to know myself.

I had the greatest difficulty suppressing my mirth, but in the end I walked away after telling him I'd met myself in Florida several months ago and been invited to visit if I ever got up in this area.

He'd invited me in to talk about our mutual friend but I felt sure I could never maintain my act under those circumstances and after assuring him I was still alive and well in Florida when I left, we walked away and wandered back to the camper with its Florida license plates, and I bade him farewell.

From this encounter I concluded that there had been no hue and cry from any authorities, regarding my whereabouts, and felt comfortable in visiting Joyce's place to see how it had fared during the two years of neglect.

The garden had suffered a severe invasion of thistle, thorn and blackberry vines, which effectively protected the house from insult. The door key, a little rusty under its brick in the patio, eventually let us in, but it took a week to recover the garden from the encroaching briar and jack-thorn bushes.

Pugsley sniffed and searched around for Joyce for the first couple of hours, but finally joined me in an uneasy tolerance of the house that had been her home for a short while. Like me, I think she sensed its hollowness.

When I cautiously checked, it was evident the airfield hadn't been used for a long time either, and an industrial brush cutter and mower would be required to restore it.

The shack in the trees seemed even more deserted. I spent one whole day, removing all traces of my camera set-ups, before finally closing the door and leaving the forest to bury everything in fallen branches and pine needles once more.

At one time, I'd felt a deep desire to own this airfield myself, but now, everything reminded me too forcibly, that it had probably been the potential proximity to Joyce that had lured me.

After restoring some kind of order in her little farm, I took time to search the archives of the Forks and Port Angeles libraries for any references to the disorder we'd left in Forks. I had no inclination to return there myself but felt sure the bizarre event there must have hit the headlines sometime. Although I scanned every copy I could find of every local paper, there was nothing. I mean Nothing. I found it hard to believe that those two corpses were still lying undisturbed in an empty house for two years. Somebody, maybe 'Big shoes' must have quietly cleared up the mess. But as Roba would have said, "Curiosity killed the cat." I had no other reason to investigate. I had not been personally involved there. and eventually I told myself "Leave it alone."

Somebody had evidently cleared away the mess before the neighbors called in the local police and that somebody might still be watching.

I had been very personally involved in the even more bizarre events in Brinnon, so I moved camp to Port Townsend, and began a similar search through the Jefferson County archives there. Finding a similar dearth of interest, I went to Shelton thinking the event might have been reported there, but met a similar blank wall.

The anonymity of my unshaven self was becoming a detriment to doing business with the bank and other services in the area, so I headed back to Sequim and wandered into Fred's barbershop one afternoon when the place was empty of other customers and invited him to 'Unravel the man beneath the bush.' I was surprised to see how pale my face appeared after just a few months shielded from the sun.

At the bank, I recognized none of the tellers, mute testimony to the turnover these days. But, after checking my balance the young lady attending me was considerably more congenial.

I was almost shocked myself, to see what two years of neglect had done when she handed me the slip on which she had jotted down the total.

I retrieved the papers that Joyce had placed in the safety deposit box for me, and returned to the camper-van to restore myself to myself again.

After much thought, I hid Mr. Gingham's credentials under the mattress in the camper. I'd originally been intending to destroy them, until I realized I, was driving, his van.

Sequim is a town where the Snowbirds come back each Spring and leave each Fall. There is a well fenced mini-storage cum R-V parking area, which fills and empties with southern number-plates in rhythm with the seasons.

I parked Mr. Gingham's van there and Pugsley and I caught the bus to my own place.

I had been there for three days clearing up the debris of two years neglect, before Kamm discovered there was someone living in my place and came over to investigate.

He was delighted to see me and was in the middle of telling me all about my friend's recent visit, when Pugsley came trotting round from her kennel.

He stared from her to me, back and forth several times until the penny dropped.

"It was You?! With a DOG?! I don't Believe it!' He roared, giving me a brotherly hug.

We spent much of the rest of that day exchanging news, and I gave him a condensed version of my adventures in the sailboat, which I knew would soon reach most of the other pilots who knew me, and be easy to duplicate if necessary.

During the course of the conversation, he asked me if I had been able to contact the young woman with the red Ferrari who had been asking for me shortly after I disappeared.

"Said you used to take her flying." He explained, seeing my surprise. "Came two or three times and finally left a note for you. I'll see if I can find it." He added as he left.

I hadn't really expected him to come back so soon. The letter had been delivered over two years ago and Kamm, being the busy man he is, would have inadvertently buried it under one of the piles of invoices or other documents he habitually stacks all around his office.

When I expressed my surprise that he'd found it, he proudly asserted he now had a 'model' office since he'd converted 'Everything' to the computer.

"No more files full of A-D notes and Service Bulletins.

'Everything'; FAR's included, are on the computer now. It only takes a few seconds to find things instead of hours of searching through books and pamphlets. You'd never believe the mountain of paperwork I burned a few months back."

"Did you ever get the telex I sent from New York?" I asked, studying the envelope he had just given me. He looked blankly at me for a few seconds, trying to remember.

"Oh yes. I tried to send you a reply but there was something wrong with the connection, I think." He was still searching his memory when I replied.

"No Problemma. I hadn't expected a reply anyway."

"Ah! That reminds me. You owe me seventy five bucks".

"I do?"

"Yes. I've paid your DPAA membership for the last three years." He said, smiling at my chagrinned expression. It was the one obligation, I'd not covered.

"Bless your heart. I completely forgot about it." I exclaimed, pulling out a hundred dollar bill from my wallet and handing it to him. "What would I do without you looking after me?"

Absent mindedly, I stuffed the letter in my pocket with the wallet as I was putting it away.

A few days later, in the post office to buy some stamps, I was standing in the queue of people waiting to get served, when I pulled out my wallet and found the letter.

Having nothing better to do, I opened it and studied Mary's neat writing. It was dated the day I'd left for Eureka.

The queue moved forward and I shuffled automatically along with it, reading.

Among other endearments, Mary had noted that she'd been trying to reach me for a couple of weeks, and was about to take up a new job, in Spokane. She would like to talk to me as soon as possible, as she was certain I'd be delighted to learn that she was pregnant, and what did I think of the names, Stuart Henry, for a boy or Erica Mary, for a girl?.

"Are you feeling alright Sir?" The postal clerk behind the counter asked anxiously, and I wondered why she seemed so concerned about me.

"Certainly!" I replied stiffly. "Could you please tell me when the next bus leaves for Spokane? I need to buy a ticket."

For a moment, she looked at me as if I were potentially dangerous and then she turned and spoke to the man at the other window. He came over and asked if he could help me.

"I need a ticket for the next bus to Spokane."

"This isn't the Greyhound Office Sir." He said quietly.

"This is the Post Office. We don't sell tickets. And anyway, Greyhound doesn't come through here any more. Hasn't in fact for almost two years. If you're anxious to get there quickly, I suggest you try the airline out of Port Angeles."

I mumbled my thanks for this information and left.

Pugsley, sleeping in the car, sensing my disorientation, jumped up and gave my ear an affectionate lick as I sat down and closed the door. I put my arm around her and hugged her to me. Her fur felt warm and re-assuring. Real and good. I knew she would support me again, just as she had done throughout our unsuccessful search for Joyce.

"I guess we'll simply have to drive over to Spokane and see if we can find the rest of the family." I told her with a sigh as I turned the key.

*   *   *

The letter had not been posted, so there was no date on the envelope; but it had been hand delivered to Kamm, only a couple of weeks after I had "disappeared."

I added and subtracted in my head the significant times and finally decided that her child would now be almost two years old. Stuart Henry or Erica Mary, whichever it was. My Son or my Daughter? There could be no question that Mary was carefully and positively letting me know she was sure it was my child.

I felt a strange sensation of elation and apprehention, mixed. Elation, to think I might have sired a child which had been denied to me so many years ago, when the doctors declared I was sterile; and a nagging fear that somehow it was going to be stolen away from me once more, by the bizarre series of events that had pre-occupied me for the past three years.

What would be the surname she had given? Had Mary gone off and got married to some younger man who she had collared, to provide for her illegitimate child? Had she gone through with the pregnancy when she failed to be able to reach me? The fearful side began to escalate as I pondered the many unknowns. I simply had to find out! The normal qualms a man might feel regarding his responsibility for the pregnancy didn't arise. I was single, and in the event it was established that the child was truly mine, I would be delighted to do the honoutable thing. Money was certainly not a factor. During the period I had been away, I had successfully sequestered the money, or at least three quarters of it, into legitimate bank accounts or investments. The original stack was still lying undisturbed, under the peat moss down in the garden shack. I had already checked and confirmed that item.

I could not imagine why I had asked for a bus ticket, in the Post Office, of all places! Something must have slipped in my head. If ever I had urgently needed to go to Spokane before, I would normally have flown there in my Luscombe. Well; the Luscombe was three years "out of Annual", so it would be some time before it was re-licensed, and I couldn't wait. Bent on getting over that problem, Pugsley and I went home. I unearthed a bundle of hundreds from the peat moss, packed a few changes of underwear, and some clothes, before catching the bus back to town to unearth 'Mr. Gingham's camper van'. Once I got the van started again and changed my wallet and identity, back to match, I realized I had completely forgotten to. 'Close up the house'. Back at the house, I shut off the water, etc., and Pugsley and I set off late that afternoon for Spokane.

I had absolutely no idea where to start looking for Mary. By the time I reached Discovery Bay I was feeling hungry, and stopped in at Fat Smitty's for a giant hamburger. If you've never had one of those, it's a treat or a test, waiting for you. I ate as much as I could and took the rest out for Pugsley. I set it beside the van while she wolfed it down and gave her a drink of water in her bowl. I won't let her eat in the van for obvious reasons. I then set off on our first diversion, to the old house of Mary's Grandmother, at Beckett Point.

The old couple who answered my knock on that symbolic, and still rusty, door knocker, were unable to give me any exact information, but explained that they had bought the property almost two years ago from Mary through a realty in Port Ludlow, which, naturally, was closed by the time I got there.

Rather than return to base for the night, I drove down to the launching ramp at Mats-Mats; and we spent a quiet if somewhat sleepless night there beside the tranquil water inside the harbor. Pugsley seemed happy to be beside the sea once more, and went on a little excursion to explore the beach before settling down for the night. During the stillness, I remembered a few of the details Mary had given me about her interests in Spokane, just before the disastrous events that had led to my sudden and unplanned departure. That was almost three years ago.

She had been studying to become licensed as a masseuse; and I remembered once more the intense pleasure that had stemmed from her touch on that fateful afternoon on Stuart Island. You might think that had been the start of everything, but it wouldn't be quite fair to her, as I had, despite the difference in our ages, fantasized intimacy with her long before that event. I minimized my sense of responsibility for the consequences, by ascribing the romantic circumstances, to our invigorating nude swim in the sea, and the consequential warm-up in the cabin, in front of the fire, stretched out together naked on the huge bearskin rug the owner had spread before the hearth. My only sense of obligation to him, whoever he was, was to someday replace the wood we had burned. I still hadn't done that yet. However, it occurred to me that if my search turned out successfully, I might actually owe him far more than I could ever hope to repay.

That momentous incident had occurred, shortly before the horror that occurred a few days later, of which Mary was totally ignorant. It was really the turning point in all of our lives, resulting in my impromptu departure with Joyce. Mary had left the area to take up her course of study at Gonzaga. Her decision to do this, had been a relief to me at that time, for she had been 'coming-on' a little too possessively, which had alarmed me slightly. Things had changed rather radically with the receipt of her letter. Somewhere in the depths of my ruminations, I must have become irrational, and decided to skip the search at the realty office, and go straight to Spokane in the morning.

I awoke to the sound of heavy machinery. The daylight was pink in the camper window and the air felt fresh on my face. Somewhere nearby, a rock crusher was at work and the sound of trucks moving past the camper brought the realization I had camped in the vicinity of a quarry. I remembered pulling off the road beside what I thought was the launching ramp at Mats-Mats. It had been blissfully quiet in the early nightfall and even semi romantic when the moon rose over the sea.

Pugsley got up from her bed under the table at the sound of my movement and yawned. I am always amazed at the way she can sleep though the external uproar and yet spring to life the moment I move in my bed.

On board the 'Sugarcane', the sail-boat we had lived on in the Carribbean, she was a puppy. She slept on the bare floor of the cockpit. Now, at three and a bit years, and ashore in the camper, she had a bed. Whereas I could not have risked a soft rag mat at sea, possibly blocking the scuppers of the cockpit floor during a storm; on land, I could no longer justify depriving her of such creature comforts. She had selected my old sea Pea-jacket and commandeered it one night after our 'Coming Ashore'. Henceforth, although I could not just leave it under the table all day, she would scratch at the floor and whine if I forgot to put it down for her at bedtime.

Last thing before going to sleep, I had intended to return to base and conduct my researches from there, rather than drive off into the dawn in search of someone I assumed, might be looking for me. Mary Lykes might be Mary Something-else by now and I might be fouling up an otherwise contented nest by butting in. Even if the child was truly mine which, in the cold light of day, I doubted, Mary might have found a surrogate father. Young and beautiful as she is, a determined woman could easily accomplish that. I wouldn't mind having a dollar for every time had been done, even when the guy knew the facts.

Then, consider the child. Perhaps he or she would find themself as the firstborn of a family with younger brothers and sisters.

How would they like it if some old geezer came along and proclaimed them to be his son or daughter?

I went about the day's chores with my mind still preoccupied. Coffee for me, hot. A saucer full for Pugsley, cool. Followed by, a walk down to the water's edge for me and a swim for her. Back to our mobile domicile for a bowl of corn flakes for both. We took a leisurely tour around Mats Mats, and arrived at the office of the Real Estate in Port Ludlow just as they were opening up. The people who had bought Mary's house in Becket Point had given me this address and I was hoping someone there, could tell me where Mary lived. Some correspondence with her must have occurred in the course of the sale and even if only a Bank account number was available, it would help.

The realtor, an attractive lady in her early fifties, was guardedly cautious about passing on any information she had until I explained the circumstances and finally showed her Mary's letter, which she read a couple of times before deciding. Finally she got up and went to a file cabinet and took out the file on the sale. The closing date was five months after I had left for the trip to Florida and points beyond.

The Fax I sent to Kamm from New York, would probably have been mentioned to Mary when she came to deliver her letter to me. Possibly that would have been enough to prompt her to sell out at Beckett Point. Doing so, would certainly have provided her with funds while she was unable to work. How sad are the circumstances we inflict on one another unintentionally.

Mary must have been showing distinct indications of her condition by that time, although the lady realtor herself seems not to have been aware of this, and the last communication from their office was two weeks after Closing. Also, Mary, to my relief, was still using her maiden name, Almost exactly two years and eight months ago. How much could have changed in the interim?

I wrote down the address, and then as an afterthought, asked the lady if she could give me a bank number or Mortgage Company reference, just in case Mary had moved in the meantime.

"I probably shouldn't, but you strike me as a man who would

not abuse the information." She looked me straight in the eye as if questioning her recollections of Mary's youth versus my obvious age, and I hastened to assure her I was only interested in doing whatever I could to help Mary.

"The last time I saw Mary was about a week before I left for Florida and I didn't have a chance to tell her I was leaving. It was a rather sudden emergency." I added seeing the quizzical look. "You see she had just left for Spokane to resume her college courses, and she hadn't sent me her new address," The eyebrows were still raised, so I put my foot further into my mouth by continuing the recital, "I had only met her a couple of weeks before that. She kept coming round to my place so we could go flying."

By this time the eyebrows were about to disappear into the hairline and I felt embarrassed when she started laughing.

"Sounds as if you two were flying pretty high Eh?"

I just wished I could remind myself to take my shoes off before putting my feet in my mouth. So I continued with the story of my life and we were both laughing when I left.

As I was going out of the door she handed me her business card and invited me to take her flying sometime.

It wasn't until we were crossing the Hood Canal bridge that the penny dropped. I realized, that once again, I had "Gone off half-cocked", and shuddered at the memory of another time when that had happened. I pulled over into the parking area at the east end of the bridge, sat and thought about what needed to be done first. Finally I started up the engine again, turned around and headed back across the bridge, to the Mobile home. I could make more progress in the search for Mary by enlisting the help of the lady realtor, and the telephone before rushing off into the blue like an overexcited child.

It was Friday,and the idea of plunging into the weekend traffic to Spokane, in search of Mary and whatever children she and I might have conceived, seemed decidedly futile as I thought more deeply about the ramifications involved. First of all I was old enough to be her grandfather and although this hadn't given her reason to reject me on that sunny afternoon on Stuart Island, it didn't make sense for me to rashly assume that by some miracle I had made her pregnant. Even though her letter inferred that while she was not exactly accusing me, she did want to indicate she considered me as the potential father.

For thirty years of married life, I had believed myself to be sterile, while my wife had been declared fertile. We had discussed the lack of children and how to live our lives together without that aspect of a marriage. Her career as a registered nurse and mine as an engineer were considered as sufficient reason to finally accept the condition.

Her sister had four children and we were often visited by that family. While they were infants, my wife, whose name was also Mary, and I enjoyed them as if they had been her own. However, with, I confess, gradually lessening enthusiasm for the experience, as they grew up. Towards the end, when the two nephews were busy getting into trouble with the law and the two nieces were busy getting into trouble with the lawless, we became more comfortably adjusted to our own situation. Tragically, she died childless.

I admit my attraction to Mary Lykes, had been distinctly biological, tempered only by a reluctant realization of the inequities in our ages. The events on Stuart Island had been as much of a surprise to me as the letter itself. I'm not saying I was not absolutely ecstatic at the afterthoughts, or my suppressed hopes for a repetition of the event. But I believe in being practical in setting goals or expectations.

Mary had left for Spokane shortly after the Stuart Island event. In the interim, she had made no mention of any early warning signs she might have been aware of and I can not bring myself to think she would ever be so desperate as to try to deceive me on that subject. There had been no subsequent letters or phone calls. I'll admit I was absent for a long time shortly after she left for Spokane. Also, allthough there was a tapefull of phonecalls on the answering machine before it quit working, for lack of space to record any further, there was nothing from Mary before or after the date on the letter. Presumeably she had wanted to announce her news personally and I just hadn't been around, so she gave it, in the form of a letter, to Kamm to deliver. I hadn't asked Kamm whether he had shown her, the fax I sent him from Florida, saying I was leaving for England, before or after he handed me her letter, and after reading it, I was glad I had not opened any 'avenues for speculation' on his part.

Despite the enticing thoughts engendered by her letter, I decided to give myself a little more manoeuvering room, by writing a reply to the return address on her letter, before taking any hasty or il-considered steps in this new dance.

Spokane itself has never seemed appealing to my mind as a place to live. and Division, the street address she had given on her letterhead, was even less appealing. I have driven along that road myself and my recollections are of a depressing area in which I would not chose to live, and I could simply not imagine Mary picking it as a place to live, much less to raise her child. In the two years I had been away, even if circumstances at that time, had forced her to live there, she would by now have moved. After much dithering, I sat down to write a letter which I hoped would convey the facts without seeming to accuse Mary of some underhanded dealings in trying to foist the responsibility onto me.

> *My Dearest Mary,*
>
> *I cannot begin to tell you how delighted I am to finally get back in touch with you. Kamm gave me your letter the day I returned and my heart is heavy with the realization of the time we have lost.*
>
> *The old airplane is looking as dejected as I feel. The tires are flat, and must be replaced and Kamm insists the engine should have a complete overhaul after sitting idle and unprotected for such a long time. As soon as I can hear from you, I would like to come and visit with you.*
>
> *Erica Mary or Stuart Henry, must be approaching two years old by now, and I am longing to see your child*

and perhaps, to meet the father, if you think that would be acceptable.

I wish. I wish. I wish. But wishing alone, could never accomplish the miracle it would need for your supposition to be correct. My wife of thirty years, died childless although the medical authorities declared several times in the course of our efforts to do so, that she was perfectly capable of conceiving a child. I was the one who was deficient. I can have no children. That, I fear, is my lot in life.

Your devoted friend, Henry.

I sincerely wished and even hoped, that her inference of my being the father of her child could be true.It would be a marvel if it were proven to be the case. I realized I might have to submit to a blood test, despite my certainty that doing so, would only prove that I was not the father. It was not even a win win situation. Truthfully, I was not sure I wanted to know. I addressed the envelope with the hazy, smudged, return address given on the letter-head, and added a 'Please Forward', just in case. Then, with a strange tingle of anticipation, drove to town and mailed it at the post office to be sure it didn't have even the smallest chance of getting lost between there and the mailbox across the street.

The next three weeks simply flew by. There were so many things to attend to, I was never able to think about getting an answer to my letter.

Although money was now no object, I steadfastly refused to splurge on extravagent purchaces. The Moonbaby, as we had named my old 1947 Luscombe, was in the process of an engine overhaul and Kamm and I worked daily on that project. When not engaged on that, Pugsley, my sweet Heinz57 canine companion, and I were off to the little hamlet of Joyce, to look after Joyce Reynold's little farm and garden. We also made periodic visits to the R,V. Storage in town to, 'Check the tires', on the camper van and its valuables. Although most of the residue from Chip's treasure was safely in various banks, there was still a considerable amount in cash which I was again hoarding under the peat moss pile. Almost every bank in town had a savings account, into which I made regular small deposits in cash.

I developed a routine. Monday morning's, I went to town with five envelopes, each marked with the address of one of the banks and containing an assortment of bills plus a deposit slip to that account. I kept a register of each deposit, varying the amount deposited in accordance with the computer's deposit record, which was determined by a simple algorithm I had worked out on the computer, so that the total deposit came to exactly $2,000.00. I still had a pile of cash to dispose of without raising anyone's eyebrows.

The monthly bank statements went to my P.O.Box and since they all came at different times, there was small chance that any one postal worker would get interested. Had I used my mailbox across the road the mailman might have noticed the steady flow of bank related correspondence. In the course of a year, I hoped to accumulate $104,000.00 After all. I now had a family to think of and felt it would only be prudent to prepare for education expenses and the like.

Call me a fool, say I'm sentimental, senile, whatever you wish, but 'Hope springs eternal in the human breast' is as true today as the day it was first uttered. I took Mary's letter and mounted it and the envelope in a picture frame and set it on my desk with a photo of her that I had taken, it seemed, so long ago. Then, to add salt to the wound, I slipped a similar but much older portrait of my original Mary, into the same frame. If somehow, a miracle had occurred, I wanted some way for her to share it with me.

The letter was at least two years old, the return address on the envelope was faded and barely readable, probably the result of being cramed into my pants pocket for a few days, and the letter itself carried only a pencilled heading. Mary probably wanted to hide all semblance of formality. The implications, were certainly clear enough. Our impromptu ride at Stewart Island had been bareback after I had explained my sterility. It has happened to many men I know but somehow, I still could not accept that she would try to lumber me with another man's responsibilities. But, who knows how far a desperate woman may go in such a situation,?

One thing was for certain. I had to find her now, for my own, and possibly the original Mary's, peace of mind. Staring at the collage, I finally realized, I had become obsessed and needed relief.

Erica Mary or Stewart Henry. A clever juxtaposition of her name with part of my surname transposed, if it was a girl. And, the fateful location, with my first name, for a boy. I re-read the letter several times, trying to detect any hint of blame but the phraseology was totally devoid of it. Why hadn't there been any other letters in the two years? The child would be eighteen months or more by now. Possibly, Mary had come over to visit me and found me gone. No word from me might have suggested to her that I had skipped town on getting her news. Nothing could be further from the truth. I could feel the onset of a sense of excitement within me at the thought that after so many years of sterility according to the medical profession, a miracle had happened. I wanted so very desperately, to believe in her, despite all the cautions and caveats that whispered in the other ear. I was determined find her, and perhaps, a son, or a daughter, of my own.

*   *   *

The luscombe was finally ready for a trial flight. The rebuilt engine also needed to be 'Run-in' for about an hour. Kamm and I had religeously lock-wired all the nuts, particularly those of the oil system. She had a brand new set of tires and a fresh paint job, after all the corrosion had been eliminated. I wheeled her out of the hangar intent on making a couple of hours flight, after which, we would empty out the break-in oil and replace it with a fresh batch of the proper weight oil for continuous use.

I cruised out to Joyce and made a couple of passes over Joyce's pasture which, by now, Pugsley and I had successively mown down to almost the status of a lawn. During that process, Pugsley had chased off all the deer who had moved in during our absense. I had not realized that she was so territorially aware, until one afternoon, when we had finished mowing, I noticd her marking the boundaries in a surprisingly systematic doggie way. Maybe she was warning the deer to keep out. I hoped they would co-operate, for with those tall trees at each end, nothing could be more disconcerting while taking off or making a landing on Joyce´s confined landing strip, than having to make a sudden abort, or a ´go-around´, because of deer on the runway.

On this trial flight, I did not want to get too far from a potential landing strip and although I was tempted, I refrained from flying out to the San Juan Islands for a sentimental journey down memory lane, until the engine had been run in and checked. I had more important plans to consider. A two hour flight across the Cascade mountains to Spokane, as soon as it was safe to do so.

Despite the high noise level in the Luscombe, Pugsley was soon content to sit in the right seat and look out of the window at the world below with no restraint. I was pleased to know it would be no problem taking her with me to Spokane and /or beyond. I did treat the two of us, to a few low level passes over Beckett Point, just in case Mary had returned to the house where I had first met her. She might just happen to see the airplane and come running up to the house looking for me. How lazy or infantile can one get?

The landing at Diamond Point, was so good it gave me goose bumps. Apparently, almost three years of no flying, had not severely dulled my reactions.

There had been no response to my letter. I regretted not having registered it. I was still floundering around at square one and decided I needed to go to the address in Spokane and hopefully make personal contact with whoever was there at that address, and ask if they, or anyone else, could lead me to a new scent.

Also, I was beginning to think about my money laundering game and wondered if I was simply offering myself up as an easy target to anyone who might be investigating the disappearance of close to two million dollars of hard cash.

I tried to put myself in the position of an investigator and wondered whether there might be a danger of liberating too many of those bills in one small locality, all at once. Whoever had packaged that stack, and I didn´t think it had been Chip or a close acquaintance, probably had records of the numbers on the bills.

I had been shuffling them, two or three apart, so as to reduce the possibility of some alert bank teller spotting a sequence and reporting it. Now, after noticing that some of the packs of bills were all numbered in sequence, I widened those gaps by staggering my selection from different packs. Somebody had to have a record somewhere.

On the day before departure for Spokane, I noticed an unfamiliar car, one with those opaque windows, cruising up and down the road past my place as I worked out in my work shed I doubted if anyone could see me in there, but what alerted me, was the way it seemed to slow down outside my entrance, each time it passed. Somebody in that car was definitely looking for someone or something.

My place is an old mobilhome converted into a dreamy little old fashioned campsite with lots of trellis and fiberglass, not much of a target for thieves so who were these guys? After they had passed and could no longer see the shed, I left on my bicycle and rode across the fields to the road and came cycling past my entrance from the other direction. The car was parked further up the road around the bend and out of sight of my house. As I cycled past, I noted the numberplate. It was a California plate PRF 798, I had a momentary creepy feeling it had some connection to Praif Inc. My erstwhile employer two and a half years ago for all of approximately two days. I tried to appear oblivious to the car, cycling nonchallently by it, as if I had not noticed anything unusual and continued past my entrance on a roundabout route to my hangar, making sure I was not followed. I parked the bicycle inside and walked over to Kamm´s house and had a cup of coffee with him.

The conversation started off with him giving me a fairly detailed summary of local events in my absense, until it seemed to subside into rather emotional vortex, revolving around the current homeowner's association activities.

I suspect it frayed on his sensibilities as I am personally not in favour of the association at all. I laid it on pretty thick, that I could not find one activity the association was engaged in, which in any way benefitted any of the homeowners. Except perhaps, those on the board of directors, who presumeably got some sort of Ego Trip out of being able to say they were "On the board". I mentioned my sighting of the Californian car prowling the area, pointedly noting that the association didn't even provide any kind of security service, or for that matter, any other service to justify their imposed dues.

Having rattled his cage sufficiently, I then made up for it by paying him in full for his work on the Moonbaby and walked across the taxiway to the back of my yard.

Nothing had been tampered with around the house or the outbuildings as far as I could see. There was no sign of the car. I even checked to see if it had left any tire tracks in the Cedar needles which cover everything in my driveway, but found none. I felt relieved that the occupants had, apparently, not been digging too deeply into my affairs. Probably Kamm was right. They were only sightsee-ers, or perhaps potential home buyers. I silently hoped they had nothing to do with that particular Californian company . . . I shuddered, remembering the terrible consequences to Joyce, of my interfering with their activities.

Packing for the flight to Spokane, kept me from thinking about anything else and by evening, the Moonbaby was loaded with baggage, filled with fuel and ready to go. However, the nagging sense of impending trouble refused to leave me entirely.

In the Post Office, forms had been duly filled in and deposited to divert my mail to the Box number and I took a final trip into town after supper to check on any last minute deliveries in the P.O.Box. Nothing from Mary there. Nor, to my relief, was there any indication that my movements were being followed. However as I was planning an indefinite absense I also took the bundles of wrapped up bills out of their hiding place at home and deposited them under the pile of old under-clothes and brick a brack in the camper at the same time.

The storage unit provides me twenty four hour access and I knew nobody followed me there so I felt it was safer than leaving it at home, where some sleuth might find it if they searched my home in my absense. Everything in the Storage was in the name of Victor Gingham from Florida so it would not be associated with me, by anyone checking up on Henry Errickson.

On the basis of "Least said, soonest mended", I had not told Kamm anything about the contents of Mary's letter, or of my intentions of leaving for Spokane.

Pugsley made no protest at awakening before dawn. We had our morning ritual coffee and cereal for me and milky dog biscuit for her and I let her out to get comfortable while I shaved and showered. Locked everything up and we jogged over to the hangar in the pale cold light of the dawn. Pugsley doesn't bark but she runs around excitedly before any excursion and I usually wait until the moment before boarding to tell her to, "Gopee! Gopee! QuikQuik!" and, bless her, she does. We were about to start a two hour flight in an airplane with no toilet facilities, this precaution was imperative for both of us.

The early dawn is in my opinion, the best time of the day to fly. The air is so still before the thermal action gets going, there are no bumps at all after the wheels leave the ground. And even two hours after sunrise the thermal action is minimal at the altitude necessary for crossing the mountains.

With the general drift of the upper level air towards the east, we made good time and landed at Spokane International in one hour and fifty minutes after take off. The tower directed me to the small plane area and advised me the local fixed base operator would be open in an hour. We chatted a while on the ground frequency and I learned from him that there were also rental cars available at DeerPark.

I thanked him for the information and said it would probably suit my purposes better to go there, so we started up again, and flew to Deer Park about twenty miles north. There, the field is not a major jet airfield or controlled so my ancient aircraft was better suited to operate from there than mingling with the commuter traffic at the International.

Pugsley of course, had to take an emergency potty break at the International and simply hated to mark up the nice clean tarmac. Fortunately the tower was not included in that interchange. So we were able to leave without having to carry any excess baggage or a blemish on our record.

Deer Park was still in dreamland when we landed and I had to make my own way to the tie down area. Pugsley and I sauntered around among the airplanes sniffing tires and peering into cockpits respectively, until signs of life appeared.

When the local airport café opened up we went in and ordered breakfast.

The lady who served us, took an immediate liking to Pugsley who had curled herself obediently at my feet under the table and even made her a slice of brown toast with cream cheese which Pugsley devoured with delight, even to licking up the last of the crumbs from the linoleum.

"She is a remarkably well trained dog. We don´t usually encourage them in here but there´s always an exception to the rule. Have you had her long ?"

"Since she was a baby." I replied. Noticing the raised eyebrows at my choice of words, I continued, "She was a little puppy when we bought her, but she´s a grown up lady now." The eyebrows went up again. "She´s also a wonderful ice breaker. I´m kinda shy meeting strangers but she seems to have the knack of making immediate friends."

I, we, were the only customers at that moment so the waitress who, I discovered, was also the proprietress, came over and chatted freely about places to stay, rental cars, and several other items I wanted to know about the area. All of which, apparently, she could handle.

"Where's your wife?" She suddenly asked. I was so surprised I hesitated in answering just long enough to give her the wrong impression when I replied.

"I don't have one." and the eyebrows went up again.

"Divorced?"

"Dead." I said softly, watching the effect, and hastened to add. "Ten years." before she could say how sorry she felt for me, and trying to suppress my mirth at the up and down fluctuations in those expressive black eyebrows, which peaked over the black pupiled eyes, bestowing a pixi-like appearance to her delicate facial features. I had guessed her age as late thirties when they were up and early forties when they were down. She was quite attractive and possibly even interested, but very busy with her mental arithmetic, trying to equate the 'We' with the 'Puppy' and the current age of the Dog. With the rest of the information I had given.

The arrival of two more customers drew her attention away from me giving me time to finish my poached egg on toast. I sneaked a couple of small pieces down under into a soft appreciative mouth, while the lady's attention was elsewhere, and got my fingers licked clean. People often wonder why I eat toast and jam with a knife and fork,

She had provided me with a map of Spokane when I told her of my quest. In view of her apparent interest, I spiced up the story that Mary was my granddaughter who I had not heard from for almost three years, and I wanted to leave everthing I posessed to her in the will I was trying to set up. That apparently spiked her interest further. When I told her my age she was very flattering. Saying "You don't look that old. I know men of my own age who don't look as good. And you're still flying." I hoped she wasn't going to enquire further into the legality of that so I changed the subject back to my immediate needs. To rent a 'Tie-down" here at Deer Park, and a place for Pugsley and myself to lay our heads, for the next few days or weeks, as long as the search might take.

"Does your Granddaughter work?" She asked.

"I don't know. Last thing I heard, she was planning on going to enrol at the "U" here to qualify in Manipulative Therapy with the idea of setting up as a masseuse."

"Well, if they don't know anything at that address you have, you might try the yellow pages. She could be working in one of the health spas." How wonderful it is I thought, to have a second opinion available. I thanked her, paid for the breakfasts, rented a car, after promising that Pugsley would not tear up the upholstery, and said I would be back later in the day to check out a place to stay. I wanted to leave myself a little manoeuvering room. She directed me to the office of the FBO and I paid for a week's Tie-down for the Moonbaby.

Before we set off towards Spokane in a rented Toyota with only 1,250 miles on the odometer. I began to learn about new cars. When I couldn't even get the gearshift into reverse, to get out of the parking lot, I began to doubt the validity of my pilot's license let alone my medical. I switched it off. and shamefaced, returned to it after learning I had to put my foot on the brake before putting it in reverse. I hoped there weren't too many other safety tricks the teenagers know, that I had still to learn about new cars. Later, at a gas station, I had to have the attendant show me the little lever almost under my seat which releases the gas cap cover. When he saw my problem and came over, he said. "Trying to open it with a screwdriver will only set off the alarm . . . Sir".

By the time we reached the highway and scooted across the traffic to go South, Pugsley had snuggled down into the footwell on her side and was watching warily from its safety as I struggled with the driving. By the time I pulled up in front of the delapidated old mansion which corresponded with the address on Mary's letter, she had closed her eyes and gone to sleep.

The old three story house, which had doubtless once been a well kept family residence, was now a typical drab boarding house with five small appartments. None of which equated to my concept of what Mary would have selected for long term quarters.

Especially after her child came along. My only hope was that someone, perhaps the mamager, if I could find one, might know where she had moved to.

She didn't know, neither did her companion, an unkempt individual in his mid forties who made only a momentary appearance and left as soon as he figured I was legit. They had only been there themselves for six months. Nobody matching my description of Mary had come or left, since they took over. I asked if there were any other renters in the building who had been there for a couple of years or more and might have got to know Mary and possibly have some information. She was sorry but the previous manageress who had been there for many years had passed away before they came. There were two long term residents, an old retired electrician who still occuppied the attic apartment and a younger working couple who lived on the second floor. I asked if it would be possible to talk to them. No problem, except they were all out when I called. They were usually home by evening, so I thanked her and said I would come back later.

I was not too disappointed as I had expected something like this as a start to my investigations. I next tried the university registrar. After some delays, a smart young lady called me into her office and I went through the second recitation of my story. Yes. A Mary Lykes had been registered in the medical section at that time, and had completed the first stage of the required course. She had not re-registered for the following semester. They had no further knowledge of her whereabouts as she was no longer enrolled. "Yes." She had received a certificate of completiom for that section of the course. "No." I drew a blank asking if she had any special room mates or fellow students who might have known of her subsequent plans. Miss Martin was sorry she could not help further, she was very busy, and suggested I try tracing her through the registration of her car. Another avenue opened up. I thanked her and left.

As I was walking through the hallway to the exit, I passed the student notice board and another avenue opened up. I went to the car, Pugsley was asleep but burst into life when I touched the door. I had pen and paper so despite her desire to help, I wrote a note asking if anyone knew Mary's whereabouts, and if so, to get in touch with me at, for want of a local number, my Sequim phone number, and pinned it to the board.

Next stop was the Public Library. All that afternoon I studied the yellow pages for Spokane and areas around it, jotting down all the massage parlors and fitness center phone numbers.

Before heading back to Deer Park and the airport café, Pugsley had to have a little run around at a small roadside park.

Vivienne, was just getting ready to close up shop, when I arrived. She had not emptied the coffee so I had an egg salad sandwich with the coffee and gave her a resitation of my day's activity which didn't seem too impressive considering the results.

I needed access to a phone for an extended survey of the Massage and Fitness establishments which I wanted to do tomorrow and a place where we could set up a base, however temporary it might turn out to be, and I was secretly delighted when Vivienne offered me a room and board set-up, in her own house, on terms I could hardly refuse. I followed her to a cosy ranch style house about five miles North of the Deer Park airport. I could have full use of the place as she and her son, lived there alone and were both away all day. She at the restaurant, him at a garage in Valley.

I would pay a month's rent in advance and enough to cover my telephone bills. The house was on a ten acre lot about a mile and a quarter, east of highway 395. Her son, Jake, a corruption of Jaques, lived there as well and worked as an auto repair mechanic at a small garage in Valley, about fifteen miles further North and was absent from seven in the morning until about six at night so the house would be empty as far as I was concerned all day.

I met Jaques, that evening. He was a strapping young fellow. Tall, slim, well built, tanned and hansome enough to have had a career in Holywood. About the same age as Mary. 'My Granddaughter'. He had done a couple of semesters at the 'U' towards an engineering degree but when his father, Vivienne's husband, died, he had given it up for the time being to earn enough to keep the home going. Their land was a nice level area and they kept a great vegetable garden which supplied them and also provided a small income from sales to her restaurant and a few others in the area. With their combined incomes and sales, they were finally getting solvent. He had not seen Mary during his time at the 'U' and expressed his disapointment when I showed him her picture. He established an instant friendship with Pugsley and I liked him as well. He told me he had completed the first two years towards a science degree before being forced to take a full time job and regarded his mechanical work as a "hands-on experience". As soon as he had the family's debt for their property paid off, he intended to finish the degree. I liked his forthright way of thinking and told him I admired his courage and wished him well.

We spoke of my professional experiences and he laughed when I told them I was a retired airplane design engineer and had developed a case of 'Mechanic's Contempt for Engineers', whenever I had to work on my car.

Despite the developing aura of friendship, I also sensed a tendency to suspicion which I put down to a son's protective instinct where male associates of his mother were concerned.

Vivienne, her husband Jaques and their son had originally bought the property with the idea of setting up a bed and breakfast establishment around the perimeter of the property and there were four completed cabins along the eastern perimeter and several more partly built. They explained that they had been forced to stop work on these for lack of funds. Jake was for setting me up in one of the completed cabins where I would have full freedom of operation without impacting their lives while I sensed that Vivienne wanted to get a closer association going. I thought about it for some time before opting for Jake's suggetion. He gave me a tour of the area and I was genuinely intrigued. The first three cabins were fully furnished with all the simple necessities except the telephone which I needed. I suggested it would be O.K. with me in one of these, so long ad I could use the house phone during the day. They both agreed this would be fine and I moved my small belongings into the first cabin and set up the base I needed. Breakfast would be ready between six thirty and seven in the morning at the house.

They undoubtedly had their discussions after I left for the night, because Pugsley, who had slept quietly on a folded rug on the deck, became excited at six thirty, when Jake came over with an extention telephone on a long cord which he had strung across the lawn from the house. I checked it for connection, thanked him and he left for work.

I fed Pugsley and settled her in the covered deck as her new quarters before going over to the house for breakfast. Vivienne and I made light of Jake's posessive behaviour over our breakfast and she gave me a key to the house. "Just in case you get hungry," she said, before leaving for work. Pugsley and I watched as her car disappeared down the road and then I took her on a walk around the property so she could define in her own way, the boundaries. Once that was clear I took her back to our cabin and walked her around it twice and settled her on her rug with the command to stay while I walked off, got into the car and drove away in the same direction as Vivienne had gone. It was too early to begin calling business establishments so I went on a short shopping expedition in the business area of Deer Park. In Safeway, I bought food for both of us and a notebook in which to record the phone conversations etcetera.

Pugsley came bounding out of her lair as I pulled up at the cabin and I caressed her and told her what a good girl she was to affirm her status in the new surroundings. That done, I stored the provisions I had bought and set my 'Office'up on the covered deck since I would have to wait for Jake to make access to put the phone inside. I could not presume on making holes in the cabin walls for telephone lines if I wanted to reassure him as to my designs on his mother. As I contemplated this new development, I suddenly realized that I was no longer under the influence of my old friend Roba's spirit. In fact thinking back, I had not received any further intervention in my affairs since the night after my trip with Mary to Stuart Island, when he had appeared at my bedside to admonish me for the last time. I felt a wave of sadness sweep over me. It was strange. All the time I had spent in the last three years wandering the globe, I had not really mised him. Why now? As though motivated by my thoughts, Pugsley came over and laid her head on my foot. I immediately felt better as I stroked her. The phone rang driving all other thoughts out of my head. Instinctively I picked it up.

"Henry?" The voice was familiarly unfamiliar

"Jake.?".

"I called to see if everything is working O.K".

"Yes everything is fine, I'm just killing time until businesses open up before starting the survey. Vivienne left for work some time ago. Pugsley and I are just sitting enjoying the sunshine. I was wondering if there's a chance we can run the phone inside somehow, so I can have it on the table, for making notes etcetera ?" There was a silence as he considered so I continued. "Right now, while the Sun is out, it's nice and warm but if the Sun goes in, I'd prefer to be inside."

"Oh sure . . . I was just thinking where I could run the wire in. D'you mind if I do it tonight, I can't come back at the moment as I'm in the middle of a job,"

"Sure, no problem. I'll be going out later anyway. See you this evening."

I hung up, wondering what he would say if he knew Vivienne had given me a key.

As soon as the clock showed nine o'clock I began my solo Telethon. By ten, I was beginning to have my doubts of ever finding anyone who had ever heard of Mary Lykes and I was fed up with the smartasses who thought she did, 'like'. So, I changed my tactics and asked if they had or remembered having had a young masseuse on their staff called Mary who matched my desription. There were a couple of false starts with Marys currently working but not the one I was looking for. I began wondering if she had used another name. By eleven, I was half way through the list I had made in the library and needed a coffee or some other stimulent to boost my morale. Telemarketing would never suit me as a source of income. However, practice was making me perfect and just before twelve, I hit pay dirt, as an old miners might say. Mary had worked there for several months before leavng to have a baby. I said I would be at the establishment to speak directly with some of the ladies there if possible.

The salon was in a small town, twenty miles north on the highway, called Chewelah and I found it shortly before one pm.

The lady who had answered my phone call remembered Mary as a vivacious auburn haired youg woman who was studying at the university and only worked in Chewelah once a week to obtain practical experience.

She was living in Spokane and came out on Saturdays in a red sports car.

Although I was able to speak to several of the customers that afternoon, none of them were able to give me any more information than I already had so I left my card with the manageress and asked if anyone chanced to meet her please ask her to get in touch with her grandfather in Sequim. I added, Henry Erickson. Just so she wouldn't be confused with any other grandfathers she might have. I remembered her having told me at one time, that she preferred older men. The mention of her car, reminded me I had a picture of it somewhere, with her sitting on the folded top. Perhaps the number plate would be readable. I doubted if she would have sold it unless she had been seriously strapped for money. Which, from what I knew of her, seemed unlikely.

Ferrari dealers?? Another Avenue opening? It was a long drive, but, I went back to the phone books. In consequence I got back to base a little late for dinner. However, I had some good news to relate to Jake and Vivienne, who were both intensely interested in my searchings. Particularly Vivienne, who noted that she knew the little beauty salon in Chewelah. Although I didn't realize it at the moment it happened, I also sensed a sudden flash of interest in Jake as I mentioned the red Ferrari.

Jake had bored a small hole through the wall of my cabin and threaded the phone wire through. The phone was sitting on the fold down desk inside. Pugsley had helped, he said, so he had taken her for a run around the property as a reward. I couldn't ask for better service than that.

After studying the map of the area from Spokane, North to the Canadian border, I was struck by the nearness of Valley to Chewelah.

As part of controlling and recording the various aspects of this operation, I had bought a five subject school notebook with a bright red cover and a box of tabs to help find the different sections.

Section one was a log of daily happenings. Section two was destined to have several sub section tabs for the various repetitive expenditures. Section three was designated to record developments in the search and already contained two pages of address and phone numbers with a sub section devoted solely for phone numbers, dates and times of calls I had made. Originally I had intended to use my lap top computer for all this record keeping, but it soon became obvious that a hand-written record would be more convenient. My old Epson was a little too old and fat for that level of activity. If the battery had still been chargeable it might have been possible but not now.

Also, I decided that for the person to person contacts, more pictures were needed, particularly the one of Mary and her fire engine red Ferrari.

Why, I wondered, had I never made a mental note of her license number? It would now cost me half a day to fly back to Sequim to retrieve it. But, what is half a day in a search which was already twenty seven months behind schedule?

I lay awake for a long time that night, reviewing the various aspects involved. I could call Nora Transome, if she was still in P.A. but the thought of her response to a request for researching another mysterious license plate number might provoke a lot more questions than I could answer satisfactorily.

Quite a few people might still be wondering what had happened to me.

I decided to keep my return to the area as low profile as possible. I even began to regret shaving off my beard. Besides, I could walk into almost any license agency or police station around here and ask them to get those details. All I needed was that number. Despite my good intentions, this search had already gone off half cocked. I needed to back off and take things easy.

Pugsley, who somehow always seemed able to sense my mental state, gave a soft sympathetic whimper. I got up and went outside to check.

It was a calm warm night with a million stars above and a small crescent moon. Ideal for flying and I was tempted to go right there and then to the airport and fly back to Diamond Point. In years gone by, when the gliding club moved their summer operation to Fancher Field just on the east side of the Columbia near Wenatchee, I had regularly flown my older (1941) ragwing Luscombe, across the mountains, back to Renton after the gliding finished on Sunday evenings. It was only half this distance and often on arrival over the coastal zone west of the mountains, the clouds extended from the mountains to the sea coast in a solid ceiling of white. In those days . . . . But I was younger then . . . . Here, stretched out dreamily in the chaise lounge, with Pugsley curled close beside me, there didn't seem so much urge to go right now . . . I could talk with Vivienne and Jake at breakfast and possibly go after checking the weather.

Sometime in the night, the air turned distinctly cold. Pugsley crawled off the cold plastic of the chaise, onto her blanket, while I stumbled into the cabin and slid under the luxury of a down comforter on a soft warm bed.

In the morning, a dense fog had settled over the landscape. Flying was out of the question. The Moonbaby is not equipped for legal I.F.R. Airlines would not accept Pugsley unless she went as cargo, in a cage. I did not want to subject her to such an indignity. I discussed my dilemma with Vivienne and Jake at breakfast and I could almost have kissed him when he offered to take her with him to work, and look after her for two or three days. It might take me that long to do what I told them I planned to do on my computer in Sequim. They were both sharing my sense of excitement over making a set of posters on it by scanning my pictures of Mary and printing a number in colour. We would distribute them in selected locations where Mary might be known. I was so excited myself, it would have been difficult for it not to have spread to them.

After breakfast we went in Jake´s pickup to the garage in Valley, where he took some pride in showing the place. Not only to Pugsley and myself, but also to his mother who had followed us so that she could drive me back to the house. Pugsley settled down with Jake holding her leash, once I had assured her it was O.K. and I would come back soon. Living on board a small sailboat cruising the Carribbean for two years with me, had built a strong sense of trust between us.

As I was opening the door of my car, Vivienne handed me a small bag and gave me a swift peck on the cheek saying, "This will keep the wolf from the door until you get home. Take your time and don´t worry about Pug. We´ll take good care of her." I thanked her and set off for the Spokane airport. Although the patchy fog required close attention to driving, my mind wandered to thoughts about the relationship which I sensed was developing at least from her side. I had sensed Jake's concern and a certain protectiveness in the way he responded to it, and I was careful to keep my side of the affair at as low a key as possible, consistent of course, with keeping her assistance going. Jake was close to twenty four, with two years of college. Vivienne was forty six by her own admission, with two years of widow-hood. Although I had taken an early retirement, I was closing in, far too swiftly, on sixty seven. Mary would be twentyfive, with a two year old to look after. I had no idea of her current status. After two years plus, with no word from me, even if the child was mine, she might still have found herself a husband. I could visualize the distinct possibility of being relegated to the position of an old uncle at best. Fog outside, and a fog inside. On the drive back from Valley to the house, we had discussed my poster idea and she had wisely advised me to 'Take my time and do it right this time.' I wondered just how many times one must 'do it right' before doing it right.

Horizon Airlines delivered me safely to Port Angeles in about an hour and forty minutes. The taxi took six minutes to drop me at the bus station in P.A. and the Clallam County Bus Service deposited me at the corner of my street in another hour and a half. I just had time between busses at Sequim, to slip into the Post Office and collect my mail from the box.

My mobilhome showed no signs of any prowlers and apart from needing the heat turned on, was soon back to normal even without Pugsley trotting around to keep the deer out of the gardens.

I went straight to work sorting out the photos I had of Mary and her car.

The best one, where Mary is sitting on the back of the folded canopy, didn't show all the numberplate behind her foot. I kept searching until I found the oldest one of them all, the one which I had taken the morning I met Mary at her gransmother's house on Beckett Point. I had only taken it to record the numberplate of the impatient young red headed witch, whose strident horn had shaken me up after I stopped at the top of the hill leading down to the point, to admire the view over Discovery Bay.

By the magic of computers I was able to scan the pictures into the computer in high resolution. Then, cut, expand or decrease the size, then paste selected portions, wherever I wanted them on the page.

I pasted the expanded view of her and the car into the top left of the page, and the cropping of the numberplate also expanded to a good readable size below it.

On the right side at the top, I printed the word "Reward" in big bold letters to catch the eye and below that, $100.00. for information leading to the recovery of the car.

Below that, my name, Henry, with Vivienne's phone number followed by my E-mail address.

I know that's not strictly Kosher, but then, I'm not Jewish either.

In the unlikely event that Mary herself should see the poster, I knew she would understand. And, knowing her, if she had a husband, she'd probably send him to collect the reward.

In my excited condition after seeing the final result, I ran off about five more copies before realizing it would be cheaper and quicker to take it to a print shop for about another twentyfive copies.

I skimmed through the mail sorting out the slug of bank statements which had come in and entering all the details in the computer.

There was one strange letter. It had been posted, from George Town.in the Cayman Islands. My first thought was it must be from someone I had met during my voyaging out there but I had never mentioned or given my address in Sequim to anyone. It had no return address on the envelope. When I opened it, there was only a dirty piece of mud smeared cardboard inside with the words, "Thanks for the sugarcane." scrawled across it.

I stared at it for ages trying to decide who had sent it. I truly didn't believe that after this long, either Chip or Joyce had somehow survived, and wanted to let me know in this bizarre fashion. From the franking on the stamp, it had definitely been posted recently from out there in George Town. Did they know I was back in Sequim ? The questions tumbled over each other in my head and I resorted to a long lost craving for a shot of Rum to help me level off.

I suddenly felt myself in acute physical danger. Chip, I am sure would stop at nothing to get that money back. It simply had to have been him behind that card.

I had never mentioned anything or told anyone in my travels, about the boxes of money. Nor the trick I had played on Chip and Joyce after I deduced they were, or at least Chip was, intending to 'ditch' me and keep the money for themselves. Only my last minute piece of histrionic behaviour saved me from losing my own share. Chip must have felt desperate to get away before I could carry out my threat to snatch their two boxes as well, just to keep them honest.

'Yes,' I decided, 'Somehow that lucky devil has survived, and is coming after me.'

Well . . . . He, or They, don't know about ´Spokane´. I hadn´t mentioned, even to Kamm that I was planning to make this trip over there. I had nothing referring to it in my computer files if anyone should break in here, I surmised that Joyce must have told Chip my Box number. I would empty that by giving a key to Mail Boxes Too, to collect it every day and hold it until I returned . . . Where from? Mexico? Sure! Why not? If you´re going to lay a false trail. Do it thoroughly . . . Sure . . . I felt better immediately.

I ran my usual 'closing down the shop routine,' and caught the last bus to town. Just in time to catch the Mail Boxes Too, before she closed for the night. The Bus to Port Angeles had already left so I called a taxi, and took a single engine charter flight to Seatac to pick up the Horizon Air flight to Spokane. This time, I didn´t forget to take all my pictures and posters in my briefcase. I arrived in Spokane late that evening.

A long day and I was still too excited to feel tired. The lights in the house were out but Pugsley was still using her blanket and came joyfully out to greet me. I took her for a good long walk around the property to let her know we were ´officially´ back home together, and went to bed.

During a somewhat disturbed sleep, a plan of sorts was forming in my mind. The letter from George Town had assumed even greater significance than had been given to it in Sequim. In fact it governed my whole plan of action. With the financial resources Chip and Joyce had between them when they actually set out on that flight, I thought they would, by now be virtually penniless. Unless Chip had already salted some of his loot, which he hadn´t mentioned to me, in a Cayman Islands Bank, all he or they had between them, was what he had already pocketed from the box. (Which, incidentally, was supposed to have been my share.) Discounting the few dollars Joyce had from the money I´d given her, I estimated it would be less than thirty thousand dollars. In the intervening years in the islands that would not have lasted this long. His taunt, must have been a luxury item in their budget.

I had sailed into George Town and almost every other harbor and bay where castaways might have made it to shore.

Their aircraft had not been equipped with an emergency life raft. If they went down in the sea, they must have been rescued in a very short time and possibly been living amongst a native population somewhere in some very out of the way island for me not to have found some trace of them.

So why now was I getting such a message. I felt sure there would have been no indication of interest from Mr Bigshoes of PRAIF Inc. in the Sequim area, Unless!? Unless Chip had suffered a "Change of heart", after finding the money missing, and decided to go back to base and turn me in as the thief.

The more I thought about this idea, the less likely it seemed. It didn't match Chip's way of thinking. It seemed more likely that Joyce might have sent me a secret warning. But why so long after the event? No wonder I hadn't slept well. Bringing Mary and her leter into that equation. Or vice versa, keeping her out of it, seemed to dictate a further spell of ´incognitoism.´ My heart told me I needed first to find Mary and my gut feeling said she was living somewhere over here. East of the mountains. I would therefore be better off, shifting my whole operation over here until that mission was accomplished. I also needed to keep my lowered profile. So, with the hounds still in the Caymans, I needed to get my posters distributed widely as soon as possible. I needed time for the scent to dissipate before the hounds arrived.

Another precaution might be to open up a few bank accounts over here to continue sifting the $100 bills into the ´legit´ system since I was no longer able to make my routine deposits in the vicinity of my home in Sequim. I decided to quietly run a survey of the local banks in the area of Deer Park.

I showed my print-outs to Vivienne and Jake at breakfast next morning much to their surprise as they had not heard me return during the night. I may have missed something about Jake´s reaction when he first saw the poster but he asked me if he could take one with him to display at the garage. "Garages and Highway Gas Stations, might be good places to display these," he said, rolling it up carefully to avoid creasing it. "There's plenty of traffic between Spokane and Coleville where a traveller might just recognize either her or the car."

Vivienne said she'd also like one to put up in the airport café.

After Jake left, she casually remarked, "He's quite taken with your granddaughter I think". I must have displayed surprise, for she added.

"A mother's intuition, perhaps."

I was preoccupied thinking about accessing my E-mail and asked her if she would mind me taking out a subscription to the local internet server and she replied "Jake already has one." She wrote his E-mail address down on a piece of paper.

"Call him at work and ask him if you can use his computer to get on line. I'm sure he won't mind." I smiled my thanks and added, "You make me feel more like one of your family than a renter. You are both so kind."

"Would that be so bad?" she laughed, and I felt, rather than discerned the plea in her words. I laughed to cover my confusion and replied,

"It's a very nice family. I would hate to spoil it." I was thinking of how much I had already impacted the various families I had become involved with in the last three years. Devastated might have been a better choice of words.

She reached across the corner of the table and put her hand on top of mine. "I'd be willing to take that risk," she said, raising those eyebrows and looking right into my soul. I turned my head and clumsily sighed.

"You'd better find out a lot more about me first."

To break the subject before it went too far, I looked around for Pugsley and asked

"Where's Pugsley?" Vivienne laughed at my clumsy diversion and replied, "Wher've you been all morning? Pugg went off to

work with Jake. Didn't you see her get in the pickup with him?"
I shook my head slowly, saying,

"I don't know what you two are doing to us, but I like it, and
so apparently does Pugsley," and she squeezed my hand until I
realized how strong she was.

"You'll get used to it." She laughed, getting up. "I've got to
go to work ". Her eyebrows almost disappeared into her hair as
she turned, adding cocquettishly over her shoulder, "D'you want
to come with me?" I could feel that warm, warning, sensation
arising as I smiled my "Thanks but no thanks . . . I've got work
to do, too."

The stationery shop on Main Street, did a nice job of copying
my poster and I paid ten bucks for sixty copies and set off to find
places to post them, starting at the Post Office. Every supermarket,
drug store, and Garage with a notice board, between Deer Park
and the outskirts of Spokane got one. I got another hundred
printed off in Spokane and headed off South west toward the Tri
Cities for about twenty miles then returned and went thirty miles
west on Interstate 90. Jogged north as far as Davenport. Returned
to Spokane on highway 2 East,into Idaho on I.90 to Kellogg for
another hour and finally returned to the library for a list of gas
stations in the area twenty five miles around Spokane.

By sundown, I had found places for all except about twenty,
which, as I headed homeward, I figured I could split between
Vivienne and Jake to distribute. If they were going to become
family, they might as well work. After all a fisherman doesn't just
spread bait. He has to wait with his rod in his hand in case a bite
has to be reeled in. I felt as if I had been chumming, the way
some of them attract their special target, like sharks. I shivered
involuntarily at the thought of the 'sharks', I might end up
attracting.

The next two days were a shambles as I tried to balance my
time on the phone, between waiting for calls and using the phone

to continue my telethon with the emphasis on massage parlours. Compared to the cost of the posters, the nebulous bills for phone calls were probably building up seriously higher. Especially as the calls went further afield. Also, they took up valuable time, possibly while eager bounty hunters might be tryng to get through to me with the vision of $100.oo, fogging their glasses.

To solve that problem I bought, and with Vivienne´s consent, installed, an answering machine on my extention in the cabin. However, for an answering machine to earn its keep, I had to be off the phone, or better still, off the premises.

I bought some more copies and began a planned circular tour of all the Massage and Fitness centers asking my questions and delivering copies of my poster. It probably cost more on gas but it at least kept me from the tension of waiting around for calls during the daytime. When I had time in the late evenings, after I escaped to the cabin, I began comparing the rapidly increasing costs of these various tactics.

I had asked on the answering machine, as on my poster, for the caller to leave a name, a phone number and an address. Instead of answering all the calls each night, I could add a circuit of visitations to the addresses as part of my tour of the M and F centers.

Such big plans and so few fish. It reminded me of an episode when I had been snorkeling in a lake some years ago. There were two trout flirting at the base of a large rock and a fisherman dangling a piece of bread or such on his hook a hundred feet further along the shoreline in a spot where there were absolutely no fish. I intervened, and told him about the fish I had seen. He moved to the rock and caught them both. I remembered regretting my action later. But, as the days passed with no results, I wished there was an equivalent ´fisherman´ somewhere around to help me.

The bond between Vivienne and myself was gradually strengthening and I caught myself lying awake, thinking about her.

After almost three years of cruising alone with Pugsley as my m ain companion, I was finding it nice to have someone to really talk things over with. To share stories of the day and the past with, and, to think about the future with. But, while Vivienne's past had been devoid of major upsets, apart from the loss of her husband Jaques, my past had some huge rocks in it which I sensed might soon come tumbling down, on me and whoever was attached to me, someday. Before I let anyone, Mary, Vivienne or anyone else, tie themselves to my chariot, they'd better know the real risks involved.

Visions, of Barbara's body, in the bath, and of Joyce, joyfully taking off to disaster with Chip, still perturbed my conscience, from time to time.

Several days passed in this routine, before the expected flood of eager informants began as a tiny trickle. Between the three of us, we had distributed close to two hundred copies of my poster without a single response and I was beginning to think it was the wrong approach to the problem of locating a missing person or car. Vivienne tried to boost my morale, counselling patience.

Meanwhile, Jake had sparked our hopes by mentioning he thought he had actually worked on Mary's car and was diligently searching through the sacks of invoices the garage owner kept in an old fifty five gallon oil drum at the back of the garage, in case of an audit from the income tax people. When Vivienne and I had questioned him about this practice, Jake had stated that the owner cum secretary cum manager and Chief mechanic, Mr Whitland, kept his daily records in an exercise book, using only the receipt number and the amount paid to identify the entries. All other information, like customer name and address had to be found from the actual receipt copy. Mr Whitland hadn't been too helpful, or enthusiastic, about Jake's search, and searching itself was a slow process, as the sacks themselves were not clearly marked as to the year or any other identification. They were merely folded over and taped after the air had been squeezed out of them. Mr Whitland had said the law required him to keep records for five or seven years and according to Jake, there must be twenty years worth of sacks in the bin. He could only search when not working on some project so progress was "kind'a slow". Mr Whitland had once told him that if the IRS wanted to question his records they were welcome. And it was evident that some of the lower sacks had gotten wet as the barrel only had a piece of weathered plywood as a cover. I wasn't holding my breath waiting for a successful outcome to that search. Vivienne had told me, in response to my comments, after Jake left, that the practice was typical of the people over here. "They're not really Rednecks." She said. "Just a little pink under the collar."

Every morning after breakfast, I fired up Jake's computer and checked my E-mail from the remote access to the olympic server and usually found nothing except spam which had been segregated and had to be accessed from a specified secure website.

Today there was a reply to one of the posters.

The sender address was from one of the major T.V. stations in Seattle and the gist of the message was an invitation to me to come and be interviewed on T.V. regarding the search I was conducting. I printed it out and left it on the table beside the printer for Jake and Vivienne to see when they came home that evening. I was really excited at the prospect of possibly being on T.V. and having Mary actually see the program. I could imagine the Media, milking the poignant story of a lonely grandfather searching for his missing granddaughter and her child. But, as the day progressed, I became more and more aware that to do this would expose me to the possibility of other, not so friendly viewers, becoming aware of my whereabouts.

I had decided that morning, to spread my net northward to the Canadian border, and was in Coleville when this re-evaluation hit me. The picture of Vivienne or Jake picking up the print of the E-mail came to mind and I turned around and started back to Deer Park at full speed. The thought of getting a ticket with it's potential for further increasing my visibility slowed me down just before the State Patrol pulled me over. I was profusely penitent to the officer and came away with a verbal warning and an enhanced awareness of the close shave. Never the less, once out of his sight, I shaved the speed limits all the way back to the house.

Vivienne's car was in the driveway and I new it would be useless trying to get out of contacting the TV anchor. Unless . . . Unless she hadn't seen the E-Mail copy yet.

Pugsley met me at the door of the car and Vivienne met me at the door of the cabin. She had just brought the copy over for me. and was brimming over with enthusiasm for me to go on TV-

Probably all of you have seen this lady on T.V. so I will avoid mentioning her name or describing her to you beyond saying she reminded me of Marilyn Monroe. She met me in the foyer of the T.V. station and discussed the terms of the interview in her office. After that, I was examined by some cosmeticians. They brushed and dabbed a little coloring powder on my face here and there before ushering me into a small studio, with some furniture you have also seen. There were also, all kinds of lights and microphones and wires strung on the opposite walls, which you have not seen, but no cameras. When I mentioned this to her she pointed to several small portholes in the walls and explained that the cameras were out there and it was entirely up to the engineers to decide which one would be recording our meeting, "So don't stare at them." She warned. I felt rather like some microbe under a microscope and said so. At which she laughed heartily, told me to relax, and assured me it would not hurt. I fervently hoped she was right.

She asked me a few questions as to why I was doing this search and I told her as simply as I could, about having left suddenly, to attend my Mother's funeral and take care of the subsequent disposal of her effects in England. Marylin asked me why I hadn't told anyone I was leaving, and I laughed, a little harshly I suppose, explaining that speed had been the essense of my motivation. "The telegram I recieved from the hospital indicated mother was dying and had asked to see me. There were no other relatives except Mary and she had just left that weekend to find new lodgings in Spokane. I had not heard from her."

"Were you in time to see your mother before she died?." I shook my head sadly", reminding myself I was there to create pathos. "She was too far gone to speak or see me, but I held her hand and kissed her and I think she knew I was there. It was only a few minutes before the nurse moved in to cover her with the bedsheet and declared she was dead. "Marylin" shook her head sadly and I was so entered into the spirit of the discussion, I added, watery eyed, "All that rush and anxiety for one last kiss." She handed me a kleenex. I had already explained to her about the disposal of mother's house and furnishings and how I had used the money to buy a sailboat and cruise the Carribbean for the next two years. I mentioned a few high points of the cruise and explained how, after returning home, I had retrieved a letter from my granddaughter written just a day or two after I had left, saying she was going to college in Spokane. It was the last contact I had with her. My letters, sent to that address had not been answered, and having no other relatives, I wanted to locate her and bring myself up to date with her affairs. Also I added in case they actually used this interview, that there was some money my mother had left in her will, to be given to Mary.

"What's with the car?" she asked, and I explained that I thought Mary had taken it after I left and since it was such a highly visible item, and I felt sure she would still be driving it around, I had added it to my poster as a focal point. Something people might recall seeing it, before they recalled meeting or seeing her. 'Marylin' looked at me with those big inquisitive eyes and asked,

"Did she steal your car after you left?" I nodded my affirmative, saying,

"One could say that. "

"Are You saying that?" she asked, effectively trapping me. So

I replied prevaricatively. "What else can I say until I see her and find out the Facts?"

The whole interview lasted less than five minutes before she thanked me for coming in and it was all over.

I washed my face in the men´s room and was about to leave when the lady at the reception desk beckoned me and handed me a cheque for two hundred dollars and asked me to sign a 'Waiver of Further Interest.' form. "Just in case we broadcast it." She explained. That stopped me in my tracks.

"You mean it might not be shown on T. V. ??" I said in surprise. She smiled, nodding her head as if everyone who ever went in for an interview asked the same question. "You mean I came all the way over here from Spokane at your. I mean this station´s invitation, and got paid two hunded dollars for a five minute interview which may not even be shown.?" She continued smiling and nodding her head. I shook mine to emphasize my lack of understanding, and headed out before she could change her mind about the money.

Half my worry about being too highly visible slid away right there, and I decided to spend a little time at the mobile in Sequim before heading back to the search area. The TV station is only a few blocks from a bus stop where I could catch a bus to Boeing Field, where I had landed in the Moonbaby at 09.00 hrs. after a smooth flight from Deer Park. So, I walked. I waited, and took the bus ride for twenty five cents, instead of trying to hail a taxi and pay six or seven dollars.

I gassed up the Moonbaby and flew to Diamond point in twenty minutes versus the three or four hour trip by road and ferry. As soon as I had parked the airplane in the hangar, I looked in on Kamm, but he was too busy working on an engine rebuild to stop for coffee. We spent a few minutes discussing the repairs and I left him with an awareness of my presence, without having to account for any of the time I had been away, even supposing he had noticed. The mobile home, was just as I had left it and only took a minute or two to reactivate. The longest operation was brewing up a cup of coffee while I checked the answering machine, and found it had no pertinent messages.

The interview had been scheduled for 10.00am. And I figured I could make a swift run into town, get everything I needed done, and fly back to Deer Park before dark

By one o'clock, I had collected my mail, arranged for the, 'pick up and hold' program to continue until further notice, and had my lunch in the little cafe across the road from the auto parts store.

By three o'clock, I had made my rounds of the banks, closed up the mobilehome once more, and by four o'clock, I was airborne on my way back to Deer Park.

At six fifteen, I was back in the cabin waiting for Vivienne, Jake and Pugsley, to come home.

Vivienne arrived about five minutes after I had settled down to go through the package of mail, which I had not had time to examine before leaving Diamond Point. I put the letters down and went over to the house. From the amount of pressure she and Jake had applied in convincing me to make the interview, I was sure she'd want to hear all about it. I was right. She made me a cup of coffee and we sat down on the veranda while I answered her questions. When it came to the appearance of the T-V-personality, I said, that with all the skilled professional help that lady received she was still nowhere near as lovely as Vivienne herself. (Score 100 points for Henry.) Jake was not handy to put the brakes on things. As though she sensed my relaxation on that score she asked if Jake had come home yet, in case, I supposed, she thought he had gone out again. I didn't know of course, but it occurred to me, that if Pugsley was with him, as I presumed, he would have left her at home, knowing Vivienne would soon be home.

"He's not usually this late." She said, checking her watch before going inside to phone the garage. A few minutes later, she returned looking a little worried.

"There's no answer from the garage."

"Pehaps he went shopping." She shook her head.

"He would have called and left a message on your machine, if he was going away for parts or anything like that." She asserted. "He knows I'm a worrywart. Besides, He's got Pug with him."

She still appeared worried so I got up and put an arm around her shoulders and hugged her.

"Quit worrying." I said soothingly. "He's a grown up man now. He can look after himself. You would know if anything serious had happened, Mothers always do." She relaxed and smiled but made no move to disentangle herself from my arm and I wondered if I has sprung a trap on myself. Or, just made another 100 points.

It had been one full and fast moving day, and perhaps the momentum of it had carried me a little too far. There was no overt evidence of that, so I mentally counted my points and sat back down in my chair.

"I think I'll put supper on anyway." She said, heading back into the house.

"I've got some mail to look at." I called out as she left, and took my cup across the lawn to the cabin. There was no flashing light on the answering machine and I'd already checked for poster responses.

After discarding all the junk mail, and setting aside the bills and magazines, I picked up another letter from George Town. It contained another mudstained piece of a cardboard box with two photographs face to face with piece of kleenex between them. The whole package inside the envelope, was wrapped in a kleenex. There was no message on the piece of cardboard like the previous letter. This envelope had also been franked in George Town, just one week ago.

Both photographs showed an aeroplane which I recognized at once as the DH84, sitting upright, on a small sand bank, with its wheels buried in the sand. The tail appeared to be supported on a pile of assorted objects, not readily defineable without a magnifying glass.

One, was a long shot, taken in the evening, from a position in the water, and the elongated shadow of the photographer on the beach was not identifiable . . .

The other photograph, showed the same airplane from close up.

I simply can not describe the waves of emotional turmoil I felt sweeping over me, as I recognized Joyce, smiling in the sunlight, leaning nonchalantly against the wing, beside the right engine nacelle of the plane. I was happy to see she appeared unharmed and presumed it must be Chip's shadow on the other print. Thus, my pleasure was badly contaminated with apprehension as to where they were at this very moment. I felt a sudden urge to be looking over my shoulder all the time. What an explosive ending to an already turbulent day I thought.

I probably sat at the drop leaf table with my elbows resting on my knees and my head in my hands for twenty minutes, trying to make sense of the two letters and the two pictures. How and when had the wreck happened? Where?, I learned from the carefully printed words on the back, was 'Dead Albatross on Big Banana.'

I didn't recall seeing such an island marked on any of the detailed navigation charts I had on board the "Sugarcane". The name I had given to the thirty six foot sloop I had bought in Fort Lauderdale. I had not connected that name with the muddy thank you card I'd received the previous week.

I had only chosen it because my yacht, had in effect, become the substitute for the sugarcane I had substituted for Chip's money in the two Mobil Oil boxes. It was their money which had eventually paid for the boat.

There was no way on earth he could have known that. No. He was being sarcastic and hinting revenge. Trying to spook me. Successfully too, I must confess. But why had he waited two and a half years to do this? He and probably Joyce, were safe, somewhere in the Caymans waiting for me to surface somewhere. It amazes me to think how we could have crossed paths in the Carribbean without seeing each other. I had made no bones about the fact I was looking for them. If they ever got wind of someone searching for them they'd probably have assumed it was Bigshoes, perhaps, and gone to ground, so to speak.

That quirky thought made me laugh out loud, startling Vivienne, who jumped, and startled me, back to the present reality.

She had come over to call me for supper and had been observing my apparent despondency, hesitant to disturb me further about Jake not having come home.

"I didn't want to worry you." She said in a strained tone. But Jake and Pug haven't come home or called. And its after dark already." A fact I hadn't noticed until then.

She had me worried now, in case Jake and Pugsley had been involved in a serious accident. I hate to admit I was more worried about Pugsley. Jake would have had his seat belt on but Pugsley didn't wear one when riding in a his Pick-up. I suggested she call the State Patrol.

Trooper Lyman Jennings, had just confirmed for her, that no accidents had been reported, when the headlights of two cars came down the road, turned into the driveway and parked. The lights went out and a second or two later Pugsley came bounding in and started her welcome home dance in my lap. Behind her, Jake came in looking mighty pleased with himself, accompanied by a lady with two small children hanging on to her hands. Jake embraced and kissed his mother which obviously she hadn't expected him to do and I heard him excitedly telling her "I found her!! I found her!!"

I am not clear whether I fell, or Pugsley pushed me, into the chair, but the next thing I knew, was hearing someone saying "Hi! Gramps!" and holding Mary with her two cildren, in my lap.

After the first wave of 'Bedlam' subsided, Vivienne Jake and Mary went into consultation with Jake dominating the program, explaining to Vivienne how he had discovered the receipt for the work he had done on Mary's car in Mr Whitland's filing system.

It had been a slow afternoon and he had gone to the address on the slip and found Mary with the two children at home. He showed her the poster and she admitted it was herself and had been delightrd to learn her "Grandfather" was searching for her and temporarily living in the Deer Park area with him. Her first reaction had been to go visit, but after learning that he was away that day in Seattle to go on T.V. with his search. She had agreed with Jake's suggestion to bring the children and have free occuppancy of the cabin adjacent to her grandfather's and surprise him when he returned from Seattle. She could hardly wait, she declared, to see his expression when he met her and his great grandkids.

Jake was enthralled with Mary from the moment of meeting her again. When she had brought the Ferrari in for him to fix the brakes, Jake had noticed her as nice looking, but a bit overweight. He had been too busy with work to follow up on the meeting and had forgotten about her. Only when he saw the poster Henry had made, did he recall the car. He began searching the records which were over a year old, to see if he could locate an address. He had been reticent when speaking about it to his mother or to Henry until he had a chance to, as he described it, 'Suss it out'.

Mary, who had set up a small Massage and General Cosmetic Culture, in her cottage, had agreed to postpone her appointments for the next day to comply with Jake's suggestion. She was almost as excited to get his news, as he was with finding her. Since he had first seen her, she had slimmed down to an extremely attractive figure herself and Jake was bewildered with his sudden eagerness, to get to know her better.

Henry in the meantime could only listen with half an ear, to their conversation as he was absolutely dumbfounded, by the similarity he percieved in the little boy, who had been introduced to him as, Stuart Henry, with a picture he remembered of himself as a two year old.

Although he had no such comparison he could define between the little girl, Erica Mary, and his recollections of old family pictures. She had Mary's auburn hair colouring but there was a fragile delicacy to her facial structure that reminded him somewhat, of his own mother's features. He thought he could detect a similarity to pictures of her as a young woman.

All thoughts of blood or DNA testing, flew out the window.

He began to hope his letter, never had, or ever would, reach Mary.

While the younger adults talked, Henry sat contentedly holding Erica Mary, half asleep on his chest, while Stuart Henry sat on his right knee, chattering on about the excitement of the night ride in the car.

The use of the word "Gramps", had alerted me to the extent of the discussion between Jake and Mary that had taken place during their meeting. Only two or three times previously, had she used that epithet when arousing me, after I had fallen asleep during her massage sessions. Normally, she called me Henry.

Obviously, the question of the paternity of her children would, if it had not already been answered, soon arise. I did not think she would have already named me as the benefactor after reading the poster Jake had shown her. I had included no mention of our relationship in the poster. Jake probably inferred it on meeting her, and her use of that epithet might have been intended to let me know she would, for the moment, play along with me on it.

She already knew I had no previous children and I did not want to cloud the issue by trying to define our genealogical relationship in conflict with whatever she had said to Jake.

Vivienne's interest in my status, had already been demonstrated in our original meeting so any wild excursions had to be avoided if possible.

Stuart was winding down so I hitched him up into my lap and couched him in my right arm against my chest and lulled him to sleep.

To complete the picture, I closed my eyes pretending to fall asleep myself.

Vivienne, Jake and Mary unloaded the baby's cribs from the pick-up and set them up in the cabin adjacent to mine and then quietly ate the supper Vivienne had prepared, without waking us. What woke me, was the photo-flash, of Jake snapping a picture of our contentment

Mary carried Erica, I carried Stuart, and Vivienne and Jake escorted us across the lawn to our respective cabins. We all participated in putting the babies to bed.

Languidly, I pleaded physical and emotional exhustion with the day's events. After givimg Mary as long an embrace as I could, commensurate with my paternal status, for the benefit of Jake and Vivienne. I petted Pugsley, who otherwise might have felt ignored in the midst of all our family celebrations, and closed the door.

Although I had felt elated from the experience of finding my children, and realizing the miracle I had prayed for, had been granted. Not only once, but twice. I somehow felt exhausted knowing the search was over. Added to that, I was too tensed up from my anxiety concerns regarding Chip's activities, to sleep. Somehow, he knew I had returned to Sequim these two letters from George Town were proof of that. If he had come to Sequim to find me there, he would have had no hesitation in accosting me, nor in killing me if necessary before or after he recovered what was left of the money. So what was the point of his cat and mouse game.?

And how might it also affect the safety of Mary and the children so recently discovered, and now, so potentially close to being lost ?

Cooped up inside the cabin, the air seemed to be full of question marks, every breath seemed to fill me with more of them. Outside, in the fresh night air, dressed only in my robe, I lay down in the chaise lounge. Pugsley lifted her huge head and looked at me without getting up. I sat and stroked her head talking softly to her, as I had so often done, back on board the Sugarcane.

She and I used to hold long conversations in those days of solitude, as I tried to clarify some problem, or make a decision on where to go or what to do next. She always gave me the right answer to my questions with her soft eyes, so full of calm wisdom.

"What are you doing out here? Trying to catch your death of cold?"

Mary, dressed in a long flannel nightgown, just seemed to have floated in, to join in the conversation. "I could hear you talking from in there." She said, indicating the cabin next door. "Come on you silly man. Back inside" she commanded, pulling me to my feet. Pugsley laid her head back on her blanket as if satisfied the right answer had been reached.

I would have liked to end the story there snuggled warmly in bed with my Mary, but she wouldn't linger long enough.

Once she was sure I was warmed up and had promised to stay in bed like a good little boy, she left and went back to her cabin, to be there for them, in case either of the children should wake up in unfamiliar surroundings.

She was wise, like Pugsley.

Mary had cancelled her appointments for today in order to give herself time to talk with me. Vivienne said we could have the run of the house if we wished. Mary wasn't too anxious for staying away from her home but the babies cribs had been brought from her house on the road from Chewelah to Usk, just a few miles out of Newport. Almost at the Idaho line.

Jake insisted he would take an early departure from work and bring the crib's headboards and springs themselves, in his pick-up, to her house that afternoon around five. We gathered up the matresses and blankets and all the other esentials and loaded them into my car. After I washed up the breakfast dishes.

Pugsley came with me in my car despite Stuart's objections as he wanted to ride with her. As we followed Mary's Audi the short ride to her house, it seemed incredible that with all the posters we had plastered around Spokane, she knew nothing of my activities until Jake arrived the previous evening and showed his copy to her.

My letter had been sent on to her and she had not replied to it, feeling devastated at my asertions that I could not have been responsible.

I assured her that after seeing the resemblance between Stuart and my own baby picture. I had absolutely no doubt that the required miracle had indeed happened, just as she said.

I even described how I had put the letter and her picture in the frame with my own wife Mary's photo, so that she too could share my joy. If it turned out to be true.

"You still love her don't you?" She said softly.

"Of course. When you love someone you can't just stop because they died. The change that love makes in you, is always there. Your feelings may change once you get over the emptiness, for sure, and you can love another person at least as much, maybe even more."

"Yes I know." She replied, my friend Henry once told me what love is. I thought it was very beautiful."

We sat in silence for a few minutes, watching the twins playing with Pugsley.

Do you love Pugsley?"

I thought for a moment, wondering what had prompted that question.

"Of course I do we are inseparable. However it's purely platonic! We've been together ever since she was a baby. I mean a puppy. She's almost four years old now."

"You didn't have her when I first knew you. And I've known you that long."

"It's a long story, which I am afraid you are going to have to know before you make up your mind what you want to do with me."

"Before I! Make up My! Mind? Does that mean you've made up your mind?!" The hot tempered Ferrari driver was still alive and I laughed.

"Of course. What I would like to do, would be to, marry you . . . . But, as I said, there is a whole lot you need to know about me. What I've done, and what I've been doing, since you left for Spokane. You might not even want to live with me as your grandfather!" Mary's eyes were wide with concern and I knew I had her undivided attention as I related all the gory details of the events leading up to my departure.

"Well . . . I'm glad you got that off your chest Henry . . . You're more concerned what these people might do to me and the kids aren't you? If we were together as a family. Is that it? . . . I mean is that all of it ?"

"No." I said thoughtfully, as my mind flashed back to the night my old departed friend, Roba, had visited me in my sleep and verbally chastized me for consumating my lascivious romance with Mary. I remember his very words, spoken with such a tone of disgust, before his image vanished.

"My God Henry! You're old enough to be her Grandfather!"

When I finished telling Mary about it she laughed. "I always knew there was something spooky about you." and she added, "That was his opinion. Not yours. Or mine . . . And there's not much he could, or can, do about it now. Is there?"

It often amazes me how little one has to do to upset an applecart by saying something. But I couldn't help myself, and said.

"Nobody really knows how much the souls of the departed can influence the souls of the living, But, on many occasions, I've wondered about just how much influence Roba has had over my affairs since his death.

Maybe I should feel thankful in some way to him, for our miracle. After all, it was his advert that started the whole ball rolling."

Mary made no response to my remark. She sat meditatively studying me while all the things I had told her filtered down through her mental sifting devices. Then she broke loose and went to answer the doorbell. Jake had arrived with the cribs.

One of the first things I had noticed on arriving at her house, was the absense of the red Ferrari. "I sold it a year ago when I bought the Audi" she said laughing, It wasn't exactly the vehicle for a solo mother with twin babies to cart around."

"Do you miss it?"

"Not so much. The Audi is a pretty peppy little car. Besides, I got a real good price, from a collector, which covered the Audi and enough for the down payment on this house."

The house was a three bedroom rambler, set well back from the road, in a five acre lot. Mary had arranged two of the bedrooms as massage and cosmetic salons and had already established a small private clientelle, of previous customers from the Salons in Chewelah and Coleville, where she had done her basic apprentice-ship. The master bedroom had one single bed and the two cribs. As I learned more about her financial arrangements, I saw a place where I might be able to help.

However, the posters had implied I was also looking for 'My' car. It occurred to me that I should be going around retrieving these as soon as possible to avoid spending too much time answering hopefulls wanting the reward, or, the possible annoyance of the current owner.

After Jake and I had finished re-installing the cribs to Mary's satisfaction, I solemnly presented him with a One hundred Dollar bill. He looked at me in surprise. "The reward money." I said. He handed it back. "Keep it." He said, looking me squarely in the eye. "I was part of the search team." Then smiling sideways at Mary, added "My reward was the pleasure I got in finding Mary . . . And her Grandfather." Was it my imagination, or did he lay a little more emphasis than necessary, on that last word?

Thinking back later, I realized that Mary probably felt the same way about both of us.

I tried to develop a 'Ho Hum' attitude to the developing situation. It wasn't really in my hands to control . . . Probably Roba was right. I felt hurt. But also, that I deserved to be.

The next three days, I travelled the countryside, cleaning up my litter, putting over three hundred miles on the car in doing so. I also called the T.V. station in Seattle and told the lady interviewer, that the search was over. I doubted whether they would ever have shown the ´clip´ in any case, but I still saw no reason to expose myself more than necessary.

Those three nights, Vivienne and I dined alone, since Jake had apparently found a more appealing restaurant for his evening meals, which lasted until quite late before he came home each night.

Although I had stopped in at Mary´s each day for a visit with the kids, Mary herself seemed to be somewhat stand-offish, and I realized that she was having some difficulty equating our shenanigans with those of the other six ladies, to whom I had been obligated to return letters.

Perhaps she had discussed it with Jake as he too had seemed a little more distant.

Only Vivienne seemed to be maintaining her level of interest. I wondered how long it would take for Jake to say something of a cautionary nature to his mother. I hoped Mary had not been too indiscrete, but as the days passed and my only excuse I now had for prolonging my visit, was the presence of Mary and the kids, I wondered what to do. I needed a good heart to heart with her but her work and the continued visiting by Jake limited my chances. Perhaps if I 'broke camp' and went back to Diamond Point it might provoke some action from her. I suggested it to Vivienne. I was surprised at her reaction.

"To be frank Henry, I´m not looking forward to your leaving. I don´t think I´ve enjoyed being around anyone quite so much. Not since Jaques died. Do you really have to go.? Mary´s fine. Clearly she doesn´t need you. Hasn´t for at least the last two years. But, you should spend a little more time if you can with your great grand kids. Get to know them. While they are still so young and so beautiful. I almost wish they were mine." I debated mentally, before saying, with a smile.

"They just might be, If Jake gets his way. I think he has definite designs on Mary."

I knew from the way Vivienne smiled that she was already aware of that trend. "Would that be so bad?" She asked, taking hold of my hand, with the most pixie-like smile I have ever seen, adding, "Then you and I would be related as well . . . wouldn't that be nice.!"

'It certainly would be ´ I thought without saying it, and wondered if I dared ask her to come over to Diamond Point with me, for a couple of days so I could fill her in privately on all the ramifications that might involve. Then another thought came to me. If she flew over there with me, Jake and Mary could work out their plans without our interference. Or, it just might jog Mary to weigh her memories of our times together, versus Vivienne´s possible chances of capturing me.

The voice within said. "Go for it!" I did. She said "Yes."

The Westbound flight normally takes almost a half hour longer than the Eastbound, because of the general Easterly flow of air across the mountains. The weather report had correctly indicated "Patchy morning fog". Which was mostly gathered in the valleys and had not yet covered the strip at Diamond Point. In the absense of any wind, the touchdown was almost imperceptible. The Moonbaby rolled at idle to the hangar and Vivienne, totally enthralled with the flight, helped me to push her backward inside and close the heavy doors. Hand in hand we walked through the wet grass to the back entrance of the lot and down the garden path to the front of the Mobilhome.

"You live here?" The tone of the question implied disbelief, so, I simply opened the door and bowed to invite her to enter my humble abode. I left her to look around while I went through the routine of turning things, like the water and electricity, on. Then I showed her around. So far, we had come no closer than holding hands and I was determined not to push things further than necessary. Accordingly, when I showed her the bedroom, I said she could sleep there and I'd sleep on the couch in the room at the far end, where the T.V. lived. She made no comment, but her eyebrows were eloquent in challenging that arrangement.

I showed her where everything was and left her to make us some instant coffee while I checked around outside, for signs of intruders, and the answering machine inside, for any significant messages. She made no verbal comment on the clutter of my little office, but her eyebrows could not resist the temptation.

"This is Bluebeard's den." I growled solemnly.

She was fascinated with my desk picture collage and minutely examined the pictures of both Marys. Then she read Mary´s letter and her whole manner changed as if I was suddenly contaminated with a foul odour. "What does she mean? 'You'll be happy to know.?' etcetera?' it sounds as if she´s trying to implicate you as the father."

"I am the father!. And I was, and I still am, happy to know it."

"But you said she was your grand daughter, and she even called you Gramps when she came to the house."

"I know. Jake must have shown her the poster and told her, that her Grandad was looking for her. She was among strangers. Remember? Also, she knew by the name on the poster that it must have come from me and I must be giving out the word that I was her Grandfather."

"Only she, knew for sure, that I was the father of the children. Even I wasn´t sure then, and I had sent her a letter indicating I didn't believe I was. The other day, she told me how devastated she had been, when she got my letter, almost three years later, saying I couldn't be."

"Why couldn´t you be?" Vivienne interrupted.

"Because my wife and I had tried for years and years, to have a baby. Somehow, she just couldnt get pregnant. She had been examined and repeatedly declared fully capable of conceiving. So the failure was blamed on my sterility."

"Why are you so sure now.?"

"Let me show you." I said, picking the infant portrait of myself out of the box of old, sepia tone family photographs and handing it to her. I heard her gasp, "Is that you.?"

"It was taken when I was two years old."

"Why don´t you marry her then?" She acused me.

"She doesn´t want me to. I already asked her. First, I think, because of my letter. After the long period of self doubt and loneliness, it somehow changed her concept of me. And secondly, because I really am, old enough to be her Grand father. And thirdly, because I think if we back off enough, she and Jake may have a chance to hit it off together."

"And you`d be Home Free ?"

I clapped my hand over my mouth and took a deep breath to steady my face before replying.

"I can´t believe you said that.!" I said quietly, trying to control the hurt from my voice, before adding, "He doesn't need to know I am the father. And even if he found out later, from You or from her, I don´t think it would influence his affection for her.".

"Why don´t you ask her to have a blood or DNA test.?"

"Because I am afraid to. It could only prove I was wrong. I don´t want to know if that is the case. Besides, I have already told her, that I think the miracle, I claimed, in my letter, would be needed for me to be the father, actually took place."

"You´re holding all the 'Proof' I need.! Right there! In your hand.!"

I think she was a little too shocked, and possibly regretting her hasty words for she didn't have anything more to say.

We left shortly after that exchange and drove in a rather subdued mood, to town where I picked up another wad of letters.

After lunch, and a little grocery shopping, we returned and I sat down with her and told her the whole story. All about the seven letters, and the severe consequences of my subsequent involvement with the various writers. I showed her the two letters and the photographs and explained the misgivings I had about Chip and his probable threat to my life and possibly those near to me. My stock had already gone down in her eyes as a result of learning about my involvement with Mary and telling the rest of the story hadn't helped. Of course, I really hadn't expected it to, but I rather liked her and decided it would be best to lay all the cards on the table first. If she still wanted to be in the game after seeing my hand, she'd have only herself to blame if things went wrong.

I apologised for all the falsehood I had concocted at our first meeting and asked her if she would have helped me as much if I had told her the truth then.

"What are you going to do now?" She asked when I had finished.

I hadn't any idea, and said so.

"It looks to me as if someone is watching you up here and sending word of your whereabouts to this person who is sending you letters from Georgetown."

I would suspect this Joyce character may have come home and is sending word of your being back here, to Chip."

"No. That doesn't fit in with her way of doing things, she lives a good hour's drive from here and she hasn't got a car, as far as I know. If she came home without Chip, she'd have come right in on the bus and confronted me here in my own house. I'm more afraid it is someone from the company who was behind all that clandestine activity at her airfield. Maybe Chip went back to California and laid the blame for everything that had happened to their operations there, on me.

I showed her the pictures of the airplane and Joyce. Then I remembered I had been going to borrow a magnifying glass to study the pictures with. I took them into the study. Put my jewellers bonnet on and studied the photos under the strong light.

First thing I noticed on the close up of Joyce beside the nacelle, was that the starbord, and possibly both engines, were without propellers. On the long distance shot, examining the pile of odds and ends propping up the tail, I saw they were among the cans and sacks, apparently being used to pull the tail down. I then directed my scrutiny to the nose of the airplane and sure enough there were crinkles in the skin consistent with a nose-over on landing in the soft sand. Definitely a surviveable landing.

Chip must have taken them off in order to load enough weight to the tail, to pivot the plane back into a level position. Otherwise, the airplane didn´t appear to have much damage. I tried to imaging what I would have done in his place. The fact that someone had sent me the piece of cardboard with the reference to sugarcane meant they had found out the money was gone and knew I had it. They also knew I was back in my home and the second letter had been sent to inform me they had survived and knew I was home. There had been no signs of life or occupancy at Joyce´s farm or the airstrip, for a considerable time. Indication ? They were short of money and couldn´t get home? No. I couldn´t buy that.

Chip couldn´t even try to trace me through the pick-up we had driven to Florida. It had belonged to Barbara, and if anyone went to ask her where it was, they´d be out of luck, and probably come under suspicion for murder.

Besides that, any police investigating her death would have been after anyone who might appear to be connected to her and her dead husband. I didn´t want to involve Vivienne in all this so I said very little and just enough to let her know that there was a menace behind the scenes which I hadn´t fathomed out yet.

"Why don´t you go and see if Joyce is home?" She said after I had told her my side of things. I thought about it and said,

"We could fly over and see if there are any signs of activity there, before making a ground reconnaisance."

She wasn´t impressed. I sensed she preferred to think of me as bolder.

I wished we had been able to bring Pugsley with us. She could have approached the house while I kept in the background observing. I did not think Joyce would use the old blunderbus on me if I came prowling around her house, but I had no doubt that Chip would come to the assault stage much more readily. A frontal approach, was therefore out of the question.

The thought of sending Vivienne to reconnoiter was dismissed immediately it came up. In fact the more I thought about establishing contact with either of them the more I realized it was a wrong approach to solving the mystery.

One catches a stalker, by displaying the bait momentarily. Then disappearing and circling behind him to stalk him. Of course, you have to locate his position first if you can, to know where 'behind him' is.

In my long-winded way, I tried to explain all this to Vivienne but after studying her reaction, I decided the best place for her in my program, was back in her own house doing her thing and wishing she could catch me somehow. I realized that someone had me under observation and was relaying the information to someone else in George Town. Someone who might already have left there and come here to operate. Chip would do something like that.

I needed to get her out of here before whoever was watching found out where she fitted in.

"Perhaps, it wasn't the best idea for you to come over here with me. I wouldn't want Chip Mason getting the idea you were involved. He isn't the kind of individual I want anywhere near you, or Mary, or the children. At present, nobody in his organization knows anything about your or their existence."

Vivienne laughed. I had known she would of course. I started saying I thought we should go directly back to Deer Park, but she came and put her arms around me as she would comfort a disturbed child and told me not to worry so much about her. I wrapped my arms around her and held her close, looking deeply into those dark mysterious pools of intelligence and committed myself by saying with all the sincerity I could muster in my voice,

"Honey, I could never forgive myself if anything happened to you" . . . Or Mary and the Kids" I added as an after—thought. Her reaction to this could have been predicted like the sunrise. She reached up and kissed me with a fervor which she couldn't control. After a while it became the inevitable 'sinrise' of a most enjoyably intimate experience for both of us.

Our mutual interest now thoroughly established, I decided to evacuate the locality as soon as possible and roused Vivienne an hour before dawn for the flight back to Deer Park. We had talked, after recovering last evening, about moving my base on a more permanent location at her house. The 'Opposition' must remain convinced I was still resident here in the mobilehome alone, but I wanted to set up surveillance equipment to monitor the premises during my absence and did not want them seeing me around this area purchasing it. I still needed to determine who was watching me and reporting to the man in George Town. Besides, Vivienne needed to be over there to watch over her financial interests until I could leave here. I decided it would be best if she went back by commercial Aviation. That would leave me free to return to the mobilehome with the equipment, set up the traps and follow over in my own transportation. I did not even want either of us, to use the telephone until we knew, who and what, we were dealing with.

I cranked up the luscombe and we flew to Renton field and took a taxi to Seatac for her flight home. She said she would rather go directly to the café, so I gave her the cash for her taxi fare from Spokane and tenderly saw her aboard the Horizon Air flight.

With the aid of a friendly taxi driver, I went shopping in various specialty electronic stores and returned with my booty to Renton before flying myself back to Diamond Point.

I spent the rest of the day, setting up a series of small video cameras, carefully concealed and operated by motion sensors, which were already in place, providing the access to the property with night lights. For daytime coverage there are now little units about the size of a tennis ball with their own built in motion sensors and an internal T.V. transmitter which sends the pictures directly to a video recorder. I spent time during the day to check these out by moving around the property myself and then watching the pictures on T.V. It was most interesting. Had this capability been available three years ago, when I was doing a similar exercise at Joyce's house; all of our lives, would have been totally different.

In preparation for the move to Deer Park, I got up an hour before dawn next morning and drove to the R.V.Storage. I was definitely not followed and was able to liberate seventeen packages, filling a brown paper Safeway bag, from the stash. I drove straight home and packed them, along with my computer tower and the flat screen, with a selection of floppy disks and some files from the filing cabinet, in the luggage compartment of the moonbaby. In place of the computer, I hooked up the old 286 tower and monitor to the printer. There was no room for that in the airplane. Had a quick breakfast and took off for Deer Park. It.s funny how differently alert one gets when constantly checking for a possible stalker. I even remembered to squeeze in my desk picture collage in case the place was searched.

Vivienne was delighted to see me in the airport café when I arrived. The presense of other customers precluded too overt a welcome and after a second breakfast, I left for the cabin and my task of setting up the computer and shuffling the hundreds.

I opened one of the packets of bills and began to stack them in thirteen piles. As each bill was picked up in my surgical-gloved hands, I crushed it into a crumpled ball and then smoothed it out before putting it on top of the others in the pile. The last nine, I crumpled, then folded in half twice and stuffed into the back section of my wallet. These I designated my ´small change generators´.

Each of the thirteen piles was put away in a blank envelope and placed back in the box of mailing envelopes in my briefcase. The rest of the envelopes were then packed in, compressing the stuffed turkeys safely out of sight on the far side, under the half open lid. I could leave the box open on my desk and doubt if anyone would take a second look at it. If they needed an envelope, there were a few left sticking up ready to pick. That done, I went shoping for a new color printer and some presents for Mary and the children, as well as a box of K9candy for Pugsley.

I was lucky to catch Mary between appointments and had a pleasant, if somewhat distant, chat with her after the children were satisfied with their presents.

It was important to emphasize that I would never intrude in her affairs since it was evident she had no desire to marry me. I only wanted to be allowed to be their GreatGrandfather, and have at least that much affectionate connection with them, if the truth had to be suppressed for their and her sakes. I asked if she had told them who their father was or had been and I could sense the relief she felt.

"Have you told Jake? I asked. and she blushed slightly shaking her head negatively.

"Well" . . . I hesitated, realizing that the more I carried on with this line, the further I could end up putting myself, away from my own children and I wondering in the back of my mind, how my own Mary might have felt, if she were here. "Well . . . Hasn't it come up between the two of you?" She looked so unhappy then, I was compelled to put my arms around her and ask again.

"Sweetheart you must tell me!" I pleaded. "Just so I don't accidentally screw things up, by either claiming them as my own or pretending I don't know who the father was. Jake and Vivienne are not fools honey."

I like them both, and I wouldn't want to be driven away now that they have been so instrumental in bringing us back together".

She was trembling, and I feared she was on the point of breaking down and I was afraid things might get, 'Out of hand', so I said, in a much more paternal tone.

"Mary my dearest, even if you have already committed yourself to a falsehood, It would be best if we all sat down together and told each other the truth."

"Both Vivienne and I've been observing Jake. He's crazy about you. and we're almost certain he'd like to hitch up with you. Which means he has already accepted you with the children. And, I continued, driving the knife right in to the hilt. "He'd be a better choice for a husband than I would." She buried her face in my shoulder and cried. Between sobs she said,

"Henry, I love you." For a moment I was stunned. But I gradually realized that she really loved me as a father figure. I tilted her chin up and said,

"I love you too. But what happened in that magical moment

on Stuart Island was a miraculous mistake. We have to be realistic now for the sake of the chldren and go forward with our lives in a sensible manner." Her eyes were swimming as she looked up at me and I went on before she could protest. "What happened then can't be undone thank God! I'm thrilled to have been their father. I can also be their Grandfather, and their Great Grandfather. Think about it! I am almost three times your age. Despite the euphoria and the haunting longings, to relive that rapturous event on Stuart Island, I love you more as a daughter than as a mate. You don't need to tell anyone I am a crook. As I told you; almost immediately after you had left for Spokane, events, simply got wildly out of control. What happened, was an accident, committed in the face of a deadly attack. However what happend after that, could possibly link me, as an accessory after the fact, to the murders, of three other people, which that lunatic had committed."

"I don't know what else they could suddenly dump on me if I ever were to be charged, but regardless of how we feel at this moment, our children need a solid home, with a loving father and a loving mother to give them a secure sense of un-blemished identity."

The sudden ringing of the doorbell announced the arrival of her next client, so I hustled her into the bathroom to wash her face while I went to answer the door.

I ushered the lady into the salon Mary had been preparing when I arrived, and went back to playing with Pugsley and the twins. When I realized how late it was I remembered how Vivienne and I had decided to leave Jake and Mary as much space as possible, I knocked on the door of the salon and called out to Mary that I was on my way home and would get in touch another time.

"I'll take Pugsley with me!." I called out through the door.

I again shaved the speed limits all the way to the airport café and arrived just in time to catch Vivienne closing up. Her car was in the shop at Valley, Jake had driven her to work, and she was just getting ready to call and ask him to pick her up before going out to Mary's. He apparently raised no objections when she told him I would take care of that chore and she laughed, and winked at me, when he said he was glad he could have more time with Mary and the children.

I hustled her and Pugsley off, to a nice little Bistro I had discovered during my paper route. While eating, I told her the plan I had hatched during my wild moments on the road, to spend the night with her in a romantic visit to Coeur d'Alene Lodge.

After the meal in the Bistro, we drove contentedly through the mountains enjoying the colours painted on them by the Sun, setting behind us.

An hour later we were sipping a glass of Harvey's Bristol Cream on the veranda over-looking the lake. The full Moon was coming up on the far side, illuminating a golden sheen across the water with it's mystical glory.

Pugsley, who, where Harvey's is concerned, has absolutely no self control to, savour the flavour, was asleep on the mat with her head in the saucer. Vivienne was contentedly snuggled in my arms and entranced with the world. I was reluctant to move lest I should fracture the infinitely tranquil beauty of my surroundings, and was almost asleep myself.

When the night air began to over-power Harvey's warmth, we snuggled down together in a dreamily soft bed and slept like an old married couple.

I learned, some weeks later, that Mary and Jake had been similarly disposed, like a young married couple.

In the chastity of infancy, the twins were likewise content in their cribs, with their double doses of Good Night Kisses.

While lying awake on my back, with Vivienne's left leg encircling my mid section I daydreamed about finding a way to handle the future encounter I visualized myself having with Chip.

He would be solely interested in finding out where and how I had hidden the money he considered as his.

Believe me, in a normal middle income situation, such as I

considered mine to be. One million seven hundred thousand dollars, in one hundred dollar bills, isn't easy to spend without raising someone's eyebrows. Vivienne's went up and down of their own accord so often, that another twitch, stimulated by that amount of available loot, would probably have entangled them permanently in her hair. I hadn't wanted that to happen, so I hadn't told her and decided not to change my mind on that subject. Not now anyway.

If Chip thought I had spent it he'd try to exert pressure on me to part with something of value I had bought. He had believed me to be a crook anyway when he had decided he needed a new partner. I could tell him I gave it away. He wouldn't believe me. Can't blame him. I wouldn't believe that myself. Not without irrefutable proof.

Proof.!? . . . I liked that idea. Perhaps I could generate some irrefutable proof for him. Like what? Like Thank-You Letters, from various charitable organizations?. With receipts on Letterhead paper.!. If Chip could be convinced the money no longer existed . . . Better yet if he could be induced to convince himself . . . to find out for himself . . . the ideas got better and better . . . and as I got more and more excited with these thoughts, Vivienne's leg seemed to get more and more excited with the results.

After a week, although I had made no definite promises, I was more or less established as a permanent resident in the cabin. While the others were all working honestly for a living, I did considerable research into the subject of acknowledgements for charitable donations.

Using actual samples scanned into the computer, I had made reproductions and even generated a few ficticious Charities myself. By copying and selectively editing them to indicate the gratitude expressed for my great generosity, I managed to develop a file of 'Good Deeds' showing how I had disposed of several hundred thousands of Chip's share of the loot. and was ready to fly back to Diamond Point, to "Play-back" the video recorder and 'Salt' my office files for potential intruders to discover.

To assist whichever moron found the 'File', with his arithmetic, I pasted inside the file cover, a hand written account sheet listing the Charity, the Date, the Amount and a column with the appropriate progressive 'Totals to Date' . . . The inference being, the money was flowing away at an impressive rate and serious action was needed if this philanthropic drainage was to be 'plugged'. That word, reminded me forcefully, that hopefully, Joyce had not been motivated to mention, the soap which she had exchanged for the kordite, in the cartriges of Chip's revolver.

The pre-dawn flight to Diamond Point with Pugsley wrapped in a small blanket because of the cold at altitude, went without incident and I parked the moonbaby in her hangar just before sunrise. On reaching the back entrance to the property, Pugsley suddenly darted off in front of me sniffing at the sheds and pathway as if scenting a deer. Then she led me to the work-shed housing my saws and after I let her in, she went straight to the big table saw and sniffed at the metal base under it.

Sure enough, the boxes of Mobil Oil I had directed Joyce to hide there under the sawdust, were gone. There was no other indication of anything else that had been taken and I conjectured that Joyce or both of them had been there and recovered the boxes thinking they contained the money they were after. I then went to my workshop. There was no indication it had been entered and the video recorder hadn't been touched. I took out the cartridge and looked at the reels, to see if it had been turned on. Sure enough, there was indication of it having been run for a short while. I carried it into the mobilehome and put it in the recorder under the T.V.

The recorder in my workshed, had been set to mark the time of recording. When the tape started, the header title showed it had first responded to the camera facing the garden. A deer and a fawn were browsing on the young maple trees on the lawn for a few minutes at about 9:15 pm. They moved out of camera range to feed next door. A pair of racoons came trotting down the pathway and scampered up the cedar tree when the yard light came on blinding the camera. Several other animals, mostly the neighbour's cats came on stage as they foraged through the garden and I was getting a bit disenchanted with this disjointed animal show, since the film stopped automatically after ten second of sensing no motion. Suddenly, the video switched to the header labelled 'Driveway' and a car drove in and doused its lights in the parking.space. It was barely light enough for the camera to record but I could definitely make out Joyce's figure and that of a large male accompanying her. I did not recognize him but he was larger than her and Chip was smaller and not as tall or young as this guy seemed to be. They went to the saw shed and the film went blank for a few seconds. Then came on again as they triggered the motion sensor on the return to their car.

On screen, it looked as if the were only gone for a few seconds, but by re-running the tape and checking the clock displays, I found it was almost fifteen minutes before they reappeared.

Both were carrying heavy boxes which I recognized as the Mobil oil boxes she had hidden in the sawdust under the saw, for me, the day before that fateful flight began.

Definitely, Chip must have had got himself some burly assistant, and Joyce was evidently still on his team.

The car drove away and the video returned to the recording of the movements of the dawn foragers. I had been away four days and when setting up the recorder with the time display, I had somehow omitted to set the date in as well so I could only estimate by the sequence of the episodes, which day they had visited. I estimated it must have been early Sunday morning, from six fifteen to six thirty. Well before any of the neighbours would have been up and about.

They had gone directly for those boxes, which I thought was strange, as I was almost certain Joyce would have remembered that those boxes only had cans of oil in them. Perhaps she had looked inside, when she hid them, and knew different, without telling me.

I hoped they hadn't opened any of the cans of oil, as I thought back to the violent explosions that had occurred after I had thrown the four 'empties' into the sea, off the cliffs in Oregon.

If they had !? . . . Perhaps the consequences, might be visible from the air, if I were to fly over.

I decided to take Pugsley with me. She would know Joyce, and even if Joyce didn't recognize the grown up Pugsley. Any sudden reaction by Pugsley might alert me in time to possibly avert an ambush if I decided to land. Also she knew the place since we had been there on several occasions cleaning up the airfield as well as the house and garden areas.

Joyce at least, should have been pleased, if not delighted, to find her home in such good condition. After almost three years of neglect, who knows what kind of a mess she would have been expecting to find when she returned. She would know immediately who had done the clean-up. That was probably why Chip had started this campaign of harrassment.

We took a trip into town, first, to pick up the mail and replenish some of the perishable food supplies. I had not given Vivienne any hard and fast return date and we were to communicate by E-mail only since I did not want her phone number showing up on my phone bills. That accomplished, I set up the old Windows 3.1 computer and wiped out the E-mail address book and the waste baskets, just in case the burly guy or whoever else they had on their team, was computer literate. I also salted the filing cabinet with my Good Deeds Documentation.

I loaded the moonbaby with fuel, and this time, made sure to take the binoculars and my Olympus OM1 camera, with its telephoto lens installed. Not having a good high resolution digital camera, ment resigning myself to waiting a couple of days before the prints would be available from CostCo for viewing.

We took off at two thirty p.m. into a cloudless sky. Thirty minutes later, the airfield at Joyce's place was directly below and moonbaby was slowly circling the target at about five hundred feet while I popped the shutter of the OM1 at every different scene. I covered the house and garden as well as both ends of the airstrip and its approaches from the road. The open parking area between Joyce's house and the road, appeared to have a car parked there and I wanted to be able to get a view of the license plates but that would necessitate landing, as the angle shot from up above was obstructed by tree tops. When the film ran out, I tried reading it with the binoculars. However, the buffeting from the slip-stream past the cabin window, plus the concentration on maintaining height and flying speed long enough to read it clearly, was too severe. Having circled almost overhead for several minutes I had still not seen any signs of life other than the parked car. Joyce had not had a car when I last saw her. Chip had driven me in a his Rolls Royce, in California and that car in Joyce's 'Parking', was no 'Rolls'. I wondered what Chip had done with the 'Rolls' before we started out on our impromptu escapade. After he disappeared from Bigshoes's radar, I would suspect Bigshoes might reasonably have 'impounded' it, after it became obvious he had no intention of returning. Thus making it necessary for him to obtain a different car. If that car in the parking, was Chip's of course. I made a few more tighter turns around the house hoping the noise would lure someone outside to take a look. Joyce would know the airplane as I had not changed the paint colour and there aren't too many school bus yellow luscombes flying around the area nowadays. Then I gave up and returned to base.

Strongly suspecting this noisy display might have provoked some kind of reaction, I re-set all the security devices before Pugsley and I set out by road for a closer look; dropping the roll of films off for processing at CostCo 'en passant'.

I parked the old midnight blue Olds, outside the café at Joyce. I settled Pugsley down in the car as I did not want to arouse any interest in her, and went in for a quick snack until it got fully dark. The cafe was empty, except for a couple in a booth at the far end, who I could not see, except for the man's shoulder. I parked myself in the booth by the door so I could check on anyone coming in. After I left, I fed Pugsley the few scraps I had promised her, and we set off, walking close hauled together, down the road towards Joyce's house.

I had forgotten just how dark it got on that road, but Pugsley managed to keep me from wandering into the ditch on either side. As we approached the house, I shortened the leash even more to warn Pugsley to silence and we entered the parking area. The light which was on in the parlor window, provided just enough illumination for me to read the number plate and determine the make of the car.

I repeated the number in my head several times to ensure remembering it as a Washington plate number 706 DMY. At least it wasn't a California car. That was some relief.

I thought about making a closer inspection of the house but remembering how easily Joyce's old blunderbus could go off, I decided to let the enemy come to me.

We left as quietly as we had come.

I had parked close to the the café entrance, and was opening the car door for Pugsley to get in, when the café door opened. The couple, who had been seated at the back of the room when I originally entered, came out.

Pugsley immediately jumped out and ran to the woman wagging her tail frantically excited. The man moved to intervene but Pugsley eluded him and went to the woman she recognized. I had trained her not to jump up at people but the moment I called her back by name, Joyce recognized her, and bent down and hugged the dog to her. The man, who I then recognized as Joyce's burly companion from the video. Turned toward me and in the light from the café, I could see his friendly face for the first time. He was a large man with an Anglo-Indian appearance, and the moment he began speaking, his dialect confirmed my first impression.

"It's Henry!, Ramesh". Joyce cried out in a voice full of surprise and pleasure. "And this is the little puppy I left behind . . . Lordy, haven't you grown up into a beauty?" she exclaimed, rubbing Pugsley's cheeks between her hands. "She has grown up into a lovely lady, Henry." She said turning her attention towards me while still fondling the dog. "I suppose that was your airplane we saw circling around this afternoon." There was no point in denying it so I replied. "It was indeed, and we, Pugsley and I, were so surprised to see a car at the house, we drove out this evening to visit. There was a car there, but you weren't home, were you?"

The big man chuckled extending his hand for me to shake. "We were out having a wild night on the town instead. Eh? My name is Ramesh; and I gather, from what Joyce just said, you are the Henry she has mentioned from time to time. And this loverly dog is the puppy she left behind." He added as Pugsley came round to me in response to my call. His handshake was firm but the hand was soft, indicative of a sedentary occupation.

I sensed Joyce's disappointment in Pugsley's ready response to my summons, and realized I'd better establish my claim to her, before Joyce could voice one. "Yes". I said firmly. "She was originally our puppy, but Joyce went away and left us about three years ago, and now she's mine." I looked straight at the two of them so they'd know I meant it.

"Where's Chip?" I asked directly to Joyce and she winced before saying quietly. "Chip died." I didn't want to say anything that might display my true feelings, for I could see she had been hurt by his loss, so I murmured, "Oh . . . I am sorry", in my best funeral parlor voice. I was, for her sake. For my own petty self's sake, I was relieved.

"How did that happen?" I asked gently, and was a little surprised when it was Ramesh who answered.

"He died in my hospital, of a massive infection of Necrociitis." Then, as if to explain, he continued. "When he came to me, the necrociitis was too far developed, for us to have any hope of curing it." I think it was for Joyce's sake he added. "Even if we could have halted it, he would have been miserably crippled for the remainder of his life." I decided not to probe the question any further until I could look up Necrociitis in my old copy of the Merk Manual and find out what it was.

Sensing a long story to be covered, and still somewhat confused, as to who or what was the behind the reason these two had raided my property, only three days ago, and walked off with some highly explosive loot, whether they knew it or not. I decided to terminate the discussion before they could invite me into a potential trap. Speaking casually, I mentioned that it was already late and getting later. We had a long drive home, and this was not the best location to discuss what obviously was a long and complex story. Also, that I would be delighted to host the dinner at my place tomorrow if they would care to come round, say about eleven o'clock in the morning, since I had a tendency to be a late riser. I asked Joyce if she remembered how to get to my house and she answered, pensively,

"How could I possibly forget?.."

Obviously there was no doubt about Where, Ramesh fitted into the puzzle, but How? And When? And Why? Were still unanswered. In some unchivalrous way, I also wanted to ask if they had opened any of the cans of oil they had stolen from my house, but this was not the time nor the place. I thought it would be more fun to confront them at my place, by casually asking Joyce, if she remembered what she had done with the boxes of oil I had asked her to put under the table saw, and watch their reaction.

I said goodnight, and as soon as Pugsley was settled down, got into the car myself, effectively avoiding any overt demonstration of familiarity. Put on the seatbelt, started the engine and backed out of the parking space, and drove slowly away. In the rear view mirror, I could see them in the light from the café window, watching for a few moments, before walking off, arm in arm, into the darkness.

Eleven o´clock and the sound of a car entering the driveway aroused me from a short nap in my old leanback chair. Dinner was already cooking on the stove and wine chilling in the ice bucket. Since I didn´t have a silver one I used a plastic bucket with an aluminium foil trim around the rim. The table was set with its assorted place mats and the best U.S. Navy silverware. Folded paper towels served for serviettes. and each place had its own wine glass and waterglass so there would be no mistaking the glasses during refills.

All very 'Posh' to impress Ramesh, who I guessed from his accent, came from a wealthy Indian family background, I was eager to learn how Joyce and Chip had encountered him.

Pugsley had greeted them at the car. Perhaps they had wondered why she hadn't greeted them last Sunday. They didn't mention it, so I left them to guess.

Ramesh was enchanted with the Camp atmosphere of the mobilhome, surounded by its out buildings and trellis covered pathways, with Wisteria and Virginia Creeper shielding it from the Cedar grove in which it lived. Just as though he had never seen it before. I thought, maybe it had been too dark on Sunday morning for a real inspection so I took them on a tour, thinking I might make one of America's funniest videos. At least for myself.

Years ago, Joyce had made a couple of working visits. The first, when we 'salvaged' Barbara's Enrique, and the second when she came up to deposit the goodies under the table saw for me. On both occasions, she probably had very little time to really nose around.

The meal, roast ham with it's heaped covering of lightly browned chunked potatoes, quartered onions, slices of celery, tomato and carrot, and whole mushrooms. All baked together in the dutch oven, was a roaring success, assisted with the two bottles of Gewertstrameiner. There was no need to introduce the 'Scherezade' to induce them to talk. For dessert, an impressive Key Lime Pie, which I had picked up at the all night supermarket last evening on my way home, completed the delusion I was also an excellent chef. Who says a single man can't survive, and live well on his own cooking.? That 'dish' with the variant of beef or pork instead of ham, alternated with a big pot of vegetable soup, can keep me alive and well for several weeks of isolation. If the roast and the soup are made on alternate days, they start fresh, keep well in the refrigerator, and can be 'nuked' in a few minutes, whenever required.

Feeding them well, led to a more congenial atmosphere and as I continued to keep a coolness towards Joyce, I did nothing to provoke any sense of rivalry with Ramesh.

"My infatuation with Joyce was mortally wounded, the moment Chip showed on the scene. I have never before, or since, witnessed two adults, falling instantly in love with each other, the way they did." I declared, when he finally brought up the subject of my relationship with her. "At first, I was devastated, but by the time they arrived at the rendezvous in Louisiana, I had rationalized my feelings down to a minor disenchantment." I smiled at them as I said this, before adding, "After they failed to show up in the Everglades, I was more worried about her safety than anything else. Especially when it became obvious that something critical, must have occurred, to prevent them from returning to the last rendezvous to collect the money."

"We didn't know you had stolen it." Joyce said quietly, to my surprise. "I'm glad Chip never knew either." she added, with a little more emphasis, as though to infer she blamed me for his demise.

"The poor chap died miserably enough without the added torment he would have suffered if he had known that." Ramesh injected before Joyce could add it to my score. With a solemnity I felt for her, I replied, "Well that's a relief, I wouldn't have wanted to feel responsible for torturing a dying man." Most of the story of their ill fated flight came from Joyce, but in regard to the subsequent events, Ramesh did most of the talking. His factual narrative, was spiced up with occasional bursts of corrections from Joyce, who was cuddled up to him on the couch.

I had suggested we retire to the end room as it was smaller and more comfortable than the kitchen, where the sight of the dishes piled in the sink was a constant distraction for Joyce, who kept wanting to get up and wash them up, whereas, I wanted them to sit and talk with me, about the events leading up to their returning together to her farm.

They were both grateful, and impressed, that Pugsley and I had taken time to work on clearing it up and keeping it nice for their return. Joyce could not get over learning that I had paid her taxes, electricity and water bills, for the whole time she had been absent. I simply said I had never given up hope, and set up the routine payments for her place and mine, from my bank account while I searched the Carribbean for her and Chip. To allay Ramesh´s concern, I shrugged, "It was the least I could do for a friend, for who´s ´difficulties´, I had felt more than somewhat responsible." I didn´t mention, that in the event she had never returned, I could, in about four more years, legally, have laid claim to the property after having paid the property taxes etc. for the last seven years.

Another reason for holding the conference in the parlor was the fact that it was being televised. I had set up my little 'spies' in both rooms, and after recording the two hours around the table in the kitchen cum dining room, I had to excuse myself to change the tape in the recorder in the shed. The parlor was cosier as well, helping to subdue the extranious noises that might otherwise conflict with the recorded conversations.

I had to make two more trips to the shed to change tapes. Each time as the two hours passed I had more and more difficlty controlling the urge to look at my watch as there is no wall clock in that room. However I managed to slip out for 'Replenishing the Harvey´s, taking a leak, checking the dog, etcetera.'

By the time we had exhausted ourselves relating our stories to one another, it was beginning to get dark and I was concerned about them driving all the way to Joyce. Ramesh and I were beginning to develop a friendship, so I stopped the flow of liquor and began to concentrate on sobering everyone up for the trip home. I had offered to let them sleep in my bed while I kipped down on the couch, but Joyce would have none of that. We demolished the rest of the Key Lime Pie, had some strong coffee and we eventually parted as friends as the sun went down. Ramesh and I shook hands warmly and I submitted to a hug from Joyce before they set forth on the forty mile drive home. I tidied up and went to bed, fervently praying they would make the trip safely.

I spent the next three days, digesting the taped conversations and the left-over roast ham, while writing the rest of the story.

As transcribed from six hours of video tapes:-
The Saga of Chip and Joyce
After dropping the keys of the pickup to Henry, Joyce realized Chip had not been merely teasing Henry by his sudden take-off. It was also becoming obvious to her that he had no intention of making their next rendezvous. She felt dismayed that someone for whom she had developed such an intense attraction, could be so devilishly treacherous. Henry, already disconsolate over the loss of her affections, would be further dismayed when he and Pugsley reached the Everglades only to find they had been totally abandoned. When she challenged Chip with this betrayal, he merely laughed.

"He'll make out O.K." He said, pointing over his shoulder. "He already took his share. You don't think I'm going to let him take my share too. Do you? I don't trust him any more," he added, reaching across to hold her hand. "Not with our share that is. Those two boxes hold almost a million dollars in cash. Do you think we'd ever see him again if we left him with all of it? . . . In his present frame of mind?"

Joyce said nothing. In her present frame of mind, she was busy trying to compare her betrayal of Henry's love for her, to Chip's perfidious behaviour. True, they had never specifically declared themselves to be 'In love' with each other, even during their moments of ecstacy, and despite the extent and depth of their involvement in each other's lives. His kind and caring behaviour towards her and even his offer to share his take in this escapade with her, had been no more than her feelings towards him. Certainly, she had felt flattered by Henry's sexual attraction to her but her own attraction to Chip, the moment their eyes met, had been different. Overwhelming in fact, and to find Chip reacting to her in exactly the same manner had seemed incredible. It had been her first experience of 'Love at first sight'. She had literally

'Changed horses in mid-stream' without a second thought. However, she also realized, she would have to sustain a certain loyalty to Henry At least as far as not admitting, or even mentioning, anything to Chip about her's and Henry's involvement in the events which had led to the death of Chip's previous partner in this nefarious operation. 'Honour amongst thieves ?', she thought It was merely a matter of self preservation. She and Chip had been so euphorically entwined during the previous two days drive from Garden City to the Louisianna rendezvous, they had spent litle time in sharing individual histories and Henry had warned her not to mention anything about her connection to the airfield to Chip lest he become suspicious about all these 'fortuitous meetings'. With this new turn of events, if she revealed anything, Chip would suspect she had been a 'Plant' and possibly reverse his attitude towards her. For the present, she would have to say nothing and watch her step. On the drive from Garden City to Louisiana, Chip had been so full of plans for their 'future', his, her's and Henry's, on Grand Cayman. Now it had become only 'his and her's'. It could be extremely dangerous to risk upseting his plans before they were completed.

Three hours after they had taken off, Chip decided it was time to begin transfering the fuel from the cans in the cabin, to the wing tanks. They had been flying over the sea for some time and Chip had been busy with the radios, making frequent adjustments to them and drawing lines across the chart in his lap. Joyce, loth to distract his attention from this by asking questions, had assumed the lines were associated with some sort of radio beacons. The chart had a series of little pencilled triangles on it and a line joining these, which no doubt represented their track across the sea. The line seemed awfully short compared with the size of the pale blue area depicting the ocean.

Although, before they had got ready to fly, Henry had carefully explained the process of transferring the fuel to her, doing it in flight, was another matter. The four Jerry Cans, as he had called them, were strapped in pairs to the two seats immediately behind theirs. At the outer side of the seats, between the seat and the sidewall, a short pipe with a valve on it stuck up from the floor. From behind the seat, she had to reach down, unscrew the cap from the top of this pipe, attach a clear plastic hose to the open end, put the free end of this hose into the bottom of the can, open the valve and squeeze a rubber bulb in this hose several times to start the fuel siphoning into the wing tank. The instructions had not been very dificult to follow, but Henry hadn't told her how hard it was to actually open the Jerry Can lid. It simply wouldn't budge, no matter how hard she tried. In the end, she had to call Chip and ask him to show her. His reaction to this, was her first indication of how fragile his adoration of her could be. As soon as he left his seat, the airplane began to wobble. The floor seemed to tilt up and sideways, causing her to grab the back of the seat to keep from sliding to the rear of the cabin, and a sudden strange sense of unreality attacked her. Chip pushed past her, reached down, snapped the spring lock from the cap on the can and spun the cap off. It all seemed like one motion to her and his look of annoyance as he scrambled back to his seat, coupled with the sudden waft of gasoline fumes did little to calm her stomach. Once the gasoline was flowing from the can to the tank, she had to remain standing to hold the tube securely into the neck of the can watching the level in the can go down by peering through the opening with the aid of a flashlight. It seemed to take forever to transfer the fuel. Chip meanwhile, had re-estabilized the world on an even keel and her stomach's rebellion went into temporary remission. Now, the fumes she was forced to inhale, if she breathed at all while close to the opening, were making her dizzy. When the bottom of the can came in sight and the last tiny waves in the liquid sloshing across it disappeared, she had dificulty extracting the hose and transferring it to the second can. When that transfer was completed, she almost collapsed while trying to put the caps back on the empty cans. Engrossed in taking radio bearings, Chip was startled to find her stumbling back to her seat as if she was drunk. He realized immediately what had happened and carefully strapped her back into her seat before opening the cabin window beside her and holding the airplane in a slight skid, to create a strong draft of cold air across her face. He needed a way to hold her head from lolling forward across the control wheel, if she passed out completely.

Her white scarf, the gift he had bought her on the drive, had gone when she had thrown the truck keys out to Henry. He now had to push her elbows under the shoulder straps as a temporary solution and trim the airplane slightly nose down so he could leave the seat and go aft to the bulkhead and get one of the bungee chords holding the money boxes in place.

Henry, in his rage, had torn the center box off the bulkhead and its dangling bungees would now have to be used to hold an even more precious cargo in place.

Chip had cursed Henry at that time, and had started the take-off, before Henry could carry out his threat of taking the other two boxes or preventing the take-off by driving the pick-up in front of the airplane. In the heat of that moment, he hadn't realized he still had the pickup's keys in his own pocket. Joyce had pleaded with him to turn back, but he had refused and finally compromised by flying back over the runway once more to allow her to drop the keys to Henry. She had used her scarf for a flag to enable Henry to find and retrieve the keys. Henry had taken his share of the loot. He also had the truck and her dog and could 'Go to hell' now as far as Chip was concerned. The bungees, he used now to tie her head to the back of her seat, to restrain it from falling forward if she became unconscious. He kissed her gently and settled back to the job of flying them to safety. The plane had developed a distinct list to starbord, since Joyce had not attempted to transfer the fuel from the other two cans behind his seat. He would probably have to do the transfer himself. He shrugged slightly as he levelled the wings. He had done this transfer solo a number of times in the past and could do it again if necessary. The fuel system had a crossover valve connection. For the wing tanks to be either isolated, or joined, allowing the fuel to balance itself across the airplane, or all be directed to one engine if necessary. It had been closed when Joyce transferred the fuel from the first two cans to the right wing tanks. Rather than leave his navigation, he decided to run with the unbalanced condition for the moment. They could transfer fuel from the left cans later. He fully expected Joyce to be recovering very soon. By his calculations, even allowing for the small deviation from course her malaise had occasioned, they were well on their way to making a landfall in a couple of hours. Even if they missed the Caymans entirely, the long island of Jamaica lay across their path, not too far to the south-east for emergencies.

He scanned the engine instruments and settings, noting everything was still functioning as it should, and began taking another set of radio beacon bearings. From time to time, Chip glanced across at Joyce to see how well she was recovering from the effects of inhaling the gasoline fumes. She looked pale and ill and he wondered if he should try to make it to Miami where she could get medical assistance. To do this would seriously endanger the success of their scheme to reach asylun in the Cayman islands with the money. There would be all kinds of officialdom to contend with . . . It was already too late to consider diverting back to the Everglades rendezvous. Henry wouldn't be arriving there for at least another day, if he arrived at all. Chip harboured no delusions as to whether Henry believed the reasons he had given for carrying the extra fuel instead of leaving the empty cans for him to take in the pickup to refill at their next rendezvous. The man might be a little deranged from the sudden switch in his love life, but he was no fool and must have realized Chip had decided to try and abscond with the girl, the plane and his share of the loot. Hence all the histrionics and desperate behaviour.

He decided to press-on to the Caymans. The weather report from Havana, in Spanish, seemed to be talking about a hurricane developing in the Atlantic off the coast of Africa. Miami weather hadn't mentioned it. Chip decided it would probably not affect the Carribean for another day or so and dismissed it. His bearings from Tampa, Miami and Houston were coming in sufficiently strong to assure him the fixes depicting their progress towards the Cayman Islands were reliable. It was time to complete the fuel transfer. He trimmed the airplane slightly nose heavy and biassed against the unbalance to compensate for his moving aft, and climbed out of the seat. Joyce was stirring but still appeared dazed and barely responded when he bent over her and kissed her. He opened the crossover valve and began the transfer.

He was just closing the cap on the second can, having completed the transfer, when Joyce came fully back to consciousness and glanced across at his empty seat. She tried to turn her head to see where he was but found it strapped to the back of her seat with the bungee chords. In a panic, she wrenched her arms out from under the restraining straps and reached up to free her head from its tethers. Her hand struck the control column in front of her, driving it forward. Bent over the back of the seat, screwing the cap back on the pipe in the floor, Chip was flung violently against the framework of the cabin ceiling, while Joyce, finding herself trying to float out of her seat, grabbed the control-wheel for support, pulling it vigorously back towards herself. In consequence, Chip was slammed down head first into the Jerry cans. Squeezed down into her seat by the increased gravitational force, Joyce's head came free of the bungee cords and she lurched forward again, pushing the controls forward and propelling Chip up against the cabin roof once more. The next backward movement of the control wheel brought Chip's inert form flying over into the pilot's seat with his feet landing across Joyce's forearms, disengaging them from the control wheel and pressing them down into her lap.

By the time Joyce had disentangled both arms from under chip's legs, she had recovered enough to realize that all these gyrations must have been the direct result of her movement of the control wheel, and she jerked her hands away from it as if it was red hot. The airplane magically stabilized itself into a shallow dive. As the engine speed built up into a high pitched whine, she remembered Henry explaining to her that fore and aft motion of the control wheel controlled the speed. She cautiously took hold of the wheel once more and began holding a slight back pressure until the sound of the engines seemed to return to normal.

To her horror, she realized Chip had been badly hurt. He seemed to be unconscious, lying limply across their seats with his feet in her lap, with blood all over his face and head. Added to her concern for him, was the sudden realization that she was now virtually alone, in charge of this airplane. Where it went and how it was to get there. This was definitely not the time to panic.

Joyce had never flown in her life before the trip from Port Angeles, Washington, to Garden City, Kansas. That had been an adventure in itself. Henry had given her enough money to go First Class, He wanted to ensure she got the best treatment and assistance from the airline, to compensate for her lack of experience. She had revelled in the comfort and special attention, the airline people had given her, after she told them it was to be her first flight. They had assisted her with everything. Porters had carried her luggage and Couriers had even accompanied her from one plane to the next, at both Seattle, and St Louis. It had been a wonderful experience. Her second flight, in the very airplane Henry had fantasized about stealing, and flying off to Paradise with her, was turning into a real live nightmare. Instead of Henry, sitting in the other seat, excitedly describing their flight to the islands, in a stolen airplane, she was sitting under the legs of an unconscious man she had only known for a couple of days, in a stolen airplane she had no idea how to fly, and lost, somewhere over the middle of the ocean. Was this to be her punishment for deserting Henry? Somehow, she felt this predicament would not have happened, under his control. However, wishing would not help either herself or Chip, and she could do little to keep the airplane flying with Chip's legs weighing her down. One by one, she lifted them off her lap and tucked them into the space between the seats. Their slackness convinced her that Chip was unconscious and his left arm seemed to be caught between the control and the seat preventing her from being able to pull the wheel back enough to stop the airplane from gathering speed each time she relaxed her pull on the wheel. She undid her seat belt and climbed over the back of the seat to where she could reach over and get a hold under Chip's armpits and literally drag his body over the back of the seat to lay him on the floor between the two rows of seats. He was bleeding from a gash on the top of his forehead. The only thing handy to bandage this was her skirt, she slipped it off and wrapped it as tightly as possible around his head and wedged him between the seat legs before scrambling over the top of his seat and flopping into it with the control wheel in her hands. For some time she seemed to have no control over the roller coaster action until she remembered Henry explaining what the big wheel on the side of the lever box between the seats was for, and that the airplane would usually fly itself if you trimmed it. Gently she turned the top of the wheel backwards, until the nose came up to the horizon, and let it stop there. The engine noises seemed to settle down to what had been their normal sound and the airplane seemed to have its left wing down a little and be turning to the left. On the back of lever box there was another wheel set across it, which was for adjusting the level of the wings according to Henry. She moved the top of this wheel to the right and the wings levelled off. Watching and correcting the level and the up-down movements took a little getting used to but eventually everything seemed to stabilize itself and she had time to attend to Chip, the man she loved. The first man she had ever really fallen in love with, was now lying helpless behind her on the floor between the seats and she desperately wanted to go back and help him. But each time she got ready to move to his side, the airplane became agitated and she could only look over the back of the seat and try to talk to him. Gradually, her natural pragmatism took over and she realized that she could do nothing until the airplane came back to earth. If she couldn't make it do that, there was nothing she could do for either him or herself and they would die together in the final crash. Much as she thought about the poetic beauty of this, it was not the picture either he or Henry had painted in her mind and she did not want to simply submit to the present circumstances.

The little clock-like dials on the panel in front of her all seemed to be reading different times. She checked her watch and saw that it was almost one o'clock. One of the airplane's clocks was in agreement with that. The other, had only ten hours on it's dial and a closer examination showed the word 'Altimeter' on it. After some study of the numbers and the positioning of the hands, she decided the altitude must be seventy five meters. She didn't really know how high that was, except when she looked over the side the sea seemed to be a long way down. 'O.K.' she told herself, "When all its hands come to zero, dead or alive, I'll be down on the ground." The thought was quite comforting. Alongside that clock, was another with only one hand and some pieces of red, green and yellow tape, stuck around the rim of its glass face. The numbers on its face read from Zero to 200 and it was marked, 'Airspeed'. With the airplane riding nice and steady as it was at the moment, this hand was reading 125, and the initials 'mph' she decided, meant miles per hour, just like a car. However, unlike a car, there was no sensation of speed. The sea appeared to be almost motionless and with no clouds in the sky, the airplane didn't even seem to be moving at all. Also, there was no white line for her to follow. She had no idea which way she was going. The airplane had been turning when she took over control, but where it was heading right now was something she would have to find out. Chip had said they were supposed to be going South East.

Years and years ago, Charlie had shown her and the girls, how to find South from the sun, if they ever got lost in the woods, by using the watches he had bought them that Christmas. "Point the hour hand at the sun, and divide the angle between that and the direction twelve o'clock is pointing, in half." He had said, "That's due South, and remember, the road outside the house runs due south from the highway." She had checked it herself several times when walking back from the store. At that time it had seemed insignificant. Just one of those little useless bits of information one gathers. In her present predicament, she felt she could forgive Charlie for everything he had ever done to her and the girls, for it. Right now, she decided, the difference between one o'clock and noon was insignificant, the sun was almost directly south and though she couldn't actually see it because the upper wing hid it, she could slowly turn the airplane with the little wheel on the lever box, until the nose of the plane pointed in the right direction. Southeast? Chip had said they were heading Southeast.

Charlie had also had a scheme for determining which way was southeast by spreading the fingers and pointing the ring finger at the sun. However this was not easy to do while carrying the baskets of groceries and she had forgotten which hand to use. "The sun comes up in the east and goes down in the west." She chanted. "So, if I move the airplane a little more to the right, the sun will go west and I'll go towards the east." The sun was high overhead and fearing she might turn too far, she moved the wheel until the sun was just to the left of the division between the windscreen panels. Chip, she knew, had been plotting their position on his chart and he had stowed it in the side pocket before getting up to manage the fuel transfer. However, she didn't know how to read the chart with its multitude of different symbols and in any case she had to continuously be correcting the plane's direction to keep the sun where it should be. The next time she looked at her watch, she was surprised to see it was half past two. A slight bumping feeling in her seat alerted her to the probability that Chip was moving and she carefully turned around to kneel on the seat and look over the back without bumping the controls. Chip was trying to move the end of her skirt from his face and she reached down and uncovered his face for him. He stared at her and she was intensely relieved to see his eyes were focussing and apart from a puzzled expression they appeared normal. She reached for his hand and helped him to sit up and gradually he managed to stand up supporting himself on the cans beside him. Her skirt was firmly stuck to his head and she told him not to pull it off or it would start the bleeding again. Carefully she folded the lose material away from his face and draped it over the back of his head.

"What happened?" He asked, motioning her to move out of his seat into the other seat. "You fell and cut your head on the can." She told him as she slowly helped him round into his proper seat and begin to resume control of the airplane. "How long have

I been out?" She looked at her watch again, trying to calculate. "About two hours." "And you've been flying the airplane that long?" He asked, smiling incredlously as he adjusted the trim to compensate for the changed balance their movements had caused. "I had to do something while you were napping and I forgot to bring my knitting." She laughed, overcome with relief at his recovery. "I just kept going Southeast like you said." Chip almost had tears in his eyes as he remarked, smiling admiringly at her.

"You really are a fantastic woman! Give me a hand to tie this head gear out of my eyes will you? I'd best get a radio fix to find out where we are."

The sandbar swept in a crescent towards the sun. Such ripples as he could determine from this height would mean landing against the glare. Even if the surface was firm enough to support the wheels it would be almost impossible to steer the Dominee in such a tight curve without engine power.

"Do your belt up tight honey and say your prayers." Chip tried to make his words sound encouraging but his smile lacked conviction. The bitter taste of failure was drying his throat and the thought of her air sickness having brought his carefully planed scheme to this ignominious end, ate insidiously into his feeling of affection for her.

Joyce had admitted 'messing about" with the radio, in hopes of finding help, while he lay unconscious on the floor, and, perhaps because of the injury to his head, he now found difficulty in remembering the frequencies for the VOR signals he had been using before the upset. When he found some again, the bearings were at such a small angle to one another that they made a long thin intersection. They could be far off, to either side, of the track he had plotted on the chart. He was still trying to locate a station to give a definite cross he could plot, when the starbord engine started running out of fuel. He had opened the crossover valve when making the transfer from the left hand cans and the port engine still had fuel but Chip had no doubts it would soon run out as well. He trimmed the ship left wing down and eased the fuel mixture as thin as he dared, noting the altitude was holding steady, just over seven thousand feet, and went back to the radio. They were below five thousand feet, with both engines silent, when Joyce drew his attention to the sand bar.

"I think that's an island down there." she said, pointing hesitantly, sensing his suppressed tension. He banked right instinctively to see it. "It's gone underneath." She exclaimed, grabbing her seat, as he swung the airplane back over into a left turn. "By God you're right!." He shouted with relief. "Though . . . I don't see any trees on it . . . Maybe just as well . . . It's only a sand bar but it'l be better than landing in the water." He added, concluding his survey a little less enthusiastically. "Your seat belt's not fastened." She exclaimed as she realized they hadn't put it together when he had taken over the controls again. He was concentrating on the approach to the landing as she reached across and began trying to fasten his belt.

"Give me the other side she yelled." as she strained across him "I can't reach it!" He made no move to engage the pin himself, but flipped it across and she barely had time to engage the pin through the closest lap strap hole and the first hole in the nearest shoulder strap, before the wheels touched the sand. Chip made a perfect three-point landing on wet sand of the lee side of the sandbar, and for a few moments it seemed the airplane would run smoothly up the sandbar. But as its full weight came on them, the main wheels sank into the soft dry sand at the crest and the plane nosed over into a violent halt with its tail up in the air. Un-braced as she was, reaching across Chip, trying to reach his left shoulder-strap, Joyce was slammed between him and the control wheel and had the wind knocked out of her. Chip was twisted out of his seat and the left side of his head smacked against the top of the control panel so hard that despite the makeshift turban around it, he was stunned.

Trapped in that un-natural position, hanging half in and half out of their seats, it was several minutes before either of them became fully aware of the silence surrounding them. The late afternoon sun's reflection from the sea, flickering on the cabin walls, created the illusion of a fire and Chip panicked. He pushed Joyce aside and began fumbling for the D-Ring to release his harness. When he pulled it out, he fell into a struggling heap between the seat and control wheel, half under the instrument panel. The violent shove and Chip's panic stricken gyrations brought Joyce to full awareness and, despite the disorienting position in which she found herself hanging, Chip's scrambling about on the floor of the airplane, tickled her sense of humour so well, she burst into hysterical laughter.

The absense of actual flames and the pealing of Joyce's laughter finally calmed Chip and he wriggled into a position where he could see her. He stopped moving and lay staring incredulously at her.

The entry door of the Domminee is on the right side of the fuselage, about eight or so feet behind the pilot's position. In the airplane's tilted attitude, they literally had to climb the walls to reach it. Hinged along the forward edge and opening outward, the door fell out and down against the outside of the fuselage, when Joyce, standing on Chip's shoulders, opened it.

The sand seemed an awful long way down and she had to climb out and lower herself down the door onto the top of the lower wing and slide down it before dropping the remaining three or four feet to the sand. She made the journey without hurting herself. Chip, bereft of anyone to climb on, had to kick some foot holds through the cabin wall panel to get up to the exit. He followed Joyce's route down the outside except that she was there to assist him down the wing to the sand. They moved away unsteadily clinging to one another and gazing around their new island home.

"It's not quite what I'd expected, but at least it isn't crowded." Joyce said cheerfully, hoping to lighten Chip's woebegone expression. Climbing out of the airplane had been difficult, especially for Chip, as he had a sense of desecration in having to damage the interior paneling of the fuselage of his precious vintage airplane. After surveying the overall situation for several minutes, he dis-engaged himself from Joyce and walked slowly around the wreck, surveying the damage and shaking his head dismally as he realized the totality of his loss. He went back to Joyce, put his head, still partially wrapped in her blood-stained skirt, against her breast, clung to her and broke into a long drawn out wail of despair. Momentarilly she was appalled. Then, instinctively, she put her arms around him and held him tightly. A small weeping child who, she realized, needed her more desperately than anything else. It gave her love for him, a strange sensation of strength and power she had not known since the days when her two girls had been little babies.

Their shadow lengthened unheeded across the sand as Joyce sat, with her arms around him on the beach watching the sun disappear into the golden fire across the sea. A gentle breeze stirred the ripples at the water's edge whispering re-assurance to her. The darkness gave way to starlight more rapidly than she had expected and the air moving in from the water felt suddenly warmer. Chip's distress had eventually subsided into the sleep of the exhausted, and she now lay back, gradually pulling him up onto herself like a cover and studied the brilliant panoply of stars above her. Never in her life had the stars seemed so bright or so close, nor, strangely enough, her contentment been more complete.

Chip climbed back up the wing, carefully cutting hand holes with his pocket-knife through the exterior fabric of the fuselage, to enable him to use the lattice of the airplane's tubular steel structure as a ladder to reach the doorway. Each hole, he cut just wide enough for his shoe to pass through and the cut fabric, he tucked neatly back inside around the adjacent tube. Watching this meticulous surgery, Joyce wondered how Henry would feel if he could be beside her now, witnessing what had, and was still happening, to the airplane of his dreams. Mentally, she pictured him driving the pick-up with her puppy Pugsley, sitting beside him. She felt a strong sense of guilt at the thought that when he reached their carefully planned rendezvous in Florida, they would not be there to greet him. All four of them had been supposed to make the last leg together in the airplane to the Cayman Islands. There, they could spend all the money in those boxes, for a place to live the rest of their lives in luxury, safely beyond the reach of the american authorities. She and Chip were probably beyond anyone's reach, but hardly in luxury or safety. Henry and Pugsley were probably safe, but definitely within the reach of the authorities and driving a stolen pick-up, which Henry had explained to her, was undoubtedly linked to four murders. That facet of the story, which Henry had only revealed to her the night before meeting Chip, had, she admitted to herself, been a significant part of her decision to fly the next leg of the journey with Chip rather than drive with Henry. She could not however, put all the blame for her present situation, on Henry. He may well have cajoled her into joining this crazy escapade, but the final decision leading to her present predicament had definitely been hers.

Chip had now disappeared from sight inside the airplane and Joyce's thoughts returned to the present situation and how they were going to extricate themselves from it. In the course of the night, the moon had passed across the sky and for the first time in her life she had been content to just lie and drowsily watch it move slowly through the stars like a venetian gondola. Its crescent, a thin silver sliver, became a shining saucer with a large plum pudding sitting on it. Mother had just poured the rum over it and Dad had lit it. The pale lilac flames crept up around the dark ball of the pudding illuminating the delicious feast they were about to enjoy. Dad had already removed the sprig of holly the pudding had been decorated with, so that it would not catch fire and she felt disappointed because it had been so pretty. She cuddled her teddy bear to her breast and wondered why her pants and legs were wet. She knew it was not her doing. It must be her teddy bear that was being naughty. She would not tell mother because she might take teddy away. The wetness felt warm to her skin except where the air was cooling her knees and gradually she realized it was all the way up from her feet to the small of her back and she woke. Teddy was still in her arms and for a moment or two she felt offended that he would urinate on her until she realized that it was Chip she was holding, and, no way on god's earth could he have done so much. She sat up slowly and was amazed to find tiny green lights sparkling all over her legs. Chip's long pants were floating between them, full of it. The toes of his shoes stuck up out of the dark water, like two tiny little black mountains with a ring of sparkling emerald lights along their shorelines. She spent some time absorbing this magic kingdom before the true reality came through to her. The sea was gradually reaching further and further up the sand and would soon completely cover their little island.

By his watch, it was 4am. and the moon was close to the western horizon. The warm night air moved so softly, it seemed to surround their wet clothes as if to steal the moisture from them without disturbing them. The sea had only come up a little way beyond where he and Joyce had been lying and was now receding again. The lump on his left temple, throbbed with a dull ache, but the cut that curved across his forehead, though sore to touch, had quit bleeding and congealed into a long scab like the handle of a bucket. Joyce had gently removed her blood soaked skirt and washed it in the sea before hanging it over the wire bracing between the wings. Relieved of his concern that the airplane would become submerged, he was now beginning to feel hungry. In his original planning, he had realized the airplane would have had to wait some indefinite time for the truck to arrive at the Everglades rendezvous, and had therefore included extra rations for the air crew. In accord with the plan, he and Joyce had picked up four bags of groceries for that purpose, on their way out to meet Henry at the Louisiana rendezvous. Even more important now, were the four plastic gallon milk jugs of fresh water stored in a box below the right rear seat. Later, when after observing Henry's irrational behaviour at that rendezvous, he had decided to ditch Henry. He had been careful not to betray this revision by explaining the extra supplies would be needed while waiting for Henry to arrive. He now congratulated himself on that piece of wisdom. With careful management they might be able to keep themselves alive until rescued. If he could restore the airplane to a level attitude it might be possible to reach help on the radio. If the crash locator beacon had gone off, help might even have been on it's way at this very moment, he thought, except for the fact that he had switched it off at the beginning of the escape and it had remained that way in case of a crash enroute. After all, the whole purpose of the enterprise had been to avoid notifying the authorities of their whereabouts. That hadn't really applied once the overwater leg had begun but he had overlooked that aspect. The realization made it more important to get the tail back down and try using the radios. He climbed back into the tilted cabin and passed some food and a jug of the water to Joyce. He bit into an apple and let his mind wander over the possibilities of all these eventualities. Should he bury the money boxes here on the island and come back later, after rescue, to recover them? Would he be able to wrap them sufficiently well to prevent the sea water from destroying the paper money? Pirates, he thought, never seemed to have had that problem.

"What are you doing that for?" Joyce asked, watching Chip adjusting the hands of his watch to six o'clock. He smiled at her before replying.

"The sun has just come up. So it's six o'clock." She studied him carefully to see if he was joking. He seemed normal enough smiling contentedly and speaking clearly, but the battering his head had received in the last few hours must surely have deranged him somehow, she thought.

"How do you know that?" she asked warily.

"I don't." He replied, amused by her concern. "But in the tropics, the days are almost exactly twelve hours long all year round. So the sun comes up at six and goes down at six. I forgot to set my watch before we took off from Louisiana, and I can't remember where I last set it. So I'm using that fact to try and find out how far south we've come." Seeing no signs of comprehension on her face, he continued. "If the sun goes down at exactly six tonight we'd be on the equator. If it's later than that, we'll still be North by some amount. There's an Almanac in my flight bag that'll tell us how far." Joyce shook her head and smiled with relief, it was comforting to know there was reason behind his actions and though she didn't know anything about navigation, she felt better knowing he did.

"Don't worry yourself honey," she said, leaning across to kiss him. We're not likely be going anywhere in the immediate future."

"We can't just stay here forever. Can we?" He asked, nuzzling her ear.

"Why not?" she giggled. "We can straighten up the airplane and live in it 'til some ship comes along. With all the money you've got in those boxes, we should be able to buy a ticket to anywhere in the world." Her light hearted attitude began to defuse his anxiety. She was right. There was no sense in screaming for help to an unsympathetic world. The weather was warm and doubtless they could fish for food, though he wondered how she would react to eating raw fish. Except for the excursion into the airplane to find some food, they had been snuggled together under the wing since the water had wakened them. The dominee had ended up on the highest part of the sandbar and though he wasn't quite certain how close the tide had come after arousing them, it had not come that far. While Joyce had gone back to sleep, he had lain awake thinking. He had concluded they must be somewhere east of, but in the vicinity of, the Cayman islands. The name had always intrigued him, whether they had been given that name because the islanders thought they looked like floating caymans from the vantage points of their canoes, or because caymans actually lived around here. Maybe they should try and level the dominee as a refuge in the latter event. Flimsy as it might be, it offered a shelter and he still had the little revolver in his flight bag as a last resort.

His mind drifted slowly over the mechanics of righting the airplane. There were some tools on board, not perhaps as many as he might like, but with help from Joyce, the propellers could be removed and tied to the tail wheel for a start. The 'Jerry Cans' could also be filled with sand and tied there. If enough weight was applied there, the airplane would right itself. What effect the wheels being buried in the sand might have, he could not imagine and put it out of his mind for the time being. He would address that problem if and when it arose. When the food and the warmth of the morning had fully refreshed them, they set about the task of righting the airplane. It was a strange sight viewed from a distance, Joyce thought, as she and Chip floated in the water looking back at the airplane. They were completely naked, having surrendered pants, shirt, skirt, blouse socks and underclothes to the need for more bags to hold more and more sand which was now piled up under the tail. She imagined it like a giant wasp with its claws buried in its victim in the process of depositing her cluster of eggs on its back. Perhaps it would fly away when it was finished and leave them there to watch over the eggs until they hatched. She thought of describing her impressions to Chip, but decided against it. Some other time she thought, when the stress has gone out of him. When the tail had finally come down, it settled firmly on top of the motley conglomeration of improvised sandbags they had managed to hoist up and secure to the tailwheel. The cabin floor was as level as if it had been in flight, and the door almost as inaccessible. Chip had collapsed on the sand from a mixture of relief, exhaustion and unfulfilled achievement. Joyce, had taken his hands and pulled him to his feet, declaring it was better than living in a cabin with a tilted floor. She hugged him to confirm her delight and then dragged him away for a swim, as much to revive his spirits as to satisfy her own need for relief from the irritation of the sand and the sun.

"We can build a staircase up to our apartment by the sea and even shut the door at night my love." She said. When he started to explain why they couldn't do this, she clung with arms and legs around him and planted her lips firmly against his until he responded, carrying her progressively into the shallows on his knees, until they rolled together exhausted on the beach. Much later, they stood watching for the green flash he said would appear the exact moment the sun went fully below the horizon.

"Six twenty three." He said, staring at his watch . . . "Near as I could see anyway. I'll look it up in the Almanac tomorrow. Don't let me forget."

"I'll write it down." Joyce replied, scribing the numbers in the sand with her foot.

With the airplane level, the weight, with the propellers removed, held the tail so firmly on the pile of sandbags, they were able to remove their sand filled clothes for washing and wearing. They also extracted one of the Jerry cans for use as a door step without disturbing it. When the Moon rose out of the eastern horizon they held each other close together and watched until it shrank back to moonsize above the silhouette of the airplane. Sleepily, they clambered up into the cabin and closed the door, before arranging a makeshift bed of seat cushions and clothing, on which they cuddled together for the night.

Several hours later, Joyce awoke to find herself cold and alone on the hard floor. Chip had gone, yet the door of the cabin was closed. She called out to him softly thinking he might be in the cockpit area, trying to use the radios to get help. He had been concerned over the batteries running down because some things had not been switched off in the confusion after the landing. At that time, she had refused to let him fuss over this in his exhausted condition. Now, hearing nothing, she realized he was not in the airplane. Alarmed, she opened the door, jumped out and ran around the airplane, searching the dark shadows under it and calling his name. The starlight gave just enough light to see he was nowhere around. Fighting back the panic rising within her, she set off along the shoreline following the wavering green phosphorescsnt lines of the water's edge, calling to him and stooping frequently to scan the horizon across the sandbar and across the water for his silhouette. Nothing. Not even a disturbance of any kind in the smoothly breathing starlit surface of the sea. By the time she had circled the entire island and returned to the airplane, her intestines were cramping severely and for the first time in her life she felt the paralyzing infantile sense of being completely lost and alone.

Joyce stumbled to the water's edge, squatted and relieved her pent up feelings. She waded a few steps into the sea and washed herself carefully, relishing the warmth of the water and the soft soothing coolness of the night air. Her panic had subsided as she rationalized that Chip must have been circling the island at the same time she was. Probably they had both been going in the same direction at opposite ends, which was why she hadn't seen him anywhere. She contemplated reversing direction but she had exhausted her anguish and decided that she would just have to get back into bed and wait for him to come back, chiding herself for her childishness in panicking the first moment she couldn't find him. When she climbed back into the cabin, the first thing she saw was Chip lying curled up on their makeshift bed. Her immediate irrational desire was to kick him for not answering her calls and causing her so much distress. As she suppressed the impulse, relief at finding him safe, spread through her, shaming her for over reacting to such slight provocation. Chip, wherever he had been, probably just hadn't heard her calling. Always so courteous and caring, it would not have been like him to deliberately ignore her. She lay down and curled herself protectively around him. In the morning, he explained how he had been on top of the upper wing with one of the windshield wiper blades, carefully squeegeeing the dew which had formed there into a small sponge and squeezing it out into one of their plastic mugs. He proudly presented her with the mugfull of rather cloudy water which she reluctantly tasted.

"It's a bit salty." She said dubiously.

"I know. But it's not as bad as the sea water and after we clean the dust off the wings, it'll be better. We can even filter it through some cloth later on. Our water supply isn't going to last much longer. We've got to collect whatever we can each night. There's about two hundred square feet of fairly smooth surface up there and I just wanted to experiment with a way of collecting the dew. Very soon, it may be all there is to drink. Today I also found out that we'll have to set some kind of collecting device along the trailing edge to direct the water into."

"Why?"

"Sponging doesn't work too well. It doesn't pick up all the water like the squeegee does. also, it's dificult to squeeze all the water out. Maybe I could have sucked it dry, but I didn't like the muddy taste." Chip replied, his face confirming the unpleasant memory.

"I could hold a mug under the places where you collect the water." Joyce volunteered.

"Yeah. That might work. We'll just have to learn by trial and error. More trial and less error in fact if we're going to survive. Also, we'd better learn how to fish too." Joyce remained silent. Chip's sober expression left little room for doubt. She was on the point of asking why they hadn't already been rescued, when he continued with an even more depressing announcement. "The batteries are dead, the radios don't work and I'm afraid we're here for a long stay."

As the days went by they developed a routine. On windless nights, they collected what dew there was, as soon as it formed. Once they rejoiced in making three collections through the night. Just before dawn, they fished until the sun rose. After eating, they rested, made love and sometimes slept, in the only shade there was, under the wing. Chip at first seemed resigned to their condition, but when almost all the 'civilized' food was gone, he became restless and spent long periods scanning the horizon through the binoculars from a vantage point he made by cutting foot holds through the fabric of the fin until he could climb up and perch himself on the top of the fin. After a few days of this, he developed a blister on the end of his tailbone which became infected, causing him a great deal of pain. Rest and love making became virtually impossible, much to Joyce's concern. She tried treating the sores with everything in the little first aid kit without relief. After another week, Chip was in such pain, he could barely stand up and his attitude became increasingly irritable with every attempt to help him. All the work of collecting dew fell to her. All the fishing and serving of the raw fish, she did, but nothing seemed to please him. In desperation, she collected some of the sea weed off the reef and made a compress of the squeezings from this in a sock tied across the sores, hoping the natural iodine and other juices might heal the injury. The pain declined but was replaced by a gradual enfeebling of his left leg, which resulted in him being unable to stand up. Three days later, the pain had gone but the left leg had no feeling and little movement. Chip blamed the seaweed treatment as the cause of this and accused Joyce of deliberately trying to poison him. His moods alternated between anger and self pity, one moment he'd be cursing and swearing to kill her, then suddenly crying and pleading for her help. She became reluctant to go near him lest he tried to vent his anger physically, although she knew he was too weak to do her much harm. However, the horror of possibly having to fight with him for her life, where once she had been able to hold and love him was too much for her to contemplate. Shocked and bewildered, she withdrew to the far end of the sandbar with her hands over her ears to shut out his faint cries. By sunset he had fallen into an exhausted sleep and Joyce was able to drag him into the cabin, wash the sand off his body with sea water and stretch him out, face down, on the seat cushions. This done, she took a small drink of the remaining water and sat in the cabin doorway with her legs dangling outside, gazing sadly at the dark line of the horizon through the struts and wires of the wings. Once again, she realized, she was going to have to 'fly this airplane' herself.

The faintest breath of a breeze off the water, rustled the pile of drying seaweed she had gathered and stacked on the wing against the fuselage wall. Without thinking, she reached out and picked a strand of it and put it in her mouth for something to chew on. The stars were out and twinkling now that the twilight had faded into the full depth of night and the horizon was clearly visible against them. She sat staring blankly at the point where the black silhouette of the wingtip strut, bisected the horizon, chewing the stringy fiberous weed and wondering if it would affect her in the same way it had affected Chip. She didn't much care now anyway. A bright star, right on the horizon, went behind the strut and she moved her head slightly to bring it back again. It went behind the strut once more and she leaned the side of her head against the edge of the cabin door and wondered why. The other stars simply went straight down until they seemed to fizzle out in the water. Maybe this was another satellite like those Chip had shown her moving through the other stars across the sky. A little while later it came out from the other side of the strut and continued moving steadily away from it.

Her mind drifted back to the night when she and Henry had stood on the pier at Port Angeles, gazing out across the water after the meal in the restaurant. There was a similarity between her present mood and the agony generated then, by the events that had preceeded that meal. Henry had taken her there to get her mind off the tragedy. This time there had been no meal and no Henry. Chip's injury and its results were not quite so tragic, but she felt the same sensation of being helpless to do anything about it. Her dog Patch, her precious companion of so many lonely years, gone. Killed by that hideous monster who had also murdered her sister in law. She had felt glad. Viciously glad, that accidentally or otherwise, Henry had killed him. She leaned the side of her head against the lamp standard. Henry on her left had his arm around her waist, but somehow she felt reluctant to snuggle against him. The cold metal of the lamp standard against her temple felt more secure. Henry had brought all this trouble down on her, by bringing back that silly letter which she had written years ago and had forgotten about.

As she and Henry had gazed out across the placid black water between them and the distant causeway that ran out to the lighthouse. A lone fisherman in a small boat came home from his night's fishing outside the harbour. She could not see the boat itself but the light on the masthead moved across the silhouette of the causeway like a lonely star. Chip, asleep on the floor beside her, replaced Henry. The metal frame of the doorway replaced the lamp standard, and immediately she realized that the star moving across the horizon was a boat.

She scrambled to her feet, grabbed Chip's flight bag from the back of the pilot's seat and jumped out of the airplane. She found the binoculars and hastily scanned the horizon. It was a boat. No question. She felt in the bag for the flares Chip had shown her, desperately trying to remember exactly how he had told her to set them off. She held the spike handle of the flare as tight as possible and pulled the striker strap down and away from her as he had demonstrated. For a moment nothing happened and she wondered if it was a dud and what to do next. "Hold it up high." he had said and as if in response to this thought, the flare suddenly spurted a red flame and lots of smoke. She held it as high as she could and a bright star suddenly exploded from it and soared like a rocket into the sky leaving a long trail of red smoke behind it.

"See it! For God's sake!" She screamed at the top of her voice as the flare ejected a second white star which seemed to light up the entire island. As the flare burned down, it became too hot for her to hold and she stuck it quickly in the sand and jumped back away from it in case it ejected another star. Had the people in the boat seen the flares? She wondered as the darkness returned. Half blind from the brilliance of flares, she staggered to the airplane and felt along the wing for the binoculars. She could not see the boat any more even after her eyes had re-adjusted to the darkness. Should she light the second flare? There were only two of them in the bag. She continued scanning the horizon, thinking to herself, that from the position of the light when she had first seen it, the boatman had most likely had his back to her when she set off the flare. Better to wait until tomorrow or another sighting before wasting their last chance to summon help. Long after the residual traces of light from the flares had faded from her eyes, she searched the horizon for the faintest hope that her signal had been seen. When this too faded completely, she crawled dejectedly into the cabin and despite the fetid odours surrounding him, curled herself around Chip's back. He was deeply asleep and though she caressed his head and neck, he remained unconscious of her presense or her affectionate caressing. Eventually, still clinging to these remnants of secuity, sleep gently erased all awareness of her sadness and loneliness.

Pongo Itacruze saw the red flash out of the corner of his left eye. For a moment he wondered if it had been real or another imaginary sensation, like the tic he sometimes felt in that eye.

He turned his head just in time to see a red star sinking towards the sea illuminating what appeared to him to be a double arch of pink clouds on the horizon. When the light died, the ghostly white loops remained for a while, still faintly visible in the starlight. He had never seen anything like it before and could not imagine what had caused it. There was nothing he knew of in that direction, except the barren sandbars they called 'Banana Fritters'.

His uncle Barney, had once shown him the group of sandbars, named, he said, because they looked like slices of yellow banana, frying on an iron griddle. Most of the smaller bars were only visible at the extreme low of the tide, but they set up ripples in the ocean around them because the waves bounced back off them, making smaller waves moving in the opposite direction. The interference between the two sets of waves formed a pattern one could see from a boat. Learning the patterns, was how the islanders could find their way across the oceans.

First, learning the patterns around their own island. Then, as they moved further beyond the horizon, learning the new patterns in the vicinity of other islands. Pongo, only eight years old at that time, believed everything his uncle told him. He readily understood the naming of the islands, having watched, lying expectantly on the sand beside the cooking fire the delicious plantain slices sizzling on his grandmother's iron skillet at eye level. 'Perhaps the pan was too hot and the fat had popped just as he was passing.' He thought, laughing aloud at his own joke, and thinking how Maris would giggle when he told her.

Had he not been instructed on these night voyages, to return with the two barrels of rum without delay, he would have chosen to go over to the sandbar and see just what was happening there, but orders were orders, and Uncle Barney would be angry if he returned late. He did not know what else was in the two wooden barrels he was carrying in his boat, besides rum, but on previous occasions, he had seen the men who had taken the barrels from the boat on his arrival at the beach, pouring the rum into empty steel drums. This sacrilegeous activity, had mildly aroused his curiosity, but he knew better than to question the strange behaviours of the men of the village. Later, when he became fully grown and established as an adult. he would doubtless be told.

On one occasion, he had seen the men strip the emptied barrels of their iron hoops and remove the end panel to take out some blocks which appeared to be wrapped in white cloth. These blocks were passed around and apparently pleased the men who made approving gestures on examining them. One night, while amorously engaged, lying, on top of Maris with a warning finger pressed across her lips, watching this performance, he had hoped to see where they finally put them. He had searched in the daylight with no succes, and now, the fear of being seen himself restricted his movement so much that again, he had been unable to see what the men did with the blocks. Although his curiosity was now thoroughly aroused, he made no move to get a better view for fear he and Maris would be observed and have to find another secret bivouac for their trysts. Worse yet, the elders would know he had been with her before they had been accepted into adulthood and there would be hell to pay for both of them if that was discovered. Thenceforth, any night when he was sent on the 'Rum Run', he told Maris he would be too tired to Tryst with her afterwards for fear she would accidentally betray their secrets if she observed the men at work. This newest secret, which in his mind he labelled 'The Ghosts of Banana Fritters", he would not tell to anyone. Instead, he would go back alone. In the daylight, when ghosts were powerless, and find out what was causing the fat to splutter. It would be his secret. His alone. He wouldn't tell Maris even as a joke. She might tell one of the other girls and it would eventually reach their uncle no matter how secret he said it had to be.

That night he slept fitfully and woke early. The dawn had not yet signalled it's coming but Pongo could not rest. The Ghosts of Banana Fritter were calling him. He got up and went to the boat, refilled the gas tank, and put a gallon carton of water in the bows under the seat. Then he helped himself to a couple of hands of bananas, which he set on either side of the water jug. As a last item he selected some curls of copra from the pile and set this where he could reach it from his steering position and pushed the boat out into the water. He rowed away until he felt far enough from the village to start the motor and set course by angling across the dominant wave pattern for 'The Fritters' as he thought of the area where Main Banana Fritter was located. Uncle Barney would assume he had gone fishing when they found the boat gone, and expect him to return with some fish. Accordingly, he set one of his lines with a small strip of dried dorado skin on the hook and trailed it so that it lay on the face of the second wave of the wash behind the boat. There he could see it skipping occasionally off the edge of the wake where he knew it would attract the attention of any mackerel disturbed by the boat's passing.

Pongo's boat was a sixteen foot long wooden, ship's life-boat, which had been cast up on their island many years ago. Originally it had been a double-ender, but when his uncle had 'acquired' the outboard motor, he had cut off the stern end and rebuilt it with a transom on which to mount the ancient single cylinder British Anzani outboard. It cruised smoothly across the tranquil sea at the one setting of the throttle and the simple engine seemed to run forever on a tank of mixture. The long night forays to bring the rum casks to the island usually took two full tanks. But, since this was suposedly only a fishing trip he had not risked getting and loading the extra tank. By the time he reached the area where the reflected waves from the sand bars had become discernable, and he knew he was approaching the location of the 'Banana', he had caught three fine fish. He pulled in his line and shut off the motor for fear of arousing the 'Ghosts' who, he thought, might be getting ready to flee the daylight. The dawn was just beginning to colour the eastern horizon and Pongo wanted to be very careful not to run aground on one of the many shallows around the islands. Even more important, was the feeling that from this angle, with the light behind the island, he would be able to see 'them' before 'they' saw him, for, although Uncle Barney's training had provided him with confidence and understanding of the ways of the ocean, he had also acquired from him, a genuine fear of the unknown. He stood facing the bows and leaned slowly forward on the oar handles, rowing steadily towards the light, taking care to make no sound. Neither with the oar blades in the water nor with the shafts against the thole pins which were wrapped with coir cloth so that the wood of the oars would not squeek when rubbing against them. When Main Banana Fritter came clearly into view, he was astonished to see the strange silhouette of a structure rising out of the sand near the northern end of the sand-bar.

There had been just the faintest breeze during the night and Joyce, working prone on top of the wing had been disappointed with the meager 'catch' she had been able to scrape off the taut fabric with the two wiper blades. Chip had not woken up to help her for the last two nights and though she had developed a little more skill in corralling the dew to the trailing edge, she found it almost impossible, working alone from above, to catch all the water that ran over the edge. Especially as the only container they had for that purpose was an empty soup can. Apart from having to work lying down to avoid breaking the wing fabric, she had to sweep the undulating surface in front of herself and then slither forward over the scraped area to the next section, collecting each 'panel's-worth', before moving on. Without a helper, this meant squirming back every so often, over the scraped area with a full can of the precious water without spilling it. Climbing down off the wings and taking the can to the cabin where they had set up the filtering system. The two of them, working together, had been able to gather about a gallon of water on a still night, and somewhat less if a breeze came up. It was taking her ten times as long working alone she estimated and the resulting 'catch' was about one tenth of what they could have been getting. Yet there were still two people to drink it and she felt bad having to deprive Chip in his present condititon, but she realized she had to keep functional herself or they would surely both die of thirst. She was about to make her last trip to the cabin with the almost full can when she heard the crunch of something in the sand behind her. She craned slowly around and saw a boat aground on the beach on the other side of the airplane. A young man clad in ragged sawn off jeans and a tattered tee shirt was just getting out of the boat and she watched him pull the boat up onto the sandbar. For a few moments, she thought it was her imagination playing tricks on her for she had wishfully dreamed of such an event, and now she was afraid to make a sound lest this apparition should disappear.

When Pongo's boat returned to his island, it was met by a swarm of naked brown natives curious to know who the strangers were. Joyce, a tall smiling white woman, in tattered clothing was helped from the boat and led ashore by a group of women and children, while Chip was lifted out of the boat and carried ashore by the men. Their luggage, consisting of his flight bag and the single case of clothing Joyce had been alowed to bring with her on the airplane plus the two boxes of money which Chip had refused to leave behind, were passed from hand to hand ashore and carried by a variety of adults and children behind the procession as they moved towards the village. The fish, forgotten in the excitement over the strangers, were finally found by some children playing in the boat, and taken to the old ladies of the village. Pongo was led away by uncle Barney for interrogation.

The average height of the native women seemed to Joyce, to be about four foot six and that of the men about five feet. At her height, five eleven in her bare feet, she towered over everyone in the village. While the women, jabbering excitedly among themselves around her, urged and pressed her forward, she could only look back over their heads to where the men carrying Chip marched behind them. She glanced frequently over her shoulder, anxious to check that they were not getting separated. She could not make out what they were saying, or even if they were addressing her, although the two older ladies who were leading her by the hands, seemed to be addressing her directly.

She had never heard such incomprehensible speech before. Partly Spanish and partly Indian or maybe African she supposed. All the words seemed to end in 'ee' or 'ooh' which their high pitched voices rendered more like singing than speech. An undulating sound with the 'ee's rising and the 'oo's falling and most of the utterances commencing with a sharp 'A' as in 'fat'. Her inability to understand words didn't seem to matter. Simply smiling and allowing herself to be led seemed to please them for they laughed and smiled continuously, almost as if overjoyed to have her company. Only her concern over Chip prevented her from relaxing completely. This too seemed to convey itself to them for the two women repeatedly patted her wrists and stroked her forearms each time she glanced back, as though to assure her that her man was being taken care of properly by his bearers.

The relatively short beach on which they had landed, led up to a dense stand of mangrove trees and coconut palms through which a shaded pathway wound its way between the trees into the jungle. They had been walking relatively slowly because of her reluctance to lose sight of Chip and the narrowness of the pathway itself. Underfoot, the reddish ground was hard and beaten flat by the frequent foot traffic although the occasional root, denuded of soil, would have presented a stumbling block if they had not pointed them out. Accustomed as she was to going barefoot around the farm, the roots presented only minor discomfort and it amused her to think that the sole member of the party wearing shoes was Chip, and he was being carried by barefoot bearers.

After a while the trees began thinning out into a more open area where an occasional patch of sun on a thatched roof suggested habitation. The path widened, and soon developed into an open sunlit clearing with several thatch covered dwellings visible in the surrounding forest. Joyce was enchanted. Chip had eulogised the island life, as had Henry before him, but this was far more authentically native than anything she had imagined from their descriptions. In most of the dwellings, women with small children looked shyly out at the procession as if afraid to come outside. In the middle of the clearing was an area obviously used for fires and cooking and there were a couple of tripod structures, presumably for hanging up a large pot over a fire pit. She hoped the old movies of cannibals and boiling pots were only a myth. There were no signs of wires, T.V antennas, or other modern equipment of any kind in view. She was entranced and gazed around with delighted interest which the women leading her picked up on immediately. However, when they reached the mid point between the edge of the trees and the central fire-pits, the women directed her towards a larger hut on the left, whereas the men carrying Chip, abruptly veered off towards a different hut at the other end of the clearing.

She turned and shook off the hands holding her and ran to him, shouting "No! No! No!". She grasped his hand and held on tightly as the entourage stopped and milled around, all jabbering together and trying to gently separate her from Chip's hand until she began stamping her foot and yelling at them. The bearers, set Chip down gently and she had to crouch down to retain her hold on his hand while the natives all backed away a few feet leaving the two of them in the middle of a circle that had suddenly become silent. She sat beside Chip and lifted him up to where his head rested in her lap and glared around her at the silent faces as if defying anyone to touch him.

A few moments later the ring of natives parted and an old lady wearing a grass skirt and carrying some kind of a club made from bamboo and a carved coconut, came waddling through. Around her neck hung a woven necklace of hair, from the end of which, dangled a walrus tusk that swung from side to side, in rhythm with her pendulous breasts. From the alacrity with which the natives gave her a path, Joyce deduced she must be someone of great authority to them. Possibly the chief's wife.

She beckoned Joyce to come away from Chip but Joyce shook her head vigorously, indicating she had no intention of leaving him. "He's my man.' She said, pointing to emphasize her words and gently stroking his forehead. She smiled at the old lady hoping to convey her thanks for their help but also her determination not to be separated from him. The old lady smiled a rather toothless grin and for a few seconds the battle of wills seemed about to end in a peremptory order to come away from Chip. Then the old woman stepped back and gave the silent group of natives a simple command. Without a sound, the women all moved off towards one end of the clearing leaving the men who had been carrying Chip squatting around him in the positions they had occupied previously as if waiting to continue their work, while the remainder of them walked off in the opposite direction towards a large hut at the other end of the clearing. Thus, in a couple of seconds, the old lady had displayed her command over the whole village and indicated clearly to Joyce the fact that the men and the women had definite separate territories. The men who had been carrying her cases and Chip's flight bag and the two boxes, had departed with the others, leaving these articles un-attended, on the ground. The old lady pointed to them and seemed to be asking if they were to come with her or to go with Chip. Joyce was confused and more concerned with Chip's injuries than the luggage. She drew the old lady's hand towards Chip's middle and made a sign for the men to turn him over so she could show her the damage.

When she saw this she began giving sharp commands to the men who once more picked him up and began carrying him while she, keeping a tight grip on Joyce's hand, walked her along behind them. This time they moved in a direction different from either the men's or the women's quarters and soon reached a large fenced shelter where there appeared to be some kind of a field hospital set up with several low slung cots under the shade of a palm thatched canopy. A large brown native wearing a little apron over his loin cloth and a pith helmet on his head, came out to greet them.

Around his neck hung the universal symbol of a doctor, a stethoscope. Joyce breathed a sigh of relief as he immediately focussed his attention on Chip, directing the bearers towards a section of the shelter with a white metal table where, under his direction, they laid Chip and gently removed his clothing. Only then did she remember the luggage and Chip's precious boxes of money. It was as if the old lady was reading her mind for she immediately turned to Joyce and motioned for her to stay while she went off to see to whatever was happening in her realm of jurisdiction. Evidently it hadn't extended fully into this part of the village, for the doctor hadn't even so much as indicated his awareness of her when he saw the bearers carrying Chip into the compound. He had cast a cursory glance at Joyce herself and she had sensed a momentary flash of interest in his eyes before he turned his total attention to Chip. Viewed from the rear, the doctor appeared amusingly nude, plump and soft, as if he spent most of his time sitting or lying around. She judged him to be about her own age and height but undoubtedly he was almost twice her weight, especially since their privations on the sandbar had reduced herself and Chip to little more than skeletons. She could not get near enough to touch Chip as the doctor and three atendants working on Chip were constantly in motion, exchanging commands and responses in their peculiar lilting tongue. Evidently the doctor was very concerned about the wounds on Chips spine and from what she was able to see they had removed her seaweed poultices and were washing the caked and encrusted area very thoroughly and carefully. Chip, who had been almost unconscious when she and the boatman had lifted him into the boat, apparently felt nothing for he gave no indications of pain. From time to time the doctor glanced round at her as if about to ask her something, but each time she was about to say something, he turned back to his work and ignored her. Perhaps, she thought, he was just checking to see if she was still there, and hoped he would not send her away.

The wound, when they had cleansed all the purulence away looked terrible to her, as if the skin and flesh over the lower end of his spine had just rotted away. Here and there the tips of the bones could be seen. She felt sick, just to look at it. At least the vile smell had gone, and the doctor was covering the area with a whitish powder and some kind of yellow paste, from a jar, which had been brought to him by one of his attendants. The injury was then covered with a layer of grey gauze cloth before Chip was lifted off the operating table and carried to a bed made of bamboo frames stretched with what seemed to her to be fish netting. He was laid face down on this and strapped so he could not turn over, and a bamboo stand, complete with a plastic bag and some clear tubing hanging from the top of it, was placed alongside.

The doctor then inserted a hypodermic needle in the vein in the back of Chip's left hand and attached the I.V.tube from the plastic bag to this and taped it there with a couple of turns of half inch wide masking tape. One of the assistants, then strapped Chip's wrist and forearm to the side frame of the litter he was lying on. As if, finally satisfied with the treatment, the doctor looked up at Joyce, smiled and spoke directly to her for the first time, saying,

"Crude, but effective . . . Under the circumstances."

For a moment she was too surprised hearing English, to reply. The doctor's voice was deep and strong and his words were strangely cultured as if he had learned them in a foreign country. "Is he alright ?" She asked hopefully. The doctor's smile faded. "Obviously not . . . Would you mind telling me how he came to be, in this condition.?"

"He got a sore tailbone, from sitting on top of the tail of his airplane." She replied. "Looking for ships." She added hastily, realizing how strange her explanation sounded.

"Looking for ships?!"

"What I meant, was, Is he going to be alright?"

"Hard to tell. If the medication can arrest the spread of the necrotizing bacteria which are eating away his flesh, he may be able to walk again. If not." He shrugged, emphasizing his uncertainty.

"Can't we get him to a hospital ?"

"This is the hospital." The doctor's tone suggested a trace of resentment at her questioning his professional status. "Where are you from?" He asked quietly. "Washington." Joyce replied, and then launched into a summary of the events leading to their present predicament. The doctor listened attentively.

"Fascinating." he commented when she finished. "Have you any idea where you are now?" Joyce shook her head.

"All I know or care about right now, is getting Chip to a hospital where his injury can be treated." She said abruptly.

"Well . . . This is the only medical facility witin a radius of about three hundred miles. Your husband, has been given the only known treatment for this kind of injury." He took both her hands in his, faced her and spoke gently. "We have cleaned all of the visible necrotized tissue away and treated the exposed fascia with broad spectrum antibiotic powder. We are also administering a similar intravenous infiltration of a powerful broad spectrm antibiotic solution to arrest the spread to other areas of his body. This is precisely the treatment he would receive in any major city hospital. I assure you."

"Can I stay here with him?"

"Of course. In fact, it is the best medicine anyone can give him now. Family members invariably stay here with the patients. Do you have any personal belongings with you?" Joyce looked around, half expecting to see her suitcases and Chip's bag somewhere on the ground.

"I thought they were going to bring them here." She said, vaguely concerned at Chip's probable reaction to the disappearance of his boxes of money and the possibility the natives might be 'divvying it up amongst themselves' even as she spoke. "They were left back there on the ground."

"Don't worry. I'll have the orderlies fix a bed here beside him, and then bring your things here." At that moment, Chip heaved a big sigh which ended in a long drawn out groan of pain. Joyce pressed his right hand up to her lips and kissed his fingers. "Sleep my darling. Everything's going to be alright now." She said, as assuringly as she could.

Doctor Ramesh Gupta sat on the veranda of his hut overlooking the medical compound. His hut differed from the standard native hut of the village by the inclusion of a fine mesh screen which ran entirely around the walls of the hut. It stretched from the top of the wattle covered wall to the frame that supported the roof. Where the entry door interrupted the wall, the door itself completed the security of the fine wire mesh. He had insisted on this feature which none of the other huts in the village had. Such a luxury, it had been the one item he had insisted on when he decided to take the job of island physician some eleven years previously. When the hut was being built, he also insisted on doubling the thickness of the bamboo flooring. The standard hut had only one layer and whenever he entered, he felt a fear of breaking through. As time passed he had covered the whole floor area with the fine woven matting the villagers made. Inside, he felt safe from the swarms of mosquitoes, that bred in every depression, where water collected for more than a day, and periodically invaded the village. He had wanted to make the same requirements for his 'Hospital', but had been thwarted by the villagers who preferred their more airy style of construction. His fear of mosquitoes originated in India where he had been born and raised in one of the more affluent districts of Calcutta.

Following in his father's footsteps, Ramesh had qualified as a medical doctor there, but had grown disaffected with the hospital management, and decided to 'emigrate' to England as soon as his internship ended.

He surfaced from the 'Underground' at New Cross Gate, in London, on a cold wet November morning and after negotiating the busses, and the twisted streets of the city on foot, presented himself at his uncle's house in Bermonsey.

Uncle Shashi had written offering him a place to stay when he arrived. Uncle Shashi, also a medical doctor, had left Calcutta several years previously and was reputedly well established at Guy's Hospital. The drab cold grey city had already sapped much of Ramesh's enthusiasm and the terraced brick houses of Rotherhithe New Road, where his uncle lived, filled him with an uneasy foreboding that this must surely be the wrong address. He checked the address once more, against his uncle's letter before knocking hesitantly on the front door which accessed directly on to the sidewalk. A pale young girl, about ten years old with long black hair and large solemn black eyes opened the door partly and looked him over dubiously.

"Korshed?" he asked hopefully.

"Yes." She nodded, studying the wet suitcase he was holding, as if it might contain something malevolent.

"Is your Dada at home?" The question caused her to back up a little and she answered.

"No. But my mother is," she added hastily, as if reluctant to let this stranger think she was at home alone. This nervous child and the dowdy surroundings were inducing a measure of extreme nervousness. He wanted to just turn and run, but the cold and the wet which were already penetrating his body through his light clothing, pushed him to the point of desperation, and he slid his foot between the door and the jamb lest she should shut it in his face.

"Mama! Mama!" The girl shrieked desperately, jamming her weight against his foot with the door. He heard the sound of running footsteps and a woman's voice trying to calm the child and asking rather nervously, "Who is it?!".

"My name is Ramesh Gupta!" He called out. I am the nephew of Shashi Gupta . . . Is this his house?" There were a few moments of silence before the door opened fully and he saw his Aunt for the first time. A tall rangy woman with light brown hair and blue eyes that studied him with guarded interest.

"Aunty Maria?" He asked hopefully.

'Doctor Shashi', was at work, according to Aunty Maria, and would not be home until evening. He would be delighted to know his nephew Ramesh had arrived at last. They would have much to talk about. Meanwhile, he had been stripped of his soaked clothes, and dressed in a set of Shashi's Dhotis and a fresh pair of sandals, while they dried, over the back of a chair in front of the fire. Were these all the clothes he had brought with him? Maria had asked in amazement. He tried to allay her concerns by assuring her that he had money to buy fresh English suits and whatever else he needed. He had also discovered that she spoke only English, and that with a strange twang, somewhat reminiscent of the Australians he had spoken with, on the journey from India.

Long before 'Doctor Shashi' returned home, Ramesh had realized that much of the glowing reports Shashi had written to his family in India were false. From Maria, he learned the stark truth that England refused to recognize the credentials of Indian college and hospital graduates. 'Doctor Shashi' was chief of the male nurses at Guy's Hospital, and still going to night school, trying to pass the finals at London University. He began to understand, even sympathize with, his uncle's reluctance to tell the truth to the family back home. However, a growing concern was gnawing at his intestines, that he himself was about to undergo a imilar experience. Where would he sleep tonight? The house had only two tiny bedrooms upstairs. One where Shashi and Maria slept, and the other where the three children, Korshed and her two younger brothers shared a single bed. There was no bathroom. One apparently washed in the sink in the cramped scullery off the living room, and the toilet, was at the other end of the small garden at the back of the house. Compared to his father's house in Calcutta, with its spacious walled compound, its marble tiled floors and huge, high ceiling bedrooms, uncle Shashi's house was a 'hovel'. He was appalled, and desperately afraid of showing it, to this kind, considerat e Auntie. he had just met for the first time.

*　　*　　*

"I did not say I lived in a Palace here," Shashi retorted angrily, trying to keep his voice low and under control. "I merely said we were very comfortably situated and I would find room for you if you wanted to come." Ramesh still remembered his uncle's words. Just as clearly as if he were still sitting with him, in the pub, where they had gone to confer, away from Maria and the children.

He had not spent that, or any other night in his uncle's house. Instead, after cooling his anger at what he had considered as a sleazy betrayal by his uncle, he had gone with his uncle to Guy's hospital, where, under the cover of his uncle's position as head of the hospital orderlies, he had slept on the floor of the male nurse's locker room.

He sipped his mug of 'Fumee', his name for the local distilation of fermented coconut juice, and looked across the darkened compound to where the wife of that poor chap they had brought in this morning, was sleeping on some rush mats under his bed. 'Comfort is a relative term.' He thought, as he went inside his house and fastened the screen latch. Despite the nightcap of 'Fumee' he could not sleep. The woman's presence disturbed him. He marvelled at the way she had accepted her sudden privations without complaint of any kind so long as she could remain with her husband. He stared at the thatched roof above him, watching a gecko stalking a moth, wide awake, thinking about her and the tragedy stalking her husband. Neither of them wore any rings. She had said "His airplane," not "Our airplane." Then, later when their luggage was brought in, there were only "Her cases" and "His boxes". The airplane had run out of gas, not petrol; and they'd landed on a 'sandbar', where the 'Fisherman' had found them. She couldn't remember how long they'd been there. He hadn't asked their names or if they had any identification papers. Out here, what did it matter. She was obviously deeply attached to the poor chap, probably the other way round too, but the poor chap, wasn't likely to be concerned about that much longer. His infection was about the worst case Ramesh had ever treated and some of the victims with far less devastation than he had already sustained, had not survived. 'If the intravenous antibiotic doesn't work this time,' he thought. 'There'll be no hope of repeating it unless the supply ship, which isn't due for another week, comes inside the next two days.' She'd been so desperate for hope, he hadn't had the heart to disillusion her. 'Had he behaved any better than Uncle Shashi?'

As Ramesh had suspected on his first examination of Chip's infected tissues, the necrocis had already spread too far to be arrested. Chip died three days later in Joyce's arms.

Watching dejectedly, from the vantage of his veranda, the demise of his one and only patient, Ramesh consoled himself with the thought that, had they remained on the sandbar, it would have occurred just that much sooner, and in her debilitated state, Joyce too might have given up the strugle and also died. He felt relieved that this had not happened. He went to her and gently drew her away from the body.

"I'm so sorry Joyce." He said putting his arm around her shoulders, "There really wasn't anything anyone could have done to save him. The damage to the facia of his spinal muscles had spread too far to be stopped even with the intravenous antibiotics." She said nothing, just looked at him with a blank expression in her eyes and turned away. As she walked slowly away, he heard her muttering sadly, "All this, for a million lousy dollars and no place to spend it." What did she mean by that? he thought, recalling the two boxes of Mobil Oil. She was, guarding them now almost as desperately as Chip had done, doubtless pending the day she would set out to find civilization once more. Concerns about her farm in Washington which had been cast aside during her distress, now returned in her dreams, and became a large part of her chosen topics of conversation.

*   *   *

From a quiet chat with Pongo, Ramesh learned that the airplane referred to, had landed on Big Banana, and from Pongo's description, it didn't even seem to have been damaged. Fascinated by the possibility of owning an airplane, he decided to suggest to the old queen Kassareliah, that an expedition should be sent to try and salvage the dead man's airplane, much of which could be used or traded to their benefit. There was nowhere an airplane could land or take off on the jungle covered sector of the peninsula where the village was located, but if they could bring it into the lagoon between them and the mainland, they might be able to put a couple of canoes under it as floats, and even fly it. He knew enough about airplanes. In his early youth he had made a hobby of assembling kit models and even flown some of them in his compound. His father's dedication to Medicine had limited his hobby time and it had dwindled to nothing long before he entered medical school.

*   *   *

Joyce took one look at the all-woman house and decided to accept the offer of a bed in the Doctor's House. There was plenty of room, the place was forty feet square, and apart from four posts which supported the mid span of the roof timbers, there were no walls except in one corner, where a semi spiral of vertical corrugated fiberglass panels coiled around the shower and toilet bowl. These items were separated from each other by a huge philodendron towering up to the roof and along the rafters, searching for the sunlight no doubt. She refrained from asking whether the shower water or the toilet water was responsible for its phenomenal growth. It was also home to a colony of geckoes, which Ramesh explained, were his house guests as they captured and ate every other living insect that ventured inside the building.

"Just so they don't come searching for grubs in my bed." She growled.

"They're all very well mannered and discrete." He assured her, smiling as she erected a screen around her cot with several of Chip's pants and shirts hanging from a clothes line, as if he would thereby be protecting her from the beast in the far corner.

Ramesh, the perfect gentleman, made no comment. In fact, he sympathized with her, having lost his own wife only a year earlier. Her needs now, were the same as his had been then, and still were. Peace and companionship. Given those essentials, whatever might come of the fact they were living under the same roof, would simply be frosting on the cake. He had had plenty of time to adjust, and would give her all she time she needed.

While picking through Chip's belongings to find material for her screen, she had unintentially displayed a wad of one hunderd dollar bills she'd found in Chip's jacket pocket. She had not seemed surprised, and from the deliberate way she later stacked the two mysterious boxes of Mobil Oil under her cot, he suspected there might be more of the same, in them. No way, given the circumstances, could those boxes contain cans of oil. From the quick impression he gained, while she'd been curiously examining the waxed brown paper packet, the bills were brand new hundreds, and the wad was at least half an inch thick. If each bill was a hundredth of an inch thick, that translated to around five thousand dollars. He turned away in feigned disinterest, and left her to her own devices.

He stretched out in the hammock, eyes closed visualizing the stacks of bills in the boxes, and trying to remember his mathematics, until he fell asleep.

"How'd you come to be doctoring here?" The question he'd so often asked himself, percolated into his consciousness, and Ramesh wondered who could be talking to him as the gentle swinging motion of the hammock established where he was. He came fully awake, looking around for the voice. Joyce was sitting on the veranda floor leaning back against the wall of the hut. She looked fresh and relaxed, her hair neatly tied behind her neck with a blue and white scarf that matched her blouse and a light denim skirt. Bare feet and long slender legs stretched across the bamboo floor completing the picture.

"My Goodness! Don't You look nice." Ramesh exclaimed, dropping his feet to the floor and sitting up astride the hammock for a better view. "How long have you been there?"

"'Bout seven snores, three woofs and a couple of farts."

Ramesh burst into an unrestrained guffaw of laughter at the unexpected response. "Well I'm glad you're feeling better."

"Yeah." She replied wistfullly, "how does one get off this island and back to civilization?"

"Where did you want to go to?"

"We were headed for Grand Cayman at one time."

"You're about a hundred and fifty mile southwest of there. Chip must be one great. Uh!, have been, a great nav . . . How'd he get, that far, off course. ?"

"It's a long story.".

"We've got plenty of time."

Joyce, Ramesh decided, must be a very tough minded woman. Distraught as she had been over Chips injuries and subsequent death, she had pulled herself together in record time. True, from what she had told him of their whirlwind love affair, she had known him only a few days before they took off on their ill fated journey. Yet, her distress had not been feigned. Of that, he was positive. As a doctor, one observes grief often enough, to be a good judge of how genuine it is.

Once he had explained how utterly isolated this little community was, and how little prospect there would be of a speedy return to civilization, she had settled down to make the best of her situation. They were a month into the dry season and water was getting less available daily. She hadn't complained once. Her skin, red and sunburnt when she first arrived, had healed up nicely with the application of turtle oil and she was taking a good deal more interest and care with her appearance. She still hadn't got into the native culture but didn't fight against it either. She got by rather well among the ladies, using sign language and had also made it clear, in no uncertain fashion, that she was not available to the male population at all. Her size, speed and strength had come in handy on a couple of such occasions. Ramesh had also interceded, interpreting on her behalf. So far, where he was concerned, she had managed to remain neutral whenever any of the local ladies had come to 'visit' with him, though Ramesh himself felt slightly embarrassed at her presence when their primeval voices became raised.

*　　*　　*

When his expedition set out to Big Banana, to recover the airplane, Joyce went with it. For one thing, as she told Ramesh.

Having flown it alone for at least two hours, she probably knew more about that particular airplane than anyone else in the village, including him. For another, which she didn't tell him, she wanted to get a feel for how safe and reliable their proposed mode of transportation would be. If there was ever to be a future away from this predicament, for her, the safety of that airplane was paramount.

Excitement at participating in Ramesh's crazy scheme had aroused her hopes of ultimately returning to civilization. As they discussed the recovery plans, she realized he knew a great deal of the theory of flight, although he had never been a pilot. Also, despite his somewhat stilted manner, he was a rather impressive creature and natural impulses returned, niggling her now both Chip and Henry were both out of the picture.

The heat and the 'romantic' setting of the village life, while originally appealing, palled quickly with her isolation. In the back of her mind, the old homestead kept calling,.

Ramesh had sought out old Barney Itacruse and sat down on the beach beside him as he was repairing his net. They exchanged the customary greeting which the natives used when wishing to indicate a certain subject would be for discussion between them alone. Barney, as Ramesh well knew, was involved in the smuggling of narcotics. It had been on one of Pongo's delivery trips when he had seen the flare from Big Banana, which ultimately led to the discovery and rescue of Chip and Joyce. Ostensibly, Pongo had been out fishing when he discovered them. Barney knew different. Pongo would have taken the small canoe for a simple fishing trip and he would not have gone as far as Big Banana to fish. Barney also managed their isolated Petroleum supplies. They would need bigger supplies of Petrol to run the engines of the airplane if they recovered it. Pongo had told everyone about the airplane.

When the torrent of interest in the stranded airplane had reached Ramesh's ears, he had gone to "Queen Kash", as he called her, and explained to her that it would be in the very best interests of the island community if they did not broadcast the story. Otherwise, other natives would probably destroy the airplane taking souveniers. The airplane would be best brought intact to her village and that undertaking was something which needed the knowledge that he alone posessed. Also, it would be best done after the man Chip died, as he, the doctor, knew was inevitable. He then, with her concurrence, would organize a proper expedition to Big Banana to assess the methods and equipment needed to do this. She had been hesitant until he promised that once he had restored the airplane to health, she would be the very first person to go flying with him in it. He was very positive that he alone was the one capable of doing this. If anyone else in the village, was allowed to touch the airplane before he could salvage it, it would never be able to fly again.

The flotilla of seven canoes, twenty men, three to a canoe, including Pongo and Ramesh, with Joyce in their canoe, set off at sunrise across a millpond smooth sea, bound for Big Banana. The canoes were laden with long stout Bamboo poles, coils of hempen rope, as well as coconuts and various tools like machettes, the one saw the vilage owned, plus some native shovels. Joyce had assured Ramesh, the tools which Chip had used to detach the propellers, were inside the airplane. She had personaly tidied up after they had levelled the aircraft.

To save fuel, Pongo, Ramesh and Joyce paddled their canoe. After an hour it became obvious that her arms were too tired to contribute fully and they eventually decided they would simply have to use the motor if they were ever going to catch up with the rest of the fleet. When they caught up, the island with its strange monument to Chip was not far away. The sight of it caught her by surprise and a flood of emotions swept over her. Memories and losses, hopes and despondencies surged through her mind until she covered her face with her hands and wept. Ramesh, who had been anticipating this, slipped quietly off his seat onto his knees in front of her and wrapped his arms around her to console her. Finally she sighed and relaxed in his arms surrendering to a new sense of security.

"I'm sorry" she said. "It won't happen again." She took her

hands down and tried to smile at him, as he gently wiped the tears off her cheeks with his thumbs.

"Don't worry. he replied, If it does, I'll be here." He asured her.

The canoe beached softly in the sandy beach and one by one they stepped into the shallow water and grasping the gunwales, lifted and pulled the boats up the beach. The villagers, Pongo and Barney included, walked solemnly around the airplane without touching it, and finally at Barney's command, sat down in a circle and watched as Ramesh began his inspection by first taking a few photographs with his little camera. Joyce held tightly to Ramesh's hand as they walked slowly around the airplane, each studying in their own way, the prospect ahead of them. After noting the various holes in the fabric he turned to her.

"The first thing we'll have to do is take her pants off." Ramesh remarked humorously. "The wheels are buried too far into the sand to try and lift her from there." He bent to examine the fairings and then asked if there was a screwdriver in the tool kit on board. When she nodded affirmatively, he went to the tail and tried to lift it with his shoulder. It wouldn't budge. He then examined the propellers both partially buried in the sand under the pile of jerry cans and sand filled clothing, which held the tail wheel firmly in place. He carefully slackened the rope tethers holding the wheel and tried lifting again. It moved, enough to assess the load there and he motioned to Barney to come over. In a mixture of English and the native tongue, he described the need to make a crib of three bamboo poles on which to tie the tail wheel, so that it could be held up, and then lowered to the sand by two men, after the pile of stuff it was perched on, had been removed. He explained with great emphasis on avoiding any contact with the tailplane or the two propellers while doing this. Barney accepted this duty and called a couple of the natives over to explain it to them. The three poles were brought and lashed in place. One man supporting each end of this beam stood waiting to lower the tail as the pile was carefully taken out from under it. Then the tail wheel, still on its beam, was lowered to the sand.

By trial and error they determined how many men were needed to lift each main wheel out of the pit it had dug and as Ramesh had calculated, six men on each wheel lifted the airplane out of the sand. Then in a carefully choreographed exercise they turned the airplane pivoting around the right wheel until the tailwheel was pointing straight out towards the water and the whole machine was moved slowly backwards until the tail wheel was gently lowered onto the middle seat of one of the of canoes which was almost afloat. Again, by trial and error, they determined that this one canoe would be enough to carry the tail and the bow of the canoe was then tied to the root of each of the undercarriage legs, after Ramesh had removed the fairings, and set them securely inside, between the seat rows.

He explained that he thought it would be best if the floating aircraft was towed backwards for better control. Barney then pointed out that the tail canoe was in the wrong way round for this, since the towing line had to be attached to the bow of the canoe. Accordingly, they turned this canoe around and attached the two tethers from the outboard mounting plate on the stern. Once Barney had been satisfied and his seamanship duly acknowledged, the team effort soon had the two main wheels firmly planted and secured on bamboo supports in the middle of two of the larger canoes. Under his careful instructions these two canoes were aligned parallel, and were firmly lashed together forming a catamaran, with long bamboo poles across the bow and stern. Once they had the whole rig afloat Barney again insisted that a third canoe be placed under the middle of the poles of the catamarin making it into a trimaran. The two outer canoes, he argued, were being pressed too deeply into the water for safe towing. Getting this third canoe under the loaded poles seemed to Joyce to have been the most difficult of all their operations. It was carried out by all the natives in the water heaving and splashing about with much shouting and laughter the main part of the process. Finally when Barney and Ramesh were both satisfied everything was in order, Ramesh assisted her up into the airplane and nimbly followed her inside. As the evening breezes subsided, they sat watching out of the side windows as the expedition set off. Barney and Pongo in the towing canoe, broke the hush that had descended on the island, by starting up its ancient outboard motor, and began moving the unwieldy cargo slowly backwards. The two remaining canoes loaded with natives, now a strangely silent escort, paddled slowly alongside. Five of the natives remained on the island. Ramesh explained, the weight of them would be too much for the available floatation. They would guard the propellers and cans etc., and as soon as the flotilla had safely beached the 'Dead Albatross', as the natives now called the airplane, Pongo would take the tow canoe back and bring them all home.

The sunset, towards which the heavily laden canoes were moving faded rapidly into the tropical night. The only sounds were from the monotonous rattling and chugging of the little British Anzani outboard. Complementing the steady dip and drive of the paddles and the soft rippling of their wakes against the hulls. Occasionally, one of the natives in the canoe outside her window coughed. Or a subdued word passed from one or other of the canoes on either side of the airplane. She could barely see the outline of Ramesh´s head silhouetted against the pale starlight beyond the window. The night wind, having died completely, left the sea as smooth as a pond. Only the air moving slowly through the open the windows, and the rythmic back and forward motion of the canoes, as the sponson canoes breasted the tiny wash, from the tail and towing canoes, enabled them to realize they were actually afloat.

For a long time, they had sat in silence until it seemed to Joyce, as though she and Chip were still flying across the darkened ocean and she relaxed into a dreamy contentment holding Ramesh´s outstretched hand.

Just before the dawn fully lightened the horizon through the cockpit window, Ramesh and Joyce awoke simultaneously, still holding hands. After a moment or two looking sheepishly at one another they both smiled, disengaged their hands and rubbed their eyes. The light morning breeze wafted suddenly in through the open windows alongside them and at the same time the motion of the water in response set the whole assembly rocking slightly and creaking as the joints between the poles and the canoes flexed. Seated, they were only able to see forward and sideways and it appeared they were still far away from land until Ramesh stuck his head out of the window and craned his neck to look aft, towards the tail. He popped his head back in, smiling excitedly at her and announced. "We're almost there!"

As the instruction manuals say. "The installation process is the reverse of the dismantling instructions." The airplane landing, was handled in the same manner. Less than two hours after the canoe under the tailwheel grounded on the beach, the Dead Albatross was high and dry in a small area of the beach, free of coconut palms and looking, without its propellers, rather like a somewhat tattered version of a modern jet aircraft.

After some of the children had demonstrated how easily the skin of this strange beast could be pulled off. Ramesh, almost beside himself with anxiety at the threat of it's total destruction, beseeched Queen Kash. to keep them off it. At her bidding, a native guard, with a cane, was stationed at about every six feet all around it. Later that day, at Joyce's instigation, small select groups of five or six children at a time, were allowed inside the airplane, to look at the controls and some of them even sat in the pilot's and copilot's seats and handled the control wheels while others watched the airfoils moving outside, in response to the wheel movements. Ramesh, reluctantly at first, explained the actions to some of the older children, who then in turn, demonstrated this to their friends and siblings. By the afternoon, half the local population had become qualified pilots, at least in their opinion. By nightfall most of the young boys were piloting small bamboo canes around the open area, banking, weaving and swooping around each other, in mock aerial maneuvers. The only difference Joyce noted, between these children's games and those that might have been played by American children, was the absence of engine and gunfire sound-effects. These children, she realized, were emulating the flight of flocks of birds. It was a rather sobering revelation, she thought.

Ramesh had other matters on his mind. He and Barney dispatched the rescue crew to return and bring back the propellers and the gas cans and any other items they might find lying on the disturbed area around the site of the airplane which had belonged to the castaways. The two canoes were to be towed there and back by Pongo who felt extremely proud of his part in the whole affair, especially after Joyce had embraced him almost every time she met him and thanked him several times in that manner for his part in the original rescue. This gesture had been observed by Ramesh and although he understood her motivation to express her gratitude, he also knew it was not being interpreted in this manner by the villagers. He drew her to one side and cautioned her. At first, she resented his remarks, thinking they were prompted by feelings of jealousy on his part but after catching a few scowling expressions from several women she began to reconsider them.

"These people have different concepts of what is appropriate behaviour between adults." He told her. "Unless a woman is closely related to an adolescent male, she does not embrace him, in public, unless she's seeking to invite him into her bed."

Two days later, the propellers and gas cans arrived safely along with the windshield wiper blades. On seeing them Joyce was again attacked with a wave of agonizing memories of Chip and their love for each other. She fought it off by washing out the sand from the gas cans in the sea. Satisfied that every grain had been removed she took them one by one to the well in the village and rinsed them in fresh water and set them in the sun to dry.

Ramesh had already discussed with Barney, the process of filling them, two at a time, at the pickup point of the rum supplier. Joyce had proffered him a couple of hundred dollar bills to pay for this. The price Henry had mentioned for gas as she recalled, was about a dollar seventeen a gallon, but Pongo didn't know what the island price was for gasoline. He always simply filled up the two battered old two gallon cans from a container marked 'Premix', for the outboard, as part of his payment for making the shipment. Maybe he could do the same for her. Ramesh was not absolutely sure if airplane engines would run on 'Premix', so he

had asked her for some money to buy straight petrol. Having
seen the thickness of her 'stash', he was amazed when she told
him there were no smaller bills available. He examined both
bills, front and back, cautioning her to be extremely discrete
about letting anyone else see her money.

"The islanders, including Barney, have probably never seen
a hundred dollar bill. You'd better keep it." He said, handing
the bills back. "They take their payment in Rum. And, if this
gets talked about, it may not; in fact it won't be long, before the
word reaches the drug smugglers who are just as likely as not, to
come over to the island some night, to 'investigate' you, your
airplane, and those two mysterious boxes. Of yours." He said,
raising his eyebrows to indicate he too had already surmised
what they contained. "How do we pay for the gas then?" She
asked sheepishly. "Don't worry yourself about that, I'll discuss it
with Barney, he'll work something out between himself and the
smugglers." He put his arm, tightly around her sagging shoulders
and added, with a smile, "We'll need your money, if and when,
we reach civilization." His use of the word 'We' stimulated her
hopes once more and she wanted to pursue the subject, but just
then Barney announced his presence by calling for Ramesh.
She slipped the money out of sight before he entered the house.

Later, in the night, after everything except the jungle creatures
were silent and the last revellers of the village had calmed down,
she lay awake thinking. In the end, she got out of her bed, went
quietly over to the hammock where Ramesh lay on his back,
snoring gently and stepped across him carefully until she
straddled him and could lower herself very softly on top of him.
He awoke with a grunt of surprise and looked up at her.

"If we are going to civilization together," she said seductively,.
"I thought we ought to get to know each other better." That night
they did.

It took almost two months of Pongo's routine trips, to bring
back enough gasoline to fill the tanks of the DH-84. Ramesh was

very uncertain about some aspects of aviation despite his understanding of the theory of flight. Most of his knowledge had come from watching movies on BBC television in England. Certainly, as a boy in India, he had made and flown models successfully. Their little engines started by flicking their propeller, the right way, with a quick jerk of the forefinger, making sure to keep it clear when it started. Undoubtedly starting a big engine with a swift swing of the hand meant keeping all of oneself, not just a finger, out of the way of the propeller, if, and particularly when, it started. But, understanding that, was not quite the same thing as standing up to a real airplane, whose engines wouldn't start because its batteries were no longer charged, and actually doing it. There was no electricity in the village, so there was no way of charging them except to send the batteries with Pongo to try and get them charged. Pongo didn't even know what he meant by that. He started the outboard by wrapping a cord around the fly-wheel and pulling it hard to spin the motor. Swinging the Prop, was something Ramesh had only seen done in first world war movies, and he was very reluctant to try starting the engines like that. Joyce was equally ignorant of the proceedure, except for having once watched Henry start up his Luscombe one day after landing unanounced at her airfield, by, as he had described it, 'Swinging the Prop'. Henry, she recalled had been through quite a performance. First he made doubly sure the engine was switched off; and then after several swings, he had gone back into the doorway and reached up to switch something he called the 'Magazines' on. The next time he pulled the prop through, with both hands, the engine started and Henry had had to race around the wing to the cockpit to keep the engine running. He had been most insistant that she stand well off to the side of the runway, in case the airplane should start to move, saying, it might chase her if it did. It hadn't of course, but Henry had said the brakes were not enough to be certain it wouldn't move and he didn't want it to, 'eat her up'. In her mind she tried to picture Ramesh doing the same thing with this airplane and realized it would be impossible.

"You would need to have someone in the pilot's seat to start the engines like that, because you couldn't run around into this airplane to switch things on and off". She told him after describing Henry´s performance. She tried to demonstrate how Henry had pulled the propeller blade down hard while stepping backward away from the airplane as he did so. But she found that it was too hard for her to get the blade to swing past the compression in the cylinders. Ramesh being stronger was able to do this but took a long time to master the backward step, to her satisfaction.

She had repeatedly asked Ramesh why he wanted to start the engines anyway? Always the same answer. "There is no point in going any further with plans to fly it, if the engines don't work when we are ready . . . First things First." Secretly, she suspected he just wanted to play with his new toy. There was no way on earth he could persuade the Queen to get the natives to cut a way through the jungle here to make a runway and she doubted if they could mount the thing on floats, using canoes, the way Ramesh described it. Lying awake almost every night now she she devised various plans to escape back to civilization. Ramesh could have the airplane. It was rightfully his by virtue of having salvaged it and as the weather grew daily hotter and more oppressive she became almost desperate to get back to her cool home on the Olympic Peninsula.

Ramesh, had been aware of her feelings and saw a way he too could get away from this situation with the assistance of her money. The two of them had spent many hours over the past few weeks, talking about her home in the State of Washington. She had cajoled him time after time with stories about the beauty of the Pacific Northwest, the quietude and serenity of her home and the easy access to the city of Port Angeles. There she had told him, was a beautiful harbor with hundreds of boats of every description and a huge Ferry boat that plied betwen there and Victoria on Vancouver Island. carrying hundreds of cars across each day. He would not have to work to support himself as he could live with her for ever if he so desired. Yet, if he wanted to continue as a doctor, there was a large hospital there in the city overlooking the harbor where his years of experience in running his own hospital would almost certainly assure him a position on their staff. It would, she told him, be a marvelous opportunity for him as he could easily commute from their home to the hospital in five or six minutes. In the boxes she assured him was enough money to keep them there, in luxury, for the rest of their lives. To stimulate his interest in her project, she mentioned that almost anyone in the U.S.A. who wanted to, could learn to fly and even own their own airplane, like her friend Henry had done. He, she declared, even lived in a community where everyone had their own airplane and owned the airfield between them. Ramesh began having dreams of getting the Dead Albatross shipped there for himself once they were established. When she mentioned the little airstrip which she herself owned, was the one the 'Albatross' had flown from at the start of it´s last journey, he was convinced. From then on, they were both effectively committed to leaving the village.

Ramesh realized that their biggest problem in getting safely away would be keeping the knowledge of her money a secret. The contents of the boxes would have to be taken out quietly, and hidden somewhere where the villagers would not suspect they had been removed. He mentioned it to Joyce and a long series of discussions took place over the next weeks, usually in the hammock. Joyce, in the manner of women preparing for a journey, had packed almost all of her wardrobe. In addition had bought the clothes she was wearing on the flight after landing in Garden City before meeting Henry there. On the subsequent idyll with Chip, he had bought her more. Apart from the residue of the money Henry had given her and the money in Chip´s Flight bag, she had nothing.

Ramesh, realizing they would need something to carry the money in, wanted to use her case and suggested she leave the clothes behind. It is hard to imagine anything more certain to guarantee a protracted discussion. Their final decision to leave the clothes and take the money in her case, came when Ramesh played his two ace cards.

One. He was overdue for 'Home Leave', having not taken the annual month's leave for the last five years, and had accumulated almost half a year entitlement, which would guarantee the arrival of a temporary replacement. So that he could leave without the Queen's special permission, which she would be unlikely to give if she wasn't assured of a replacement. A most important contribution, since he knew the ropes of travelling here.

Two, an even more important contribution, The institution's seaplane which would bring the new Doctor, and take them away to Jamaica.

It felt like a divine inspiration to Joyce and she agreed to the rest of Ramesh's suggestions to empty the case by spending the next month giving away her clothes in small individual donations to the native women, starting with the Queen. "In that way," he said, "the villagers will not feel you have been freeloading on them. Money is of no use to them here and you can buy new clothes in Jamaica."

In preparation for the coming 'Garage Sale' Joyce strung four clothes lines across the inside of the house and began hanging all her finery, lingerie and day to day clothing up to air. In order to mix with the women she had adopted and grown quite comfortable with their custom of 'nakedness above the waist'. However, the rush skirts they wore she had found too irritating, and wore either folded down slips or skirts, supported with a leather belt Ramesh had given her. However, she knew this kind of attire, would not be acceptable, even in Jamaica. Accordingly, she set aside the long black and orange dress she had bought in Garden City while waiting for Henry's arrival and the undergarments which went with it, and packed them back in her suitcase. All that remained, her rings, costume jewelery and the money she had, plus that salvaged from Chip's posessions, together with the two unopened packages of bills, she wrapped in a stained old tee shirt, stitched so it would not spill if dropped accidentally. Ramesh selected those items he felt were most probably regarded by the women as desireable and set them aside for special gifting, as he described it. "The Queen and her entourage must not be insulted by you giving things they would prefer to own, to the lower class women you have been giving your attention to." Joyce was offended, but Ramesh persisted that this donation program needed to be handled diplomatically according to the villagers, not as she saw it. Otherwise, it could lead to serious difficulties being placed in their way when the time came to depart.

"We're in their playground, we have to play by their rules, regardless of our preferences. You'd better trust me on that one Lovee". He said, giving her a warm hug to soothe her bruised ego.

The preparations for his departure involved sending his request for home leave to the headquarters of the organization and that involved Barney and Pongo in the posting of this request. Barney was concerned about when he would return. Not so much for reasons of their friendship as in the hope he would bring back all kinds of 'Goodies' when he returned. He had Barney make a list and give it to him so that he would not forget and he gave lavish promises to get these things and bring or send them back. In the back of Ramesh's mind, the money required, would come from the stack Joyce held in those boxes and he was generous in agreeing to all of Barney's requests on one condition. Barney would protect the Albatross until he returned.

In Ramesh's mind the airplane represented a sizeable fortune. He could claim it by virtue of having salvaged it. The man who had stolen it was dead and could not be prosecuted. The original owners would probably not make any attempt to recover it, since they had, apparently, been involved in an unlawful activity with it. It would be an interesting exercise in any case. He thought.

Once the 'Request' for his replacement had been accepted, Ramesh and Joyce began the process of giving away the clothing. Selecting what they thought was most likely to be desired by the village women, resulted in confusion until Joyce had the notion to ask the women themselves. With Ramesh's help she held a fashion show in his house with a panel of six of the ladies who had previously visited him as judges until she was able to sort the dresses in what seemed to be the order in which these women saw them as desireable. The order they chose was apparently just the opposite of how she herself regarded them. further confusing the issue.

Finally, Ramesh went and explained Joyce's dilemma to the Queen and asked her if she would be kind enough to receive the whole lot as a 'Thank-you gift to the village', from Joyce, to be distributed among all the ladies, as she saw fit. That accomplished, apparently to the satisfaction of all the women in the village, Ramesh and Joyce began the task of secretly opening the boxes to transfer the money packets, to the almost empty case.

At the sight of the dried mess of mud and sugarcane, instead of the neatly stacked packets they had expected to see, both were appalled.

When the second box revealed the same, they were stunned. They remained, crouched over the boxes staring alternately at the boxes and each other until Ramesh gave a small shrug and a grimace of helpless resignation, which set Joyce laughing until she rolled over backwards with her legs kicking in the air, laughing hysterically. For a few moments, Ramesh stared at her in amazement. Then, seizing the opportunity, lunged over on top of her and they clung thus together until Nature was satisfied. Finally, sane, satisfied and emotionally stabilized once more, they began revising their plans.

When the Catalina seaplane bringing the relief doctor arrived, Joyce's suitcase was loaded with small native artifacts given to her and Ramesh by the villagers who were genuinely sorry to see them leave. The pilot, one of the more devoted of Her Majesty's Medical Missionaries, whose organization suppported this service, impressed by the native display, tried hard to convince her to devote herself to his cause. The pull to return to Joyce was too strong. She and Ramesh had already decided how to use the twenty seven thousand dollars in her suitcase, for their trip home.

*   *   *

It would need another six hours of Surrepticious Video Taping to capture the story of their journeyings on the money before they returned to her farm, and since I did not think they presented as sinister a threat to me as Chip would have been, God Rest His Soul, I didn't need to spend the time. The only remaining threat was the unknown interest that Bigshoes, or PRAIF inc might have, in recovering the money. All $ 1,920,000.00 of it.

The evident lack of any further use of Joyce's airfield, suggested that another avenue for the procurement of "Neural Synapses or Ganglions" or whatever the explosive contents of these mysterious oil cans were, had been developed. I wondered if Old Baldy Watsisname, was still cruising in the Chrysalis, between Canada and ports in the San Juan Islands with an engine room full of them. That thought led to the questionmark in my head as to what Alice, in the Goliath, was doing these days. Looking back to those far off times, as I lay awake that evening after Joyce and Ramesh had left, I realized that I still needed to warn Joyce, and particulrly Ramesh, as to the dangers of opening those cans. No mention had been made of them during the visit. I had been so concentrated on getting them to talk about their Carribbean escapades that I entirely forgot to bring that subject up. Until that realization entered my head, I had been contemplating the prospects of returning to Deer Park and beginning a new life with Vivienne over there.

Some people's minds work swiftly. They are the people who are proclaimed to be able to:—'Think on their feet. Here I lay, flat on my back, staring at the ceiling and the pieces of the puzzle were falling into place, almost three years after I had unwittingly participated in the events themselves.

Somewhere in British Columbia a research firm was manfacturing mechanical gadgets which functioned like a human nerve cell and packaging them in engine oil for shipment. These things became extremely volatile in the presence of Oxygen and would explode spontaneously, shortly after being exposed to the atmosphere.

International and inter commercial rivalry was causing the flow of these gadgets across international borders, and International bureaucratic restrictions on the shipment of hazardous materials was being overcome, at considerable expense, by the pipeline I had inadvertently stumbled across. Probably on a government grant, which had been feeding the 'Cash Cow' from which Chip and his grotesque assistant, Enrique Barranquillas, had been milking the pipeline of money flowing in the opposite direction.

Alice, Monica, Evelyn, and Nora, were all part of the involuntary monitoring network, on channel 39.

Mary, Joyce and Barbara, were innocent non participants. At least Mary was entirely disconnected(Until Roba and I butted in.) Barbara and Joyce were related, and more deeply involved, innocently of course, but tangibly affected by circumstances.

Barbara was dead. Murdered by her own husband. Joyce had brushed the veil of death and miraculously escaped. But now, again because of my incompetence, she and her companion Ramesh, were still in danger. After much cogitating, I decided to fly over to her field, first thing in the morning and warn them.

Normally, I would have taken Pugsley. However I had observed Joyce, making, what I felt, was too much of a fuss over her and I didn't want to encourage that connection. Pugsley was mine, and I wasn't going to risk her switching affections, the way Joyce had done.

The early dawn ride to Joyce was, as always, a flight of fantasy for me. Cold still air and the ever changing colours in the sky as the sun rises above the Cascade mountains behind me, tend to evoke a surrealistic sense of unreality. Moonbaby wanted to climb up to heaven and I let her. When I returned to sanity, I was at seven thousand feet. Joyce's little airstrip in the forest was far below me, a litle dark green swimming pool in the middle of a glittering carpet of treetops. Dew!! Dew on the grass! I might as well try landing on ice. I remembered my introduction to landing on dew laden grass, had ended with the nose of the airplane straddling the wire fence at the end of the runway. Joyce´s runway was short enough and with high trees at each end.

I had landed there once before, with Mary, in an emergency. We had made it safely enough, though Mary was petrified by the time we stopped, just short of the trees. There was no emergency this time. I might as well just take a quiet look around as I circled down, gliding at idle, to a reasonable height, thinking what to do now. Might just as well go to Port Angeles and gas up for the impending flight to Deer Park once Joyce and Ramesh had been warned. I was making my last circuit at about fifteen hundred feet, just right for entry into the pattern at P.A. still looking at Joyce's airstrip when something caught my attention, raising goose pimples all down my back.

There were three tracks in the dew. Three parralel lines running half the length of the field. A tricycle gear. A tail dragger would only have left two tracks on take off. Something, fairly big had landed, probably during the night, and taken off again just before dawn, leaving those telltale tracks in the dew laden grass. I took a quick look at the ´Parking´, the area between the end of the runway and the road, but there was no vehicle there. A glance at the ´Parking´ at Joyce´s house showed their car still there. At least they had made it home safely.

I continued my descent into the pattern at Port Angeles. and landed there.

Horizon Airlines has an early flight to Seattle which was preparing for boarding. Asking around for rental cars, I was lucky to catch one of the taxi men who was hopefully waiting around in case anyone needed a ride. I told him my story of the dew, and asked him if he would drive me to Joyce´s house, wait for me in the restaurant, return to Joyce´s house in an hour, and bring me back to the airfield. I dug out one of my folded mad money hundreds and offered it if he would. Ten minutes later I knocked vigorously on Joyce's front door and stood to one side, out of direct shotgun line.

Ramesh, loosely covered in my old dressing gown, opened the door. He looked blearily surprised at me for a few seconds before calling over his shoulder.

"It's Henry!"

Joyce, in her mother hubbard and bare feet, came thumping down the stairs. She stared at me for a moment before demanding, rather stiffly I thought, to know.

"What the hell do you want?" Short of brandishing her shotgun she could hardly have sounded more aggressive. I was so taken by surprise I barely heard Ramesh say, "Come in."

All last night and even this morning I had been debating with myself on how to broach the subject of the cans. Their surprisingly antagonistic attitude, must have reflected in me somehow, because without further thought I answered.

"Don't open those cans!"

"You came all this way at this time of the morning to tell us that!?" Joyce snapped. "How'd you know we had them anyway?" she continued accusingly.

By this time Ramesh had put his arm around her and said,

"Calm down Lovee." And turning to me, he said. "We don't want your cans Henry. It was all a mistake." And then, after a long pause while he tried to soothe Joyce he continued, with a smile of amused interest, "Well? . . . How did, you know we had them? Anyway?"

Caught on my own Pitard so to speak, I lamely answered, "I checked under the saw after you folks left, and they were gone." Ramesh gave a short grunt of laughter, saying

"You must have known Joyce wouldn't risk opening them. Especially after what happened in Oregon". I hadn't realized until then, just how much she must have told him, but I dug myself in further by saying. "I was more concerned that you might try to see what was in them . . . How was I to know she had told you what happened in Oregon?" For a few seconds his smile disappeared while he digested that remark, and then it came back. "I don't believe you."

"What don't you believe?"

"That you went and checked to see if we had taken your precious cans. After we left." I looked at him, surprised and a little shagrinned, when he added "They aren't very precious to you, and you knew they weren't precious to Joyce either, So. Why would We, want to steal them?"

"You tell me." I said grinning "Joyce just admittted it."

"You told me those cans were worth about Ten Thousand Dollars each." She blurted out accusingly. "Remember?" She said, pointing her finger at me. "You said it. You had calculated it out. From the number of cans to the number of packs of money." She was getting all worked up, and thankfully, Ramesh was desperately trying to calm her down, but she kept on accusingly. "You took all the money. I knew you didn't want the cans so I suggested we could use them and maybe sell them since our money is almost gone, if they were worth so much."

"You are welcome to them." I said hoping to cool the atmosphere a little. "I only came here to warn you . . . Mostly to warn Ramesh, not to open them as whatever is inside them, aside from the oil, is liable to explode when it has been exposed to the air for a while."

"What is in the cans? Besides oil?" Ramesh asked quietly.

"I really don't know." I replied, thinking back to my interview with Bigshoes and to Chip's inference they contained nitro-glycerine. "The guy who interviewed me for the job of pilot for their airplane said they were elements of a synthetic nerve they were building so computers could feel and sense things exactly the same way humans do. Something inside the cans made the nerves work." When Ramesh made no comment, I continued. "He had a twisted rope-like rig set up between two huge computers. It was made up from those cans with some sort of flexible chain-like tube or wire links between the ends of the cans. Something to do with Artificial Intelligence, he told me.

Chip however, told me it was Nitro-Glycerine, I didn't really believe him. I thought he was trying to scare me into making very gentle landings." Ramesh was very intently looking at me while I was talking, and I wondered if he, being a doctor, would have known how human nerves transmit their messages. If so, he might be able to shed some light on the puzzle.

"I gather, from what you two have told me:" Ramesh finally said. "These cans are valuable only to either the people who make them or the people for whom they were made. I doubt if anyone else would have any use for them." He said, directing his remarks, first to me and then to Joyce, as if offering each of us in turn a chance to refute it "They aren't exactly saleable on the open market, like drugs or jewelry."

Since I had never attached any value to the cans myself, their only interest to me was the potential danger to me, of being found in posession of them. I had already expressed my willingness for Ramesh and Joyce to do whatever they liked to recover their monetary value from the very small market he had defined. My only interest had been and still was, in alerting both of them to the physical danger involved in opening them. I was on the point of bidding them farewell, when I remembered the tracks in the grass.

"Are the airplanes still landing and taking off in the night?" I asked suddenly. Joyce nodded her head. "The strip appears to have been kept mowed all the time we were away."

"That's not what I asked." I said trying to keep my tone from sounding rude, "I meant, have you heard any airplanes taking off recently? Like last night for instance?" Ramesh picked up on that immediately. "We slept pretty soundly last night. I don't remember hearing anything until you banged on the door." His tone indicating he felt it was a bit ungentlemanly for me to have done so. "Why do you ask?"

"I saw tracks of an airplane taking off, in the grass, earlier this morning." They both stared at me as if unable to understand what I had said. Joyce had a look of dismay on her face.

Finally Ramesh asked. "You flew over here this morning?" I

nodded. "And landed here?" I shook my head. "Then, how did you get here?"

"I took a cab ftom P.A . . . I left the airplane there."

"At the airport?"

"At the airport. Yes."

"How are you going to get back there ?" Joyce asked and Ramesh gave her a strange look of surprise. I suspected he thought they would naturally expect to ferry me back, without question.

"The taxi will be here in about ten minutes." I said, looking at my watch. "Since we have neglected to mow the grass for the last three weeks, it must be about six to eight inches tall by now, and the tracks in it should be easy to find, if anyone wanted to measure the width of the tread itself, and the span between them, so we could find out what kind of an aircraft took off. It took off towards the road."

Joyce slumped down in a chair and covered her face with her hands, moaning "Oh! No!. No! Not again!"

Ramesh went and put his arms around Joyce. He turned and looked at me anxiously, saying, "Why can't we just give them their cans back.?"

I looked at both of them with a silly smile, asking. "Now, why didn't I think of that?"

A couple of toots on a car horn, alerted us to the fact the taxi driver had arrived. Not being ready to discuss Ramesh's suggestion in detail or get involved in the examination of airplane tire tracks myself. I left it to them. Bidding them a rather hasty farewell, and at Ramesh's next suggestion, agreed to come back by air and discuss a plan for doing these things, as soon as possible.

Returning by air has its advantages in regard to speed, but it has the disadvantage of putting me and the luscombe in a compromised position, in the event a sudden rapid departure became necassary. I had seen no signs of activity at the strip until just now. It could have been a private pilot making an exploratory flight but I doubted that.

I had tried putting myself in Bigshoes's shoes so to speak. My supply of essential parts had been broken and obviously violated. A lot of money had been lost. I felt sure he knew the details and as I already noted there had been no 'Hooting and Hollering' about all the gruesome events that had led to my induction into the crew.

Since I had also disappeared at the same time as the DH-84, I would be the prime suspect if I ever showed up again. I had been hired on as Victor Denim, and given an address in Eureka, which, if traced, would turn out to be a motel there. I had paid cash so no credit trail would lead to my true name and legitimate address, yet someone in George Town, had sent me pictures of the airplane on a island somewhere, presumeably in the Carribbean. I had not questioned Ramesh and Joyce about those pictures, and hadn't detected any indication of them trying to trick me into revealing whether I had received them. Though they had mentioned Ramesh taking pictures. Another item of significance was their return and all these other activities coming together at approximately the same time frame. Ramesh and Joyce had a car with Oregon plates. I checked the number when they visited me to make the videos they didn't know about.

I began to realize there would have to be another 'interrogation session', pretty soon so I could pump them about their travels between Jamaica and Joyce, Washington. I didn't even know if either of them, had ever been to George Town, which is the capital on Grand Cayman island, since I had never asked if Joyce had gone there after being rescued.

I gassed up the luscombe at P.A. and returned to Diamond Point. The first thing I did, was to scrape out all the sawdust from under the saw and spread it very evenly all over the dirt floor of the lean-to shed. I used the yard broom to smooth it out completely obliterating my foot prints as I backed out to the door and closed the shed. Any intruder would have to find a broom and repeat my work if they didn't want me to know they had visited. After that, I set up a fresh tape in the recorder, re-arranged the cameras so they would monitor the house for intruders instead of forest creatures, changed the Windows access password in the old computer, turned off the water and locked up the Mobilehome and all the sheds. Pugsley and I then flew directly to Deer Park and arrived at Vivienne's house just in time for supper.

Vivienne was delighted to see us, and I hoped she was as delighted as I was, to be so welcomed. I had laid enough of my cards on the table, and if they hadn't scared her off by now, probably nothing would.

"Where's Jake?" I asked, and from the twisted way her eyebrows moved, I really didn't need to hear her answer.

"I appear to have lost my son."

"And gained a whole new family?"

"It looks that way. How d'you feel about that?"

"Personally? I couldn't possibly be happier."

"Out from under?"

"Oh! Viv! . . . How could you even think that?"

"I didn't. I don't. I just wanted to see your reaction."

"Did I pass?"

"With flying colors." She came over and literally plonked herself down in my lap. A move that surprised me no end, and led to an extremely exhausting evening, with no thought whatsoever, given to what Jake might say if he knew.

The phone woke me out of a deep sleep. I reached for it and found myself alone in a strange bed with no idea where the phone was. I was fumbling, about to pick it up, when Vivienne rushed into the room and reached for it calling out. "Don't touch it!" The remark achieved its purpose and she put it to here ear.

"Of course! Who did you expect it to be?" I leaned on my elbow trying to catch the other side of the coversation, though I knew it was Jake calling to see if his mother was alright in the house alone. "Where did you spend the night? As if I didn't know.".. She grinned at my suppressed interest. "You'd better watch out . . . You might end up having to Marry her . . . You Are!! . . . What!? . . . When?!" Viviennes eyes were streaming. Jake was rattling on with the details too excited to stop. Finally he must have asked her what I was likely to say.

"You can ask him yourself." She said, handing me the phone. There was a pregnant silence on the other end. "Who wants to ask who, about what?" I asked.

"Henry?"

"That's me". There was more silence then he asked. "Where are you? In Bed!?" I let him stew on that for a while before answering "Yes" He might as well hear it from me. I heard him say something presumeably to Mary and there was a loud peal of laughter from her. He didn't get anything beyond the "You-Ba." part said, before he too burst out laughing. I handed the phone back to Vivienne who had heard most of the interchange anyway as I had kept the earpiece away from my head and she was laughing with tears running down her face.

That evening we all got together at Mary's house for the evening meal and settled most of the details. I had spent much of the day at the airport café, drinking coffee and talking over my scheme to more or less take over the building program Vivienne and Jaques had started. She was very enthusiastic. I didn't suggest changing any of their plans, so Jake would be eager to co-operate, though I did have a few improvements in mind which I could suggest later on. When Jake and Mary heard this they were as eager to get started on it, as the rest of us including the children, who didn't undestand what all the fuss was about.

When Jake and Mary got married, I intended to open three bank accounts in the area. One for the parents and one Educational Trust. for each of the children, with Mary as the trustee. All three accounts would be fed with monthly deposits from several off-shore accounts which had been opened while I was journeying in the Carribbean.

Vivienne and I intend to take a couple of months off this winter, when the weather gets rough in the Spokane valley, to take the Sugarcane on a cruise to the Islands. I figure to replenish those feeder accounts in person.

In the interim, I needed to establish a new base in the area where the local Fixed Base Operator would not have any records of my Tie-down for the Luscombe. I found one at a little paved airfield a couple of miles north of the town of Chewelah where I could buy a lot on their taxiway and build a hangar. A local jobbing builder erected a prefab, corrugated iron Tee hangar for me there, with a concrete slab floor, in less than a week. I paid him well, in cash. He was happy, and I noted his availability for the Motel Project as we named the work at Vivienne´s.

Jake wanted to re-register for his engineering degree, when the semester opened in September. On the premise that what costs nothing is worth nothing, I talked Mary, into letting me take over her mortgage so that they could get by on Mary´s income from her beauty and massage business while he studied, and worked part time at the garage for Mr. Williams, without having to pay any interest on it. At first, she was reluctant, until I pointed out that it was, no skin off my nose, as long as they made their payments. After discussing it with both of them we settled on $400 a month until it was all payed off. The only stipulation I made was that if they wanted to miss a payment any month, they would let me know ahead of time. I opened a joint account with Vivienne to receive their payments. Vivienne was a little sceptical at first, but after we talked some more about the tendencies of the young, in today's world, she agreed to signing with me.

Vivienne, Jake and Mary sat down with me one evening when the children were fast asleep, and thrashed out the subject of the children's surname. Mary herself as a single mother, had registered them as 'Lykes'. I asked Jake how he felt about changing that to his name. It would not require a legal adoption by him if he simply stated he was the father. Apparently, he and Mary had already discussed that and agreed it would avoid a lot of red tape, pointing out, that with the possibility of myself being one day arraigned falsely or otherwise as a criminal, it would be better for the children to have nothing more than an 'emotional' connection to me.

At first I felt some regret that the children would not carry my name but on more mature thinking, I realized that for their sake, they would be better off thinking of themselves as Jake´s natural children. If he and Mary had others of their own, they would all integrate together as one family, without the implication of anyone being different.

I knew in my heart, that I could, and would have, just as much love for any more children Jake and Mary might have, as I felt for Erica and Stuart. I knew that it stemmed from my own love for Mary. Something deep in my heart that I had not been able to explain.

I wondered if she understood that. Either way, I was not going to tell her. Though I thought it might be a good idea, some day, way down the road perhaps, to mention it to Jake.

"It should be possible." I explained. "Only the four of us know the truth. Nobody else need ever know. As long as none of us mentions it to anyone, especially not to anyone who might make some stupid veiled remark later on, to the children, while they are growing up, it will not cause them any filial confusion, sibling rivalry, or psychological damage. There is so much evidence today of grown men and women, tormenting themselves with an obsession for finding their 'Biological Parent'. Usually it is a result of some thoughtless person, most probably a relative, hinting during their childhood, that the father they have known and loved all their life, is not their true biological parent." While I had their undivided attention I added, "Please, let us us all vow to ourselves right now, that we will never do such a stupid mean thing, to either Stuart or Erica."

All through the months of June and July, I had been making weekly trips back and forth to Diamond point to check on my monitoring system.

Rather than ask Vivienne to run me back and forth to the airfield, I had bought a Volkswagon Bug which I had left in the hangar at 'Sandy Precipice', as I called the local airfield since the western end of the runway, ends virtually on the edge of a cliff above the highway. However, the wind always seemed to be coming from the other end so there is little chance of going over the cliff if the brakes failed. The approach was somewhat similar to landing on runway 28 at D-Pt., where the wind tends to drop down over the steep hillside causing a downdraught one had to be alert for. Sometimes I took Pugsley but it is a two hour flight going west and she gets pretty restless in the absence of a toilet. Also, she was becomming more of a pet for Stuart and Erica and I sensed the end of our close relationship coming. She was always happy to see me when I returned after a couple of days away from her.

On the last trip in July, there was evidence of a prowler around the house in the night . . . Nobody I recognized, and no tangible evidence of any break-in. From the date shown on the video it had been the evening before I returned so I e-mailed Vivienne to say I would stay over for a couple of days to see if anything further might develop. That afternoon, I drove out to Joyce and called on Joyce and Ramesh to see if they had learned anything.

It had been almost two months since our last meeting and Ramesh was intrigued with Joyce´s account of our escapades which had led to her meeting him. They seemed to me to have really settled down together and I fervently wished they could enjoy life without the potential threats posed by Chip and Enrique´s plot.

I wanted to ask Ramesh if he still had any photographs of the airplane, that did not include Joyce, on the sandbar. And, or, while it was floating on the canoes. The other thing I wanted to ask, was whether he had, or could get, a copy of whatever death certificate existed for Chip. Those two pieces of evidence might convince 'Bigshoes' or his organization to believe Chip had absconded with the loot alone, having fired me beforehand without notifying him, and ended up in the exactly trouble he actually did land in, I thought, if such were available, I could make computer prints from them and 'leak'them to 'Bigshoes', who might thereby assume, the money was "Lost at Sea." I also wanted to sound Ramesh out, on the idea that if 'Bigshoes' learned the DH 84 had been salvaged, he might want to buy it back, from the salvage company, or maybe some insurance company might have a vested interest in it.

As soon as I could get him away from Joyce, I asked him "Have there still been any indications of night fliers using the airstrip since we had talked.about the tire tracks?" He said he personally had not heard anything. and Joyce, possibly afraid to pique his interest in the same way mine had been aroused, refused to say if she had heard anything either.

Ramesh still thought it was impossible for them to raise any cash for the twelve cans they had in the house. I wholeheartedly agreed. The idea came to me that if they were to get rid of this piece of evidence of their involvement, the simplest thing, would be to hide the cans under the cot in the shack in the woods.

While we were walking back to my car, I asked him if he had ever seen the shack in the woods where the first blow in our little war had been struck? He shook his head saying,

"Joyce refuses to even go out on the airfield."

"That´s ridiculous!" I exclaimed, angry at the situation she was in. "Dammit why not, it's her airfield, she has every right to go out there."

"She says she doesn't know if it really is on her property or not."

Ramesh's tone, inferred he accepted her view in lieu of mine.

"I thought I had shown her, the surveyer's report.!" I said without thinking. I had ordered the report immediately, following our 'Beating the Bounds' several days before the trouble started. Then I remembered. The report itself, hadn't come into my hands until after I collected my mail, on my return to the area from the Caribbean adventure. Because of the uncertain situation existing at that time, before learning of Chip's demise, I had not contacted anyone with that knowledge. I didn't say anything to Ramesh right then, to imply that I also believed she could be legally entitled to a fairly large tax refund if it was, by virtue of the fact she had been paying taxes on that parcel over almost fifty years. I thought that might diminish any loss she might still feel she had suffered through my dirty trick on Chip. And, by force of circumstance, on her. I also thought about hiring a lawyer to press her case with the county, and then realized that might cost more than the refund itself. I might just as well give the money directly to her myself . . . Something worth thinking about. Eh?

Instead of getting into the car, I asked Ramesh if he would like to take a walk with me round the airfield. I said I would like to have permission to use the field for visiting and of course he said it was up to Joyce but he didn't imagine she would object.

As we turned into the airfield parking he suddenly rested his hand on my shoulder.

"She doesn't seem to hold you responsible for what happened to her. You know." He said "I think sometimes, she still has a soft spot for you." He added, smiling.

"I had a soft spot for her at one time," I replied, looking him straight in the eye. "But somehow that went away when she ditched me for Chip." He nodded sympathetically. "You two seem pretty content with each other." I began, "I'm happy for you both. She's a very fine woman." He laughed when I said that and it was definitely a contented, rather than contradictory laugh. So I continued, "I suppose she told you about the letter?"

"She did." He said thoughtfully. "I guess she was a bit embarrassed until she realized there were other letters you hadn't told her about."

"She knew!?" It was my turn to be embarrassed, and he laughed then, right out loud at my obvious discomfiture. "I wonder how she found out:" I said lamely.

"Never under estimate a woman's intuition." He said. "They think on an entirely different level to men. Much more primeval. It goes with the territory."

When Ramesh finaly saw the heap of forest debris which covered the hut built by the aviators who had been using the airfield at night, he was amazed at how well it was camouflaged.

"I would have walked right past it if you hadn't pointed it out." He said, carefully inspecting the mound for signs of an entry door. He walked all round it examining the ground for tracks. "Very clever." He said, "They seem to have raked up so much of the fallen stuff from around the area to cover the hut that there is not enough debris to differentiate between a pathway and the undisturbed forest floor. Very clever indeed."

When I had first visited the shack while returning to the Pacific Northwest, it had appeared to me to have been abandoned and I merely removed the remains of my surveillence equipment and left the shack for the forest to bury.

Ramesh had shown me how delinquent I had been in my assessment of the situation. I had been certain the airfield had not been used, as it was too heavily overgrown with the two years of neglect that predisposed me to assuming the shack too had been abandoned. Whoever was now using the strip, must have been quite surprised when Pugsley and I came and cleared it, I hadn't seen any signs of activity. What I saw was obviously what I had wanted to see. Ramesh had seen what was. The doorway was carefully hidden by a large cedar branch, placed to look as if it had fallen against the pile, and covered the door. The butt end, was stuck in the ground and any experienced forester would have known instantly it was far too big to have fallen like that, from any of the trees locally. The hole it had purportedly made in the ground in falling, was wedge shaped so the branch could be pulled back and tilted, over center, to rest in the opposite direction, whenever access to the door was needed.

"Clever, but not quite clever enough." Ramesh remarked "Better check it for booby traps before trying to move it." He added, catching my arm as I bent to do just that. Remembering what had happened to me the last time I had carelessly prowled around this area, I shuddered.

There was nothing, as far as we could see attached to the limb or the dried fronds, so, standing well back, I reached over and lifted the branch and moved it over to the other position. The original padlock holding the hasp, had been replaced with a rusty nail, almost invisible against the brown camouflage, and with exagerated caution, I removed it carefully and slowly opened the door. Nothing untoward happened and everything inside appeared just as tidy and unused as when I had left it after removing my surveillence camera. The grey army blanket covering the cot was still hanging down to the floor as we had left it and there was nothing underneath; which gave me the idea of hiding the boxes of cans underneath the bed. Ramesh and I discussed the idea and he thought it was probably the best way to dispose of them, only voicing the fear that at some later time, some tramp might find the shack and then the cans and then . . . He shrugged his shoulders expressively. "I suppose the worst that could happen then, is the explosion might possibly set the woods on fire." He said pensively. "Our house is a little too close for comfort if something like that happened. Don't you think.?" I nodded agreement, noting the possessive he had used.

"We wouldn't like that to happen. Would we?" I agreed. "Of course, if whoever is still interested in the shack should notice the cans under the bed, they would probably assume Chip had left them there and they'd probably take them away." I offered as a suggestion for alleviating his concerns. He rubbed his whiskers thoughtfully. "It would have to appear that they had been there the last time whoever came here and somehow he had not noticed . . . What do they use this shack for anyway?"

"Didn't Joyce tell you?"

"She said you and Chip had slept there."

"That's true. We did, but only the one time, because there was an emergency. Normally they only used the shack to start up the generator, and turn on the lights for the incoming plane to land. Then they load up and it takes off again. The guy on the ground then turns off the lights and goes home."

"The bed doesn't look as if anyone slept on it, or even sat on it." Ramesh said grinning slyly, "If anyone did sit on it, and the cans were stacked under it, they'd feel them wouldn't they?" he said. I agreed, feeling we should waste no more time.

"Why don't we go get those cans right now and do as you suggest. Stack them under the bed so if the ground man comes in and sits down, to wait or for any other reason sits down, he'll feel them. They'll be discovered, and Bingo! They'll be removed." Ramesh was silent for a few moments and I feared he was about to hesitate so I added, "I think the probability of that happening is much higher than the probability of some tramp finding the shack and setting the forest ablaze. Don't you?" He nodded slowly. "Let's go." he said decisively, closing the door behind us.

There wasn't enough room to stack the cans two high, Ramesh decided, pointing out that it might have been sat on before and the piled up cans could obviously not have been there then. He set them in two rows of five each with the last two cans lying on their sides, partly wedged between the tops of the other cans. "That way" he said, brushing off the knees of his trousers. "Whoever sits there will feel his bum strike something which fell over under the bed . . . That'll make him look under to see what it was, and Bingo!" he smiled, triumphantly echoing my earlier remark.

When we closed up the shack and reset the branch, Ramesh noticed how the fronds were still full of needles, and remarked that the branch hadn't been there very long or the needles would have all fallen off by now. I cast my mind back to the time I had first visited in April. To avoid having to drive past Barbara's house, with its gory reminders, I had elected to come up via the coast road and called in at Joyce 'En passant'. After viewing the disorder in Joyce's house I had walked over with Pugsley, to hsve a look at the airfield and the shack and did not recall the door being covered at that time. Nor the following week, when we visited and cleaned up the garden and the house, and removed the cameras. The shed was in an area where the main forest coverage was mostly densely packed with fir trees and fallen 'Pecker-Poles' as the loggers would say. The cedar branch must have fallen from one of the large cedars growing alongside the road.

Ramesh and Joyce had returned only a little under a month before I visited them. Therefore, it appeared that the branch must have been placed across the door before then, or it would still be showing green needles. Ramesh assured me niether he nor Joyce had visited the shed or the airfield for that matter until the week I came over. As we walked through the Parking area of the pathway from the road, Ramesh pointed out the tree where the branch had obviously come from. The scar was clearly visible where it had been sawn off. A somewhat premeditated event no doubt

"It would be interesting to know whether anyone does sit on the cans, so to speak." Ramesh remarked as we walked back to my car. "Would you like me to bring the video recorder and the camera over and set them up to register whenever their car comes in.?" I asked him. He didn't answer directly. Then asked "Could I have a look at that surveyor's report you mentioned, first ? It might show whether the shack is also on her property or not." "Why not? I'll bring it and the recorder over tomorrow if you like." I replied getting into the car.

"Aren't you going to say goodbye to Joyce?" he asked. I made a face and shook my head indicating I would prefer to let him do the honours.

"I'll be seeing her again tomorrow." I said, wondering what had prompted him to make that remark. "Ramesh." I said, reaching through the window to shake his hand. "You've got to understand. It's all over between Joyce and me. I don't want to give her any wrong impressions in that direction . . . Don't missunderstand me . . . There are no hard feelings. I like her. I want to help her. She's a hell of a fine woman . . . But we simply have to get on with our separate lives from now on . . . You take good care of her." I instructed him with a smile, letting go of his hand. "See you tomorrow!" I called through the window as the car started moving.

On the drive home, I thought about them. They had been together on their outpost and their journey back, for the best part of two years. Much longer than Joyce and I had even known each other. I had estimated that Chip had upward of twenty-five thousand dollars with him in the airplane, which would have seen the two of them quite a long way. I remembered I had intended to set up a second 'Video Conference' to get those details but I needed to set things up for it beforehand. That meant two or more days over here and allowing for weather maybe more. I was anxious to get back to the building program as there were some refinements I wanted to suggest to Jake and Vivienne, before the work got beyond the point where the changes could be incorporated.

Getting rid of those incriminating oilcans, was a big relief to me. If I could get Ramesh to run with the ball as far as tackling the tax situation was concerned, I might be able to concentrate on the matters closer to my heart, in Eastern Washington.

One other thing I had in the back of my mind was to set up a computer, programmed to E-mail those video clips taken by the surveillance cameras, directly to my computer over the mountains, each time a clip was made. That would obviate my need to flip flop across the mountanis every so often, and incidentally it would cost very little by comparison. All I needed, was time and space to get the details worked out and the equipment set up.

The rest of the day was spent, rounding up what equipment would be needed, as well as the old cameras and wiring I had bundled up after removing from the trees and the shack. I had originally intended to leave all that, in the closet in Joyce's kitchen until realizing it might incriminate her if the house was searched by the 'Enemy'.

Next day was spent with Ramesh and Joyce, setting up the system and showing them how to operate it. A piece of brilliance on my part, led me to pick up a new digital video recorder and a twenty inch television set at Costco, plus a dozen videos from; 'Gone with the wind', 'The Crimson pirate', 'Mutiny on the Bounty' to a few 'Cowboy' movies as a start of a collection for them to enjoy. It would also help them familiarize themselves with the operation. And keep them occupied. However, since the cable system had not yet extended to their area, they were limited to mostly Canadian stations in Vancouver and Victoria. Bellingham came in fairly well but the mountains interfered with reception from Seattle. Niether of them had had a television to look at or get addicted to, in the last ten years as far as I could ascertain, so they were both entranced.

Feeling I could leave things as they were here, I drove home and loaded my goodies into the Luscombe and took off into the sunset. The darkness caught up with me as I passed over Stevens Pass following the highway 2, East across the darkened world with its string of moving diamonds and rubies stretched out along the road below me. One by one I picked major plaes like Cashmere and Wenatchee, out from the small clusters of lights around each of the little farming communities until I could see the shimmering reflection of the Columbia river, lying across my path. Soon the glowing mass of the lights of Spokane came up out of the shadows and spread out away to my right. I picked out the stream of lights from traffic moving north out of the city, along highway 395, and began my descent towards the smaller group of light around Deer Park. I had left the car in my hangar at Sandy Precipice, so I angled across the hills towards Chewelah and followed the road until picking out the landing strip with its red and green lights along the top of the cliff. Since I had been in the air almost two hours and crossed the mountains and it was now quite dark, I needed to know the exact altitude for the runway at Sandy, so I called Deer Park for an altimeter check and set in the local Barometric pressure, before beginning my approach. The exact altitude of the field iself is rather critical for me as the Luscombe has no landing lights. One has to know the zero height by the reference to Altimeter and the information on runway characteristics, shown on the map. Which, I could not read in the darkness!

With nothing but the red warning lights to aim at, my first attempt, was a little too high for comfort, so I made a "Go-around" early, as the hills are not that far away in the northerly direction. I was just contemplating turning back and landing at Deer Park, when, a car suddenly came out onto the runway, drove to the cliff end, turned around onto the taxi-way at the edge of the cliff, and stopped with its headlights directed back along the runway. I blessed the driver and using his lights, on my second approach, made a nice smooth landing.

As I about to close the hangar doors, the car pulled up outside the hangar. I went out to thank him for his assistance and realized it was a state patrol car. I walked up to the driver's window and then recognized the driver was the guy who had given me a warning a few weeks back when he stopped me for speeding. He must have recognized me at the same time as we both spoke together. "Hi. Thanks for the illuminations". I said, with a big smile, offering my hand as he opened the door. As we shook hands, he said with a smile. "You sure like to live dangerously I see." Then he introduced himself "Lyman Jennings." The name sounded familiar. "Oh! You're the owner of the airfield." I began.

"No, I was visiting with my brother Larramie. He owns this development. We saw your first attempt. Larramie asked me to come and show the runway for you. You were lucky. I was just about to leave. You'd better get your landing light fixed if you intend making night landings here". I nodded my head vigorously. "You're right there!" I replied sincerely. "I just had the hangar built," I said. "I think I'll spend a little time getting more familiar with the patttern. This is only my second landing here. It´s a bit tricky, what with the cliff out here and the canyon back there." He looked at me strangely as if he questioned my sanity.

"Only your second landing?" I nodded affirmatively.

"When was your first?!" I had to stop and think

"I don't remember the date exactly. It was when I came here to enquire about buying a lot and setting up the hangar. The airplane used to be tied down at Deer Park. I didn't want to leave it outside during the winter."

"You living over here now?" Lyman asked casually, "I noticed the address on your license was in Everett." I was surprised and exclaimed with a smile,

"I am impressed!. You have a remarkably good memory . . . I can hardly remember a man's name until I get to know him real well."

"Training." He laughed modestly, pleased no doubt by my praise. Did you buy the bug from Tom Phelps?" He asked, eyeing the VW parked in the hangar and laughing at my amazed expression.

"You're fantastic!" I gasped admiringly. "How'd you know?"

"Recognized the car. Tom and I have known each other since early childhood . . . It's a big country but a small population. We get to know each other pretty well. I've lived here all my life. Where are you located over here.?" I had been waiting for that question and replied.

"Right now I'm just renting. But I'm thinking I'll look around for a place to buy pretty soon."

"Better get with it if you want to get settled before the winter, he replied. It gets cold. Really cold, here, in the winter. Hot and dry in summer. Snowmobile cold in the winter."

"Where do you live?" I asked, hoping to divert his interest away from my activities.

"I've a little place about eight miles east of here on the road to Cusick" I had never heard of the place, and said so, but, according to him it was right up the road from the airport. I imagined one probably passed right by Mary's place on the way there and determined to look it up as soon as possible. We chatted about the best places to find some place to live and he named a couple of real estate offices where I should check, before he left. I had been trying to unload the airplane and transfer everything to the bug while we talked, and of course, my briefcase caught his eye with the big Boeing sticker and various airline logos stuck all over the lid. I explained I had travelled for the company and found it an easy way to identify the case, thereby making it less likely to get lost. I hoped.

He remarked on finding it hard to believe I was retired as I didn't look old enough. I thanked him for the compliment and wondered to myself if perhaps it had been a misfortune, For a certain young lady who lived not far from him, and who he probably knew by sight if not by name.

I closed up the hangar as soon as he left and drove out in the other direction towards Chewelah and on to Vivienne's place.

She was still up and happy to see me. I could see she was excited about something other than my arrival and after setting out a supper for me, she sat across the table smiling smugly, and in a low conspiratorial whisper, said. "Jake and Mary have finally decided to get Married."

There was a small group of Jake and Vivienne's friends as well as several of Mary's 'Patients' gathered on the lawn of her house. around a trellis arbor, specially built by Jake, and covered in various freshly cut flowers from her garden and some imported roses.

It stood imposingly across the garden path in front of the steps leading up to the deck in front of her kitchen door. Just beyond the arbor, Jake and Vivienne stood in front of the semicircle of spectators with Stuart and Erica holding their respective hands and squirming excitedly, as I escorted Mary down the steps, through the arbor to meet them, in front of the local minister from their church, who had come to conduct the ceremony.

Mary had specifically asked me, as "Her only living relative", to perform the function of giving her away. A beautiful brush stroke of irony I thought. However, as I walked down the steps with her on my arm, I felt astonishingly proud of her for that delicate, tactful, and, if you like, romantic touch.

Their vows were made and sealed with the traditional kiss and then we followed them, back through the arch, up the steps and into the house, for a great reception.

In order to pass through together, Vivienne carried Stuart and I carried Erica beside her, folowing behind Jake and Mary, and the rest of the party crowded through behind us.

Vivienne and I, for our different reasons no doubt, had to wipe our eyes as did many of the guests.

After the reception, Jake and Mary went off for a three day honeymoon at the Coeur d' Alene Lodge, in the same room that Vivienne and I had shared on our visit. I had booked it for them, and only after they had left did I mention that particular facet to Vivienne, who almost collapsed with laughter,

Once all the guests had left and the house had been tidied up, Vivienne and I took Pugsley and the twins to McDonalds for french fries and ice creams. Then, back to the house. Put them both to sleep by reading a children's storybook to them, and then tucked them up for the night securely in their cribs, with Pugsley sleeping on guard below them.

Order, peace, and quiet, finally restored, we sat out on the deck, sublimely content with a Harvey's each, thankfully watching the stars, before turning in ourselves, snuggled closely together in Mary's single bed.